BENEATH THE PEAKS

BENEATH THE PEAKS

WALTER MCKEEVER

iUniverse, Inc.
Bloomington

Beneath The Peaks

iUniverse books may be ordered through booksellers or by contacting:

iUniverse
1663 Liberty Drive
Bloomington, IN 47403
www.iuniverse.com
1-800-Authors (1-800-288-4677)

ISBN: 978-1-4620-3522-9 (sc)
ISBN: 978-1-4620-3523-6 (ebk)

Printed in the United States of America

iUniverse rev. date: 07/14/2011

CHAPTER 1

───────── ▼ ─────────

On Saturday, the twentieth day of April 2001, the gnarled old hands of Mother Nature shuffled her deck of diverse weather elements and dealt down a densely dark and drenching early evening to the city of Flagstaff, Arizona. As thirty year old associate professor Nizhoni Lydecker scurried and splashed along the uneven surface of a downtown alley she felt as though the city itself were compressed against its 12,566 foot Mount Humphreys backdrop for shelter, just as she was compressed within the sheltering confines of her raincoat and umbrella. She was hurrying to Chester's Pub in the venerable Wexford Hotel. The landmark building sat at the intersection of North Leroux Street and East Aspen Avenue in the very heart of the original downtown district. The Wexford, a two-story red brick structure, had been erected in 1897, and many famous Americans of that era, the likes of Teddy Roosevelt, Zane Grey, Jack London, and Wyatt Earp had enjoyed its hospitality. Now it offered just ten rooms for lodgers, but it housed the popular Chester's Restaurant, and one of the most active entertainment venues in Flagstaff, called Chester's Pub. The Chester's Pub section of the old hostelry regularly hosted musical groups of diverse genres, stand-up comedy acts, and poetry readings. Nizhoni was relieved to escape the dark narrow alley that led from the small Wexford parking lot where she'd parked her blue 1997 Jeep XJ Cherokee. She turned left onto North Leroux, and hastened to the Wexford's door. She entered the lobby, sensing the welcome warm dry air of the space. She strode past the doors of Chester's Restaurant, crossed the small lobby, and entered the Pub. She was pleased to see she was far from being the only person to brave the forbidding elements of this inhospitable night.

After hanging her raincoat and umbrella in the small cloakroom just inside the Pub's entry, Nizhoni surveyed the scene and saw musicians on stage preparing for their initial set, scheduled to start at nine. Flagstaff, she thought with satisfaction, has its jazz devotees, and judging by the size of the audience, I'm just one of the many fans of the Steve Shaw/Archie London Quintet.

She recalled having last heard the group in Las Vegas, the band's home base, just ten months ago. She'd been with Tyler, of course. They were in Vegas for an annual meeting of her national astrophysics society. Her sole-authored paper presentation, "Strategies for Imaging Bodies Orbiting White Dwarfs," had been very well received. Still, her recollections were bittersweet, for she couldn't help but recall how that trip had briefly spawned another spasm of false hope for her marriage. Just two months ago she finally felt forced to demand a divorce from Tyler Lydecker. She chastised herself for waiting so long to file for the divorce she should have known to be inevitable. Ty couldn't be faithful, and that was the bottom line. While she hadn't allowed hope for her marriage to "spring eternal," she regretted having allowed hope to spring for too long.

Chris Larrabee, a local Realty Execs agent and the Pub's host whenever Chester Morrison, the owner, was out of town or ill, approached her. Chris, who'd taken an introductory physics course from Nizhoni at Flagstaff's Humphreys University, greeted her with, "Good evening, Doctor Lydecker. It's a pleasure to see you again."

"And it's good to see you, Chris," she replied, while thinking she would soon be Doctor Yazzie once again. She inquired, "Is Chester okay?"

"Oh yeah. He's in Los Angeles on business. He'll be back tomorrow. He's lucky to be missing this weather. Still, the rain is supposed to move through the area by midnight."

Nizhoni smoothed the damp hair along her temples and countered, "Well, right now, it's just *awful* out there! I parked my Jeep in the little lot down the alley. I know it's for employees, but there were three empty spaces, and I didn't want to walk any farther than I had to in the downpour. Is that okay? I'll move it if you need all the spaces, Chris."

"It's not a problem. The employees are all here, so no one will be inconvenienced."

"Good." She glanced about the room and observed, "Looks like you've got a full house. Any small tables left?"

"Well," Chris replied with a smile, "we reserved a table for two up by the bandstand *just for you.*"

"Oh, darn it! I'm sorry, Chris—I should have let you know my friend couldn't make it. I didn't know until this afternoon, and it's been a really disorganized day," she offered in apology.

"Well, that's quite all right, Dr. Lydecker. You're a regular, and having *you* at a table near the stage enhances the appeal of the room for the general audience."

Nizhoni smiled, though it was nearly as much a grimace as a smile. She never quite knew how to respond to such uncalled for compliments. She certainly knew she was attractive, but she wasn't comfortable with male acquaintances telling her so. Ignoring the compliment, she offered, "I'd be happy to share a table with someone. Frankly, I'd feel a little conspicuous and uncomfortable sitting all alone in front of the band." The musicians would probably feel sorry for poor Miss Lonely Heart, she thought.

"Well then, I'll try to find someone to share your table. And," he assured her, "I'll be particular about him or her." He led Nizhoni to a two-person table, and she was pleased to find it a bit removed from the bandstand. She ordered a glass of California Chardonnay from one of the two frenetically busy waitresses, and upon its delivery, she savored a small sip.

She began to relax into the comforting warmth and subdued lighting of the room. She was pleasantly surprised to see a pretty young blond woman, smartly outfitted in a tight knee-length black skirt, a sparklingly bejeweled waist-length black suit jacket, and high heeled shoes, on stage. She was bantering with the musicians and helping with the sound check. Must be a singer, Nizhoni judged. She liked jazz singers, since they added an extra dimension to jazz programs; and she felt in just the right mood to appreciate a lovelorn ballad or two tonight. Still, she hoped the young chanteuse would choose an up-tempo tune for her final offering, for she didn't relish the prospect of returning to the dismal wet night with a hauntingly sad lyric reverberating through her emotions. Still, she told herself, a sorrowful lyric usually has a comforting element, for its "underneath" message is that you're not alone in your disappointing romance—it's all part of life, and life is a prolific and versatile composer, with a wonderful talent for penning happier lyrics for you once your personal storm has passed.

Just as the band was finishing its preparations, Chris Larrabee came to her table, leaned over and quietly asked, "See the guy in the gray herringbone sport coat and blue button-down shirt standing by the bar? He just came in."

Nizhoni looked around and studied the dark haired man who was smiling while intently watching the musicians on stage. He was of average height, rather athletic-looking, well groomed, and he appeared to be in his mid-thirties. Nizhoni thought he was quite good looking and had an air of respectability. She answered, "Yes. I see him."

"Could you share your table with him? I spoke with him a bit. He said he just came into Flag today. He seems friendly and well mannered."

"All right, Chris. I'd be happy to share my table with him."

Chris delivered the welcome news to the gentleman at the bar, and he promptly came to the table. As he set his drink down he said, "Thanks so much for allowing me to share your table."

"You're certainly welcome," Nizhoni responded warmly, and with a sociable smile. "You must really like jazz to brave the kind of weather we're having tonight."

"Guilty as charged," he replied with an engaging grin. He couldn't help registering the fact that she was a strikingly appealing woman—what a remarkably gorgeous gal, he thought. He said, "I heard on Sirius Satellite Radio's Classic Jazz channel that the quintet and June Connor would be appearing at Chester's tonight. I'm on my way to Los Angeles. I got a ride to Flagstaff from Denver with a friend who was going on to Phoenix. He dropped me off around six. I had time to look around the downtown a bit before the storm hit, and then I had a quiet dinner in the hotel restaurant. I'm planning to catch the train after the first set."

Nizhoni arched her eyebrows and cautioned, "Well, you know, that could be a problem. The Southwest Chief is due at nine-fifty every night, and the first set won't be over until ten-fifteen, or even a bit later."

"Well," he answered in a relaxed mellow voice, "I *was* worried about that, but I called the train station an hour ago, and they told me the Southwest Chief is running a full hour late out of Albuquerque. They said it should be in around ten fifty. The first set will certainly be over before that, and I'll have time to buy my ticket and hop on board. The station is just a stone's throw from here."

Nizhoni nodded and said, "Yes, and the Chief *is* late more nights than not." She paused before asking, "Are you mainly a fan of the group, or the singer?"

"Oh, I'm both . . . ah, I'm sorry, what is your name?"

"My name is Nizhoni." Predictably, she could see that the name struck him as novel, so she added, "It's a Navajo name."

"Well, it has a lovely sound," he commented. "Does it have a meaning, like a referent, or quality?"

"Not really." She didn't wish to say it means "beautiful," and have him say how apt the name was. She inquired, "And what is your name?"

"Wallace—hardly a great sounding name," he said with an engaging hint of diffidence.

"Oh, I think it's a nice name," Nizhoni warmly assured him.

At that point Archie London, the veteran trombonist and co-leader of the quintet spoke into the microphone, welcoming the audience. After a few words regarding the pleasure the band felt for the opportunity to perform at Chester's Pub in Flagstaff, he called the first tune, laid down the beat for the players with finger snaps, and the group launched into the Denzil Best swinger, "Move." Over the next hour and twenty minutes the band played a tasteful mix of jazz standards and two new compositions by Steve Shaw, the young co-leader and tenor saxophone virtuoso. And June Connor proved a delightfully facile and engaging singer. She sang four songs during the set, and Nizhoni enjoyed Connor's choice of material. There was the plaintive, pleading, and most artfully delivered, Jay Livingston and Ray Evans song, "Never Let Me Go," and it touched Nizhoni in a way that nearly moved her to tears. But Miss Connor's other selections were all carefree tunes—"Pick Yourself Up," "Devil May Care," and "Route 66."

When the first set concluded, Nizhoni's table companion excused him self and edged his way to the stage, hoping to speak with June Connor. There were a number of people clustered around the singer, but Wallace did get to speak with her briefly. Nizhoni felt June Connor had a very warm and open manner with her fans. Wallace soon returned to Nizhoni's table, and he commented, "June Connor is a really a nice person."

He checked his watch and said, "Whoa! It's ten-thirty. I've got to hustle down to the train station."

"Well, Wallace," Nizhoni observed, "it's still pouring rain out there. You know, I have to leave, too, and I can give you a ride down to the station. It's on my way, so it won't be any trouble."

"There's no need. It's only a few minutes walk from here, and I've got a raincoat in the cloakroom." He paused only briefly before adding, with a grimace, "I don't have an umbrella, though."

Nizhoni smilingly cautioned, "Wallace, the way it's raining it would take only *one* minute to be soaked to the skin. And you could get stuck at the light for a couple of minutes just waiting to cross Old Route 66."

"Well . . . okay! Thanks."

They exited the hotel, laughingly ducked under Nizhoni's umbrella, and stepped out into a night of shifting mist and eerie rumblings over old Flagstaff. And no one that knew Nizhoni ever saw her again.

CHAPTER 2

▼

In the cozy south-central Ohio town of Pleasanton, home to eighteen thousand Ravenslake University students and twenty-four thousand townspeople, clinical neuropsychology professor Redmond McClain and his artist wife, Jennifer, had just returned from a three week car trip they dubbed their "2008 weddings vacation." It began with a two-day drive to Boston to visit their daughter, Kate, and son-in-law, Drew Payson. After spending four days in Boston, they drove to Hartford, Connecticut, where, on Saturday, June seventh, they participated in the wedding of their only son, twenty six year old Jeremy, to Vanessa Hampshire. The following Monday they headed for Cape Cod, where they spent five gloriously carefree days in Provincetown. On Friday, they traveled to Brockton to attend the Saturday wedding of Redmond's former graduate assistant, Tim Bailey. Tim had married his lively and attractive Humphreys University psychology colleague, Margo Layne, in her hometown. On their return trip to Pleasanton the McClains enjoyed three exhilarating days in Lake George, and then the beautiful scenery and warm hospitality of several excellent small wineries located between Canandaigua and Hammondsport in the Finger Lakes region, just southeast of Rochester. And, yesterday, after a restful night in Rochester, they'd driven back to their home at 134 Shadowy Lane.

Now, at six-fifteen on Saturday evening, the twenty-first day of June 2008, they were in high spirits and enjoying their stroll up the gentle rise of Sycamore Street. Anyone observing the attractive couple conversing warmly as they strode along would almost certainly underestimate their ages, those being fifty-two for Redmond, and fifty-one, for Jennifer.

Redmond, called "Mac" by close friends, was six feet-two, and weighed a stable one hundred and ninety pounds. He'd been a good athlete in his youth and played minor league baseball during the summer prior to beginning grad school at Minnesota State. He had slightly curly black hair, engaging blue-green eyes, and regular features. He moved with a smooth agility, smiled readily, and projected a calm and reassuring manner. And with few exceptions, he tended to root for the underdog in both sports and life.

Jennifer was a slender five feet-eight, and, like Redmond, a picture of admirable physical fitness. She wore her reddish blond hair at shoulder length, had deep-green eyes, and high cheekbones. In addition, she possessed a beguiling repertoire of smiles, laughs, and generally ingratiating expressive behaviors. Redmond took delight in her ability to imitate the manner and vocal characteristics of others. She was a talented artist with a Masters Degree from Minnesota State, and had taught art classes at several colleges and in various community service settings. Jennifer shared with her husband a lively enthusiasm for major sports, classical and classic jazz music, history, nature, and learning in general. She considered her work to be painting, and had sold many paintings at good prices.

Both Jennifer's and Redmond's parents had become comfortably well off over the years, and Redmond and Jennifer were only children. Their parents helped them with investment seed money early in their marriage and gave them sound investment advice. Though they never considered themselves wealthy, and were not inclined to conspicuous consumption, the fact was that they had substantial financial wherewithal. And both Jennifer and Redmond were easy-going and good-natured, a congruence that meant they very seldom had a serious disagreement.

The McClains had been at Ravenslake for only two years. The first year, academic year 2006/2007, Redmond was there on a faculty exchange from Bain-Cottrell University in Seattle. He had been a full professor at Bain-Cottrell for eighteen years and was well known within his neuropsychology research area. Then, during the summer of 2007, after they returned to Seattle, he received an offer to join the Ravenlake faculty. After analyzing the pros and cons of the move, Redmond accepted the offer. The subsequent year convinced the McClains they had made the right decision, for they were very happy in Pleasanton.

Tonight they were headed to the home of friends, Eve and Ted Gundersen, for a casual backyard cookout. The Gundersens had also invited Ellen and Steve Muir, close friends of both the McClains and themselves. Eve and Ted owned the very successful Pleasanton restaurant named The Huddle, located, as tens of thousands of Ravenslake grads could readily tell you, at the northeast corner of Main and East High Streets. The Huddle had been established by Eve's parents in nineteen sixty. Eve was forty, five-five in height, with a slender-to-medium build, attractive facial features, lively brown eyes, and brown hair. She projected an extraverted approachability, was very secure and likeable, and, thanks to these qualities plus a penchant for participation in civic affairs, she was also an elected member of the Pleasanton City Council. Her husband, Ted, age forty-two, was a big man, standing six feet four, with a broad but lean body, a firm face, and uniformly jet-black hair. He had a deep bass-baritone voice and, like his wife, he was sociable and outgoing. Ted had spent eighteen years with the Pleasanton Police Department before retiring four years ago in order to help Eve manage their busy restaurant.

Ellen and Steve Muir were in their mid-forties. Ellen hailed from Chicago and Steve from Johnstown, Pennsylvania. They'd lived in Pleasanton for twelve years. Ellen, the head librarian at Pleasanton's Lange Library, and a regional history archivist at Ravenslake's Kingsley Library, was five-feet-seven, blue eyed, a natural blonde, and an avid Ravenslake Ravens sports fan. Her husband Steve was a cognitive neuropsychologist and a colleague of Redmond's. Steve had a good wry sense of humor, was a dedicated teacher, and a quite good golfer.

When Redmond and Jennifer reached the Gundersen's home Redmond suggested, "Let's go straight to the backyard, hon—they'll be outside on a great day like this." They went to the yard gate and proceeded around the side of the house to the small, attractively landscaped, backyard.

Ted welcomed them with a hearty, "Hey! Welcome, Mac and Jen! It's good to have you guys back in town."

Eve, Steve, and Ellen all offered greetings, as well. Eve added, "There's cold beer in the ice tub, and Chardonnay and Bordeaux Red in the wine chiller. Help yourselves! And tell us about your trip! Was it fun?"

Redmond smilingly responded, "Well, I can tell you it feels like we've been gone for more than just three weeks. We did so many things, and saw so many places!"

Jennifer chimed in, "And yes, Eve, it was all fun. But, I have to say, when we pulled our trusty Sable onto University Avenue around seven last evening it felt *very good* to be home. We saw lots of interesting and scenic places on the trip, but, nice as all that was, it's great to be back in our congenial little college town!"

Ellen asked, "And you got your son, Jeremy, married without any significant hitches, I trust?"

"Yes El, Jeremy and Vanessa got hitched without any hitches," Jennifer replied. "And we had time before the wedding to spend four days with our daughter Kate and son-in-law, Drew, in Boston. Our parents were there for Jeremy's wedding, and we had a grand family get together. The wedding and reception were *very* elegant. Vanessa's parents are prominent in Hartford, and they spared no expense. And now, Vanessa Hampton is Vanessa McClain! They both looked so happy. They left for their honeymoon right after the wedding reception."

Ellen asked, "You had a second wedding to attend on your trip, didn't you?"

"Yes, we did, El," Redmond replied. "The weekend following Jeremy's wedding we attended the marriage of Tim Bailey and Margo Layne. Tim was a doctoral student at Patten University in Pittsburgh during our sabbatical year in the Burgh. He was assigned to me as a half-time research assistant that year. He graduated the following year and he's now at Humphreys University, in Flagstaff, as an assistant professor."

"And," Jennifer added, "Tim met his future wife, Margo Layne, also an assistant psych professor at Humphreys University. We got to know Margo during the Fall Break we spent in Flagstaff last year, and she and Tim came up to the Grand Canyon for a surprise visit with us during the Christmas recess. We're very fond of them. And, their wedding was fun because we also got to see old friends from Patten at the wedding—Joe and Sarah Tedesco, our buddies from grad school days, and also Peg Carpenter, the chair of the psych department at Patten."

Redmond asked, "So, what's been happening in Pleasanton while we were gone? Anything exciting?"

"Well," Eve replied, "nothing to compare with the murder case you guys were involved with before you left on your trip! But, let's see. Well, first of all, Giselle is still doing fine with her pregnancy. Her due date is August fifteenth."

"Oh, that's good to hear," Jennifer said happily.

Giselle Hanford and her husband, Earl, were the next-door neighbors of Redmond and Jennifer. The Hanfords had been married for just a year, and Giselle was pregnant for the first time, at the age of forty. She was one of Pleasanton's best-known and most beloved citizens, being a direct descendant of Nils Johannsen, the early eighteenth century businessman who owned much of the land that became Pleasanton. He was the namesake for both Johannsen State Park and its Johannsen Lake, located just three miles north of town. Giselle was one of the wealthiest people in Pleasanton, and a celebrated alumna of, and benefactress to, Ravenslake University. Her husband, Earl, was the Dean of Ravenslake's Switzer Business College.

Eve continued, "And, while you guys were away the renovations and improvements of the uptown business blocks that I spent the better part of last year haggling with store owners over, finally got underway. New sidewalks and the repaving of High Street are in progress. High Street is completely closed to traffic from College Avenue to Beech Avenue. But we'll soon have a new smooth concrete subsurface under our venerable red cobblestone street."

Ted noted, "Yeah, that's gonna be real nice."

Eve continued, "The goal is to have all the new street lighting and store front sprucing up finished before the fall semester rolls around and the freshmen and their parents flock into town."

Ellen, looking characteristically cool and comfortable in a light blue short-sleeved blouse, khaki shorts, and sandals, pushed her long blond hair back over her shoulders, and said in her soft and pleasing voice, "And most of the shop owners, those that hadn't upgraded their store fronts in the last twenty years or more, are going ahead with the City Council-approved designs and colors. The renovations should please alums when they visit Ravenslake this fall. Everyone knows uptown had gotten a bit dowdy."

"Well," Jennifer said with a happy smile, "that all sounds terrific! And we can thank Eve for her hard work and patience in securing the agreements of those shop owners."

Steve raised his drink and called, "A toast to Eve, our hard working Pleasanton City Council woman."

"To Eve," they all said as they raised their drinks and took dutiful sips.

Eve smiled and said, "I won't say it 'was nothing,' guys, but once the main restaurants got in line, the other shop owners caught the enthusiasm. So, in the end, it went pretty smoothly."

"You're being too modest, Eve," Ellen assured her, and the others all agreed.

After a brief pause, Steve commented, "Well, this is a gorgeous evening."

"Sure is," Jennifer concurred.

Steve noted, "But before the fall semester rolls around, Pleasanton has to go through the blistering heat and stifling humidity of July and August. It's essential to get away in August. You don't want to get worn down by the heat and humidity just before the fall semester gets underway. So, El and I plan to escape some of the worst of it by heading to the cool climate of Tahoe City for a week."

"Hey! That sounds great," Redmond said. "The scenery at Tahoe is spectacular, and the night life, with casinos and shows, is also great."

"Yes," Steve responded. "We'll rent a car, and after our Tahoe week, we'll drive over to Coos Bay, Oregon. Coos Bay is right on the Pacific shore."

"That sounds cool, in both senses of the word," Eve observed.

Ellen added, "We'll be staying in my cousin Stacy's beachfront home for two weeks. She's going to be in England for a conference and some sightseeing. We'll use her home as a base from which to take some trips to interesting coastal towns and tourist attractions."

Ted commented, "Man, that sounds really nice. You're lucky to have a cousin that lives in such an interesting area, El."

"*And*, one that travels a lot," Ellen said with smile.

"Yeah, it all sounds great," Ted granted, "but it'd be *way* too hectic for Eve and me. We're just going to do what we've done for the last four years now—take a nice lakefront cottage on Lake Bellaire in Michigan for three weeks. We'll rent a little powerboat, fish a lot, play a lot of golf at the beautiful Shanty Creek course and other courses in the area, and, naturally, we'll hit some of our favorite restaurants. See, when we go on vacation we want to slow down, not speed up like you guys," he said to Ellen and Steve.

Eve asked Redmond and Jennifer what plans they had for an August escape from Pleasanton's heat.

"Well," Jennifer responded, "we've been thinking of heading back out to Flagstaff and its cool summer climate. There are lots of things we love about the area. In fact, Flagstaff has moved to the top of our short list of possible second home candidates. We have a pretty good idea just where we'd like to have a home there. It's an area just a little ways outside the northwestern city limits, and just off of Highway 180, the road that goes to the South Rim of Grand Canyon National Park. Of course, we haven't looked into prices of the homes there yet."

"Well, Jen," Ted offered, "I understand Arizona real estate had a big downturn in the last few years. Maybe it's a lot more affordable than it was."

"That would sure be nice, Ted," Jennifer replied.

Eve changed the subject by noting, "Teddy, it's time to fire up the grill."

As he raised himself from his chair, Ted said, "Right—but it won't take long to prepare my entrée. We're having maple-Dijon mustard and chives glazed chicken breasts, baked barbeque beans in serious hot sauce, corn on the cob, potato salad, and a baked cornbread casserole with sliced green chili peppers." He added, with a deep chuckle, "You might wanna keep the cold beer or ice tea handy. And dessert will be Eve's home baked apple pie, with vanilla ice cream, if you like." The others all expressed approval and anticipation of the forthcoming repast.

By eight o'clock they'd all enjoyed the meal, including apple pie and ice cream, and were savoring cups of strong Tuscany Blend coffee that Eve purchased from the Grounds for Thinking coffee shop. Eve said, "I think this is my favorite of all the coffees Kelly Wilson blends for his shop."

"It's one of my favorites, too," Jennifer said. "And I like the Carolina Mountain Blend and Highlander Cream ones, as well."

Ellen inquired, "Jen, are you going to continue to work your two hour a week stint at Grounds for Thinking? The reason I ask is I know you're planning to devote more time to your painting and the launching of a series of prints of local scenes."

"Oh sure, I want to continue working at Grounds. Those two hours allow me to see lots of our friends and acquaintances that come into the shop; and there's good exercise in walking uptown and back every Tuesday afternoon."

Eve chuckled and noted, "And it gives you and me an excuse to meet for coffee and a pastry once a week after your work; but let's not start that until school begins, Jen. Everything's so scrambled in terms of activities now. Ted and I have a ton of work to do for the restaurant. We have the ongoing renovations of the dining room at the Huddle, planning for the big weekend events of the fall, recruiting student workers, and so forth. Plus, I'm busy helping Heidi with all her preparations for going off to Purdue for her freshman year."

"That's fine, Eve," Jennifer replied. "But I look forward to our Tuesday afternoon coffee or tea sessions once the fall semester gets underway. And I wouldn't want to quit on Kelly Wilson. He relies on me to price the second hand books the shop takes in. I enjoy my little two hours of 'work.' It's an easy activity, and Kelly lets me hang some of my paintings in the shop, as he does for other artists, as well."

Ted observed, "The social contacts must be the main attraction of the job for you, Jen. I understand your pay for the two hours a week is a free sandwich and salad on Tuesdays, and free coffee anytime. And as far as the exercise involved in walking uptown from Shadowy Lane is concerned, you don't need it to keep fit, given that you guys jog three days a week, weather-be-damned, and you work out in your basement gym pretty regularly."

"Well," Jennifer responded, "our vacation interfered with our exercise routine, but we'll get back on schedule. And I do love to walk, as well as work out. There's something about walking around Pleasanton that's good for my mood. Seeing all the energetic students, the classic old and magnificent new buildings, the many trees and old homes, and knowing something of the history of this little town and of our two-hundred and six year old RU—well, it's uplifting. And, it often makes me think of things about life and time . . . all kinds of things, really. So, walking stimulates my thinking and appreciation of our life here, and any exercise in it is just a minor secondary benefit."

Ted observed, "You know, Eve and I are RU grads, and Eve was born here. So, although we love Pleasanton, and we do sense the history of it, I, at least, don't have any contemplative reactions to walking about town."

"Maybe it's because you've spent so much time here, Ted," Jennifer suggested. "Or maybe I'm just overly responsive to the histories of places. When we were on sabbatical in Pittsburgh I almost felt, at times, that I was living both in the present *and* during the days of Andrew Carnegie and Henry Clay Frick. Of course, I was reading all about Pittsburgh's history. Maybe I'm just too imaginative!"

"Well, imagination is a good thing in an artist," Ellen commented.

Redmond noted, "You know, a person can feel that the past is over, and pretty much ignore it. But you can also include the past with the present, and sense the relationship between them; and I think that's cognitively and emotionally enriching."

"That's a good way to look at it, Mac," Steve observed. "When the past has created wonderful things of the present you can appreciate them more if you think about how they came to be, and of the contributions of various people. And even when the past has created terrible things, such as great violence against people or places, it can still be cognitively enriching—like in trying to understand how it all came about."

"Okay," Eve exclaimed. "This conversation has gone from Jen appreciating the history of Pleasanton and RU, to 'great violence against people and places.' Steve baby, *your* drinks are cut off!"

They all laughed.

As the twilight sky dimmed they set about cleaning up the outdoor eating area, returning utensils and dinnerware to the kitchen, loading dishes in the dishwasher, and putting leftovers in the refrigerator. Then they settled into the family room of the house and had either an after dinner drink or another coffee. They talked about various things that were going on in town and at RU. They also noted that they'd all received their Ravens football tickets for the upcoming season, and were looking forward to a great year from the Ravens squad.

At ten-fifteen the McClains and the Muirs thanked Eve and Ted for an enjoyable evening, a delicious meal, and warm sociability. The guests said goodnight and strolled out to Sycamore Street. Jennifer said to Ellen, "Let's get together for lunch sometime this week."

"That'd be great, Jen. How about Tuesday at the Dutch Kitchen? Most of the restaurants on East High are closed because of the street construction."

"Fine, El. Noon?"

"Yes, noon at the Dutch Kitchen. See you then."

Redmond and Jennifer waved goodnight to Ellen and Steve and headed east on Sycamore. As they began the gentle downhill walk to their home Redmond said, "I think we should go ahead and make reservations for a three week vacation in Flagstaff. We know the weather will be great, even bracingly cool in the evenings—a perfect retreat from Pleasanton's late July and August weather. We could look into the prices of homes, and, of course, we can do great day trips to the Canyon, Sedona, Prescott, and maybe Las Vegas, too. We haven't been to Vegas since '93. I think two days and nights would be enough in Vegas. We could see a show, and perhaps find a good jazz club in town."

"That would be wonderful, Mac."

"I'll get on the web and check it out tomorrow."

"You could check out activities and events in Sedona as well, sweetheart. I'd really like to spend a few days and nights in Sedona."

"You got it, Jen!"

CHAPTER 3

▼

On the following Tuesday morning Redmond and Jennifer awoke at their usual six-thirty time, and with only a cup of coffee to fortify themselves, they ran the three miles of the more demanding of their two morning running routes. It took them down the short block of Shadowy Lane to University Avenue, along the east boundary of campus, downhill to the turnoff into Pepper Park, along Tawee Creek to their turn around point at The Bluffs, and from there they retraced their route back to 134 Shadowy Lane. Then, after showering and dressing, they enjoyed their breakfast of tomato juice, scrambled eggs, two strips of very crisp bacon, wheat bread toast with strawberry jam, and a second cup of coffee. Following this, they took their usual assortment of vitamins.

Redmond then remarked, "I'll be at school all day, hon. I've almost finished the manuscript I was working on before the distractions of June, and I'm determined to polish it off this week. Then I'll email it to Jeff Singleton at San Francisco State for his input, and let him have a shot at suggested changes." The manuscript was just one of a number of multi-authored papers still emanating from the data of a massive ten-year, multi-center, Alzheimer's Project Redmond had headed up while at Bain-Cottrell University in Seattle.

"That's fine, darling. I'm just planning to do a bit of weeding and some rearranging of the front flowerbeds this morning; and I'm having lunch with Ellen at the Dutch Kitchen at noon. After lunch, I'll walk up to Grounds for Thinking and price the used books that came in during our eastern sojourn. I'd also like to drop by Phil Regan's Art Shop and talk with him about the prints and sketches of town and campus scenes other artists have sold here over the years. Eve tells me Phil knows all about those efforts, and who might still be trying to ply that trade."

Redmond smiled and said, "You know, it's good to be getting back into our routines, isn't it?"

"Yeah, it really is. It's a reassuring antidote to that unanchored feeling I was beginning to get from three weeks of car travel. I can't imagine how some people manage to keep their minds straight while just knocking about. I mean, it was all fun, but I have an actual *need* for my more regular routine."

"Me too, babe. See you around five."

At exactly noon Jennifer finished her walk to the south campus area by entering the Dutch Kitchen. The modest-sized restaurant was busy with RU summer faculty and uptown business people now forced from their usual East High Street restaurants by the street closing. Ellen was already there and seated at a small table next to a window facing out on the beautifully green and freshly mowed RU women's field hockey venue. As she slipped into the chair across from Ellen, she asked, "Been here long, El?"

"No, Jen—just arrived a few minutes ago, and luckily this table opened up. It's really busy here today." As Ellen looked for a waitress she saw a new female acquaintance smilingly approaching their table. She greeted the woman, saying, "Hi Lindsey!" She added, "Let me introduce you to my friend. This is Jennifer McClain; and Jen, this is Dr. Lindsey Marston."

Both Jennifer and Lindsey smiled and said it was nice to meet the other. Ellen informed Jennifer, "Lindsey has just joined the RU faculty in the English department. And," she said to Dr. Marston, "Jennifer is a local artist and the wife of Dr. Redmond McClain, who's in the psych department."

Dr. Marston asked, "So, your husbands are both in psych?"

"Yes," Ellen responded, and then she asked, "Are you getting settled-in okay, Lindsey?"

As Jennifer listened to further exchanges between the two women, she found herself studying Lindsey Marston. There was something singular and impressive about her, a suggestion of energy even in her static stance and relaxed facial features. She appeared to be in her mid-thirties, about five-five, with an admirable figure, and a lithesome grace to her movements. Her hair, a shiny warm auburn hue, was casually cut to shoulder length, with an attractive slight curl toward the neck. Her skin appeared flawless, her intense blue eyes were bright and probing, her facial features seemed perfect, and her manner was direct and confident—in all, an attractive and formidable sort of woman. Jennifer thought that while Lindsey Marston was a bit prettier, she resembled the celebrated nineteen-forties and fifties movie actress, Bette Davis, famous for her many roles as strong, haughty, scheming, even vengeful, women. But then Jennifer silently chastised herself for the unwarranted implication that Lindsey Marston was haughty, scheming, or vengeful. No justification for that—just an errant impression from nowhere, she told herself in mild self-rebuke.

Dr. Marston smiled winsomely and said, "Well, I must run. See you later, Ellen." To Jennifer she said, "It was nice to make your acquaintance, Jennifer."

"Pleasure to meet you, as well, Lindsey."

Dr. Marston gave a little wave of the hand to Ellen and Jennifer, rejoined the two ladies with whom she had lunched, and they exited the restaurant.

Ellen said, "I met Lindsey when she came to the library last Friday to see what we have to offer students, and I learned a little about her. She's apparently an expert on British women writers of the eighteenth and nineteenth centuries. Regrettably, our little town library doesn't have an abundance of books by or about eighteenth and nineteenth century British women writers."

"Seems like an interesting specialization," Jennifer observed. "Is Lindsey married?"

"Widowed," Ellen replied. "She told me her husband had worked in the same area of scholarship, and they published several books together. She volunteered that he was killed in a multiple car accident in a mountain tunnel near Salzburg, Germany, while attending an international conference. I have to say she said it rather stoically. She doesn't seem to be the flighty or sentimental type."

No, certainly not, Jennifer thought.

Ellen took a sip of tea before exclaiming, "Oh! And she came from that college in Flagstaff."

"Humphreys University? Really?"

"Yes. I gathered in talking with her that she wasn't all that fond of Humphreys, and is delighted to be at RU. She said Pleasanton is 'so refined.'"

"Well, you know, Mac and I spent the '99/2000 academic year on sabbatical at Humphreys University. That's how we got clued into the attractions of Northern Arizona. And while Humphreys isn't RU, it's definitely a good school."

The two friends talked about other things as they ate, and at twelve-fifty they paid their checks and stepped out into the pleasantly warm midday air. As she retrieved her car keys from her handbag Ellen offered, "Can I drop you at Grounds for Thinking, Jen?"

"No thanks, El. It's a nice walk up to Grounds."

They exchanged parting words, and Jennifer headed toward the coffee shop at the corner of South Elm and West Walnut. As she strode along the moderate upgrade toward Grounds for Thinking she appreciated how pleasant the weather was, and how pretty the flower-adorned yards of the gracious old homes along Elm Street were. I can understand, she mused, how Lindsey Marston could find Pleasanton more agreeable than Flagstaff. Pleasanton is a quieter town, off the beaten track. It has beautiful old homes, all manner of large mature trees, a perfectly impressive Georgian Colonial campus, and a general air of refinement. And Flagstaff has a rougher texture to it. It's an old lumbering and railroading town, and nowadays it's a Mecca for tourists. But the natural landscape and feel of Northern Arizona are as awesome and rewarding as are the verdant lawns and cultured aura of Pleasanton. She sought some deeper characterizations of the two places. She thought of Northern Arizona, with its Grand Canyon and ancient volcanic Peaks, as testament to the long evolution of the earth and the eventual emergence of conditions that nurtured life, while Pleasanton seemed testament to the much more recent evolution of humans and their singular intellectual and esthetic needs and inclinations. She decided, with a little smile of resignation, that these generalizations failed to capture the deep essence of the two places. Still, she couldn't help feeling there was something cogent in her thoughts about them, and that, in any case, she was drawn to both of them.

When she entered Grounds for Thinking she found the scent of the exotic coffees being brewed on this day most pleasing. She said, "Hey, Joel," to Joel Wallen, an RU junior and Pleasanton native, now embarking on his second year of working the counter at Grounds.

"Ah," Joel said expansively, "the wandering book appraiser has returned to our ivy-covered towers from the corrupt East Coast!"

Jennifer laughed and said, "We had a great time on the east coast, Joel. And I don't think it has the corner on the corruption market! But now I need to put some prices on recently acquired used books."

Joel smiled and said, "I believe there are quite a few books stacked on your desk and a few on the floor."

"Good! I'm ready to get to work. I've had lunch, but I'll need some caffeine to get started." She glanced at the chalkboard listing of the coffees of the day, and ordered the Sumatra Lowland Blend.

Joel drew and delivered the coffee to the counter and Jennifer took her cup and headed to her little ten by fourteen foot office at the back of the shop. As she passed by the cake and scone display case and the pre-wrapped sandwich and salad cases, she noticed that it was a very quiet day at Grounds. She couldn't help thinking how busy the shop would be once the fall semester started. She looked forward to that happy prospect. She entered the long back hallway that led to the small parking lot in the alley, passed the supply room, and at the next door she entered her little office.

She snapped on the light and sat down at her desk. A quick glance across the books on the desk and floor told her there were approximately forty books to be priced. She dutifully examined each for condition, then removed the little index card belonging to the donor of the book, and applied the shop's rule that the original price of the book and her judgment of its condition conjointly determined the value she assigned. Then she recorded the dollar amount the donor would receive toward the price of any used or new book the donor might later buy. Finally, she placed the books in their appropriate places on the library shelves, and took the credited cards to Joel at the front counter.

Joel opened the big card file drawer and began filing the cards to their alphabetic positions. As he did so he said, "It sure has been quiet here today, Jen. The summer doldrums have really taken hold in Pleasanton. I can't wait for the students to get back to town."

"Yeah, I'm with you on that, Joel. See you later."

*   *   *

When Redmond completed his walk home to 134 Shadowy Lane at five o'clock he found Jennifer comfortably reclined in a canvas sling chair on a shaded area of the back deck. She was attired in shorts, a sleeveless blouse, and a pair of old running shoes, and she was reading a book. When Redmond opened the screen door she smiled and softly said, "Hello, darling."

As he stepped out onto the deck Redmond responded, in a tender voice, "Hello, sweetie." He paused briefly and studied her before saying, "You're looking very appealing in this pleasant setting today!"

"Well, to look appealing is something I strive for, at least where you're concerned."

Redmond chuckled. "Well, you've certainly succeeded in your striving. You look great!"

Jennifer locked her gaze on Redmond's eyes while saying, "Und *yong*, Mag. Tall me I loog yong, darlink. I vant to loog yong." She said it in a playful pleading voice that Redmond considered a good impression of the great Greta Garbo.

"You don't look . . ."

"A day over thirty-seven! Right?"

He laughed. "I've told you many times you don't look a day over thirty-seven, and it's absolutely true!"

They exchanged a brief kiss, and Redmond said, "I'll get into more relaxed clothing, and be back in a few minutes. Can I bring you a drink when I come back?"

"No thanks, sweetheart. I've got an iced tea here," she said as she lifted her glass.

Redmond soon returned, attired in khaki shorts, a white short-sleeved RU golfing shirt, and sandals. He pulled a chair close to Jennifer's and commented, "Gorgeous day, eh?"

"Yes—smells great, too. The aroma of flowers from the RU Formal Gardens is drifting our way today. But, gorgeous as it is, we know all too well that miserably hot and humid weather will assault us come August!"

"Yeah, for sure. But you and I shall *escape* to the cool mountain air of Flagstaff on July thirtieth."

Jennifer asked, "Did you let Tim and Margo know we're coming to town and would like to have dinner with them?"

"Yes . . . emailed with Tim. We'll be meeting them for dinner at *La Fonda* on Wednesday, August sixth, at seven."

After a brief silence Jennifer said, "Oh, I thought you'd be interested to know that while Ellen and I were having lunch a new faculty member that El met at the Lange stopped by our table to say hello. El introduced us. Anyway, she's a new English prof. Her name is Lindsey Marston. And the point I wanted to tell you about is that she came from Humphreys University in Flagstaff."

"Really?"

"Yes. And I wondered if you ever ran across her while we were on sabbatical. Lindsey appears to be in her mid-thirties, and she's quite attractive, if that should assist your recall," she said with a sly smile.

"Marston . . . Marston," Redmond muttered searchingly. "No, I don't remember meeting any Marston at Humphreys."

"The English department apparently thinks she'll be a good addition to their faculty. Ellen said Lindsey's area is the study of eighteenth and nineteenth century British women writers."

Redmond mused aloud, "British women writers of the eighteenth and nineteenth century. Sounds like a rather narrow and obscure area, doesn't it? I can only think of two British women who *might* have been eighteenth century writers—Charlotte and Emily Brontë."

Jennifer, the inveterate bibliophile, smiled and said, "Mac, Charlotte and Emily Brontë published their only really successful books, *Jane Eyre* and *Wuthering Heights*, respectively, in the late *eighteen*-forties, not in the seventeen hundreds. They were *nineteenth* century, sweetheart."

"Okay then—I can't think of *any* eighteenth century British women writers," he said with a laugh.

"Ellen said Lindsey is quite ecstatic about being at RU."

"Well, we do have a large and talented group of people in English, not the least of whom is Langston Wallingford. I mean Langston's a Regents Professor and has written some very successful books, both fiction and non-fiction. Of course, he does have an ego to match his talents. Anyway, I can see why Lindsey Marston would be happy to be at RU. And Pleasanton is a terrific little college town."

"Absolutely."

"Didn't you have some other items on your agenda for today?"

"I did, and I dealt with all of them. I worked my stint at Grounds. There were only about forty books to price, so I finished early. And I stopped in at Phil Regan's shop, but he wasn't in. I tell you, Mac, uptown is dead. Having East High all torn up and overrun with construction equipment and workers has forced everybody out of our main business area. But, I'm sure it'll all be worth it when the fall semester rolls around."

"Yeah, I'm looking forward to that. And we've got North Carolina coming to town for the opening game on the thirtieth. The grand sprucing up of East High Street should make our visiting alums and other fans happy on game day."

"Well, it'll help, Mac. But only a Ravens win will make them *really* happy!"

CHAPTER 4

───────── ▼ ─────────

At noon on Tuesday, July fifteenth, Margo Layne Bailey, assistant professor of psychology at Humphreys University, and the newly married wife of Tim Bailey, knocked on the third floor office door of Erin James, associate professor of sociology. Hearing a pressured "Come in" response, Margo opened the door and saw Erin seated at her desk and busily scribbling a note.

"I just have to finish this little reminder to myself," Erin said, "and then we can go to lunch." She finished the note with a definitively laid on exclamation point, and energetic, "Done." She looked up and asked, "We're eating at the Union, right?"

"Yes," Margo returned. The brown-haired young women exited the office and moved briskly down the north stairwell from the third to the first floor, exited the building, and began their short walk to the Student Union. It was a nice day, mostly sunny, and with the temperature in the mid-seventies. As they walked they conversed about what they were working on. Margo volunteered that she was writing an article based on a study she'd completed during the spring term, and Erin said she was still struggling with an ungainly wealth of new information she needed to include in the revision of her introductory sociology textbook.

Erin said, "Margo, if you ever get a chance to write a *textbook*, for god's sake, don't do it! It's the most tedious, compulsive, maddening kind of activity. And just when you think you've described the definitive essence of some area or the very latest important finding, what happens? One of your colleagues somewhere in this freaking world reports a study that demolishes your 'definitive' important finding or conclusion. It seems like an endless process of revisions. But, thankfully, your publisher does set a firm deadline that ultimately frees you from the concern of not having the absolute up-to-the-minute, very latest, information on all subjects in your book. My deadline is September thirtieth, so I'm only free to be compulsive and frenetic for a few more months."

"Well, I admire your dedication, Erin. Writing a textbook is a major undertaking. I don't think I'll ever be tempted to try it. I like doing my research and writing up the results. It's simple and straightforward. You have a question, you design a study to try to answer it, and you analyze the data. If the results support your hypothesis you have a little inward celebration, and if the results fail to confirm your hypothesis you can still often get it published if the question is important and your experimental design had cogency."

"Yes. I'm looking forward to being able to devote more time to some research with my grad assistants again."

They went through the short cafeteria line of the nearly empty Lumberjack Room, and both selected a salad, a sandwich, and a soft drink. Then they found seats at a small table. The first summer session had just ended, and save for administrators and a few faculty members working at their scholarly pursuits, few people were on campus. Margo noticed that Erin was looking fixedly at something. She glanced to her left to see what it might be, but saw nothing other than the nearby south wall of the cafeteria.

Erin noticed Margo's glance toward the wall, and said, "Oh! You're wondering what I was looking at."

Margo smiled as she pushed her long hair back off her shoulders and said, "Well, I thought it might be that good looking Casey Suder, the new Business Dean, that you told me you dated a few weeks ago."

Erin raised her eyebrows dismissively and nodded negatively. "No," she said, "and I haven't heard a peep from him."

"Too bad."

"No big deal. It was just a colleague get together sort of thing, I guess. He's extremely reserved." She paused briefly before saying, "But what I was looking at just now was the painting on the wall above the table over there."

Margo looked at the painting and asked, "The portrait of the pretty Navajo girl?"

"Yes. It seems that every time I'm in this area of the room it somehow demands my attention. It's like I have to look to make sure its still there. The girl in that painting reminds me so much of a young professor, an astrophysicist, that I first met in the fall of '98, my first year at Humphreys." Erin paused before quietly adding, "Something terrible happened to her."

"Really? What was it?"

"I don't know."

Margo smiled and gibed, "Erin, you said something terrible happened to her, but you also said you don't know what happened to her—maybe you can see it's a bit, might we say . . . *inconsistent?*"

Erin smiled feebly and said, "Well, I should have said something terrible *must have* happened to her."

"Mmm . . . sounds interesting. Tell me about her."

Erin began her narrative in a soft and tentative tone, seeming as much immersed in recollection as in the act of communication. "She was a wonderful young woman. Her name was Nizhoni, a Navajo name meaning 'beautiful,' and she truly *was* beautiful. She'd already been here four years when I arrived, and had earned an early promotion to associate professor. She married Tyler Lydecker right after her first year here. Lydecker is still a professor in the anthropology department at Humphreys. I first met Nizhoni when I was assigned to a university committee concerned with the recruitment of minority students. She was very interested in helping Navajo students adjust to Humphreys. She worked closely with The Navajo Student Club. Nizhoni and I became good friends. We often had coffee together at this very table, and she spoke of lots of interesting things about her life, and a few things about her marriage."

"Well, she sounds like an admirable faculty member."

"She was. But during the fall term of two thousand she asked her husband for a divorce, and he reluctantly agreed to it. It came as a bit of a surprise, because they'd been married a little over three years, and they seemed happy. And then, they got into really bitter disagreements and legalistic arguments about the terms of their divorce. Tyler Lydecker isn't exactly wealthy, but he apparently does have some money, through inheritance. Nizhoni, on the other hand, was born into a traditional Navajo family in the little town of Many Farms, a town of fifteen hundred people. Many Farms is basically surrounded by desert, although there is a man-made lake there. It's located about twenty miles north of Chinle on U.S. 191. Nizhoni went to the Chinle School District high school in Many Farms, where, literally, ninety-nine percent of the enrollment consisted of Navajo students."

"An unusual background for an astrophysicist, perhaps?"

"Yes. But her teachers recognized early on that she was a *remarkably* gifted student. She became utterly captivated by physics, chemistry, and mathematics. She was intrigued by the questions most people are content to answer only with religious fables of one type or another—questions as to the nature of the cosmos and the origins of life and of humans on our planet."

"I suppose it could have been difficult for her if her family adhered to traditional Navajo beliefs."

"I suppose it was at times. Her family believed in the Navajo creation story, the four previous worlds, the four magical mountains, the various Navajo spirits, and rituals. But even as a young adolescent, Nizhoni couldn't believe these myths. Her parents were loving people. They never rejected her because of her disbelief, and she never rejected them because of their belief.

"During the spring term of 2001, one of her undergraduate students—Joshua Usher was his name—complained to the Arts and Sciences Dean that Nizhoni was teaching atheism. He claimed she was promoting, among other heretical ideas, the view that our planet is 4.567 billion years old, plus or minus a few million years. The student told her, during class, that this wasn't correct, and that the earth is six thousand years old. He said theologians had 'calculated' the age from the Christian bible story of the genesis. Joshua had been raised in the religious atmosphere of his father, the Prophet Jimmy Usher."

Margo smiled and asked, "Mr. Usher actually calls himself the *Prophet* Jimmy Usher?"

"Well, at least his followers do. Brian Koppel, in our department, studies the sociology of religions. Brian told me, at the time of Joshua Usher's complaints about Nizhoni's teaching, a few things about Jimmy Usher's theology. Usher leads a religious settlement located out in the semi-desert. The closest town is Lake Havasu City. He calls his colony The House of the Ascension. It's Christian, but has some beliefs that are strictly Usher's own. Usher has written his own version of the bible, based on visions and what he says were instructions he received directly from God—but it includes parts of the King James Bible, as well. The sect believes 'The End of Days' is fast approaching. As I understand it, Usher and his followers believe they'll join an army led by the resurrected Christ, and wage war against Satan and his followers, as well as those of other, false, religions. It's modeled on a story written around 79 A.D. by a man named John, although there were apparently three 'Johns' and no one knows, for sure, which one wrote it. According to the story, Jesus and his followers will win the war. The rest of mankind, and Satan, will die horrible deaths in the Apocalypse, while the winners will have eternal life in Heaven."

"And they'll all live happily ever after!"

"Yes. Anyway, the A and S Dean looked into Joshua's complaint, talked to other students in the class, and decided the complaint wasn't valid—that Nizhoni was not teaching atheism. Further, he approved Nizhoni's request that Joshua be dropped from her class because he presented his religious arguments so frequently and at such length that it interfered with her teaching of the class. The incident got a bit of publicity in town. There were a few letters from townspeople to the *Daily Sun* that argued HU should incorporate creationism into Nizhoni's Introduction to Astronomy class."

"Good grief," Margo remarked.

"Yes. But, as to Nizhoni's background, she graduated early from high school and got a full academic scholarship to the University of California, at Berkley. When she completed her Bachelor of Science degree she went on to Stanford, again on full scholarship, and got her Ph.D. in astrophysics. It was at Stanford that she met Tyler Lydecker. He was pursuing a doctorate in anthropology, and he graduated a year ahead of her. When he got his degree he accepted a position here at Humphreys. The following year Humphreys was very happy to hire Nizhoni, and she was pleased to be in Flagstaff. She had regular time on the big telescope at the Naval Observatory out on Mars Hill, as well as the intellectual stimulation of a variety of visiting astronomers that, like her, had affiliations with the permanent staff at the Lowell Observatory here in Flag. It was a great professional arrangement, and it allowed her to be reasonably near her family. And, she and Lydecker married in June following her first year here."

"But her marriage was falling apart?"

"Yes." Erin considered her words carefully as she said, "Nizhoni . . . *intimated* to me that Lydecker had a mistress, and couldn't, or wouldn't, give up seeing her." She added, "I never inquired about the details. She never said who the woman was."

Margo wondered if Erin actually knew more "details" than she felt it proper to reveal.

"But," Erin continued, "Nizhoni wasn't a timid person, and since she felt she'd been terribly disrespected by her husband's philandering, she hired an attorney and filed for divorce on the grounds of Lydecker's adultery, and incompatible differences. Tyler Lydecker's parents lived in Muncie, Indiana, but they had an impressive vacation house out on U.S. 180, the road to the Grand Canyon. They were quite well off, according to what Nizhoni said. Tyler's mother had died several years before Tyler and Nizhoni married, and Tyler's father had developed heart trouble. One of the consequences of his condition was that he could no longer deal with Flagstaff's seven thousand foot elevation. He *gave* the newlyweds his Flagstaff vacation home as his wedding gift."

"Wow! Not a bad wedding gift."

"Yes, that was great—but Arizona is a community property state, and moreover, the gift house was deeded in the names of both Tyler and Nizhoni Lydecker. Nizhoni confided that, given these facts, she was pressing Lydecker for possession of the house as part of their divorce settlement—compensation for pain and suffering, she said. She also threatened to make public the details of his adultery, and to reveal the identity of the woman with whom he had his affair if Lydecker didn't accede to her demands."

"My inclination," Margo said with a smile, "is to say, 'Go girl!' And you're right—she doesn't sound at all timid."

"No. And as further evidence of that, during the same period, she told me she was considering filing a sexual harassment suit against someone here at Humphreys. I guess it's fair to say she was agitated and ticked off during that period."

"Harassment against whom?"

"She . . . never said. But she was *very* angry about it."

Again, Margo wondered if her very discreet and proper friend was holding back on the information as to the identity of Nizhoni's harasser. Margo asked only, "And all this stuff, her divorce, the harassment, and the atheism flap were happening at pretty much the same time?"

"Yep. All during the Spring Term of 2001."

"Musta been one hell of a time for her!"

"Yes . . . but, you know, she never seemed to feel defeated by it. In fact, she often seemed energized by it all."

"That's remarkable!" After a brief pause Margo asked, "So, just what was the terrible thing that *must* have happened to Nizhoni?"

"Well, I suppose the thing was . . . murder."

Margo's eyes widened and she caught her breath. "Good heavens!" she muttered.

"But no one really knows what happened to her. What is known is that she went to the Wexford Hotel to hear a jazz group. It was a Saturday night—April twentieth of 2001, to be precise. And it was the stereotypic dark and stormy night of murder mystery stories, with heavy rain, blustering winds, thunder and lightning!"

Margo was finding Erin's story more than just a little interesting.

"Nizhoni had learned to love classic jazz while she was a student in the Bay area, and she'd planned to go to Chester's Pub to hear a group from Las Vegas. She had arranged to go with Gwendolyn Kline, who is still here in the music department's Jazz Studies Program. But Gwendolyn sprained an ankle pretty severely while jogging that afternoon, and wasn't up to accompanying Nizhoni to Chester's.

"Nizhoni went to hear the jazz group at Chester's Pub by herself. The manager of the Pub that night was a young man named Chris Larrabee, a local realtor. He usually managed the club when the owner, Chester Morrison, was out of town. I knew Chris because I'd bought my condo through him. According to Chris, Nizhoni stayed at the Pub through the first set, but left sometime shortly after the set ended. Chris was busy and didn't actually see her leave, but he said Nizhoni had agreed to allow a man to sit with her at the table she'd reserved for two—you know, for her and Gwendolyn. Apparently, the band was popular and there was a bigger crowd than could be seated. So Nizhoni and the man were seated together throughout the first set."

"And Nizhoni left and disappeared into the blackness of the night?"

"Sadly, that's exactly what happened. She was never seen again. She had mentioned to Chris Larrabee that she parked her Jeep in that tiny lot behind the Wexford, but her Jeep wasn't there. It has never been found."

"What about the man that sat with her? Did they find him and ask if he had any information?"

"No. Chris said he'd never seen the man until that night. He said it was possible that Nizhoni and the man left together. He noticed that Nizhoni and the man were both gone before the second set started, but he couldn't say if they left together or not. He described the man as of average height and weight, casually well dressed, and polite." Erin took a sip of her drink before adding, "Chris moved to Kingman a couple of years ago."

"Well, it's a sad and mysterious story. I'm surprised I'd never heard of it."

"You know," Erin said in a resigned and reflective tone, "Flag is a place where memories can be short. People come and go, and crimes aren't uncommon here. Lots of tourists and transients, rolling stones among them, rattle through Flag on their way to or from Los Angeles or back east. There were some articles about Nizhoni's disappearance in the *Daily Sun* around the first and second year anniversary dates of the disappearance, but after that, interest in it seems to have faded away."

"Did the police try to find out if her Jeep was ever re-registered in any other state, or if her credit card or cell phone had been used after that night?"

"Oh sure. But her Jeep was never re-registered, and no use of her credit card or cell phone ever occurred."

"How unsettling, and sad," Margo said gloomily. Then her attractive face brightened and she ventured, "Tim and I know two people who'd love this story. I don't mean they'd love hearing about Nizhoni's personal tragedy. What I mean is, they'd probably be *fascinated* by the mystery of it, and would love trying to figure out what happened on that terrible twentieth of April, 2001."

Erin squinted a bit and her lips formed a tight little bemused smile, as she asked, "You know Sherlock Holmes and Dr. Watson, perchance?"

Margo chuckled. "No, no . . . just a psych prof and his artist wife, in Ohio. Tim was his assistant at Patten University in Pittsburgh. They were at our wedding, and they're very nice. Actually, they'll be in town in August, and we're having dinner with them." She glanced at her watch and said, "But we'd best eat up and get back to the Social Sciences Building."

"Right. I've got to revise that damned chapter twelve."

CHAPTER 5

━━━━━━━━━ ▼ ━━━━━━━━━

For Jennifer and Redmond most of the month of July was quite enjoyable in Pleasanton, and the dreaded intensely hot and muggy weather arrived only within the final week of the month. Still, that week of blistering heat and humidity was enough to make them very happy to be heading off for Northern Arizona on this early morning of Wednesday, July thirtieth. Their Southwest Airlines flight to Phoenix arrived at Sky Harbor Airport at nine fifty-one, and at ten-forty Redmond directed their rental car off the westbound I-10, and onto the northbound I-17. They were familiar with I-17, having traveled it while on sabbatical at Humphreys University, and on subsequent trips to Flagstaff.

Jennifer commented, "It's a nice, if warm, morning for our two and a half hour drive to Flag. The high in Phoenix today is supposed to reach 110 degrees."

"Well, fortunately, Jen, in Flagstaff, the predicted high for today is 74. And by the time we go out for dinner tonight, it'll be in the high sixties. So, we're headed for delightful cool days."

"And," Jennifer added, "for air that's agreeably scented by Ponderosa and Coconino Pines; and it's still monsoon season, so we may even get some of those delightful and capricious, brief, rumbling afternoon downpours that seem to come out of nowhere." She paused before adding, "I love everything about *northern* Arizona weather."

"Me too, Jen. Still, Flag has its faults. You can argue, pretty convincingly, that it has too many tourists, especially in the summer, and also anytime they have heavy snows at the Snow Bowl, when hordes of Phoenicians rush up to Flag to ski."

"But if we lived in Flag during the summer or whenever we had a fall, spring, or semester break, don't you think it would be great to have a house of our own just outside of town? We wouldn't have to worry about downtown traffic if we had a place out in the pines somewhere close in, but not *too* close, to downtown."

"Well, don't get me wrong. I enjoy Flagstaff, the canyon, and lots of other places in Northern Arizona. But I also enjoy Pleasanton."

"Well, so do I, Mac."

"I don't think I'd ever want to live solely in Flag in retirement. Pleasanton has a different range of pleasures, including the beautiful autumns, interesting men's and women's sports, great performing artist series, charming old homes, and reasonable proximity to Pittsburgh, Cincinnati, and northern Michigan—all nice places to spend a bit of time. I'm sure I'd rather spend fall in Pleasanton than *any* other place."

"Darling, I agree with all of that. I'm just thinking there'd be enough periods when we could dash off to Northern Arizona and enjoy our own place. Honestly, I'd love to spend a major portion, if not all, of summer in Flag."

Redmond nodded in agreement. "I think summers in Flag would be neat. And Christmas in Flag would be nice, too. It would be great to have a big enough house that Kate and Jeremy, their spouses, and future children could enjoy it, and Flagstaff."

Jennifer looked at Redmond and smiled. "Sounds like a nice place you'd like to have."

"A nice place, but not a particularly big place."

"Mac, sweetheart, let's face it. We have more money than we need, and more than we ever thought we *could* have. We have a very nice, but not extravagant home, in Pleasanton. It has a nice little woods behind it and the RU formal gardens are close enough to see and smell the flowers; it's perfectly located within walking distance of uptown and every campus building and sports venue at RU—and it's *paid* for! Barring extremely unfortunate and unlikely circumstances, we're going to inherit more money in the years to come, though, hopefully, that will be many years from now. I know you don't want to ever feel like an aspiring plutocrat, and neither do I. But we're talking a nice, fairly roomy, comfortable, woodsy place, and *not* a pretentious manor house."

"You're very persuasive, sweetie. I can't argue with anything you said. And as long as we're going to be here awhile, we'll have some time to look into the general Fort Valley Road area, or maybe some other areas we don't yet know about. It could be an interesting way to spend some of our time."

"I'm for that."

They drove on in silence for a few minutes. Then Redmond said, "You know, this is going to be a nineteen day vacation. We're going to be bouncing around from one place to another."

"Good! I'd hate to spend nineteen nights in one hotel room."

"Well, tonight and tomorrow night we're staying at the Comfort Inn on Beulah Drive, just down from the Hilton. Then we'll be in Vegas at the Luxor on the first and second—that's Friday and Saturday nights."

"Oh good," Jennifer said. "We stayed at the Luxor the last time we went to Vegas—when it first opened in '93."

Redmond continued, "When we get back to Flag we'll be at Little America for five nights."

"Little America should be nice, since it's out in the pines," Jennifer noted.

"Then, we have two nights in Sedona at the *Piedra Rojas Resort*. It looks good, by the way."

"Great."

"Back in Flag, we'll have another four nights at Little America. And finally, the last four nights we'll be at the Flagstaff Hilton. We'll fly home on Tuesday, the nineteenth."

Jennifer smiled and said, "I think that totals up to six places and five bounces. You did a great job of finding lodging, under the circumstances, sweetheart."

"This might have been a good time to have a home in Flag, I suppose."

"Yes. But I do like the idea of staying in Sedona for two nights."

"Yeah, me too, Jen. The *Piedra Rojas Resort* website advertises that they have a nice lounge, and a singer/pianist named Ridley Raintree. I've heard of her, but never heard any of her recordings. She and her jazz trio will be performing on Saturday nights during the summer. We could give her a listen on Saturday evening."

"That'll be nice."

"And in Vegas we're doing the Lewis Black show at the MGM Grand on Friday, and," he announced with pleasure, "on Saturday we're going to hear the Johnny Trujillo Septet at a club called, The Jazz Interlude, off the Strip, on Pecos Road."

"Well, I'm looking forward to those two nights. I'm sure Lewis Black will be funny. We've seen him on TV a few times, and he always cracks everybody up, including us. And it'll be great to hear some really top-flight jazz players in a relaxed club setting. When we heard the Trujillo group in Seattle we had a nice conversation with Johnny between sets. Remember?"

"Of course! It was the summer of 1999. And you have to like Johnny. He's a really great guy."

*   *   *

The McClains' first two days in Flagstaff proved very relaxing. The weather was congenial with deep blue skies, some fluffy white clouds, daytime temperatures in the mid-seventies, and on both Wednesday and Thursday there had been intense late afternoon monsoon downpours that lasted twenty minutes or so and were followed by spectacular rainbows. They found the Comfort Inn to be agreeable, and they ate at some of their favorite Flagstaff restaurants. They had also taken a day trip to the Cameron Trading Post to see its dramatic stark scenery and the historic Post's rug and jewelry offerings.

On Friday they checked out of the Comfort Inn around eleven o'clock, loaded their luggage into their rental car, and drove the two hundred and forty-nine miles to Las Vegas. They found the Luxor an exotic retreat. And on Friday evening at the MGM Grand they laughed so hard at Lewis Black's feigned spasms of outrage and irritation over everyday follies and frustrations that their jaws ached at times.

Now, at eight thirty on Saturday evening, they walked into The Jazz Interlude. They were shown to a table located just left of the center of the room and only a few tables from the stage. Redmond ordered a scotch and soda and Jennifer requested a gin and tonic. While they awaited their drinks Jennifer noted, "This is a really nice, well lighted, well appointed, and very clean room—unlike some jazz clubs we've been in."

As they chatted about what a nice day it had been, how they'd enjoyed the fabulous pool at the hotel, the beautiful weather, and the good dinner they had just relished at a Carlton Steak House, patrons of the jazz club drifted in and were shown to their tables. At five after nine Johnny Trujillo welcomed the audience, introduced the members of his septet, and called the first number—Clifford Brown's great jazz standard, "Joy Spring." Over the course of the next hour and twenty minutes the members of the band demonstrated their consummate virtuosity in both the solo and ensemble playing of jazz classics and new compositions. And the band's featured singer, June Connor, proved she could hold her own among such talented players. She demonstrated fluent improvisational skill in scat singing on up-tempo tunes, and exquisite phrasing and depth of mood and meaning on ballads. Her daringly slow rendition of the languid, longing, George and Ira Gershwin song, "The Man I Love," totally captured the audience from the opening line to the closing word of the piece. As the applause died Redmond said softly to Jennifer, "Wow! Has anyone *ever* delivered the emotion of that song better?"

As the first set ended, Jennifer said, "What a great session that was! We've got to hear the second set."

"Absolutely," Redmond agreed with a happy grin. "Another drink?"

"Yes—play it again, Sam," she said with a sensuous smile and perfect Ingrid Bergman-like enunciation.

At just that moment Johnny Trujillo leaned over their little table and said, "I know you two, and I remember our discussing something about my very youthful days in Woody Herman's band. But, I can't remember where or when, as the Larry Hart lyric goes."

Redmond was quite surprised and very pleased, and he responded without hesitation, "It was in Seattle, Johnny—at The Lighthouse, in the summer of 1999!"

"Right! That's it! The Lighthouse, near the pier." He borrowed an unoccupied chair from an adjacent table and seated himself.

Redmond said, "Of course, no one could expect you to remember our names, but I'm Mac McClain and this is my wife, Jennifer."

The veteran tenor saxophonist said, "I didn't remember your names, but 'what's in a name,' as the Bard put it. I did remember your faces and our conversation. That's two out of three, and for a sixty-seven year old senior citizen, that's pretty damned good," he said with a warm chuckle.

They told Johnny how they had lived in Seattle up until two years ago, but now lived in Ohio, and were visiting Vegas for a few days as part of a three week vacation in Northern Arizona.

Jennifer commented, "I think you've still got most of the same musicians you had in your band in 1999, except for one or two of the guys. It's a great band, by the way. We really love it."

"Thanks so much, Jennifer," he said with a gracious smile. "This band is exactly the same group I had in Seattle, *except* that Jimmy Donahue wasn't with the band when we made that tour. Duke Hartsfield was our alto player on that swing."

Redmond said, "I remember the alto player we saw in Seattle, but I never knew his name. He played so great on 'Body and Soul.' Anytime I hear that song, I recall hearing him play it."

"You know," Johnny said, "I always gave Duke a featured solo on that song. He was the *only* soloist on 'Body and Soul.' Duke isn't without his faults, but when it comes to music he's as close to perfection as any alto sax player can get. He *owns* that song, far as I'm concerned. I hear Duke went to Paris to work with Chet Condoli and stayed there. Chet's a big celebrity in France, and Duke and Chet go way back. They were together in the Gene Fielding Band when they were practically kids. And I hate to admit it, but more Europeans than Americans appreciate jazz these days. Duke never got the recognition he deserved, over here.

"But that's how it is for jazz musicians these days. Even here in Vegas, it's far from being the place it was. There's a lot of what I call minor league music here today, and it seems the more simplistic, repetitive, and banal it is the more popular it is. When I came off the road from Woody's band, Connie and I moved here because there were scores of great swing and jazz players, world-class musicians of the very first rank—right here. And there were plenty of jobs for everybody. Then the casino owners decided to go to all recorded music in the big shows. They didn't want to deal with the musician's union, and they were looking to cut costs—that's the way of *this* world. But, I tell ya guys, the music scene was fantastic prior to that!"

"It must have been terrific in those days," Jennifer offered.

"It was paradise, Jennifer! But hey, I don't want to get maudlin. We're still swinging." He stood and said, "It's great to see you two again, Mac and Jennifer. Anytime you're coming to Vegas, please check out my website to see where we're playing. It has my email address, too, so drop me a line if you have any reason to do so—or just to say hello."

The McClains promised they'd do that. Johnny returned his borrowed chair to the adjacent table, and moved to the bar to greet other fans.

After finding the second set of the septet just as enjoyable as the first, Redmond paid his tab and added a very generous tip. As they left the club Jennifer said, "This has been a terrific two days. I'm so glad we decided to visit Vegas on this trip."

"Yeah, Jen, it's been fun. And I only lost my limit—two hundred dollars, at blackjack."

Jennifer detected the disappointment in his voice. As they stepped away from The Jazz Interlude she put a hand on his shoulder and said soothingly, "Don't fret about that, sweetheart. Your wife won two hundred and eighty bucks at the slots!"

CHAPTER 6

▼

While Jennifer and Redmond were happily driving from The Jazz Interlude back to the Luxor, Emerson Yazzie, a thirty-six year-old Coconino County detective, was feeling uneasy in his apartment in Flagstaff. What troubled him tonight was the nagging and painful question of what could have happened to his cousin, Nizhoni, seven years ago. He thought over all of the essential facts. Nizhoni had shared a table with an unknown man who could have been responsible for her disappearance. A police artist's sketch of the man, based on Chris Larrabee's descriptions, never led anyone to claim the man resembled someone they knew. Nizhoni had, atypically, been alone and vulnerable in Chester's Pub—an inviting victim for a predatory monster.

But no one knew if the man at her table left the hotel with her or not. Any chance of determining his identity through fingerprints or some crucial bit of DNA had vanished with the washing of drinking glasses and the many hands of employees and customers that arranged or simply touched the chairs and tables in Chester's Pub. Several days passed between Nizhoni's presence in the Pub and the painful realization that she had not simply driven away for the remainder of the weekend. One might consider the possibility that she could have been one of those few people that suffer sudden amnesias and wander off without knowing who they are or where they belong. But Emerson Yazzie knew that vehicles are not vulnerable to amnesia. Nizhoni's 1997 XJ Jeep Cherokee had vanished quite as completely as Nizhoni. The Jeep had been Tyler Lydecker's before he got a newer one. He'd used it on his anthropological digs in the rugged central Nevada high deserts. Lydecker had equipped it with rugged Quadra-Trac capability and steel skid plates to protect its engine, transmission, and gas tank. Emerson recalled, with just a fleeting sad smile, how much Nizhoni had enjoyed putting that Jeep through its paces in the very rugged desert hills around Chinle.

The man in charge of the investigation, Chief Eric Hansen, now retired, had put in place regular monthly searches of car registration databases in all of the states and in Canada and Mexico. Those searches were still being faithfully executed. But the Jeep Cherokee was never registered anywhere. Emerson wondered if it could be hidden in some extremely remote canyon or building, or buried, or sunk in some deep-water lake, or possibly disassembled and scattered—there's just no telling, he thought. And like her jeep, his cousin's credit card and cell phone accounts had also been monitored, but no one ever attempted to use them during their defined periods for use.

And then Emerson's mind turned to the question of why this crime happened and who might have committed it. Nizhoni could have been abducted and murdered by the unknown man who'd shared her table at Chester's—a possible case of opportunistic sexual sadism. And what about Nizhoni's husband, Tyler Lydecker? Lydecker claimed he'd been alone at his Walker Lake dig site in Nevada when the disappearance took place. Still, the man had enough money that he could have *bought* the abduction and murder of the wife who was threatening him and causing him grief. After all, husbands turn out to be responsible in the killings of wives more often than not.

Emerson Yazzie felt there was good reason to regard Lydecker with suspicion. Lydecker had reacted with intense anger to Nizhoni's divorce action. She accused him of infidelity, and Lydecker had not challenged that. She had her lawyer demand possession of the home she had co-owned with Lydecker. She told her family that Lydecker threatened her and had vowed he'd never let her have the house that had once been the Flagstaff vacation home of his parents.

Some suspicion initially fell on the student, Joshua Usher, who had railed against Nizhoni's teaching of "atheism" in her classes. Emerson and Chief Hansen interviewed Joshua Usher ten days after the disappearance. Joshua said that on the night in question he had eaten a very late meal, alone, at the Lumberjack Pizza shop, just a half-block north of the Wexford. He stated that when he left the pizza shop and was approaching the Wexford he saw Dr. Lydecker holding an umbrella and turning down the alley toward the parking lot. Asked by Chief Hansen if Dr. Lydecker was in the company of a man, Joshua said he did not see a man, but that his only glimpse of Dr. Lydecker was while she was turning the corner. He said she could have been with a man who had turned the corner a step ahead of her. Joshua also said he didn't want to overtake Dr. Lydecker because he didn't want to have to speak to her, or to snub her—he felt she had wrongly dismissed him from her class, and he didn't wish to interact with her in any way. So, he ducked into the Wexford for a couple of minutes to allow her time to leave the area before he walked down the alley and past the little parking lot on his shortcut route back to his dorm. He said that when he did venture down the alley he saw Dr. Lydecker's Jeep leaving the lot. Emerson felt that Joshua had been truthful during the interview. He simply couldn't imagine Joshua killing anything.

Some had wondered if Nizhoni committed suicide because of depression over her failed marriage. Could she have chosen to drive her husky Jeep off a cliff and into some inaccessible ravine on the vast and desolate landscape of the Navajo Nation. A damned silly idea, Emerson thought. He knew his cousin's character and how precious and interesting she held life to be.

Emerson had turned such thoughts over in his mind on scores of occasions, and once again they failed to throw any light on the two questions that haunted the Yazzie family—what in the world happened to Nizhoni, and why? He couldn't answer these questions, but he vowed he would find the answers, and see that the person responsible for the crime was apprehended and punished.

CHAPTER 7

─────── ▼ ───────

When Jennifer and Redmond returned to Flagstaff on Sunday, August third, they went directly to Little America, a sprawling five hundred acre resort set in the pines off Butler Avenue, about a mile and half from downtown Flagstaff. It was a little before three when they arrived for what would be a five-night stay. They registered, went to their room, and were favorably impressed by its size and appointments.

Jennifer said approvingly, "This is a really huge room, Mac. And there's this big window that looks out into the Ponderosa Pines!"

"It's very nice, Jen; but, it's been over six hours since our breakfast. I'm starved."

"Me too. We've eaten in the Pinecone Café here a number of times. Let's hit it."

The large restaurant wasn't busy, and Redmond requested a table at the back of the room, next to the floor-to-ceiling window wall. They took a table with a close-up view of the pines, and ordered simple lunches. As the waitress left, Jennifer said enthusiastically, "Oh, look at the Aberts squirrels running around beneath the trees. They're so cute!"

"Yes. And the Ravens like to fly around in these big pine trees."

They watched the antics of the squirrels and the comings and goings of the Ravens, and then they enjoyed their lunches. As they lingered over coffee, Jennifer said, "This 'bouncy' vacation is really much more fun than staying in one hotel all the time."

"I agree. Everything about our stay has been fun. And I made a dinner reservation at the Country Club Estates restaurant for tomorrow night. It has a great view over the golf course to the high hills east of the city. And we know the food is good."

"That's great, Mac. You think of everything."

"Well, I've been known to slip up sometimes."

"When?"

"I guess you've forgotten the time in Pittsburgh when we were on the subway heading over to Station Square for our Three Rivers Dinner Cruise, and I discovered I'd forgotten our tickets. We had to get off at Station Square, wait for the inbound train, go back to the William Penn, and start all over."

"Okay," she granted, "You *usually* think of everything. And we still got there in plenty of time, before *The Majestic* sailed."

"And it was a beautiful cruise, especially the part where we sailed up the Allegheny past that great tableau of illuminated skyscrapers and all. Pittsburgh, along with Flag, the Canyon, and our cozy Pleasanton, is certainly one of our favorite places."

Jennifer nodded her concurrence, but noted, "You know, Mac, we've had some pretty threatening events occur in some of our favorite places. How in the world has that come about all of a sudden over the last few years?"

"Beats me. We haven't gone out of our way to expose ourselves to danger. We just seem to be observant and I guess we love a mystery. You've liked mystery stories all your life, and you still read a lot of them. Maybe that has something to do with it. And then we speculate with each other about all sorts of things, including, I guess, possible crimes. And we've come up with things that made us curious about some particular crimes and then we sort of figured them out. Its gotten to the point that Ted told Chief Doyle, in Pleasanton, that you and I have a talent for solving crimes."

Jennifer chuckled and said, "And to the point that my seventy-four year old mother wagged a finger in my face and said, 'I don't want you to be involved in any more mysteries.'"

"Well, hopefully our little run of involvements with crimes is behind us." He paused before saying, "Would you like to take a ride out Fort Valley Road after lunch to see if it's a place where we might like to have a home sometime."

"I'd like that. I know those places at the base of Mount Humphreys are way bigger and more expensive than we'd ever want. But I'd like to see them. Of course, there have to be desirable homes in Flagstaff that are far less expensive than those."

An hour later they were driving past the Museum of Northern Arizona on highway 180, and shortly thereafter they came to the area of homes on the left of the road called the Cheshire Development. Redmond noted, "Cheshire looks like a nice area, especially the homes farther back and up on that pine-covered ridge over there. I think that's the area they call Cheshire Heights."

"Yes, but up ahead on the right, on the lower slope of the mountain, there are homes with really good-sized lots. You can see that most of the properties have corrals for horses, down toward this road. They're probably on five acres or more. There are a few roads like that one just ahead of us that go up to the homes. Let's take this one, Mac."

Redmond slowed, turned right onto Bristlecone Lane, and drove slowly along the ascending road into the densely treed area above. They passed only two houses on the left and three on the right before the road ended. "I've got to turn around here, sweetie," he said. "The road's narrow, so I'll have to jigger around a few times." When he had the car turned back downhill he said, "I'll drive slowly by these homes and try to imagine living in them."

At the first house on their left, the one that sat highest on the slope, Redmond slowed the car and intended to roll slowly on by it, but Jennifer said, "Wait, Mac! Stop. I want to look at this place. It looks older and smaller than the others. It looks more charming than the newer and bigger houses, doesn't it?"

"Yeah," Redmond allowed. "Looks kinda neglected, though—might be strictly a vacation home."

"It does look a bit neglected, but it has a certain charm about it."

Redmond allowed the car to roll forward a bit in order to read a redwood sign with yellow lettering. The sign was close to the road and was suspended by leather ties from a wooden post-and-arm structure. He pointed to it and said, "Well, maybe 'The Lydeckers' here would be willing to sell this old place cheap."

"None of these properties have for sale signs, Mac. And I'm afraid even this older one would be way more than we'd want to spend for a very part-time residence. These houses are all nice, and the newer ones are probably in the range of six to ten thousand square feet. This oldest house could be as small as three to four thousand, maybe."

"I'd think so," Redmond said. He took his foot off the brake and allowed the car to continue slowly down the slope. He said, "You know, sweetie, these areas are pretty remote. I'm not sure I'm ready to live in the deep, dark, woods, with thousands of feet of dense pine forest above our house. These are houses for *mountain* men."

"Yes, that's right. Bears could come down to our house," Jennifer said with a teasing apprehensive expression.

"Yeah, and for all we know, a Sasquatch could be living right up there, just above the oldest house."

Jennifer chuckled before saying, "But, just out of curiosity, I would like to know what kind of prices people ask for these places."

They looked at the other houses as they slowly descended the grade, and at the end of the little narrow road Redmond turned right onto 180 and suggested, "Let's drive out a little farther and see how it looks." They passed five more roads leading to homes that were only partially visible through the trees, and soon there were no more little access roads. They turned into the empty Arizona Snow Bowl lower parking area, got the car turned around, and headed back toward Flagstaff.

They returned to Little America, and as they entered their room Jennifer said, "Maybe we should talk to a local realtor and inquire as to what kind of prices those big houses command. I'm just curious. And I'm sure a realtor could suggest some other areas for a vacation house."

"Sure. No harm in that, hon."

CHAPTER 8

▼

At eleven o'clock on Wednesday morning Redmond and Jennifer visited the local Realty Execs office and spoke with Shirley Evans, the realtor Jennifer had phoned on Monday afternoon. Jennifer had told Shirley of the McClain's desire to have a vacation home in Flag, and had indicated some essential requirements they had for such a residence. Shirley, an attractive woman with sixteen years of realty experience in Flagstaff, suggested a number of areas the McClains might like to consider. Redmond and Jennifer were impressed with Shirley Evans, and following a light lunch at the Call of the Canyon restaurant, they spent some time checking out various areas of the city that Shirley had suggested. By mid-afternoon they had decided that the two areas they liked best were the Cheshire Heights and the Country Club Estates. They thought these would be the most promising areas to explore if and when they decided to seriously commit to owning a vacation home in Flag.

At seven in the evening they headed for their dinner appointment with Margo and Tim. Redmond parked in the *La Fonda* lot, and as he and Jennifer headed for the restaurant entrance Redmond noted, "There's Tim's red Jeep Wrangler, so they're already here."

They found their young friends at a rear table, and they all exchanged warm greetings. As they seated themselves Redmond smilingly said, "I believe it's been two months to the day that we last saw you two heading off on your honeymoon to The Ojai Valley Inn and Spa. How was it?"

"It was fabulous, Mac," Tim said with a big smile. "We had *the best* time! If we ever make enough money to stay there again, we will," he laughed.

Margo, looking relaxed and happy, said, "It was so gorgeous—a big, incredibly ingratiating Spanish villa on over two hundred-twenty acres, deservedly one of the top rated resort spas in the world, with a famous golf course, pleasant areas for horseback riding, a picturesque congenial little town nestled right up to the foot of high Topa Topa Mountain peaks, the sweet scent of orange groves everywhere . . . and all just fifteen miles from the Pacific Ocean."

Jennifer chuckled, turned to Redmond and said, "I want to go *there*, Mac. Margo has sold me on the place!"

"It *does* sound great," Redmond smilingly agreed.

"Everything about the place was perfect," Tim said. "But it makes getting back to work difficult. We keep asking ourselves, 'Why can't we be there today?'"

Margo chimed in, "But the answer is obvious—we don't have the dough, or the time, really."

Jennifer responded, "And you know what? After a few more weeks of that life you'd probably get restless, question yourselves, and feel the need to get back to real things, and to your work."

"I suppose so, Jen," Margo allowed. "But it was the *greatest* two weeks."

Tim said, "So, now we're getting back in the groove, or should I say, the grind. We're getting ready for our classes, writing papers, and planning research projects. And actually, we're enjoying all that."

"Good to hear," Jennifer said.

Margo asked, "And how long have you guys been in Flag?"

"We've been on vacation eight days, two of which we spent in Vegas," Redmond replied. "We've enjoyed it a lot. The weather back in Pleasanton has been really hot and humid while we've been gone."

"It's hard to beat Flag for summer weather," Tim stated.

They ordered margaritas and said they'd like to look over the menu a bit more before ordering. The margaritas arrived and soon thereafter they placed their orders with a friendly young waitress.

Jennifer inquired, "What have you guys done about your housing situation? The last time we were here you were still single and both of you had a condo in the Mt. Elden Condominiums."

Tim pushed his undisciplined red hair back off his forehead and said, "Well, the prices right now are down below the purchase price on my condo, so we decided to lease it until the prices, hopefully, go back up some. We've got a graduate student and his wife in it, and we're living in Margo's place."

"In *our* place, Tim," Margo said.

Tim smiled and said, "Yes, our place."

Redmond asked, "So prices have dropped here, as well as in Phoenix?"

"Yes, but not as much here as in Phoenix," Margo responded. "I don't believe prices have fallen more than fifteen percent here."

Jennifer volunteered, "Well, Mac and I decided we should look into the possibility of buying a vacation home in Flag. I mean, we come here during spring and fall breaks, and now we've been thinking we might like to spend at least part of the summer here. So, we talked to a realtor about that this morning."

"Seems reasonable for you guys," Tim observed. "You already spend a lot of time here, and maybe you could come for the Christmas Recess. You fly to the South Rim for a few days before Christmas most years."

"True enough, Tim," Redmond replied. "And then we've usually gone to Telluride for five days or so. Skiing has always been part of our Christmas holidays, and we could do that at the Snow Bowl, or down at Sunrise. Even if we didn't have enough snow in Arizona, we could drive up to Durango to ski."

"That sounds good, Mac," Margo said. "Have you seen anything you'd like to buy?"

"Not yet—just thinking about it."

Jennifer added, "We'd thought we might like to buy a house out on Fort Valley Road, in the area just before the Snow Bowl road."

Tim grimaced a bit, and said, "You're talking *big bucks* out there, Jen."

"Yeah, that's what we found out from out from a realtor this morning," Jennifer said with a chuckle. "But now we're thinking Cheshire Heights or Country Club Estates."

Their meals were delivered and enjoyed, and as they paid their bills Tim noted, "It's still early, guys. How about we stop for a nightcap at Chester's." The others agreed, and fifteen minutes later they parked just off West Aspen Street and walked the short block to Chester's Pub, in the Wexford.

There was no entertainment scheduled for the Pub area of Chester's on this night, and only a few patrons were watching a televised baseball game. Tim led the others to a table away from the TV, and they ordered beers. Redmond said, "I see they have a stage. Do they have music groups here sometimes?"

"Oh yeah—pretty much every Friday and Saturday when the students are in town," Tim responded.

Margo said, with a portentous smile, "Well, that reminds me of something I'd fleetingly thought you two would find interesting. And it concerns this very Pub Room."

Jennifer smiled. "I detect an enigmatic note in your voice, Margo. What's the story?"

"Well," Margo began, "it was a dark and stormy Saturday night, that night of April twentieth 2001."

All except Margo chuckled. Redmond commented to Jennifer, "Just a year after our sabbatical here, hon."

Margo continued, "There was thunder, lighting, rain, and blustering winds over old Flagstaff. And on this fierce foreboding night a very beautiful thirty-year old associate professor of astronomy braved the inauspicious elements, and ventured into this *chamber* to hear a jazz group from Las Vegas. Her name was . . . *Nizhoni*. It's a Navajo girl's name, meaning 'beautiful.' And the moniker fit the gal as perfectly as the best-fashioned key fits its most precious lock. She'd planned to come to the Pub with a female colleague, but the colleague hurt an ankle that afternoon and had to back out. There was a good crowd in this room on that ebony evening, and the manager of the Pub asked Nizhoni if another customer, a man, could share her table for two. She agreed to that. They listened to the first set of the jazz group. When it was over Nizhoni retrieved her raincoat and umbrella, and headed for the door."

Margo could see that the others were listening attentively. She dropped her voice and slowed her vocal pace to conclude her story, saying, "And when the beautiful Nizhoni stepped out of the old Wexford Hotel the night became an encompassing cloak of impenetrable darkness that locked her in its embrace . . . and it *never let her go*. It was Nizhoni's finale, and there was no encore."

No one spoke for a few seconds. Then Redmond asked, "You mean she disappeared and no one knows to this day what happened to her?"

Margo resumed her chipper non-mystery story voice to respond, "That's right, Mac. Her Jeep Cherokee was gone, too. It took a day or two before anyone realized she was actually missing. And it all happened more than seven years ago. And for all the years since, authorities regularly check state vehicle registrations nationwide to see if her Jeep has been registered somewhere. But it never has been. The manager of the club said he didn't know the man that sat with Nizhoni that night. He didn't notice if Nizhoni left with the stranger or not, but he did notice both were gone shortly after the first set ended."

Jennifer asked, "So there was no 'natural' suspect, no one who'd threatened her or given her a bad time about anything—like, maybe a boyfriend or ex-boyfriend?"

"Well, there was her *husband*. She was in the throes of an ugly divorce from a man named Tyler Lydecker. He's an anthropology prof at HU. And according to the account I've heard, and I caution that this is imputed only by *gossip*, Nizhoni apparently knew he had a mistress he wouldn't give up. So she filed for a divorce and asked for outright ownership of the house they'd held in joint tenancy, a house that had been a gift from Lydecker's father. She also threatened to reveal the name of the 'other woman' if Lydecker didn't agree to her demands. She was *very* angry with her husband because of his adultery."

Jennifer said, "You know, we were looking at houses on one little lane off Fort Valley Road last Sunday, and there was a house that had a sign in the yard that said, 'The Lydeckers.' It was at the end of the road, and it was clearly the oldest of the houses on that lane. I wonder if it could have been the home of Nizhoni and the husband she was divorcing?"

Margo said, "It could have been—Erin said their house was along 180, and that's Fort Valley Road. Anyway, Dr. Lydecker is still at the university, but I don't know him. I've heard he said he was working alone at his dig site in central Nevada the week Nizhoni disappeared. He's a cultural anthropologist and spends a lot of his time at the site. The site he discovered is the most western of ancient Anasazi sites ever found in Nevada. Anyway, no one was ever publicly identified as a suspect or person of interest, as far as I know.

"There *was* a student who had caused something of a ruckus about Nizhoni. He'd complained that she was teaching atheism in her introductory astronomy class, and he argued with Nizhoni so frequently and at such length during class time that she had to drop him from the course. The dean talked to other students and to Nizhoni about it, and he backed Nizhoni's decision to drop the student. The whole episode got some coverage in the *Daily Sun*. There were some letters to the editor about the incident that were published in the paper."

Redmond commented, "Religious fundamentalists, even many non-fundamentalist religious persons, deny well-established scientific facts. A majority of the Republican contenders for their party's nomination for president this year deny the validity of anything resembling the theory of evolution. Knowing that many of their party hold to the biblical story of Adam and Eve, they fear contradicting the bible. They don't seem to know, and don't want to know, that Darwin's work now provides the very basis for the whole field of modern biology."

Tim noted, "And then people wonder why our nation has fallen so far behind Western European and Asia countries in the life sciences, and so many other fields of scientific inquiry."

Jennifer said softly, "And, being an astrophysicist can make you a target of criticism from fundamentalists."

"And being beautiful, as Nizhoni was, isn't an unmixed blessing, either," Margo observed. "Erin James, a friend in the sociology department who told me this story, also told me that Nizhoni was thinking of lodging a sexual harassment complaint against someone at HU at the same time she was divorcing Lydecker. Erin and Nizhoni were friends, and Erin heard this from Nizhoni herself. But when I asked Erin who the harassment charge was against, she said it was all over and done with and she didn't wish to repeat it."

"A proper attitude on Erin's part," Jennifer allowed. "But I wonder if Nizhoni could have been emotionally upset, or depressed. I mean, with all the stress she may have been under, could she have committed suicide? Could she have driven her Jeep into a lake, or off a cliff out in some remote part of the desert? The Navajo Nation is vast—over twenty six thousand square miles, with very low population density and few paved roads."

"Seems unlikely," Margo replied, "because Nizhoni was active, and not withdrawn or in a funk. And the manager at Chester's that night said she seemed to be in a pleasant mood."

Tim observed, "I suppose it's possible no one will *ever* know what happened to her."

Redmond asked Margo, "Are the police still pursuing this case?"

"I don't know, Mac. The story seems to have faded away. Certainly there would have been a lot of coverage of it in the *Daily Sun* at the time. And they wrote feature stories about it for a few years, around the anniversaries of the disappearance. But it seems little known nowadays. I've been here three years, and I never heard of it until Erin James told me the story this summer. The likely scenario, in most people's minds, might be that the mysterious unknown man she shared her table with could have been the murderer. And because Nizhoni was a *really* great-looking woman, people are inclined to think it could have been a case of sexual opportunism and sadism on the part of the unknown man. But the manager of the club didn't know him, and he didn't actually see the man leave with, or immediately after, Nizhoni. He just noticed they were both gone fairly soon after the first set ended."

Jennifer commented, "It's upsetting, but intriguing at the same time. It could be a murder mystery story, like *The Mysterious Unknown Man*, or *The Strange Disappearance of Professor Lydecker*."

"How about," Redmond suggested, "*Jazz was Overture to Murder*."

Margo looked very pleased as she said, "I sorta felt you guys might find it interesting."

CHAPTER 9

▼

On Friday morning Redmond and Jennifer had their breakfasts in the Pinecone Café, and then packed their bags in preparation for the third of their five bounces. This one would be to the *Piedra Rojas Resort* in Sedona. At nine-forty, Jennifer said, "You know, Mac, we won't be able to get into our room till two or three, so we don't have to be in a hurry to get to Sedona. We could head down the hill for lunch around twelve-thirty or one."

"Okay."

"I was thinking about the story Margo told us at Chester's Pub. Maybe we could run by the *Daily Sun* office and find someone there who could search the paper's records for stories about Nizhoni Lydecker for us."

Redmond smiled. "Sounds as if the story has made you curious about Nizhoni's strange disappearance. Maybe because we were able to learn the real fate of the student that disappeared from his Ravenslake dormitory way back in nineteen-sixty five, you now think we could somehow throw light on the disappearance of Nizhoni Lydecker."

"Well, I don't see that as at all likely, Mac. I'm sure there are city and county detectives who think about the case frequently, but just don't have enough to go on. It *is* a puzzling story. And there have to be relatives and friends of Nizhoni who are troubled by it most every day."

"But didn't we just talk about our need to avoid 'mysteries?'"

"Sure, but the underlying concern there was about not putting ourselves in danger, darling. I'm not proposing we play detective and hunt down a killer . . . if there ever was a killer. I'm just curious about it. And I haven't had any mystery books to read for almost a month. It could be an entertaining story to think about. And, silly as it may sound, her being a professor *and* a jazz fan makes me feel a sort of kinship for the woman."

"It's certainly a mysterious case," Redmond allowed, "and we've got nothing on our schedule. So, let's go and see what we can learn about 'the strange disappearance.'"

"Why not? It'd be nice to have something to just sort of research."

At ten-thirty five Redmond parked their car in the small lot of the *Daily Sun* office on Thompson Street. When they entered the office a middle-aged woman sitting at a small desk behind a high counter greeted them with, "Good morning. What can I do for you?"

Redmond said, "We're interested in reading any of your paper's articles or reports about a disappearance that occurred in Flagstaff in two-thousand one."

"The Nizhoni Lydecker disappearance?"

Redmond smiled. "Yes, that's the one. I guess it's a fairly frequent request, since you knew immediately what we were interested in."

The neatly groomed and efficient looking woman came to the counter, smiled indulgently, and responded, "Well, there aren't any other disappearances anyone has inquired about since I've worked here, and I've been here since before it happened. We don't get many requests for copies of those articles anymore. One of our reporters collected all that stuff together a few years back, and made a sort of archive of it. I can sell you a copy of the whole file for three dollars and fifty-cents."

Jennifer asked, "And that includes everything that's been in the paper since the disappearance happened?"

"I think so. Nothing has been written on that case in a long while."

"That's fine, then," Redmond said. He pulled a five-dollar bill from his billfold and handed it to the woman, who quickly returned his change. She went to a file cabinet, located the proper file, and withdrew the requested pieces from a folder.

"It'll take me a few minutes to copy these things," she said as she disappeared through an open door at the back of the room. Redmond and Jennifer heard the whir of a copier, and a few minutes later the woman reappeared. She handed a new file folder to Redmond, who opened it and glanced at the photos and articles, all reduced, where necessary, to fit on eight and a half by eleven sheets.

The McClains thanked the helpful clerk and returned to their car. As Redmond started up the engine, he commented, "Well, that didn't take much time."

"No, it was very efficient. How about a coffee at Barnes and Noble? We can read these articles there."

"That's a great place to read," Redmond replied. He drove the few blocks down Santa Fe Avenue to its intersection with Milton Avenue, and parked in the lot of the impressive new building that was the Flagstaff Barnes and Noble store. Redmond ordered two tall coffees of the day, and they found a little table along the wall near the ordering counter.

Jennifer glanced up at the mural of famous authors painted above their table and said, "We're sitting under Dorothy Parker and John Steinbeck this morning, Mac."

"Yes, and I hope they won't drop any coffee or cigarette ashes on us," Redmond joked as he glanced at the mural.

As they read through the materials they'd received it became clear that Margo's narrative had captured the essential elements of the story. There was more detail, of course, about Nizhoni's family background and educational history, and her position at HU. And there was more detail about what the manager of the Pub room that night, Chris Larrabee, had told the police. They learned that Nizhoni was something of a regular at the club's jazz events.

Larrabee had also worked with a police sketch artist to come up with a drawing of the unknown man who'd sat with Nizhoni that fateful night. The *Daily Sun* materials included a photo of the drawing. Redmond and Jennifer looked at the drawing, and Redmond ventured, "He looks like the actor, George Clooney . . . his face is a little longer than Clooney's, I think."

"I don't suppose there are more than a couple hundred thousand men who look about like this," Jennifer joked. "He's rather good looking . . . doesn't have any unusual features."

"He sure doesn't look like a sadistic killer."

"No, but neither did Ted Bundy!"

Redmond nodded and allowed, "True. Bundy was good looking, and it's thought he may have killed more than twenty young women."

Jennifer looked at the only photo of Nizhoni in the file. It was a posed black and white photograph of her sitting at her desk, and was part of a feature story about her having received a five-year research grant from the National Science Foundation. Other pictures of her in the various articles were just reduced copies of that picture.

Jennifer studied the larger photograph and said, "Like all newspaper photos, this isn't a crisp picture of her. But it's good enough to validate Margo's description of her as being beautiful."

Redmond studied the photograph briefly. "Looks like a movie star from back in the fifties or so. I can't think of her name."

"Jennifer Jones," Jennifer said while staring at the photo.

"Right! *Duel in the Sun,* with Gregory Peck, and *Portrait of Jenny*, with Joseph Cotton . . . great flicks!"

"And many other good films into the seventies. She won an academy award for *Song of Bernadette*. But she also had some tough things to deal with. Her first husband, and the father of two of her children, Robert Walker, a fine actor himself, died tragically. He was being treated for alcoholism and died from an interaction of medications prescribed to treat the disorder. And her daughter from her second marriage, that to the famous producer, David Selznick, committed suicide in her twenties."

"You obviously know more about Jennifer Jones than I do," Redmond allowed.

"I was what you could call a fan of hers when I was in my very early teens. I suppose it was partly because she was named 'Jennifer.' In any case, it's clear from this picture that Nizhoni *was* a very attractive woman."

Over the next half hour they read every word that had been written on the subject of the disappearance. They learned that the Lydeckers *had* lived on Bristlecone Lane off of Fort Valley

Road, that Tyler Lydecker was a member of the anthropology faculty, and that county detective Emerson Yazzie, who had worked on the case, was a cousin of Nizhoni.

Redmond said, "I wonder if Emerson Yazzie might be a relative of the U.S. Forest Service Ranger, Jim Yazzie, who helped us through that harrowing experience we had at the South Rim back in two thousand-five."

"Well, Yazzie is a very common name among the Navajo people, Mac. But, it's possible."

They put the newspaper materials back in the folder, set their empty cups on a small table reserved for that purpose, and returned to their car. Redmond noted, "It's only ten fifty, but we may as well head down the switchbacks to Oak Creek Canyon."

"Right. We can kill some time before we have lunch. I'd like to look at some rugs at Ortega's. If I could find a gorgeous Burnt Water Rug at the right price, I'd buy it."

"I like looking at rugs, too," Redmond said. "And after that we can come back to the main drag and have a Mexican lunch at the Oaxaca Restaurant."

"Sounds perfect," Jennifer said.

*   *   *

By four in the afternoon the McClains had looked at rugs at Ortego's, and although Jennifer had seen one she really liked, she decided there would be plenty of time in the future to choose a couple of Navajo rugs for their possible Flagstaff home. They'd also had lunch, registered at their hotel, played the short nine-hole par-three golf course on the resort grounds, and were now reclined in their swimsuits on canvas sling chairs by the pool. There was a family with three young children actively enjoying the water, and an early-thirties couple lying on towels on the pool decking.

Redmond asked, "Need some more SPF 60 for your face, hon? The sun still has a kick to it."

Jennifer smiled and said, "Mac darling, we just got out of the pool. When my skin has dried, I'll put a little more on. I'm as eager as you are to keep my thirty-seven year old looking face from looking thirty-eight," she kidded.

The early-thirties couple were laughing and joking with one another. The blond woman jumped up, scooped some water from the pool with a large plastic soft drink cup, and flung it on her companion. He yelped good-naturedly, and then chased her halfway around the pool before capturing her and throwing her into the water. He jumped in after she resurfaced, and they pushed each other laughingly, and said teasing things to one another. As the woman pulled herself up out of the pool, Jennifer said quietly to Redmond, "Those must have cost her a bundle."

Redmond smiled and responded softly, "We're living through, 'The Era of Overexposure,' Jen. And what's that saying? Oh yeah—get a room!"

"My thought exactly," Jennifer murmured.

The couple apparently had the same thought, for they soon collected their belongings and headed to the cottages area.

Redmond commented, "That woman looked somehow familiar to me, Jen."

"Of course, Mac. She's a 'type.' You've seen lots of busty young blond women who look like that, sweetheart."

"Yeah," he said with a smile, "I guess I have."

CHAPTER 10

▼

As the McClain's relaxing two-day stay in Sedona neared an end on Saturday evening, they'd had a good low calorie dinner, taken a turn around the grounds of the resort, and at eight-forty five they headed for the Turquoise Lounge to hear the local pianist/singer, Ridley Raintree. As they entered the room they saw it was of modest size, but with warm colors and good lighting, and with a slightly elevated and contoured stage near the back of the room. The stage was empty except for a handsome Baldwin high polish ebony grand piano, a drum set, and a string bass resting on its side. The room was crowded with an audience of diverse ages, and Jennifer and Redmond were shown to a small table next to a wall.

"Well," Redmond observed, "Miss Raintree appears to have something of a following." They ordered drinks, and as they sipped them they talked about the fact that they had only nine days of vacation left.

Jennifer remarked, "I'm absolutely loving this trip, Mac. I feel a bit spoiled, though. I mean, we've stayed and eaten in nice places in Flagstaff, and here in Sedona, and, of course, in Vegas. And we saw Lewis Black, Johnny Trujillo's septet, and a great singer in June Connor. And it was nice being with Tim and Margo."

Redmond took a sip of his scotch and soda and said, "Well, I don't feel spoiled in the least, sweetheart. We've earned this getaway. We were under a lot of stress in the spring, then we had two weddings to attend in New England, had to drive all over the place, and then had a month of working on our house and yard."

Jennifer smiled and said, "Okay then, we've earned it and I won't feel even a tad spoiled! I do feel grateful, and I'm looking forward to our day trips around northern Arizona that we've got planned for the rest of our stay."

Their little chat was interrupted by the softly amplified voice of a well dressed silver haired man on the stage. He said, "Welcome, Ladies and Gentleman. Tonight the Turquoise Lounge is happy to present an evening with Sedona's own Miss Ridley Raintree and her trio, featuring Jeff Hadley on bass, Keith Falconer on drums, and Ridley Raintree on piano and vocals. Let me point out that Ridley has a terrific new CD, titled *The Ridley Raintree Trio at Jazz Alley*. It's a fabulous recording of classics and some of Ridley's own wonderful compositions. The CD will be available for purchase only during the intermission, at a table adjacent to the lobby entrance. And Ridley will be happy to autograph your CD." He paused, and then said with rising volume, "And now, settle back, and please give a warm Sedona welcome to Ridley Raintree, Jeff Hadley, and Keith Falconer—The Ridley Raintree Trio!"

The musicians came on stage to generous applause, smiled and nodded to the audience, took their places, and without further preliminaries launched into a very fast and swinging rendition of John Coltrane's composition, "Moment's Notice." When the piece was finished the audience rewarded the group with enthusiastic applause. Redmond said softly to Jennifer, "They didn't waste any time establishing their credentials—first rate players!"

Jennifer silently studied Miss Raintree. She looked to be in her mid-thirties, average height, a good figure, black hair, high forehead, creamy white skin, nicely proportioned facial features, and, probably, green eyes. And on the second song of the set, "They Can't Take That Away From Me," Miss Raintree displayed her considerable vocal talent. When the set concluded an hour later with Billy Strayhorn's beautifully rendered elegant mood piece, "Daydream," Redmond and Jennifer applauded enthusiastically.

"I'd like to buy her CD, Mac," Jennifer said with a smile. "She's very talented."

"She certainly is, and so are Hadley and Falconer." He added, "One of us should hold our table."

"That's fine, Mac. I'll get the CD, and I'll ask her to inscribe it, 'To Jennifer and Redmond.'"

"Good. I'll order us another drink. You want to stay for the second set, I assume."

"Oh, yeah! Definitely."

Jennifer made her way to the lobby and got in line to buy the CD. When her turn came she paid for her CD and then handed it to the seated Ridley. Jennifer volunteered, "My husband and I loved the first set tonight."

"Thank you," Ridley responded. She smiled and asked, "Are you visiting Sedona?"

"Yes, we are. We're from Pleasanton, Ohio."

"Oh, that's where Ravenslake is. I went to Oberlin College, also in Ohio. I hope you have a nice time in Sedona." She opened the CD case and asked, "What inscription would you like?"

"Just say, 'For Jennifer and Redmond,' and sign your name, please."

She asked how Redmond was spelled, and wrote the inscription and her name on the blank page opposite the listing of songs on the CD. Ridley handed the autographed CD to Jennifer, who thanked her, and then returned to the Turquoise Lounge.

She showed the CD to Redmond, and he said, "It's a good picture of her on the cover." He checked the list of songs on the CD and noted, "There are a lot of good things here." Jennifer opened the case and showed him Ridley's inscription. "That's nice," he said.

The McClains enjoyed the second set, and following the last number of the evening, the patrons began exiting the Turquoise Lounge. Redmond suggested, "Let's just sit here a bit, rather than standing in line to get out. I still have some of my drink."

"Me too, darling. I must say this was a pleasant surprise. I figured Ridley Raintree might be just a torporific local celebrity."

"Yeah . . . I didn't really know if she would have real *chops*," Redmond said, "but she certainly does—and she was *refulgent*!"

Jennifer looked a bit unsure of his meaning, but Redmond smiled and said, "Just trying to keep up with your 'torporific,' sweetheart. Refulgent—you know, shining, or radiant."

"Well, 'torporific' isn't as obscure as 'refulgent.' But I do like, 'refulgent,'" she admitted.

A few minutes later they finished their drinks and headed toward the door. They were surprised and pleased to encounter Ridley Raintree and a man, perhaps her husband Jennifer thought, also heading toward the door. Ridley's companion was about six feet in height, had brown hair and eyes, and handsome facial features.

Ridley smiled and said, "Good night, Jennifer and Redmond."

"My goodness, you remembered our names!" Jennifer responded.

Ridley gave a little laugh and said, "I've always had a good memory for names."

Redmond addressed Ridley, saying, "I have to tell you, we really enjoyed hearing you and your group."

"Well, thank you so much. I could tell you did. It isn't hard to tell who in the audience is really into the music." She asked, "What do you do in Pleasanton?"

"I'm a psychology professor at Ravenslake, and Jen's an artist."

The man with Ridley shuffled his feet and seemed a bit impatient with Ridley's interaction with the McClains. Ridley said, "Oh, Jennifer and Redmond, this is my long time friend, Tyler Lydecker. He's also a professor—at Humphreys University in Flagstaff."

Redmond shook hands with Tyler, and said, "It's nice to meet you."

Lydecker nodded perfunctorily. "Same here," he responded. "Have a good evening," and he and Ridley exited the building.

Redmond and Jennifer walked slowly to the door. "Small world, wouldn't you say?" Redmond asked.

"Small world, indeed!"

As the McClains strolled along on the way to their unit, Jennifer said, "I wonder if he's still haunted by Nizhoni's disappearance."

"Well, who knows what he feels. At the time she disappeared they were apparently going at each other hammer and tongs, as they say. But once she disappeared it could have hit him real hard. To have a beautiful and brilliant wife like Nizhoni suddenly and mysteriously gone, and almost certainly murdered, could have been extremely tough to deal with. At least, that's what I imagine."

"But *you're* a sweet guy, darling. He could have been quite different. Still, there's no way to know, really." A few paces further on, she asked, "You remember that Margo said Nizhoni believed Lydecker had a mistress he wouldn't give up?"

"Yeah?"

"I'm wondering if that sharp thorn in her marriage might have been Ridley Raintree. Ridley referred to him as her 'longtime friend.'"

"That occurred to me, too, hon. I hope it wasn't the case. I liked Ridley—a very talented gal."

"Yes, and brimming with *refulgence*," Jennifer observed.

Redmond smiled and said, "*Absolutely* brimming." After a brief pause, he said, "You know, Jen, the police must have considered the possibility that Lydecker could have been behind the disappearance. Given their stormy divorce negotiations, checking on his whereabouts would have been a priority. According to the *Daily Sun* article we read at Barnes and Noble, he said he was doing solitary work at his dig site in Nevada. Even if he were, he could have paid some nefarious villain to remove her."

"I'd bet against that, Mac. Since they were on the outs, why would she have told him where she was going to be on that night? And even if he knew where she was going and had hired a thug to do the dastardly act, that miscreant would have had to follow her to Chester's and wait for her to go to her Jeep. So, that all strikes me as unlikely—not out of the question, but certainly questionable. The disappearance of Nizhoni, if it were a crime, seems more likely to have been a spontaneously initiated event, a crime of opportunity, and probably a sexually motivated one. And that's why the suspicions about the unknown man who, by seeming happenstance came to share a table with her, seem the most credible."

"Yes, but maybe it wasn't happenstance. One could wonder if the mystery man could have been hired by Lydecker."

"I don't want to go there, Mac. That's too gruesome."

"Yeah."

She slipped an arm about Redmond's waist and said, "Let's not talk about such a gloomy subject on such a perfect evening. Look at all the stars overhead! They seem so bright and close tonight."

Redmond scanned the sky with its hundreds of visible stars. "Well," he said, "they may look close, but, of course, they're incredibly far away. The nearest 'star' visible to the naked eye is actually two stars, Alpha Centauri A and B, seen as a single star by the naked eye. They're 4.22 light years from earth. Although we can see even more stars than these when we're at the North Rim, the stars here tonight *are* amazing. And Sedona is an enchanting place, sweetheart. So," he said softly, "let's be enchanted, while we may."

"Let's."

CHAPTER 11

─────── ▼ ───────

By Monday, August twenty-fifth, Redmond and Jennifer had been back in Pleasanton for six days. They'd run earlier this morning, and now, they had just finished breakfast. Redmond was preparing to walk to his Stoddard Hall office. It was the first day of the 2008 Fall Term, and when he left the house at seven-forty five he was feeling the excitement that the opening of the new academic year always aroused in him. He was dressed in a favorite dark blue suit, button down white shirt, a rather subdued red rep tie, and black Rockport shoes.

As he walked along he thought it was good that most Ravenslake faculty retained an unspoken allegiance to the tradition that professors should be well dressed in the classroom. He always felt a bit offended when professors went to undergraduate classes wearing jeans and a tee shirt, as they did at some schools. It was part of the general trend to look unpretentious or "laid back." And yet, he thought it failed utterly in that aim since it looked calculated and sloppy. Further, he thought there is this annoying trend among young adults, and regrettably, way too many older adults in our society, to try to look not just casual, but hot. He was thoroughly put off by fifty year old women sporting unkempt long straight blond hair with black roots, overexposed breasts, cut-off shorts that revealed *way* too much, with tattoos, and pieces of metal pinned in their lips, nose, cheeks, or other locations. If they want to look appealing, he thought, they should *not* try to look like eighteen-year old girls gone wild. They should learn the skills of good grooming and tasteful attire. And men, especially actors, now seem to think a five-day growth of whiskers and jeans with holes at the knees will really be a turn-on for women.

It was fortunate, he thought, that most Ravenslake students and faculty understood the relationship between appearance and success, and were, in fact, typically highly motivated for success. He recalled, approvingly, that Agatha Christy's old and amazingly insightful crime solver, Miss Marple, always said the secret to good taste in apparel was that it should be *appropriate* to the occasion. And there was damned little appropriateness, he thought, in striving to look hot in the classroom, or in the grocery store. But today the air was sweet, students were excited and busily heading off to classes in what Redmond judged to be generally appropriate attire, and so he put aside his little pet peeve of the moment.

He entered Stoddard, turned left down the first hallway, and popped his head into the departmental office to say "Hey" to Grace Feldon, the department secretary, and to Jill Isley, a returning student worker. He checked his mailbox, and collected several single-page, variously colored, announcements and a few envelopes. Then he returned to the main entrance area of Stoddard, took the elevator to the fourth floor, and walked to his office. He set his briefcase on his desk, gazed out his window at the scene below, and thought how grateful he was to be able to work in such in an agreeable setting as the RU community.

He read the announcements and his letters. One letter was from Jeff Greene, a fifth year student, freshly embarked on his internship year to the Brentwood VA Hospital in Los Angeles. Jeff simply related that he was pleased with his internship placement and excited to be in the City of Angels, and he expressed appreciation to Redmond for his teachings and for writing a letter of recommendation for him. Good young man, Redmond thought.

His phone rang. It was Steve Muir. Steve said, "Hey Mac, you able to have lunch with Tony and me at noon?"

"Sure," Redmond answered. "Meet you by the department office, at twelve!"

"Good—twelve sharp."

Redmond thought over his assignments for the new term. He had two three-hour a week courses to teach. One was an Introduction to Psychology class, and the second course was the graduate course in Neuropsychological Assessment. He liked both courses and was happy with his assigned class meeting times.

In addition to classroom work, he would have a third and a fourth year student to supervise in relation to their psychotherapy and assessment work with university students or community clients. The third year student would be working in the department's Psychology Clinic on the first floor of Stoddard. The fourth year student would be assigned to the Pleasanton Elder Care Center and Nursing Home. Jeff Greene had served in that placement last year, providing psychological assessments of patients, and short-term supportive counseling to spouses of the patients. Many of the patients at the Care Center, as most people called it, suffered from Dementia of the Alzheimer's Type, Vascular Dementia due to strokes, or other neurological disorders.

He'd also be supervising the Master's Thesis and Dissertation research work of several other students, and was assigned to two departmental committees and to one university committee. And of course, he had his own research to conduct and was still analyzing data and writing papers based on the massive Alzheimer's Project he'd led at Bain-Cottrell University in Seattle. Finally, he had to attend the biweekly departmental meetings on Wednesdays at four.

At noon he met his regular luncheon companions, Steve Muir and Tony Carmazzi, and the three friends walked to the Student Union's Pheasant Room for lunch. Once seated, they gave their orders to a student waitress, talked about the classes they'd been assigned, and then they all spoke about what they'd done in the way of vacationing during August.

Following that, their talk turned to the prospects for the Ravens football team, and the upcoming first game of the season against the Tarheels of the University of North Carolina. Tony said, "Well, I hope we have a good crowd for the game. Pleasanton is small, and the towns around it are smaller than Pleasanton, so we need our grads and other fans to make the trip here if we hope to fill the stadium."

Steve observed, "UNC is a quality opponent. I think our fans will turn out to cheer the team on."

Having enjoyed their lunches and further conversation, the three friends returned to their afternoon duties. At five o'clock Redmond began his walk home to Shadowy Lane. While the weather for his morning walk to Stoddard had been pleasant, his walk home was less agreeable. He thought the temperature had to be in the low nineties, and the humidity in the seventies.

When he entered the front door he called, "Hey, Jen. I'm home," but he soon determined that she wasn't in the house or on the back deck. He removed his coat and tie and draped them over a kitchen chair. He got a cold can of Dr. Pepper from the refrigerator, and then he went to the family room, turned on the music system, selected the classic jazz station from Sirius Radio, adjusted the loudness to a moderately loud level, and sat back on the sofa. He was pleasantly surprised to hear the disc jockey announce that the next tune would be "Milestones," played by the Johnny Trujillo Septet. He liked the rhythmic surging lines of the classic piece. The deejay said the tenor solo would be by Trujillo. Redmond enjoyed Johnny's tenor sax solo, but there was also a briefer alto sax solo, and Redmond wondered if it was by the current alto player, Jimmy Donahue, or the alto sax man from the earlier group, Duke Hartsfield. It was a swinging little solo, but Redmond hadn't heard enough of the playing of either alto man to attempt a conclusion as to which player it was.

Then he heard the garage door opening, and shortly thereafter Jennifer came through the mudroom and kitchen from the garage, and said, "Hey, sweetheart. You beat me home!"

Jennifer sat down beside him, they exchanged a brief kiss, and she asked, "So, how was the first day of the new academic year?"

Redmond clicked the music system off, and said, "It was, you could say, routine. I met with my Intro class, went over the syllabus with them, and gave a talk about psychology as a science and profession. They asked quite a few good questions about the clinical side of psych, the training of clinicians, *et cetera*. Being mostly freshman, quite a few of them always think they might want to become clinical psychologists. I even had a couple of students who wanted to know how much money clinical psychologists typically make. I told them the usual range of fees for psychotherapy, and they seemed to think the fees were high enough to interest them. Of course, there are those who are planning to become really wealthy business people, great titans of finance."

"Great potential wreckers of the economy," Jennifer responded.

"Then I had lunch with Steve and Tony, worked on some data for a paper, and had a very warm walk home." He took a sip of his drink and asked, "And what have you been up to?"

Jennifer removed her shoes, sat back and said, "Well, this morning I visited our next door neighbor, who has a healthy and cute as a button baby girl! Giselle had her on the fifteenth, while we were away."

"Wonderful," said Redmond. "Of course, they knew it was going to be a girl."

"Yes, they did. And the baby was seven and a half pounds, nineteen inches long, and robustly healthy."

"What's the baby's name?"

"Haylie Anne Hansen."

"Well, that's a terrific moniker. I like it."

Jennifer agreed, and after a brief silence, said, "And I just got back from meeting with Phil Regan regarding my idea for making prints of some kind from my paintings of local scenes. He gave me some encouraging advice and information."

"Great! What did he tell you?"

"Well, the first thing he told me was that, as far as he knows, none of the artists who've sold prints of local scenes and buildings have done anything new in the last twenty years. So, the field is open for a new round of paintings."

"That's good, Jen. There have been a bunch of new buildings added to the campus, and a lot of changes in the appearance of uptown over the past twenty years."

"And landscape and landmark paintings can be rendered very differently by different artists. A true artist's eye and imagination tend to guarantee individuality of the paintings."

"Did Phil suggest a method of producing prints?"

"He suggested a relatively new computer-based reproduction technique called Giclée printing. Basically, they scan your original artwork with a complex digital camera system, and reproduce the painting with pigment-based inks on archival paper or canvas. The result is of very high quality. Phil showed me a few examples. I swear they looked just like originals, Mac. And he told me many of the greatest art museums are now having exhibitions of prints made with this technique. The prints are archival and, with proper care, will last for centuries."

"What about the costs? Can you make some money doing it?"

"I don't know about making money, but I'm sure I couldn't lose much. For an image size of fifteen by twenty inches, on canvas, it would cost me thirty bucks a print. Phil would frame them with simple but attractive black or cherry wood frames for four dollars each, or if people wanted more elaborate frames he could charge accordingly."

"How many would you have to buy to get that thirty dollar price?"

"The minimum order would be fifteen prints, but I'd like to do a limited edition of seventy-five prints. So, the cost for seventy-five framed prints would be two thousand, two hundred, and fifty bucks. But they'd be gorgeous gallery quality prints, and we think they could sell for a hundred and fifty dollars each. Phil would get twenty-five dollars per sale, including his framing charge, leaving me with one hundred twenty-five dollars of income per sale. If I sold only *eighteen* prints, I'd cover the cost of my prints. If I sold all seventy-five, maybe over two or three years, I'd clear nine thousand-three hundred and seventy five dollars."

"Well, that would be nice!"

"Phil suggested I try it with just one or two paintings and see how it goes. If they sell readily, I could order a second edition. And I could gradually add prints of additional paintings, as I create them. Even if they don't make a lot of money, they could enhance my rep and maybe allow me to sell some oils or acrylics."

"Well, you sold two oil paintings last year for five and six thousand. So, if the Giclée prints help spread your reputation in Pleasanton and among Ravenslake alums, that could pay off."

"Yes, and the uptown bookstores, the RU Bookstore, and Phil Regan's Art Shop could all sell them. So, I'm inclined to give it a shot!"

"Well, that sounds good to me," Redmond said with a smile. He added, "You've been busy today, sweetie. I suggest we eat out somewhere in our renovated uptown."

"That would be great. But first, I'd like to shower and change into something cool and casual. And since we ran early this morning, and it's hotter than Hades outside, I think we can drive uptown, rather than walk."

"With ya on that, babe."

At six thirty Redmond pulled the red Sable into one of the oblique parking slots on East High Street, just in front of the College Inn. They entered the CI, as students and locals called the College Inn, and seated themselves in a tall wooden booth near the front of the establishment. The restaurant was cool, and only a few patrons were dining. Their orders were taken, and while they waited for their food, Langston Wallingford, accompanied by his new English Department colleague, Lindsey Marston, entered the CI and headed for a booth nearer the back of the room.

As they approached, Jennifer saw them, and she smiled broadly at Langston and his companion. She said, "Hello Langston," and added, "and to you, Lindsey. It's good to see you both."

Langston and Lindsey happily reciprocated the greeting.

Jennifer said. "Lindsey, you haven't met my husband, yet . . . this is Redmond." She said to Redmond, "This is Lindsey Marston."

Lindsey smiled and ran her gaze over Redmond before saying, "Well, hello Redmond. It's a pleasure to meet you."

"Same here," Redmond said with a smile. "I understand you've joined our faculty from Humphreys University. Jen and I were at Humphreys on sabbatical back in '99/2000. Were you there, then?"

"Oh, sure," she replied. "I was there from ninety-eight until I came here. But our paths never crossed, obviously. I have a good memory, and," she said rather slowly, "I'd remember you had we met."

Jennifer felt there had been more than a hint of flirtation in Lindsey's slight stress on the word "you," and her fixed eye contact with Redmond.

"Well, we enjoyed being there a lot, Lindsey," Redmond replied. "It's a beautiful area of the country."

"Yes, it's nice. But I find Pleasanton very agreeable. I have such wonderful colleagues in the English department, like Langston here." She beamed at Langston.

Langston said, "Well my dear, our department is delighted that you've joined us." Then he quickly said to Redmond and Jennifer, "Most pleasant to see you, Mac and Jen," and he guided Lindsey, with a light touch between her shoulders, further toward the back of the restaurant.

The McClains enjoyed their dinners and then returned to their car. As they drove past the businesses along East High Street and then the upper campus, Jennifer said, "Mac, did you notice that Lindsey Marston was a bit flirtatious with you when you asked if she'd been at HU while we were?"

Redmond glanced over at Jennifer, smiled, and said, "Really? No, I didn't notice anything like that."

Jennifer, speaking toward the car's roof, said, "Men are so unobservant! I mean, really, Mac—'I'd remember *you* had we met,'" she said with a little toss of her hair, accompanied by a fatuous smile.

Redmond chuckled. "Well, I guess it could be seen that way."

"You bet it could be seen that way. Langston steered her away pretty quickly after that." She added, after a few seconds, "Do you suppose there could be a romantic attraction there on Langston's part? I mean Langston's sixty-two or three, and she's probably mid-thirties, I'd say."

"Well, remember that Langston dated Helen Turner at one time, and she's a bit more than twenty years younger than he is. Langston is distinguished, looks a bit like the actor Hal Holbrook used to, and comes across as courtly and ingratiating."

"He's good at buttering people up, if that's what you mean," Jennifer said flatly. After a brief silence, she commented, "You know, when Ellen first introduced me to Lindsey, I had a momentary impression that she was the sort of woman Bette Davis played to perfection—selfish, manipulating, and capable of being cruel. Of course, I know there's no real behavioral reason to think ill of Lindsey, but there's something about her that puts me off. And, I know that's probably unfair of me."

"Sweetie, if there is one thing I know about you it's that you are *not* unfair. And you have that woman's intuition thing that sometimes amazes me. So, let's just keep an open mind about Lindsey Marston and see if woman's intuition has misled you in this instance, or not."

CHAPTER 12

▼

On the morning of Saturday, August thirtieth, Redmond and Jennifer happily entered The Huddle for their usual game day brunch with the Gundersens and Muirs. On this particular Saturday, Tierney Thornhill and Skip Craddock, both in their early thirties, had joined the group. Tierney owned the most successful of Pleasanton's realty operations, and Skip had recently become a partner in the local Potter Ford car dealership. Tierney and Skip had been dating for the past five months and there was considerable speculation among townspeople that the attractive couple would become engaged at some point in the near future.

Redmond and Jennifer snaked their way around occupied tables to the larger table the Gundersens always reserved for them. Ted greeted them with, "Hey! Good morning, Mac and Jen. Word on the street has it that we'll have a good crowd at Ross Stadium today, but not quite a sellout. And, I hate to say it, but it looks like it could be one of those drizzle games. Light showers are predicted for this afternoon."

Ellen, the group's most vociferous cheerleader at the games, was in her typically buoyant game-day mood. She said, "Ted, a little shower just makes the game more enjoyable and interesting. Today is our chance to show the Atlantic Coast Conference and the Tarheels that they'd better be ready to play when they come into Pleasanton."

Steve noted, "The Ravens and Tarheels have only met twice, both times in Chapel Hill, and we've split those two games."

Ellen responded, "We had a very young team last year, and we played them early in the season. We played them tough, although they did win. I think things will go our way today!"

The conversation turned to other topics of local interest. They all enjoyed the talk and the food, and after agreeing they'd meet after the game in the Colonial Room of the Ravenslake Inn to celebrate a hoped for victory, they went their separate ways at about eleven-ten. As Redmond and Jennifer headed east on High Street they observed that the uptown area was definitely more crowded than when they were on their way to The Huddle, and there were more Carolina fans than earlier. Redmond looked at the sky above and said, "So far, so good, on the weather question. It's mostly sunny and the clouds are white. Maybe we'll escape the rain."

*   *   *

As the clock ran down in the fourth quarter at Ross Stadium, and the moderate drizzle that had persisted since the start of the game showed no signs of leaving the area, the scoreboard read UNC 21, RU 20. Ted glanced at the time remaining on the scoreboard—"Just a minute and eight seconds left, and we got no time outs," he announced grimly to the others. The Ravens had just completed a twenty-yard pass play for a first down at the Tarheels thirty-six yard line. The red and white clad fans were all on their feet, urging the Ravens on, and the Tarheels supporters were vigorously countering the Ravens fans by yelling for their team to "hold em."

On first down, the RU tailback attempted a run off tackle, but as he received the ball from quarterback Joe Romano, he slipped on the slick turf and lost three yards. A moan went up from the home stands. "This is a tough situation," Redmond said. "We gotta throw the ball. The time is down to forty-six seconds."

The Ravens hurried to the line and on a short count Romano attempted a fifteen yard flat pass, but a Tarheel cornerback hit the receiver hard as he tried to bring Romano's pass in, and the ball fell to the ground.

Ellen was yelling, "Come on Ravens! Come on! Let's go!"

Steve said grimly, "It's third and ten, with thirty nine seconds left! We need a miracle."

Romano took the snap, dropped back two steps, and fired the ball to a slot receiver on an inside slant play. The receiver, Don Urich, made the catch in traffic and fought his way to the twenty-nine yard line, three yards short of the first down.

"We gotta try for a field goal," Ellen said urgently.

Jennifer anxiously noted, "Our freshman kicker is coming on the field! He got us two field goals today, but they were short ones. This is twenty-nine plus roughly seventeen—a forty-six yarder *in the rain*. It's a long shot!"

The Ravens hurried to line up for the field goal attempt. As the time ran down toward the final gun, the young freshman kicker from Canton McKinley High got the ball airborne. The ball seemed to leave the kicker's foot in slow motion, and all the fans stood as still as statues, only their eyes moving to track the ball.

And then the home crowd roared! The kick just managed to clear the crossbar but it split the uprights, and the muddy RU players mobbed their young kicker.

"There's still six seconds on the clock," Ted said anxiously. "We gotta kick off."

On the ensuing kick off the kicker sent the ball deep. The UNC deep return man gathered it in at the nine-yard line, slithered past three slip-sliding defenders and burst into the open at the UNC thirty.

As the runner dashed and splashed down the near sideline, Ellen screamed, "Oh no! Stop him. Stop him!"

Ted, in desperate hopefulness, said, "Ricky Springs has an angle on 'im, and Ricky's fast." But the UNC punt return man was also fast. Springs finally caught the return man at the Ravens' twelve-yard line and knocked him out of bounds. And time had expired!

The Raven's fans were wildly happy, laughing, whooping, and slapping each other on the back. Redmond said, "Wow, what an ending. What a victory!"

The others offered similar words of happiness with the dramatic outcome. Ted said, "When the return man broke through that clump of tacklers and into the clear it made my hair stand on end, and I felt chilled to the bone! Ricky Springs saved the day for the Ravens, no doubt about it."

The happy group wasted no time heading out the south exit of Ross Stadium. They crossed the little bridge over Tawee Creek, and headed up the narrow twisting extension of University Avenue to the Ravenslake Inn. Their well-practiced post-game dash to the Colonial Pub Room allowed them to beat the crowd and secure a large table. They squeezed two extra chairs in around the table for Skip and Tierney, who arrived shortly thereafter. Then they ordered beers and chips, and happily recalled various plays, hopes, and terrors they'd experienced during the game.

Ellen said, "I feared the agony of defeat most of the game, but in the end, we had the thrill of victory, baby!"

Ted volunteered, "If that ending had been any more exciting, I'm damned sure I'd be receiving resuscitation right about now."

"Well, we now lead the very short series with UNC, two to one," Tierney exalted.

As the group continued discussing the outcome of the game and offering kudos for this or that player, other clumps of happy fans trooped into the Ravenslake Inn. The English department faculty gang, including RU graduate, Langston Wallingford, arrived boisterously. Langston smiled broadly, his normally impeccably disciplined white hair and moustache now damply deranged, and, in stentorian tones, he said, "Old Ravenslake got a tremendous win today . . . an epic victory over an ACC team. It was a wonderful game, wasn't it?"

They all agreed it had been a great game, and then Langston moved on to the area where his colleagues had found tables. Over the next fifty minutes or so the Colonial Pub Room was a scene of unrestrained affability and comradeship, filled with jocular conversation and laughter. Gradually, some departed, and the conversations within the room became less exuberant, but no less companionable. A comfortable coziness enveloped the space and its occupants. Lindsey Marston came over and greeted Tierney. Tierney introduced Lindsey to Eve, Ted, and Steve, and then Lindsey smilingly asked Tierney, "Any news about my offer on the Vine Street house?"

"No, not yet, Lindsey," Tierney answered. "But we only made the offer last evening! I expect we'll hear something on Monday."

Ellen asked, "How'd you like the game, Lindsey?"

"Oh, it was thrilling . . . a little wet, but entertainingly gritty," she said. "I enjoyed it very much. It's nice to be at a school with Division I football."

Ellen said, "Good," and after a brief pause, she asked, "Which house are you interested in on Vine Street?"

"It's the last house on the street—the colonial red brick house at the end of Vine."

"That was Bob and Linda Ebersole's home," Ellen noted.

Eve commented to Lindsey, "That's a big house, and it's historic. It dates from the eighteen seventies, I believe."

Lindsey smiled and said, "It's a four bedroom, and the main areas of the house are big and *so* elegant. It was built in eighteen seventy-three, just like Langston's home. It's in good condition, but it could use a bit of renovation. I know it's a larger house than I need, but I couldn't resist it."

Ted said, "You know, Lindsey, it's on the edge of the woods that run all the way out to Pepper Park."

Lindsey smiled at Ted and said, "Well, I haven't ventured beyond the back property line, but it is wooded."

"Oh, yeah," Ted replied, "there must be close to a mile of woods, and then it comes to the park."

Lindsey leaned close to Ted and joked, "Maybe I could get lost back there, Ted, and never be seen again."

Ted chuckled and said, "Yeah, like John Traynor."

Lindsey looked puzzled. Ellen explained to her, "John Traynor was a student at RU who vanished from his dormitory, Angler Hall, back in 1965. No one knows to this day what happened to him. The John Traynor disappearance is a famous Ravenslake mystery, especially among students."

"So," Lindsey said, "Ravenslake has a spooky disappearance as part of its lore. That's interesting."

Jennifer commented to Lindsey, "Well, Mac and I visited Flagstaff this fall, and we learned that Humphreys had a mysterious disappearance, too."

Lindsey's look reflected puzzlement, or was it something else—apprehension? For a few milliseconds Jennifer saw Bette Davis standing in Lindsey's place and calculating a deception of some kind.

"A disappearance?" Lindsey asked.

"Yes," Redmond said, "of a astrophysics professor, back in 2001."

"Oh, yes! I thought you meant a *student* disappearance. I do remember the disappearance of a professor. But, it never gained the status of . . . well, a famous campus mystery."

Redmond smiled reassuringly. "Maybe the fact that it wasn't a student disappearance explains why it hasn't been incorporated into the ghost story tradition that students tend to create at old universities. Usually, in such stories, the ghost of the student still studies in the library at night, or occupies his or her old dorm room when no one is about."

Lindsey, her voice lacking its usual verve, said, "Well, today I've learned some things about Ravenslake's football traditions *and* about the John Traynor mystery. Now I'd best get back to my colleagues."

After Lindsey left and conversation at the table turned to other topics, Eve said quietly to Jennifer, "I thought Lindsey got a bit uptight when you mentioned that a professor had disappeared at Humphreys."

"Well, it wasn't a great topic to bring up," Jennifer responded quietly. "I hope she didn't know the woman well."

After another thirty minutes or so of conversation, the group broke up and headed to their homes. At seven o'clock Jennifer and Redmond rejoined Ellen and Steve for dinner at the crowded Al and Larry's Cupboard. They had a good meal, enjoyed each others' company, and spoke amiably with some UNC alums who were eating at Al and Larry's and planning to spend the night in Pleasanton before returning to Chapel Hill.

Later, when Redmond and Jennifer were home and preparing for bed, they talked briefly about how pleasant the day had been. "It was a great win," Jennifer said. She was calmly brushing her hair, and in a reflective mood. She said, "You know, sweetheart, Lindsey Marston seemed somehow thrown off balance by my mentioning the disappearance that occurred at Humphreys."

"Really? I didn't notice that. As soon as I mentioned it had been a disappearance of a *professor*, she knew what you were talking about."

"Yes, but I thought that bit of conversation made her uncomfortable, somehow. Maybe she knew Nizhoni, and found the topic upsetting to think about, and just wanted to change the subject. Still, there was something in the way she responded that made Bette Davis flash through my mind again."

"Well, if Lindsey knew Nizhoni and was upset by the topic, that wouldn't be hard to understand, would it?"

"I guess not. But Eve whispered to me that she thought the subject sort of startled Lindsey."

"I'm just a man, Jen, so maybe those kinds of things go over my head," Redmond said lightly.

"Well, it may have gone over your head—but you are much more than *just* a man!"

Redmond smiled and asked, "Would you care to elaborate on that?"

"Well, that is my intention, darling."

CHAPTER 13

▼

On Thursday, September fourth, Nadine and Rudy Baker, a retired couple, drove six miles beyond the last of the homes on Fort Valley Road to a point where they could park their car well off of Route 180, and then walk the short distance to a seldom-used Forest Service dirt road. The road ran slightly uphill into the Coconino pines, and it ended less than two miles from 180. It was a familiar pleasant routine for the Bakers, and it was designed primarily to allow their German Shorthair Pointer, Karl, to get some exercise. It was a gorgeous early afternoon, with low humidity and a temperature in the high sixties.

They parked and locked their car, and walked to the dirt road, as they had often done before. Nadine removed Karl's leash from his collar, and allowed the seventy-pound, white-ticked, liver colored hound to rove out ahead of them. Being a pointer, it was in Karl's genetic makeup to range from one grassy road edge to the other, ahead of his owners, sniffing the ground, eager to detect the scent of a bird hiding in the grass, to freeze *on point* when he detected the bird, *flush* the bird into the air on command, and wait for his masters to shoot the bird so he could retrieve it. Of course, the Baker's never shot at any of the few birds Karl pointed or flushed from the thin and spotty wild grasses along the roadside. But that never troubled Karl. He had his job to do, and even if his masters failed to do their parts, he wasn't about to shirk his duties. Occasionally, he'd venture off the roadside into the pines, but when Rudy gave a sharp whistle or a call, Karl always drifted back to their path and resumed his nose-to-the-ground scurrying from one side of the road to the other.

As Nadine and Rudy walked along they commented on the beauty of the day, and how grand Humphreys Peak looked as it towered into the sky five thousand-plus feet above them. Rudy said, "I love this really deep blue sky we get on these low humidity days." He pointed to the sky and added, "And you can see the moon almost as clearly as you can see it at night—it's about seven eighths full today."

"And the Aspen among the pines up there stand out with some yellow leaves showing already," Nadine noted with a satisfied smile.

They walked along quietly, enjoying the scene and appreciating Karl's work ethic. They saw a large red-tailed hawk and a few ravens glide high over the road, but of course, Karl wasn't interested in birds he hadn't flushed himself. As they rounded a turn in the road Nadine and Rudy were surprised to see Karl standing about six yards off to the right of the road, in a flat area partially ringed by three young Ponderosa Pines. Rudy called to the dog, and although Karl gave him a brief glance, he did not return to the road. Instead, he continued sniffing, and started pawing the ground.

"Maybe he found something," Nadine said.

"Let's see what he's turned up," Rudy suggested. He went the spot where Karl was beginning to dig.

Nadine called cheerily, "What did he find?"

Rudy moved the dog back from the spot where he'd been pawing the ground. He bent down to get a better view of what had captured Karl's attention.

As Nadine approached her husband, she asked, "Animal bones?"

"Bones," Rudy replied shakily, "but with a turquoise and silver ring." His usually florid face was ashen.

Nadine came close and looked at the bone segments of a finger Karl had begun to unearth. "My god!" she uttered.

Rudy didn't respond. Nadine asked anxiously, "Are you all right?"

Her husband took a deep breath, squared his shoulders, and swallowed hard. "I'm okay, Nadine. But we gotta go to the Sheriff's Office and report this."

Nadine fastened Karl's leash to his collar and pulled him away from the spot. Rudy glanced around and quickly found a baseball size rock and laid it next to the spot. They returned to the road and studied the area.

Rudy said, "We need to make sure we can find this place without delay when we come back." He quickly garnered three more rocks and arranged them in a triangle at the edge of the road. Then they hurried back to their car and drove to the Coconino County Sheriff's Office in Flagstaff.

An hour later the Baker's drove back out Route 180, with a Sheriff's Department vehicle close behind. When they reached the Forest Service Road site they had marked, Detectives Jim Healy and Emerson Yazzie asked the Bakers to show them exactly where they had seen what they thought were bones of a human finger.

Rudy led the detectives to the spot he'd marked with the stone. Detective Healy knelt down and looked intently at the segments of finger bones that had been unearthed. "No doubt about it," Healy said, "this is a finger of a person. The bones are separated, but they're pretty much in place, and they point up this little grade here. It's apparently a shallow grave, and this is a pine forest with acidic soil—doesn't favor the preservation of remains. The grade here isn't steep, but it would direct some water down through this shallow gully. What with the heavy Monsoon rains and snow melts we've had the past few years, these remains have begun to be exposed." He paused before saying, "There's no telling how long these bones have been here, but Forensics will be able to answer that question."

Emerson said only, "Yeah." He felt nauseous and angry. He'd seen the turquoise and silver ring beside the curled finger bone segments that were still partially covered with dirt. He didn't need Forensics to tell him how long the bones had been in that acidic red soil—seven years and four and a half months, he knew. Unlikely as it had always seemed, he'd hoped he would one day see Nizhoni again. But what was under that red soil was not Nizhoni. It was only evidence that she had once been there, terrified or already dead. His mind was flooded with memories of Nizhoni and of her heartbroken parents and grandparents. He struggled to appear stoic. He silently addressed an unknown killer, "You slimy son of a bitch. We're going to find your sorry ass and you're gonna pay for this, big time!" But the vow brought him no comfort.

Detective Healy thanked the Bakers for leading them to the site. He asked that they not talk about it to others for the time being. The Bakers pulled their car ahead, got it turned around, and headed to 180. Then Healy called the Sheriff's Office and reported the location of a probable crime scene, with human skeletal remains. He said he and Detective Yazzie would wait at the scene until a Crime Scene Investigation Team arrived.

As they waited in their patrol car, Emerson Yazzie stared through the windshield of the cruiser. There was a subtle quaver in his voice as he said to his partner, "It's Nizhoni."

Healy replied softly, "Yeah, buddy . . . I know."

CHAPTER 14

▼

At eleven-twenty on Tuesday, September ninth, Jennifer checked her email and found two new messages. One was from Margo Bailey, and the other from Sarah Tedesco, in Pittsburgh. Sarah and her husband, Joe, were old friends from their grad school days at Minnesota State, buddies whose companionship they unfailingly enjoyed at sports and cultural events during their periodic visits to the Burgh. Jennifer clicked on Sarah's message to find a suggestion that she and Redmond make a weekend visit to Pittsburgh. Joe had free tickets for them for a Friday, September nineteenth, performance of the Pittsburgh Symphony, free tickets to a Saturday night Gregg Opelka play at the Pittsburgh Public Theatre, and free tickets to the Steelers versus Cowboys game on Sunday. Jennifer surmised that Detective Sean Driscoll and Becky Driscoll, close friends of Joe and Sarah, were going to be out of town that weekend and had offered their symphony, theatre, and football game tickets for Redmond and Jennifer. Jennifer emailed back that it sounded like a wonderful three-event weekend, but that she'd have to check with Redmond later in the day. She promised to get back to Sarah this evening.

Then, before opening Margo's email she glanced at the subject line that said "New development." She opened the message and read that the new development concerned the discovery of the skeletal remains of Nizhoni Lydecker on Thursday, September fourth. It momentarily took her breath away! "*Holy Toledo*—poor Nizhoni," she murmured.

Margo's message said only, "Thought you'd be interested in this shocking development. It's been on area media a lot, and it was mentioned on CNN last night." Margo had also scanned two articles from the *Daily Sun* and attached them. The first was a short report of the discovery of the human remains by a local couple and their dog, and speculation that the remains could be those of Nizhoni Lydecker. The second attachment reported Sheriff Slater's revelations at yesterday's news conference, and responses to questions from reporters. He noted that dental records indicated that the remains were those of Nizhoni Lydecker. He also reported that the body had been nude when buried. As Jennifer read the second article she was surprised to feel tears welling up in her eyes, but she looked up, took a deep breath, and returned to the article. "God damned creep!" she said aloud. She felt a burning anger and her thoughts expressed it. How many young women and girls have to have this happen to them? How many sexual deviates does this society have, and why are they *ever* freed? And for over seven years some depraved bastard has been able to breathe, and eat, and cheer for his damned teams, and get himself all sexually aroused by his memories of this obscenity . . . and to fantasize about future opportunities to do such a thing again!

She called Ellen at the Lange Library and asked if they could meet for lunch. She told Ellen a bit about the news from Flagstaff that she found so upsetting. They agreed to meet at The Purity at twelve.

Jennifer walked uptown to the Purity at the appointed time, and when she entered the old restaurant she was happy to see that Ellen was there. As she took a chair at a table for two she forced a smile and said, "Thanks for meeting me on such short notice, El."

"No problem, Jen. I know this kind of news is upsetting."

"Well, I'm just being overly emotional for some reason. I never knew the woman, and I've only seen one picture of her." She paused before saying, "See, when we were in Flagstaff, Margo Bailey, the new wife of Mac's former research assistant at Patten University, told us the story of the strange disappearance of this astrophysics professor from Flagstaff, seven years ago."

Over the next half hour, with calming food and reassuring social interaction, Jennifer told Ellen the story of Nizhoni Lydecker as she had learned it from Margo and from archival stories in the *Daily Sun*. Ellen was very interested in the narrative. She strongly denounced the unknown perpetrator of the crime, and that made Jennifer feel that her outrage and distress had not been excessive.

By twelve forty Jennifer said, "I feel a lot better, El. Thanks so much for meeting me on such short notice."

"Anytime," Ellen said with an easy smile.

"I don't know why I got so upset by this," Jennifer offered apologetically. "I mean, outrageous as it is, we all know it happens." She added, reflectively, "Maybe it was because I'd seen her photograph and knew her story to some extent. She grew up in a tiny town on the Navajo Reservation, had proven herself to be a brilliant and industrious student, earned scholarships to UC-Berkley and Stanford, and was having a successful academic career."

"Sounds like a wonderful young woman. I can see how all that could give you a sense of closeness or acquaintance with her."

Jennifer sounded a bit relieved as she said, "That makes sense, El. I sort of felt I knew her."

They changed the topic to other matters of ongoing interest in Pleasanton, and at one o'clock they exited the Purity. Ellen headed west to the nearby Lange Library, and Jennifer began her walk east, across Main Street and down High Street toward Shadowy Lane.

When Redmond arrived home a bit after five, he found Jennifer relaxing on the back deck, reading the latest copy of *Scientific American*. He opened the screen door and popped his head out. "Hey, beautiful," he said.

"Hey, handsome," she returned. "Could you bring me a Dr. Pepper with ice, when you come back. I have . . . news to share with you."

"Great! I'll change, and be right back."

Ten minutes later Redmond appeared, with two glasses of Dr. Pepper. He handed one to Jennifer, and then slipped into the sling chair next to hers. "So, tell me the news," he said.

"Sarah emailed me today. She and Joe would like us to go to the Burgh for the September nineteenth weekend. I gather Sean and Becky Driscoll must be planning to go out of town that weekend, because Sarah has *free tickets* for us to—*get this*, The Pittsburgh Symphony on Friday night, a Gregg Opelka play at the Public Theater on Saturday night, and the Steelers/Cowboys game at Heinz Field on Sunday afternoon."

Redmond smiled and said, "My cup runneth over! Its perfect, sweetie! We'll have to leave immediately after the Steelers game to get home at a decent time, but that'll be okay. We haven't been to the Golden Triangle since last fall. I'm more than ready for the city's attractions. We can stay at the William Penn. I'll get reservations after dinner."

"That'll work fine, Mac. I told Sarah I'd respond to her email tonight, after I made sure you didn't have any problem with those dates."

"Good," he said. "And that *was* interesting news, indeed."

She looked into Redmond's eyes and said softly, "And there is *other* news."

"So? Lay it on me!"

"It's not happy news, Mac. A German Shorthair Pointer discovered the skeleton of Nizhoni Lydecker. It was just about eight miles out beyond Bristlecone Lane on 180, near an unpaved Forest Service Road. She was buried at the western base of Mt. Humphreys."

Redmond awaited further information, but when it failed to come, he said quietly, "Takes your breath away—buried eight miles from the house she had lived in." He asked, "How'd you learn that?"

"Email. From Margo."

"Man! What a shocker—after seven-plus years!"

"Margo didn't say much about it, but she sent two attachments from the *Daily Sun*. I printed them out. Let me get them."

When she returned she handed the copies to Redmond. He read the account of the discovery by Karl, the pointer. "Good dog. And good people, it sounds like," he commented. He read the longer article with no comments other than sighs and a few minimally voiced curse words, and when he'd finished reading, he said, "It's damned shocking to realize a person could do such a thing as that. To abduct someone like Nizhoni, a brilliant woman and a great beauty, and treat her like he must have, then dump her nude body into a cold muddy hole, and shovel wet dirt over her lifeless form. It's . . . sickening."

"Yes. I had that feeling, too. In fact, I was very upset and angry about it. I called El and asked her to meet me for lunch. And that helped. I realized, in talking with El, that although we knew she was missing and was probably dead, I was totally unprepared for the reality and brutality of it. Having heard Margo's description of Nizhoni's intellect, having read of her humble origins, having seen her picture and her beauty, her resemblance to Jennifer Jones, and seeing her house, and encountering her former husband, and . . . all that. It was almost traumatic for me."

"I understand, hon. Knowing that someone went missing seems like the essential fact in itself. You can't know exactly what happened to them. But it really hits home when you're confronted with the graphic realities and the grotesque perversions involved" . . . he trailed off with a sigh, and laid the printed pages aside.

Jennifer rested her hand on his forearm and said, "It makes me want to find the bastard and remove him from society, so he can never do such a thing to another girl or woman."

Redmond nodded his agreement, and responded, "Yes. But it sounds as if the authorities learned little that could help them catch the fiend. There's apparently no gun, no bullet, and no clue as to the killer."

"It seems the killer must have been the stranger she met at Chester's, don't you think?"

"Probably."

"I mean, her husband couldn't have done that to her, could he?"

"I can't imagine *anyone* doing that. We read that Lydecker claimed he was in Nevada when the crime occurred, and said he was alone, working in the high desert country of north central Nevada. Still, as we know, he could have bought the killing."

After a brief silence, Jennifer said, "Well, let's change the subject, darling."

"Right!" He stood and tried to shift his mindset. "I'll get online and check the program for the September nineteenth PSO concert, just out of curiosity."

"Good. And I thought we could have our dinner around seven. Could you grill some chicken breasts, later?"

"Of course," he replied, and he headed off to their office to get the information he wanted regarding the trip to Pittsburgh. He returned to the back deck ten minutes later and reported, "The PSO program will include a new work commissioned by the PSO, Hindemith's *Symphonic Metamorphosis,* and the Sibelius *Second Symphony.*"

"Wonderful," Jennifer said. "What a great program! I'll email Sarah after dinner and tell her we'd be delighted to see them and share such terrific events."

"Do you need to tell them we'll stay at the William Penn?"

"Not really, Mac. They know we like to stay downtown. But I'll mention it anyway."

And the prospect of their trip to Pittsburgh helped mitigate what had been a *very* upsetting day for Jennifer.

CHAPTER 15

▼

At ten minutes of eight on Monday evening, September fifteenth, Ridley Raintree sat at the Steinway in her second floor home studio and passively watched the legendary red rock formations of Sedona slip slowly into shadow. She'd rehearsed several new songs, but felt she'd just tinkered unproductively with a new composition she was struggling to construct. For the past six weeks she'd enjoyed the luxury of being off the road, and had made good use of her time. She'd completed two new compositions, one a sentimental ballad with a sophisticated lyric, and the other a somewhat dissonant and interestingly disjointed minor tune, a Thelonious Monk-inspired piece she planned to add to her group's play list. Her upcoming performance schedule was now finalized. It called for six weeks of engagements in Vegas, Reno, Tahoe, San Francisco, Los Angeles, and San Diego, all between October twenty-fifth and Christmas. Then she'd have nearly a solid month back home before embarking on a three-month east coast and midwestern tour of large-venue concert halls, name jazz clubs, and college gigs, beginning in late January.

As darkness erased the contours and colors of Coffee Pot Rock from the visible landscape, she let her arms relax into her lap as she looked beyond the piano at the dimming panorama before her. She had the thought that "Nightfall" might be a good title for the contemplative composition she'd written many years earlier, but never named. It was definitely a mood piece, but she knew she'd never perform it publicly because, and it seemed odd to think, it was a private piece—pensive, personal, and, yes, plaintive. She didn't wish to share, or *reveal*, it. And it was probably too elegiac for a general jazz audience. She frowned a bit as she sought a title other than "Nightfall." Perhaps, "Elegy for Ridley"—Stan Kenton would have liked the composition back in his day, or at least he'd have liked the title, she speculated. "Maybe Stan had his own secret sad lament piano piece, his confession of deep failings and regrets," she said softly. She played a bit of her personal piece, but her mood was restive and she felt beset by questions about her future, so she discontinued it just before the second statement of its major theme.

What troubled Ridley at this moment was her relationship with Tyler Lydecker, and the fact that he had asked her, just three weeks ago, to marry him. She'd known Tyler for almost ten years. She was not proud of the fact that she was having an affair with him at the time his wife disappeared. She had no excuse for her transgression other than that she had been young and foolish, and, she granted, horny. At that time she had been concerned that Tyler could somehow have let slip to his wife the fact of their relationship, and if that could have been his wife's reason for filing for a divorce. When she asked Tyler about that back in 2001, he assured her that was not the case, and that his wife wanted the divorce because of a variety of life style incompatibilities. But Ridley had always wondered, and felt lessened by that possibility.

Their relationship had continued, off and on, over the past ten years. Tyler Lydecker had some money, and he could be fun to be with, though he had his dark and silent moods from time to time. She had to admit that until he proposed she had never entertained the possibility of marriage to Tyler. He reluctantly accepted her response that she would need more than just a month or two to consider his proposal. She pointed out that she had professional commitments through the spring season, and needed to concentrate on those.

And then the skeletal remains of his unfortunate wife were found, just eleven days ago. What a *startling* development! Yet, it seemed to have little impact on Tyler. She recalled him being very upset and nervous after his wife's disappearance in 2001. But now, with the discovery of his wife's remains, he seemed oddly indifferent to the event. His emotional response was shallow and somehow out of tune, with unresolved dissonances that made her feel uncomfortable and wary. She knew there had been suspicions that he could have arranged his wife's disappearance. Back then she had regarded such suspicions as ridiculous.

But while having dinner with him last Friday, just eight days after the discovery of his wife's grave, she had seen his utter indifference to the discovery. Now the thought that Tyler could have bought the disappearance of his wife was less easily dismissed. Ridley knew that Tyler had been intensely angry with his wife over what he termed her "excessive financial demands." Certainly, the disappearance of his wife had paid off for Tyler. It had benefited him in terms of his avoidance of possible alimony payments and the loss of the home that he prized. Additionally, he had been the beneficiary of a substantial life insurance policy on his wife, although payment had been delayed for five years after her disappearance.

Ridley blinked, dissolving the visual memory images of her last dinner with Tyler. With no sense of conscious selection of a tune, her hands began playing, ever so softly, a spare and slowed tempo version of the old Harry Ruby/Rube Bloom song, "Give Me the Simple Life." She had decided that the next time Tyler called she would politely decline his offer of marriage, and tell him she really didn't see any future for their relationship—and she felt a great sense of liberation.

CHAPTER 16

▼

At twelve-forty on Tuesday, September sixteenth, Jennifer left the house and headed uptown for her weekly two-hour stint at the Grounds for Thinking coffee shop. The weather that had been so generously ingratiating this fall had changed overnight, and today the sky showed not a swatch, not so much as a stingy lean line of blue anywhere. And while the low clouds were brushed with only shades of gray, not black, and no rain was forecast until tomorrow, there was a gusting chilled breeze that foretold the change of seasons ahead. The many tree species that so plenteously adorned the venerable Ravenslake campus were beginning to lose some of their yellow and red leaves. And as Jennifer strode up the gentle rise of East High Street, occasional small vortices of fallen leaves danced artfully before her, while her loose reddish blond hair lashed lightly about her face and the upturned collar of her coat. She was glad she had worn her short winter coat and wool slacks. Still, she found the nip in the air a familiar harbinger of the winter ahead, a bit of nature in its proper place, for there was no season Jennifer didn't welcome and embrace. She loved and appreciated both the seasonal changes nature wrought, and the diverse and clever adaptations our human culture had devised to meet them. Constant weather, she told herself, would be dreary, regardless of its character. She viewed the chill in the air as a dear friend she hadn't met in some time.

There were many students on the sidewalk and campus walkways to her left, across High Street, and on her side of the street the sidewalk bustled with purposeful pedestrians headed uptown. She crossed Tallawanda Road and passed Tuffy's Restaurant, the popular fast food and coffee resource for generations of Ravenslake students. As she passed the Beta Bell Tower she saw Lindsey Marston and two women students on the other side of the street. They were talking and laughing, and Lindsey saw and returned the wave Jennifer directed her way. Lindsey seemed very happy, and Jennifer assumed she was heading to or from her class. Knowledge of eighteenth and nineteenth century British women writers is being disseminated, and no doubt gladly received at Ravenslake, she thought. She reminded herself that writing and publishing had been regarded as generally inappropriate activities for women even in the mid-nineteenth century. The star-crossed family of British writers, Charlotte, Emily, and Anne Brontë had, for fear of rejections based on their gender, submitted their first novels under the male pseudonyms of Currier Bell, Ellis Bell, and Acton Bell. Would their first novels have been published had the fact of their gender been known? And Jennifer wondered how much more difficult must it have been for women authors a century earlier than the Brontë sisters? As she thought of the fact that the three sisters died at the ages of thirty-eight, thirty, and twenty-nine, the latter two of tuberculosis, she felt very fortunate to have been born in nineteen fifty-seven.

She was a bit disconcerted that her very next thought was that Nizhoni Lydecker's life had been violently halted at the age of thirty, and that she was born in nineteen seventy-one. *Good heavens*, she thought, despite this invigorating weather my mind is straying to unpleasant, even morbid, thoughts today—and the common theme seems to be about women being victimized. She quickly granted the objection that women authors flourish today, and that both men and women now live much longer than they did in the mid-eighteen hundreds. Still, she thought, it *is* the case that many more women are murdered, by men, than vice versa. She made herself smile by registering the odd thought that women have to even that up! But that brief spark of grim humor faded quickly, and she hoped the man that killed Nizhoni would soon, at long last, be identified and apprehended.

When she entered Grounds for Thinking she took her place in the ordering line behind two students, and when they'd ordered and paid, she advanced to the counter and greeted Jason. He smiled, returned the greeting, and asked, "Do you want your lunch, Jen?"

"Yes," she answered. "Make it the usual, with a Highlander Cream coffee."

Jason placed a wrapped vegetarian sandwich on wheat, a covered salad, and her coffee on a small tray, and Jennifer took the tray to her office.

She saw that there were roughly thirty books on her desk that she would need to inspect, price, and then record the credits allowed to the book donors. She ate her pay, and then performed her work on the newly acquired used books, a few of which she found interesting enough to peruse. After finishing this task at two-thirty, she placed the books in their appropriate places on the shelves, and went to the front counter to return the customers' cards to Jason. Seeing he was busy, she went behind the counter and filed the cards herself. She then devoted her attention to checking the library shelves for possibly misplaced books, and, finding some, she relocated them to their proper places.

At five minutes of three she saw Eve enter Grounds. Eve waved to her and came to the back of the shop. "Hey, Jen," she said with a happy smile. "Ready for our coffee and cake time?"

"Sure am," Jennifer answered, "and how about going to The Pleasanton Bakery. It's nice and cozy on a chilly day like this."

"Sounds good," Eve responded. Five minutes later they stepped into the neat little South Main Street bakery that always smelled so sweet it seemed they could taste it. Allyson

Poggemeier, the owner of the bakery, greeted them, and after exchanging pleasantries, Eve and Jennifer ordered coffee and chocolate cake. They took their treats to the small coffee room behind the main area of the store.

There they chatted about their various activities. Eve spoke about the fact that daughter Heidi was adjusting well to her freshman year at Purdue, and had done very well on recent exams.

They also talked about local happenings, including the fact that Ellen Muir was one of two editors for the much anticipated and soon to be published book, *Ravenslake University: Two Centuries of Memories.*

Jennifer said, "It's apparently loaded with both serious and humorous incidents, interesting events, and little known stories about people and issues that helped shape the marvelous university that is our present day Ravenslake."

Eve said, "It's been a big project, I gather. Ellen said the book should be out in the spring. *And,* I heard from Ellen that you'll have two prints of Pleasanton scenes in the local book stores and Phil Regan's shop before Christmas."

"Yes," Jennifer smilingly responded. "They'll be of two campus scenes I painted last fall—the DeWitt Cabin and the old bypassed Covered Bridge out on Indian Mound Road."

"Those should be good, Jen. I hope they'll be brisk sellers."

"It would be nice if they are, Eve. I'm very pleased with the quality of the production process."

"You two gals are very dedicated to your work," Eve observed.

"And so are you, Eve," Jennifer returned. "In addition to maintaining one of Pleasanton's top two restaurants, you're the most prominent and effective member of City Council, and you're on several town/gown joint committees."

"*Whada ya mean*, 'one of the *two* top restaurants,'" Eve challenged, but with a grin that required only a chuckle from Jennifer. "Well, Jen," Eve remarked, "we women have come a long way over the past century. Not that there isn't a long ways to go, still. For example, studies show that women continue to be paid less than men within all kinds of job classifications."

"That's unfortunately true. And men murder women more than women murder men."

"*Good heavens!* Where'd *that* come from, Jen?"

Jennifer said, "Sorry, Eve. I don't mean to imply that women need to catch up with men in that department. But it's something that seems to be on my mind today."

"Should I warn Mac?" Eve jested.

Jennifer hastened to explain. "Well, when we were in Flagstaff in August, Margo Bailey—she's the young psych prof at Humphreys University that . . ."

"Married Mac's former grad assistant," Eve said.

"Yes. Anyway, we had dinner with Tim and Margo, and afterward we went for a drink to a place called Chester's in downtown Flagstaff. It's a bar that presents various kinds of music, including, occasionally, jazz players. And, to get to the point, Margo told us a true story about a beautiful and brilliant young Navajo woman, an astrophysicist at Humphreys, who disappeared."

"Disappeared?"

"Yes. Vanished without a trace, as they say. Her name was Nizhoni, and she was separated from her husband. She was last seen in that bar on the night of April twentieth, 2001. She was alone and seated at a two-person table before the first jazz set started, and the place was crowded. The manager of the club asked her if he could seat a man, who was also alone, at her table. And she said that would be fine. At the end of the first set she and the man left, but no one observed whether they left together or not. It was a night of terrible weather, with winds and rain. Anyway, she was never seen again. And her car had been driven off the lot, and it has never been found."

"And do people think it was the man she shared her table with that caused her disappearance?"

"People suspect that could be the case. No one knows who he was. And, I *should* have said she was never seen again until September fourth, less than two weeks ago."

"They found her?"

"Sadly, no. They didn't find *her*. They found only her skeletal remains, outside of Flagstaff, just off the road that leads to the Grand Canyon. She was buried in a shallow grave. She'd been naked when put into that cold muddy hole. There was no apparent damage or injury to any of her bones, and they believe she had been suffocated."

"Good heavens, Jen! How terrible. I suppose they identified her by dental records or DNA?"

"Yes, dental records within a few days, and I assume DNA, by now."

"I can see why it could give you a jaundiced outlook on men."

"There are a number of things that upset me. She was in a contentious divorce proceeding against her husband, who was also a professor. And as fate would have it, Mac and I were introduced to him at a resort in Sedona—he was with the pianist/singer who had earlier autographed her CD that we purchased during the intermission of her show. And Nizhoni disappeared from a *jazz* performance, and that somehow made it worse, more personal somehow, for me. And Mac and I had looked at a house on Fort Valley Road because we were thinking it might be a nice place for a vacation home, and it turned out that it had belonged to Nizhoni and her husband. And we saw her picture in an article in an old local paper. Her name, Nizhoni, means 'beautiful' in Navajo, and she *was* beautiful. She looked very much like Jennifer Jones, the movie actress. As a young teenager I'd been a fan of Jennifer Jones. So, this 'confluence of elements,' I guess, made me feel a connection with Nizhoni."

"You and Mac looked through a newspaper archive about her disappearance?"

"Yes, the local paper had it."

"Well, Jen, it sounds to me as if you two are engaging in a familiar pattern of being so curious about a crime that you end up getting involved with it, and trying to understand or solve it. And you've even put yourselves in harms way a couple of times by doing that."

"Well, you can't help being curious about a thing like that, Eve! But there's no way for us to get *involved* in it, really. It just makes me angry that such a terrible thing could happen to a brilliant young woman in a relatively small college town. And it isn't like such cases are rare in our supposedly enlightened country, and that upsets me, too. There are women and girls abducted, raped, killed, and thrown out in isolated places as casually as the killer might throw away an empty beer bottle. And it seems, in the sad case of Nizhoni Lydecker, there are absolutely no real clues as to who could have done that terrible thing."

"Such things upset all of us, of course. The world is an imperfect place, Jen."

"Yes. So, it's up to people to value and protect one another, and try to create a humane world. But many people are too selfish or too flawed to control their own behaviors, and they violate, rather than protect, others."

Eve smiled a sympathetic smile and said, "We can only do the best we can, Jen. Don't try to take it all onto your own shoulders. We can't wish evil away, nor protect everyone. We can only do the best we can."

"Well, let's hope our species can evolve into something more consistently humane. At the present time, our species is still too animalistic to be considered 'highly evolved.'"

"That's true, Jen, but we can't speed up our own evolution. Now cheer up, and enjoy this delicious cake and the good coffee. And let's change the subject."

Jennifer nodded her agreement, and said, "Thanks, Eve."

CHAPTER 17

▼

At six thirty on Friday, September twenty-sixth, the McClains headed uptown for dinner. It was part of their generally orderly lives that they always ate out on Fridays, and, weather permitting, they nearly always chose to walk rather than drive. As they strode by the historic Lottie Moon House, the one time home of the young Miss Moon who'd been a spy for the Confederacy during the Civil War, Redmond commented that the weather tonight was very congenial.

"And the weather has been great for over a week now," Jennifer responded. "Great weather helped make our Pittsburgh trip a wonderful weekend."

"It certainly helped, that's for sure," Redmond responded. "And what a fun-packed weekend it was. We stayed only two nights, yet we got to hear the PSO at Heinz Hall, saw a good play at the Public, and watched the Steelers outlast the Cowboys! And, as always, it was really fun to be with Joe and Sarah."

"And even though we were dragging by the time we got home Sunday night, it was all wonderful."

They entered Al and Larry's Cupboard, were quickly seated, and ordered their food. Redmond commented that the restaurant wasn't as crowded as he had expected it to be on a Friday evening.

"Well," Jennifer replied, "according to Martha Curtis, with whom I had lunch a few weeks ago, Pleasanton used to be much livelier on Friday and Saturday nights than it is nowadays. Of course, Martha does tend to find that the 'old days' were universally better or happier or more sensible than the present in Pleasanton. It wasn't the first time I've heard her expound on the subject. She and Goddard came here in the mid-sixties when there were only sixty-five hundred students on campus, unmarried students weren't permitted to have cars, the only alcoholic drink allowed in town was three point two percent beer, and the Williams College for Women hadn't yet become part of Ravenslake—and, of course, 'The Williams girls always dressed so nicely,' as Martha likes to lament."

Redmond chuckled, and said, "I suppose Martha pointed out that in those days, Friday and Saturday were the big nights uptown, whereas now a lot of students take off in their cars for other places."

"Exactly. But, you know, I heard Langston echo those same sentiments at Giselle's barbecue when we first came to town. He said when students weren't allowed to have cars at RU they were all in town on weekends, and nearly all of them turned out for athletic games and dances. He said there were lots of annual fraternity, sorority, and holiday dances, and they were quite fancy."

"Well, neither of us went to schools that had the power to refuse students the right to have cars, and it certainly wasn't the case at our schools that nearly *all* students attended games and dances. I guess this was once a very unique sort of campus, and I have to think Martha could be right—that something of value has been lost in that regard."

"You'd miss the well-attended dances if you were a student now?"

"Oh, sure! You know, they called me 'Twinkle-toes McClain,'" Redmond said with a smile.

Jennifer responded with a flirtatious batting of her eyes and a teasing tone in saying, "I'd have loved to know *you* in your twinkle toes days." Before Redmond could respond, she said matter-of-factly, "See, Mac, that was flirtation, sort of like, 'I'd have remembered *you*, had we met.'"

Redmond smiled. "So you're still thinking Lindsey was flirting with me at the CI?"

"Of course! And I want to help you be able to recognize flirtation when someone is doing it, so you won't unknowingly reinforce it. Of course, if you knowingly reinforce it, you'll be in big trouble unless you can explain, satisfactorily, why you thought it was good to do that!"

They finished their meal. Redmond paid the bill, and included a generous tip for their student waiter. As they exited the College Inn, Langston Wallingford and Lindsey Marston were just approaching the door. Langston smiled broadly and said, "Good evening, Jen and Mac. Pleasant fall twilight, isn't it? Just a slight nip in the air."

Both McClains made brief statements of agreement. Lindsey asked, "Are you going to the Kent State game tomorrow?"

Jennifer nodded affirmatively and Redmond said, "Oh, you bet. It's a critical conference game."

As Langston and Lindsey prepared to enter the restaurant, Lindsey turned and called back, "I hope we'll see you at the Ravenslake Inn after the game."

While Redmond and Jennifer were stepping away from the restaurant at a leisurely pace, Redmond asked, with a grin that he tried to resist, "Jen, was Lindsey trying to flirt with me, again, just now?"

"No. Are you disappointed?"

"No, no." He tried to sound earnest as he said, "I just have a hard time telling. How could I tell?"

"Well, first of all, she was looking at both of us when she said she hoped to see us after the game. And she wasn't looking in your eyes, or doing her slow come hither smile, and perky head toss."

"Aha! Direct eye contact, come hither smile, perky head toss," Redmond said slowly.

"*Again*," Jennifer instructed, using the long 'a' sound in the second syllable, as the British do.

"Direct eye contact, come hither smile, perky head toss," he repeated, a little faster than before.

Jennifer said, "By Jove, Pickering, I think he's got it!"

They chuckled. She said, "You're making progress, Eliza."

When they got home Jennifer said she was going to change her shoes, set a low flame in the family room fireplace, and finish the mystery story she'd taken out at the Lange Library on Monday.

Redmond asked, "Is it a good read so far?"

"Pretty good."

"What's the title?"

"*When the Bats Come Out.*"

"Kind of a spooky title."

"It has a spooky feel to it, but it's basically a murder mystery."

After a brief pause Redmond said, "Well, I think I'll get on the web. I heard a Johnny Trujillo Septet recording on Sirius recently. It was the Miles Davis composition, 'Milestones,' and Johnny had a great solo on it. Johnny's website probably has a listing of his CDs, and the titles of the songs. If there are more numbers we like on the one that includes 'Milestones,' I can probably order it from Johnny's site."

"That would be nice, Mac. We've seen Johnny and his band twice now, spoken with him on both occasions, and yet we don't have any of his CDs." She added as she headed to the kitchen, "I'm going to have a cup of tea. Want one?"

"Yes, thanks sweetie."

They talked about the importance of tomorrow's Kent State game while the water for the tea heated, and when their teas were poured and lightly sweetened, Jennifer carried hers to the family room and Redmond took his upstairs to the office/studio. He seated himself before the computer, pushed the start-up button, entered his password, and clicked on the Internet icon. When the homepage appeared he typed "Johnny Trujillo Septet" into the Google search box. The first item to appear was Johnny's homepage, with a number of options, including Johnny's Bio, Recordings, Upcoming Performances, and Photos. Redmond clicked on Recordings, and found a list of eight CDs.

He selected *Johnny Trujillo at Hermosa Beach*, and scanned the songs on the 1999 recording. "Some great tunes, but no 'Milestones,'" he muttered. As he read the other titles he thought, Wow, June Connor has two songs on this Hermosa Beach recording—"Never Let Me Go" and "Shiny Stockings." June and Johnny have teamed up for quite a while, he thought. He was *very* pleased to find that "Body and Soul," the great Johnny Green/Ed Heyman song, was included. He also checked the personnel listing to see which alto sax man was on the date, and it *was* Duke Hartsfield.

Redmond looked at two other CDs before clicking on the *Johnny Trujillo at The Jazz Interlude* recording from 2003. He was happy to see it included "Milestones," and a number of other songs he liked, including "Senor Blues," "Up Jumped Spring," and the beautiful, "I Remember Clifford," Quincy Jones' memorial tribute to the brilliant young trumpet virtuoso, Clifford Brown, who departed this world way too soon. There were also two vocals on the disc, "Cute," and "Lover Man," featuring Billie Hamilton, a singer he knew nothing about.

He returned to the initial page of the site and clicked the Photos button. There was a studio portrait of Johnny looking very suave and probably twenty years younger. Redmond smiled and thought Johnny had chosen a very flattering picture of himself. Redmond ordered the *Hermosa Beach* and the *Jazz Interlude* discs. He was just preparing to exit the Trujillo website when Jennifer came into the room carrying a second cup of tea for him.

"The tea is so good," she said, "I thought you'd probably desire another."

He smiled and said, "You do a good job of anticipating my desires, Sweetie."

"That's *my* desire . . . and that's an old song title, come to think of it." She asked, "Did you find Johnny's website?"

"Yeah, sure did. I ordered two CDs. And there are photos of band members and a close-up of Johnny." He brought up Johnny's photo.

"Whoa," Jennifer said, "Johnny could pass for a movie star in that shot. How many years ago do you suppose it was taken?"

"I thought maybe twenty."

"That's probably about right. He'd have been forty-eight or so."

"And June Connor is on the Hermosa Beach disc. She's got a couple of songs on it—'Never Let Me Go' and 'Shiny Stockings.' The recording was made at a live performance at Hermosa Beach in 1999. And, Duke Hartsfield was in the band, and he's featured on 'Body and Soul.'"

"That's great."

"And I ordered another one, a 2003 recording titled, *Johnny Trujillo at The Jazz Interlude.*"

"Where we saw him and June Connor in Vegas!"

"Yes. It has 'Milestones' on it, and there's a singer I never heard of, Billie Hamilton, on the recording. She sings 'Lover Man' and 'Cute.'"

"Great songs," Jennifer noted. "Are there pictures of June and Billie Hamilton?"

"Yes." He brought up the picture of each singer.

"Well, these gals are certainly in the tradition of great looking band singers. Any other individual pictures?"

"No, that's it."

"Put the 1999 band back up, Mac. I want to see if I can recognize your 'Body and Soul' alto player." As soon as the picture appeared she touched a finger to the screen and said, "It's this guy."

"Right," Redmond said with a grin. "The one with the *alto sax*!"

"Well, he's looking a bit sideways, so using other cues was fair play." Jennifer looked at the left-to-right listing of the players' names and said, "Duke Hartsfield—Duke is a great name for a jazz player." She leaned closer to the monitor and said, "He looks vaguely familiar."

"Of course," Redmond said, "you saw him play two sets in Seattle in the summer of 1999, after all."

"True enough! My memory is still pretty good, I guess." She took Redmond's empty cup and said, "Enjoy your tea, sweetheart. I have to get back to my book."

"Have the bats come out yet?"

"Well, Mac, I think they're getting ready too, but the protagonist isn't aware of them yet."

"That's the way murder mysteries often go, isn't it?"

"Often, Mac, but certainly not *always*."

CHAPTER 18

———————▼———————

Saturday, September twenty-seventh brought the fourth football game, and the second home game, of the season. The McClains ambled into The Huddle at five past ten for their brunch. Ellen and Steve and Eve and Ted were there, and Helen and Herb Huntsberger were with them. Helen, the town's busiest interior decorator, was forty, the same age as Eve, and she had been something of a legend among local runners who liked to participate in five and seven kilometer races. She'd given up running after marrying Herb, the chairman of the astronomy department, just last year. Helen was also known, though *not* celebrated, for her sometimes-salty language, and being more boastful about her running and decorating skills than was seemly in the eyes of some of Pleasanton's more reserved ladies. She'd also "run through" a goodly number of local bachelors, including Langston Wallingford, before finding Herb, and had subsequently set out on a self-improvement regimen aimed at increasing her vocabulary and reining in her outspokenness. But despite her foibles, she was a very genuine and kind-hearted woman, and Eve, Ellen, and Jennifer had all come to like her. They had great admiration for her work ethic. And Herb was an unflappable and good-humored guy whose stability had proven to be just what Helen had needed in a man.

Redmond said, "Good morning, everyone. Hey, it's good to see you Helen, and Herb."

Helen responded with a big smile and said, "Good morning, Mac and Jen. We dropped in for a late breakfast, and these guys asked us to join them. Great day for a football game, isn't it?"

"Delightful," Jennifer responded. "Partly sunny with a game time temp around sixty is hard to beat!"

Herb said, "I saw in the Columbus Dispatch that we're a fourteen point favorite, but Kent came close to beating Iowa, a school no one from our conference has ever beaten. I have to think the Golden Flashes are a pretty good football team."

Eve said, "That's right, Herb. The Ravens better not be looking past Kent."

Ellen, the energetic and confident cheerleader for the fans in her immediate seating area of the stadium, smiled broadly and said, "Hey, the Ravens are gonna be ready! The coaches have been on them all week to make sure they have their heads on straight and understand that this is a crucial game."

The group talked about other goings on in town. Helen volunteered, "Lindsey Marston, the new English professor, asked to consult with me regarding colonial furnishings and the renovation of the kitchen of her new home. I think the kitchen *and* bathrooms should be gutted and redone, starting from scratch."

"Well, that could be expensive, Helen," Eve noted.

"Yes, but Professor Marston is quite agreeable to my suggestions. Price doesn't seem to be a" . . . Helen searched for the right words, silently rejecting "major problem" before producing, "limiting consideration."

All right—good work, Helen! Jennifer thought.

By ten of eleven they'd finished their breakfasts and conversed about a variety of topics of local interest. Then the group broke up with friendly smiles, and the obligatory autumnal Saturday parting words, "Go Ravens!"

*   *   *

As the McClains, Gundersens, and Muirs trooped into the Ravenslake Inn they were in a happy mood. The Ravens had handed the Golden Flashes a 42 to 14 drubbing, and moved one win closer to a hoped for East Division Championship in the conference. Ted and Steve secured an eight-person table in the Colonial Room and they all applied themselves to enjoying cold beers and munchies, while they recalled big plays of the Ravens victory.

Ellen laughingly proclaimed, "All right then, guys, what did I tell ya? I said our Ravens would be up for the game, and were they ever!"

Redmond acknowledged Ellen's accurate prophecy with, "Let's have three cheers for Ellen, the oracle of the Ravens." They all raised their glasses and intoned, "Three cheers for Ellen, Hip-Hip-Hooray, Hip-Hip-Hooray, Hip-Hip-Hooray!"

"Thank you, thank you," Ellen said with a standing bow and a tip of her Ravens cap.

As the general level of conversation grew louder, Langston Wallingford, Lindsey Marston, and the English faculty's usual football crowd came in and headed for tables at the very back of the room. Langston, a 1968 RU grad who had taught at several prestigious colleges in Massachusetts before returning to RU, was known for his extravagant language and what Giselle Hanford, also an RU grad, had once termed his, "I'm more Ravenslake than you" attitude. Langston called over to the group, "This could be a team of destiny! Not the equal of the '67 team, of course, but in the upper echelons of the pantheon of Ravens football."

"They played damned well today, Langston," Ted said flatly.

"Indeed," Langston responded, and then he turned his attention to his colleagues.

While Redmond and Jennifer were enjoying their second beers, and talking of things other than football, Lindsey Marston came to their table and said, "Hi Redmond, and everyone." Redmond and Jennifer's eyes met, and Redmond detected a furtive little sardonic smile from his wife. Lindsey continued, "It was a nice game today wasn't it? No concern about losing after the first half." She took a chair from an adjacent table and pulled it close to Eve and Jennifer.

After some comments from Ellen about the game, Eve said to Lindsey, "I understand you've moved into your new home on Vine Street. I'm sure there's a lot of work involved in getting settled-in."

"Oh, of course, Eve! And there are some renovations I'd like to have done as soon as possible, especially the kitchen. I've asked Helen Turner to draw up some ideas for that."

Ted commented, "Well, Lindsey, I'm glad to see you haven't got lost in the woods behind the house."

Lindsey laughed, brushed her hair back from her cheek, leaned closer to Ted, and said, "Well, Ted, I haven't had time to explore the woods. I'm debating, though, whether or not there's enough space behind the house for a tennis court that would still leave enough room for more flowers and shrubs."

After a few minutes more of visiting with Eve and the others, Lindsey said, "Well, it's been nice chatting. I should get back to my colleagues."

Jennifer asked, "Lindsey, I was wondering if we could have lunch together sometime . . . maybe this coming week? You may not know that Redmond and I are very fond of Flagstaff and Northern Arizona. We're thinking of buying a vacation home in Flag. Since you lived there and know the town, I thought you might have some suggestions about the advantages and disadvantages of different areas."

"I'd love that," she said. "Wednesday would be good for me. Could we say noon?"

"Noon is good. Have you eaten at the Alexander House yet?"

"No, but I know where it is on Church Street. I'll see you there, this coming Wednesday."

"Great," Jennifer said with a smile and a nod.

CHAPTER 19

▼

On the following Wednesday Jennifer drove the red Sable to her luncheon appointment with Lindsey Marston. She had considered walking, but the Alexander House was a bit farther west than most of Pleasanton's restaurants, and it was a cool and drizzly day. As she drove she thought about her upcoming meeting with Lindsey. One reason she felt a need to get to know Lindsey better was her curiosity regarding Lindsey's seeming unsettledness in response to the topic of the disappearance of Nizhoni Lydecker, when it came up following the UNC game. It was surprising that Lindsey hadn't recalled immediately the disappearance at Humphreys, but then, as Mac pointed out, perhaps she could have been focused on the idea of a *student* disappearance. And, another reason for her seeming unsettledness could have been that she actually knew Nizhoni, and talk of the disappearance could have been upsetting for her. Additionally, Jennifer just wanted to learn more about Lindsey. It was even possible, she told herself, that Lindsey could provide enlightening information about nice residential areas of Flagstaff.

She parked in a metered spot on West Church, feed the meter a quarter for an hour of parking, and walked back to the Alexander House. The Alexander House, a graceful two story Italianate structure, was built in the late eighteen hundreds. It had been nicely renovated and converted into a good Pleasanton restaurant sixteen years ago, and it consisted of a number of separate dining rooms on two floors. Jennifer entered the establishment, took her raincoat to the cloakroom, and got in line behind a short queue of patrons. As she advanced to the second-in-line position Jennifer heard Lindsey excusing herself for passing a couple that arrived shortly after Jennifer had. She turned and saw a smiling Lindsey step up to her side.

As she slipped out of her raincoat Lindsey said cheerily, "Well, that was pretty good timing,"

"Yes," Jennifer said, and added, "There's a cloakroom to the left of the entry door, if you want to stash your raincoat and hat there."

"I do—be right back."

A few minutes later they were shown to a table in the Governor Wyatt Room. It was one of the smaller rooms, with four well-separated tables. They took their seats, inspected the menu, and ordered simple lunches.

As the waitress turned their cups upright and poured their coffee, Jennifer asked, "Well, how are you finding Pleasanton?"

"Heavenly," Lindsey said with a smile. "My colleagues are really nice, and so professional and accomplished. There were good people in the English department at Humphreys, too—several are established writers, and they were all dedicated teachers. Still, Ravenslake does have a larger and more distinguished faculty. And the students here are really *top notch*!"

"Had you taught somewhere before you went to Humphreys?"

"No, Humphreys was my first job. I finished my doctorate at Colorado State in the spring of '96 and went straight to Humphreys. You see, I'd married Chris Marston in June following my senior year at Cornell." She made a bit of a leering smile, and added, "He was thirty eight and I was only twenty-one."

It struck Jennifer that Lindsey's insinuating smile and challenging blue eyes were the features that sometimes gave her that Bette Davis aura of impertinent forwardness—a sort of, "See what a formidable woman I am," flaunt. Jennifer wasn't sure what to say in response to Lindsey's report of the age difference between her and Chris Marston, but Lindsey took her off the conversational hook by continuing, "Chris was a professor in the English department at Cornell. We fell in love when I was a junior. It was awkward, but I'd taken only one course with him as a sophomore, so our relationship wasn't strictly taboo. It was in that class that I decided I wanted him." She smiled and said, "And I got what I wanted. We spent our honeymoon in England that summer. In the fall he took a position at Colorado State, and I was admitted to their doctoral program. We published two highly regarded books, one on eighteenth century, and the other on nineteenth century, British women writers—all while I was still a grad student."

Jennifer read this as, "See how smart I am?" She took a sip of her coffee, and for want of something more responsive to say, she offered, "So you and Chris were both interested in British women writers?"

Lindsey smiled, her Bette Davis eyes suddenly soft and considerate, as she said, "Yes. There's something compelling about the women writers of that day and age. They were so often victims of endlessly demanding husbands, stifling religion, and an oversupply of children. Between stuffy old husbands, the shackling weight of dogmatic piety, being pregnant and looking after sickly children, you have to say their lives were hell. Yet, at times they managed to escape into soaring and intimate fictional fantasies, and to produce some wonderfully poignant and classic tales."

"I agree. There's something very admirable in that."

"Yes," Lindsey replied. She returned to her personal narrative. "Chris was a well-established writer long before our marriage. He was *very* prolific. He wrote successful historical dramatic plays and novels, as well as scholarly analytical books. Several of his plays have been performed, and very well received, in London."

"That's wonderful," Jennifer said. After a brief pause, she asked lightly, "So how did you two end up at Humphreys?"

"I have to say it was a bit of a problem for Chris, because he was happy at Colorado State. But I got a job offer from Humphreys after completing my degree in 1996—I was only twenty-five. Well, Humphreys said they'd be happy to have Chris, too, of course." She said in a confidential tone, "Really, Chris was the big fish they were after. So, we talked about it and he decided Flagstaff wasn't that different, in many ways, from Fort Collins . . . and, they gave him a *very* good deal at Humphreys."

"So it worked out well for both of you," Jennifer said with a smile and a nod of her head.

Lindsey took a sip of her coffee before saying, "You must wonder what happened to our marriage." Jennifer was grateful that she didn't have to respond, as Lindsey continued, "Well, Chris was killed in a car accident in Germany in 1999, while attending an international meeting in Salzburg. The driver was an American colleague from UCLA. It was a multiple car accident in a two-mile long tunnel. We'd only been at Humphreys three years, and married for just seven, when the accident happened."

"Oh my, Lindsey! How terrible that must have been for you."

"It *was* difficult, Jennifer. But I was fortunate that we had no children. I had a book coming out, and I chose to keep my married name because I had published under the name Marston, with Chris. And I didn't plan to ever remarry; but if, by an unexpected turn of fate, I did happen to remarry at some point, I decided my new husband would just have to agree that I wouldn't adopt his name. My work is more important to me than indulging a husband's vanity."

"You seem to be a very dedicated academic, Lindsey," Jennifer said approvingly.

Lindsey sat briefly silent, her elbows placed lightly on the table edge and her cup artfully suspended above her plate by the gracefully extended fingers of both hands. She gazed deeply into her coffee for several seconds, then locked her penetrating eyes on Jennifer's and confided, "If for some reason I couldn't teach and write, my life wouldn't be worth living." She studied Jennifer's face, gauging Jennifer's reaction; then she smiled mirthlessly and asked, "Does that sound melodramatic?"

Jennifer considered the question only briefly before answering, "Perhaps. But I suppose Redmond feels *almost* that committed to his work."

"With me," she said, "writing is something I have to do. I have a real need to write. I guess I got that from my mother. In her youth she published two books of poems, in German, under her maiden name . . . Lillian Lehmann."

"Pretty name."

"Yes, I think so. My father's name was Ellis Lavery. And mother named me Lindsey. So I'm Lindsey Lavery, daughter of Lillian Lavery, nee Lillian Lehmann." She smiled and said, "As you can hear, alliteration runs in my family. Had I had a sibling, I suppose she or he would have a name like Lois, or Lawrence."

Jennifer smiled, and then asked, "Was your dad also a writer?"

"No. He owned a lumbering and paper company."

Their conversation was interrupted by the delivery of their food. Lindsey said, "Oh, your Tenderloin Stir Fry looks very good, Jennifer."

"Yes. I've had this before, and it is good." She offered, "And your Santa Fe Chicken Salad, and Cheese Quesadillas look inviting, as well."

As they ate they continued their conversation. Jennifer related a brief version of how she and Redmond met in grad school, the various places he had taught, and the fact that they had two grown and married children.

Lindsey asked Jennifer where she had grown up. Jennifer responded, "I lived in Minneapolis all my life, until Mac finished his degree and got the job at McMahon University in Springfield, Missouri."

"Did you like Minneapolis? It has brutally cold winters."

"Actually, Lindsey, I loved Minneapolis. But I suppose people usually like the places where they grew up." She paused, and then asked, "Where are you from?"

"Reno," Lindsey said perkily. "Of course, Reno gets very cold in the winter, too. But the summers are great, and the area has a rugged charm. There are high mountains all around it. I had a boyfriend during the summer after I graduated from high school, and he belonged to the Reno Rock Crawlers off road vehicle club. He was into the club's off road forays into the mountains of the area. That was fun. He was five years older than I, and," she said in a confiding tone, "he was my first lover. Hank and I found some great places to 'get lost' among twisted junipers and pinion pines on more than one of the club's outings into the mountains."

Jennifer tried not to look surprised by Lindsey's comment, and said, "Mountains can be romantic, and perhaps especially to young lovers." She paused briefly before adding, "That really *is* rugged country around Reno. Mac and I drove through some of the area many years ago."

Lindsey decided to change the subject. "I understand from Ellen Muir that you're a talented artist, in the tradition of American Impressionist landscape painters."

Jennifer nodded affirmatively. "Landscapes are my favorite subject, but I enjoy portraiture, also. But speaking of landscapes, as I mentioned at the Ravenslake Inn, Redmond and I are thinking of buying a vacation home in Flagstaff. Of course, we'd like a nice view of the Peaks, and to have a house in the pines. Our main areas of interest are Fort Valley Road, including Cheshire Heights, the older section of University Heights, and the Country Club Estates area."

Lindsey said earnestly, "Well, it sounds as if you really know the best areas for being in the pines and having nice views, Jennifer. I lived in Country Club Estates and it was a very nice area. And I can see the attraction of Fort Valley Road, but houses on the Peaks side are very expensive, and you have to buy five acres or more of land with them. I shouldn't think you'd want the hassle of dealing with that much land with a part-time home. And you're talking eight hundred thousand to well over a million dollars for those properties."

"Well, we were concerned about both of those points, Lindsey. We sort of figured the sizes of those properties were too big and the prices beyond what we would want to pay."

"The other areas you've mentioned can have nice views of The Peaks and are more reasonably priced. Of course, those other places aren't as close to The Peaks, but the more immediate surroundings of your house can be beautiful even if all you can see are pines and blue sky. You can get a very nice house of twenty-five hundred to thirty-five hundred square feet in the older section of University Heights, or in Cheshire Heights, in the three-to-four hundred thousand dollar price range."

"Well, you've given me a good way to think about the choices, Lindsey." She paused before asking, "Dessert?"

"Oh, no . . . one has to look after her figure, if she wants men to look at her figure," she jested. "But I'd like a bit more coffee."

Their waitress refilled their cups, and, that done, Jennifer asked, "Oh, speaking about Flagstaff, have you heard the latest about the professor that disappeared back in two thousand-one?" She tried to make the question sound offhand, but she thought she saw Lindsey's face tighten a bit. Jennifer silently granted that she'd brought up a topic most anyone might find a bit unpleasant.

"Yes, I did. They found her . . . skeleton. A former colleague at Humphreys sent me an email about it." Lindsey paused before adding, "I knew the poor woman. I mean, we were on a few committees together. She struck me as a very fine scientist. It's very sad."

"Yes, it is."

*   *   *

Redmond arrived home at five o'clock to find Jennifer comfortably ensconced on the sofa before the living room fireplace, with a low gas flame burning silently, but cheerily. She was finishing up the mystery of *When The Bats Come Out*.

"Hey, sweetheart," she said as he came into the room.

"Hey to you, hon," he responded, and bent down to share a peck of a kiss.

Jennifer said, "I got an email from my mom, today. She and dad have decided to spend Thanksgiving with aunt Madge and uncle Ray in Philadelphia. And since both our kids have committed to spending Thanksgiving with their spouses' parents, our Thanksgiving in Santa Fe is off for this year. We'll be on our own for the holiday."

"Well, I understand. Your mom and her sister don't get together as often as they'd like, I suspect."

"That's true." Jennifer paused, and then switched the topic with, "I had lunch at the Alexander House with Lindsey this afternoon."

Redmond grinned and asked, "Did you tell her to stop flirting with me?"

"Oh yeah! That was the very first order of business, of course," Jennifer said with an almost straight face. "I told her I'd give her a real pummeling if I caught her doing that eye thing, smiling that smile, and doing her little head toss at ya in the school cafeteria."

Redmond laughed.

"Actually, we talked about other things. She told me quite a lot about herself. And I figured out that she's thirty-seven."

"Makes sense. As I've told you, you look to be thirty-seven, and she appears to be close to your age."

"That's what I thought, too! *But seriously*, I learned that she went to Cornell and graduated at twenty-one. And she then immediately married a man named Chris Marston."

"Really? Rather impulsive, would you say?"

"Hardly impulsive! Rather well thought out . . . calculated, even. Marston was her English professor. She told me, in relation to Marston, 'I decided I wanted him, and I got want I wanted.'"

"Well now! The legendary female predator—'I got him in my sights and I bagged him!'"

"That seems to be Lindsey! At one point in the conversation she alluded to her 'first lover,' and how she and he would purposely get lost on four-wheel drive vehicle club outings into the mountains so they could make out in the wilderness. She dated the guy during the summer following her graduation. She does like to see if she can shock you."

"Really? Part of her 'liberated woman' stance, I suppose."

"That's how I see it. Anyway, Marston was a thirty-eight year old professor at Cornell, and their romance started during her junior year. I thought she was hoping to shock me with that information, too."

"But you accepted it with debonair worldliness, I suppose."

"I accepted it . . . *indifferently*. After they married they went together to Colorado State, he to join the faculty, and she to enter their doctoral program. I don't know if she took any courses from Marston at Colorado State, but they worked on two books together, books about British women writers of the eighteenth *and* nineteenth century—and she got her doctorate at the age of twenty-five. She said Marston also wrote successful fiction, including plays, some of which have been performed in London."

"Hmm. I wonder if she gets performance royalties?"

"For heaven's sake, Mac. I didn't ask her about that!"

"Right! Why *would* you ask about that? Sorry."

"She got a job offer from Humphreys when she completed her degree, and they offered Marston a position, as well. Lindsey said, quite forthrightly, that Humphreys was naturally more interested in her husband than in her. And it sounded as though he wasn't keen on leaving CSU, but he moved to Humphreys for her. Tragically, he was only there three years before being killed in a car accident in Germany. Marston was attending an international meeting. It was a pile-up in a tunnel. Marston wasn't the driver."

Redmond said sympathetically, "Well, that's certainly a tragic thing. Lindsey had to deal with a shocking and truly sad event."

"Yes. But she didn't have any difficulty talking about it today. I think she's a pretty tough character, and a bit adventurous, as well. I mean, how many college juniors are having affairs with a professor, and especially with one who's seventeen years older than they are."

"Yeah, I wonder what her parents thought about that."

"Didn't ask, don't care to know! But, she did tell me she was from Reno. She said her father owned a lumbering and paper company, and her mother was a published poet."

"Does she have siblings?"

"No. Like us, she's an only child." Jennifer paused in recollection before saying, "She also sounds very dedicated to her profession. She said, 'If I couldn't teach and write, my life wouldn't be worth living.' The way she said it sounded fanatical, as if her work were her precious *raison d'être*. And after she said it she asked if she sounded melodramatic in the way she spoke about her work."

"What did you say?"

"Oh," Jennifer said with a smile, "just that my husband is *almost* that committed."

Redmond laughed. "Like I'm only not *quite* as far out as she is when it comes to her 'give me the academy, or give me death' stance. If I couldn't teach and write, I'd sure as hell find some other interesting activity to pursue."

"I really didn't know quite what to say. She seemed so intense about the subject."

"Well, I guess it's hard to consider a deep commitment to one's work a fault."

"True . . . *and in conclusion*," Jennifer intoned, with feigned weariness over her lengthy account, "she kept her name after her husband's death because she'd published the two books, and I don't know what else, as Lindsey *Marston*. She wanted to keep it as her professional name. And I told her a little about us—end of story."

"Well, she told you quite a lot about herself. But, wasn't the pretext for this little *tête-à-tête* to get her advice regarding good areas for a vacation home in Flag?"

"Yes."

"What did she say?"

"Just the things we'd already concluded."

"Oh."

"But, I also wanted to ask her if she'd heard the news about what I referred to as 'the professor that vanished at Humphreys.' She told me she'd received an email from a former colleague at Humphreys that told about the discovery of Nizhoni's remains. She said she *had* known Nizhoni as a colleague on committees, and she seemed sad and understandably angered at the thought of men abducting and killing women and girls."

"You see, Jen! I suggested that the reason she seemed taken aback when you mentioned there'd been a mysterious disappearance at Humphreys was simply that she found the topic upsetting."

"Yes, you were right, Mac," Jennifer granted. "She did know Nizhoni Lydecker." After a short pause she asked, "Are you hungry? Should I start supper, sweetheart?"

"Whenever you like, Jen. I'm going to change clothes and see if I have any emails. Can I help with dinner?"

"No, but you can clear the table, rinse the dishes, and stash them in the washer, as you usually do."

"You got it, babe."

CHAPTER 20

▼

The following Monday morning arrived with mid-thirties temperatures and steady drizzle for Pleasanton. Redmond, who rather liked drizzled rain, decided his raincoat and umbrella would protect him from the wetness, and he happily walked to his office.

An hour later, Jennifer drove their older gray Sable to Phil Regan's Art Shop to look over the unframed Giclée prints of her Covered Bridge and DeWitt Cabin paintings. She was very pleased with them, and she numbered, signed, and dated each print. She and Phil decided that the cherry frames looked better than the black ones they had initially considered.

Jennifer then made a trip to the Lange Library to return her copy of *When the Bats Come Out*. She talked briefly with Ellen. Learning that Jennifer and Redmond had no plans to visit Santa Fe for Thanksgiving this year, Ellen invited them to share Thanksgiving dinner with her and Steve, and Jennifer happily accepted the offer.

Ellen also shared a bit of gossip to the effect that Lindsey Marston was now dating Mike Elias, an associate professor in the English Department.

Jennifer asked, "So, Langston is out of the picture?"

"I don't really know that Langston and Lindsey were ever anything more than friends and colleagues," Ellen said.

"I assume Mike Elias is younger than Langston?"

"Yes. In fact he may be a *bit* younger than Lindsey."

"Well, bully for Lindsey, I guess. Men seem to be something she likes to collect, or at least sample."

Ellen chuckled, and changed the subject by saying, "We got a new mystery novel you might enjoy, Jen. I liked it. It's titled, *The Benton Hall Affair*."

"I trust you to know the kind of mysteries I like, El."

Ellen retrieved the book, Jennifer checked it out, and then she drove home around eleven. When she entered the house it felt chilly and damp. She turned the thermostat up from sixty-five to sixty-eight, and changed into warm slacks, a long sleeved blouse, and a red woolen sweater. She made a cup of hot black tea, sweetened it with honey, and carried it up to the studio/office. When she clicked on the computer to check possible emails she was surprised to find an email from Shirley Evans, the pleasant realtor with Realty Execs in Flagstaff. She read the message:

> Dear Dr. and Mrs. McClain,
>
>   I thought I should let you know what has been coming on the market that might interest you, so I have attached four brochures, with multiple pictures of each of the properties' features. Two of the listings are in Cheshire Heights, with beautiful views of Humphreys Peak. Another is at the base of Humphreys Peak. This is the older home you mentioned seeing on Bristlecone Lane. Dr. Lydecker just put it on the market Monday. The fourth one is in University Heights and it does have some view of the highest sections of Humphreys and Agassiz Peaks, as well as Mount Elden. All of these homes have the four bedrooms you desired.
>
>   Please let me know if you find any of these interesting. I will continue to watch for properties you might like.
>
> > Best Wishes,
> > Shirley Evans

Jennifer opened the attachments and printed colored copies of the brochures. Once she'd stapled together the pages for each listing, she sat back, took a sip of her tea, and selected the Bristlecone Lane brochure. The house was a thirty eight hundred square foot home. She thought the interior was much as she'd imagined it, with nice-sized rooms, high ceilings, lots of warm toned wood, and handsome stone surfaces. But it was, as she had also suspected, a bit on the overly rustic side. The house seemed somewhat dated, and, as she already knew, isolated. She briefly conjectured that it might have been a lonely setting for Nizhoni, and yet, Nizhoni had put pressure on her husband to give the house to her.

She examined the other brochures and decided that both of the Cheshire Heights homes had great views of the Peaks, and their interiors were very attractive, with just enough rustic elements to be charming. One house was thirty eight hundred square feet, and the other thirty six hundred.

Finally, she looked at the University Heights house brochure. It did have a bit of a view of the tops of the Peaks, and a more complete view of Mount Elden. Mount Elden abutted the eastern edge of the Peaks, but it was largely treeless since the devastating fires of nineteen eighty-eight, and it was not at all comparable to the Peaks in terms of majesty.

She opened the file drawer of the desk, withdrew an empty file folder from the back of the drawer, inserted the brochure copies, labeled the folder as "Flag Houses," and filed it behind the folder labeled, "Flag Disappearance." She withdrew the latter and took a sip of her tea.

She opened the file and recalled how she and Mac had read and discussed these newspaper articles about Nizhoni's disappearance at the Barnes and Noble store. It had all seemed so interestingly mysterious at the time. "But now," she softly murmured in sad resignation, "Nizhoni's fate is *known*, and the interesting aura of mystery has transformed into ugly reality." She scooted her chair back from the computer and looked through the meager file, passively registering only the bold print article headings. She gazed at the picture of a happy Nizhoni sitting at her office desk, only to have an uninvited spectral image of Nizhoni's unearthed skeleton flash into her mind. The evanescent image evoked a shiver, and she banished it almost instantaneously.

She quickly turned the page, and was confronted by a man's enigmatic face. She examined the police drawing with an artist's eye, and tried to imagine a model posing for the portrait. She asked herself, what did this man actually look like? The drawing doesn't capture much sense of depth—it's a rather flat depiction, she thought. She imagined a more three-dimensional version of the face, more detailing of eyebrows, and maybe a more animated, alert, look. Redmond had remarked that the drawing looked somewhat like a longer-faced George Clooney, the actor. She could see how Redmond might think that, but it does take a bit of visual license, she judged. Could this really be the face of the person who did *that* to the pretty young professor? Does this man look like a killer? Ah, well . . . that would-be killers should have a distinctive look—how much easier the task of detectives would then be! But such people would be shunned and hounded even before they killed, and great injustices might occur. There is no easy way to banish murder from the experience of human society, she acknowledged. It's an all too common behavior of our species—indeed, of many species.

At five-twenty Redmond came whistling up the front steps of 134 Shadowy Lane. As he hung his coat in the entry closet he heard the sound of cooking utensils being manipulated in the kitchen. He entered the kitchen to see Jennifer, with giant green and white oven mitts on her hands, removing a pan from the oven and placing it on a large trivet. She looked up with a smile and said, "Hey, sweetheart."

"Hey," he responded with a smile. "Lasagna! Smells terrific."

"We'll eat around six, Mac. We're having just lasagna, garlic bread, and salad."

"Sounds good."

Jennifer said, "I heard you whistling when you came in—sounded like 'The Masqueraders,' that little section just before the end of *Petrushka*."

"*Really*? Man! Stravinsky seems pretty ambitious on my part," Redmond said with a smile.

"Well, a melody is a melody no matter if it lives in a ballet score or in a blues song; and, after all, darling, you're a true virtuoso."

"Really?"

"Oh yes. And, I'm not just talking about whistling," she said with a grin.

Redmond chuckled.

As Jennifer removed the large gloves, she asked, "Would you like a glass of wine?"

"Only if you'll join me."

"Sure. There's a bottle of Chardonnay in the chiller."

Redmond poured the wine, and they moved to the family room. They settled comfortably into the sofa. "I stopped in at Phil Regan's Art Shop this morning to see my prints," Jennifer said. "They were delivered last Saturday afternoon. They look *beautiful*, if I say so myself. We decided to use the cherry frames only. I signed and numbered all seventy-five of both prints, in pencil." She added, with a smile, "I took a few breaks to avoid writer's cramp."

"You signed them in pencil?"

"Yes. Artists sign and number their *prints* in the margin, beneath the print, in pencil. The paintings themselves already have my artful little signature."

"I learn something new every day. Anything else interesting?"

"A few things. Ellen invited us to have Thanksgiving dinner with them. I accepted, of course. Their son Riggs will be home from Penn, with his girlfriend. I'll make some of the dishes."

"I'll look forward to that," Redmond said.

"And, Shirley Evans emailed some brochures of houses she thought we might find interesting. She sent brochures on four houses, including the Lydecker house on Bristlecone Lane. It just came on the market. The price was eight hundred-seventy five thousand, and the lot is two acres."

"Well, that's not for us."

"I know. Actually, the house was disappointing because it doesn't have much of a view of the Peaks at all—the forest above interferes with the view. The interior is somewhat dated, as well. I thought it might have been a lonely and isolated place for Nizhoni."

"But, as I remember Margo's account, Nizhoni wanted the house as part of the divorce settlement. Maybe having grown up in Many Farms, she preferred a house located on a good-sized parcel of land with no close neighbors, as opposed to a house on a city street."

"Or maybe she just wanted it to spite her husband. That house, even in 2001, represented a good deal of money. Margo said Nizhoni believed Lydecker had a mistress, and that ticked her off enough that she may have demanded the house mainly out of vengeance. Divorces can get really ugly."

"Well, their divorce certainly did. But where were the other houses Shirley sent brochures on?"

"One was in University Heights, and the other two were in Cheshire Heights. The ones in Cheshire Heights I thought were really nice. They're up on a pine-covered ridge, and have *great* views of the Peaks."

"Well, Jen, a great view of the Peaks would be terrific. In fact, I'd say it should be a requirement. What were the asking prices?"

"The asking price on the one I liked most was four hundred and twenty thousand, but it's been on the market for eight months. I imagine we could get it for less. The general area has lots of pines, and the interior of the house is really attractive." She added, "All the houses were four bedrooms."

"I'd like to see the brochures after dinner, sweetie."

"Okay." She sipped her wine before saying, "I put the brochures in a folder labeled, 'Flag Houses,' and I filed the folder behind the 'Flag Disappearance' folder."

"Yeah?" Redmond said inquiringly.

"I browsed through the *Daily Sun* clippings, and I saw Nizhoni's picture. It made me sad—and angry. And I looked at the police artist's drawing of the 'mystery man.'"

"The George Clooney look-alike?"

She smiled and said, "Yes. But he's hardly a dead ringer for Clooney, Mac."

"Well, his face is longer than Clooney's, Jen, but there's a resemblance. *In fact*, maybe the police should find out just where Clooney was that night."

She chuckled, and replied sarcastically, "Oh yeah—right!" She continued, more soberly, "You know, the *Daily Sun* articles said the police asked Larrabee and the waitresses about the mystery man, and they weren't able to give any information that was helpful beyond the fact that he looked normal and dressed fairly well. I wonder if they ever asked the band members about the guy's appearance."

"Well, we don't know who the band was, and even if we did, I suspect they couldn't tell any more than Larrabee told the police—that the guy looked all right. I suspect jazz musicians would most likely have noticed Nizhoni, but not the mystery man."

"Unless they thought he *was* George Clooney," Jennifer countered. "They'd have been impressed to know George came all the way to Flagstaff to hear them."

Redmond grinned and said, "Well, I suppose they would remember him if they thought he was Clooney."

Jennifer drained the last of her wine, then said, "Okay, back to reality—I'd better get dinner served, and afterwards I can show you the brochures Shirley sent."

"Good."

CHAPTER 21

$$\blacktriangledown$$

At four o'clock on Friday, December fifth, Redmond was still in his office. He clicked on the "save as" option of Microsoft Word, typed in "Alzheimer age/stage," and then clicked on "save." He exited the Word program, exited his files, and shut down his computer. He stood, yawned, stretched, and took two steps to look out his fourth floor window. A few snowflakes swirled by, but he saw no accumulation on the ground. He put on his topcoat and gloves, took the elevator to the first floor, and headed for home. As he walked he whistled bits and phrases of "Manteca," the classic Afro/Cuban tune of Chano Pozo and Dizzy Gillespie.

When he arrived at 134 Shadowy Lane he entered and called, "Hey sweetie, I'm home." He heard Jennifer respond, "I'm in the studio. I'll be right down." He put his gloves in his coat pockets and hung his coat in the front hall closet. He went to the kitchen, removed his suit coat, draped it over a kitchen chair back, got a cold can of Dr. Pepper from the refrigerator, and took it to the family room. He flipped the gas fireplace on, set it for a moderate flame, and sat down on the sofa. Being that it was a Friday, he and Jennifer planned to go uptown for dinner.

A few minutes later Jennifer came down the stairs and greeted him with a brief kiss. She said, "Dr. Pepper looks like a good choice of drink."

"Oh, I'll get you one, sweetie," Redmond said as he began to get up.

"Stay there, Mac. I'll get it. You look a bit under the weather. Hard day?"

Redmond nodded negatively and answered, "No. Not a hard day at all—a bit of a *monotonous* day, though. I spent the entire afternoon closed up in my office like a recluse. I was rechecking a bunch of data for the paper I'm writing, and as is so often the case, each analysis just suggested the need for additional analyses."

"Why don't you put some music on while I get my drink? We haven't listened to the new Johnny Trujillo CDs that came last week. I filed them under 'T' in the bottom drawer of the music system cabinet."

"I didn't even know they came."

"Sorry, sweetheart. I forget to tell you . . . it slipped my mind *altogether*."

He found the new CDs, brought them to the sofa, successfully fought the battle to remove the tight plastic wrappings, and inspected the listing of numbers. As Jennifer returned and seated herself on the sofa, Redmond said, "Let's listen to the older Hermosa Beach one first." He extracted the disc, inserted it in the player, and sat down beside Jennifer.

As the band began playing "Milestones" Redmond saw that the cover was just the first page of a thin multi-page booklet, and he flipped the pages cursorily while listening to the music. "Hey, look," he said, "there's a group picture of the band and June Connor." Jennifer moved her head closer to see what Redmond was looking at.

"June Connor looks great," Jennifer said quietly. She glanced at the band members, and exclaimed, "Holy moley, Mac! Look at Duke Hartsfield!" She placed a finger beside his picture. "He *does* look like George Clooney."

Redmond laughed. "That's just what I said about the ensemble picture we looked at on the web."

"But it's really clear in this shot. I'll be right back," Jennifer said over her shoulder as she headed up the stairs. When she returned Redmond was surprised to see her holding the police artist's drawing of the infamous "mystery man" of the fateful night of April twentieth, 2001.

Redmond used the remote to lower the loudness of the music as Jennifer said, "Excuse me," and removed the booklet from his other hand. She turned to the pictures of the band members.

"What are you do . . . oh, you think Duke looks like the drawing?"

"Well, just look, Mac! He looks very much like the police sketch. Look!"

"All right," Redmond said. "Let me look at these a little more."

As he studied the drawing of the mystery man and the photo of Duke Hartsfield he said softly, "They do have similarities. But does that make any sense, Jen? Clearly, the photo looks like Duke Hartsfield. I mean the photo *is* Duke Hartsfield. No question about that! But you can't conclude that the drawing is of Duke Hartsfield, because, after all, it's a drawing by a man who *never even saw* Duke Hartsfield. It's based on Larrabee's description of the mystery man's appearance and his critique of the artist's efforts. And you have to admit that the drawing only looks *something* like Duke Hartsfield. The nose in the drawing is thinner than Hartsfield's, and the chin isn't as prominent as Hartsfield's either."

"I know, Mac. But, it's spooky, isn't it?"

"Yes, but it's spooky only because the drawing looks *something* like Clooney. I've said that all along. We also know that there are probably a fair number of guys in America who resemble George Clooney. And lets face it—anyone who can play 'Body and Soul' with the warmth and poignancy that Hartsfield brings to it . . . well, I say, he can't be a killer."

"Yes, Mac, but we don't know *thing one* about Hartsfield other than the fact that he's a good musician. Musicians aren't immune to human frailties and foibles. We've had the experience, more than once, of discovering that respectable and seemingly well-balanced people can be driven to do unimaginably dastardly things given sufficiently pressing motives of fear, or greed, or lust."

"I can't argue with that, sweetheart. But, I wouldn't bet so much as a farthing—however much that may be—that the police artist's drawing is an accurate depiction of the mystery man of Chester's Pub."

Jennifer was silent for a few seconds, puzzling over the problem. She said, "But, isn't it relevant to consider that the so-called mystery man was at *a jazz performance* that night, Mac. They were playing Hartsfield's type of music. What do you make of that?"

Redmond reluctantly thought about that aspect of it. He said, "Well, there are, hopefully, still more jazz fans than jazz musicians in America. And, of course, sometimes guys might go to a bar, regardless of the kind of music being played there, in order to meet women!"

Jennifer sat stoically, her eyes staring vacantly at the wall across the room. Suddenly her face reanimated. She smiled, turned to Redmond, and said, "That is a good point, Mac!"

"Glad you liked it," he said with a grin.

"The mystery man might not have cared about the type of music featured that night at Chester's. He may have gone to Chester's because he knew there'd be some women there. Or, he could have gone there because he'd seen Nizhoni somewhere and followed her to wherever she was going. Nizhoni was the kind of woman that could inspire stalking by some creepy freak."

"Yes."

"So, maybe the type of music being presented is irrelevant, and it doesn't necessarily implicate Duke Hartsfield. I shouldn't have maligned him so readily!"

"That seems right to me, sweetie. But now that we've considered Duke as a potential killer," Redmond said with a chuckle, "we should try to find out a little more about him. I'd hate to have any trace of dark suspicion toward a fine alto sax player whose only real offense is that he happens to look a bit like George Clooney!"

Jennifer nodded agreement, and changed the subject by asking, "Where shall we eat?"

"Ladies choice, tonight."

"Al and Larry's?"

"Good. But let's listen to a June Connor vocal, first." He punched in track nine on his remote control, and "Never Let Me Go" played. When the song ended Jennifer commented wistfully, "That's a song and an interpretation that nearly moves me to tears."

"Well" Redmond said, "I suspect you're not the first beautiful woman to have that reaction to June Connor's treatment of the song."

CHAPTER 22

▼

At one-fifty on Thursday, the eighteenth, Jennifer was busily preparing for the McClain's usual Christmas visit to the Grand Canyon. She had devoted much of her morning to writing notes on Christmas cards, packaging gifts, and getting these mailed. She had also loaded up the birdfeeders, and dispersed an ample supply of raw peanuts-in-the-shell all around the snow-dusted backyard for the blue jays and squirrels to discover. Then she packed clothes for herself and Redmond, as well as small gifts to be given to Kate and Drew, and to Jeremy and Vanessa, on Christmas day in Telluride. It was the familiar exercise of preparing for their annual two-day stay at *El Tovar*, and subsequent five-day skiing holiday in Telluride with Kate and Drew, and Jeremy and Vanessa.

But their holiday trip would be a bit different this time because of their decision to spend this Friday and Saturday looking at houses in Flagstaff. The most efficient travel plan was to fly to Albuquerque and then transfer to a smaller plane to take them into Grand Canyon Airport. From there, they would drive a rental car the sixty-seven miles to Flagstaff tonight. On Sunday morning they would make the drive from Flag to their South Rim hotel.

Redmond turned his class grades in at the Registrar's Office at five of two and hurried home to find Jennifer bustling down the stairs and saying, "Our bags are in our bedroom. They're too heavy for me, hon."

"I'll get them, sweetie," Redmond said as he ascended the stairs, two steps at a time. A few minutes after stowing the bags in the red Sable's trunk, he backed it out of the driveway, and noted that the dashboard clock read two thirty-three. He remarked, "We'll be at the airport with time to spare, barring unforeseeable complications."

"And if all goes according to plan, Mac, we'll head for Flag in our rental car around seven forty-five, Mountain Standard Time. I checked the latest weather at noon, and it calls for clear and cold weather." She added, "The low in Flag tonight will be twelve degrees!"

"Well, hon, I suspect we'll be running a bit late by the time we get our rental car, so we might not get on the road to Flag until eight. Figure an hour and twenty minutes to drive to Flag and we'll be in the Comfort Inn on Beulah Drive by nine twenty or so."

"And we'll be hungry," Jennifer predicted. "How about we just walk to Denny's for a late night breakfast?"

"I love Denny's breakfasts. We'll have our elegant dinners at *El Tovar*, so a short walk for a breakfast-dinner at Denny's tonight sounds perfect to me. Thinking ahead, what time do we meet Shirley tomorrow?"

"Around ten, at the Realty Execs office on Cherry Street."

"And how many houses do we have to look at?"

"Tomorrow there are three—one in Cheshire Heights in the morning and two in University Heights in the afternoon. And we'll also see three on Saturday—one in Country Club Estates, one in Switzer Highlands, and one in Cheshire Heights."

"Well, that sounds easy enough." He added, "And we're having dinner with Margo and Tim at Buster's on Saturday night. I'm looking forward to that."

*   *   *

At two-forty in the afternoon on Saturday, Redmond, Jennifer, and Shirley Evans exited the last of the six houses Shirley had shown them over two days. It was a four-bedroom, thirty eight hundred square foot home on Blue Spruce Road in Cheshire Heights. In the chilly shade of Ponderosa Pines Jennifer said, "I think it's a great house, Shirley. It has a terrific view of the Peaks, and all these pines are wonderful. We'll think about it."

"That's fine," Shirley remarked. "Things are slow at this time of the year, so there's a good chance it'll be available for awhile."

They exchanged goodbyes. As the McClains settled into their rented Taurus, Jennifer remarked, "I could see us in that house, Mac."

"Me too. It's got the Peaks view, Ponderosa Pines everywhere, a beautiful long cedar deck facing The Peaks, and a yard that requires almost no care. But for now, let's get some lunch. My breakfast has worn off. I'm starving."

"I'm for that, Mac. Let's make it Chester's Restaurant."

Ten minutes later they parked the car on West Aspen and walked to the old Wexford. The small hotel lobby was pleasingly adorned with seasonal decorations, including a freshly cut seven-foot Coconino Pine Christmas tree. Chester himself was seated at the piano, softly playing the Mel Tormé/Bob Wells composition, "The Christmas Song." He smiled and nodded to the McClains. They returned the smile, crossed the lobby to the restaurant, and were shown to a table near the fireplace.

Redmond said, "There's something about house hunting that burns up a lot of calories, and makes you hungry."

"That 'something' is just *nervousness* about the weighty decisions—that's the thing that burns up the calories," Jennifer joked.

"Right. But we don't want to eat too much now, since we're having dinner at Buster's with Margo and Tim tonight."

They ordered, and then shared their thoughts about the houses they'd seen over the two days. Jennifer concluded, "I guess the Cheshire Heights house on Blue Spruce Road would be the best pick. It's really nice. Actually, I'm thinking maybe we should make an offer."

Redmond agreed, "It was my choice, too. It's tempting."

*   *   *

At seven-thirty the McClains and Baileys met at Buster's, and were shown to a table on the upper level of the restaurant. As they seated themselves, Margo, in a very buoyant mood, informed Redmond and Jennifer, "Today was the last day of our semester, and we're looking forward to getting out of town."

Tim amplified, "We're planning to spend a few days in Scranton with my family, and then we'll go to Brockton to visit Margo's folks. And on the twenty-sixth we fly to Denver and take the bus to Steamboat Springs. We'll have five glorious days of skiing and relaxing. We can't wait for that!"

Jennifer remarked, "My goodness, Tim, it sounds as if Margo has turned you into an accomplished skier. Wasn't your first time on a ski run just about a year ago?"

"Yeah, it was, Jen. I was an absolute beginner, but we were able to ski at the Snow Bowl quite a few times after Christmas last year, and, if I say so myself, I'm now a *good* skier. Of course, I'm not foolhardy enough to attack the black diamond runs yet, but I'm very comfortable on the blue squares."

Margo vouched for her hubby's prowess, saying, "Tim has a surprising aptitude for skiing, and he showed it even on his first ski trip to Sunrise last year. After just a couple of hours on skis, he came down a steep blue square run."

Tim laughingly interjected, "But I came down with my heart in my throat and a fervent prayer to the ski gods to just, please, allow me to make it to the bottom with all my bones intact!"

Tim and Margo also spoke of their academic achievements of the fall term. Both had a research article published during the semester, and Tim had been informed that his research grant submission to the National Institutes of Health had been approved for funding.

Redmond shared some information about his own publication activities, and Jennifer told of her Pleasanton Giclée prints venture. Then the topic turned to the McClain's afternoon house hunting efforts. Jennifer said they had seen one house they liked, but hadn't made an offer on it. She described it in glowing terms.

Margo said, "Sounds like you really like that house."

Jennifer replied, "Yeah, we really do. What about you two? Are you looking at houses yet?"

Tim answered, "Well, Margo and I have been too busy to think about moving this semester. We're going to put any thoughts about that off till next summer. We're pretty comfortable in our condo."

At that point Tim noticed an attractive couple approaching their table, on their way out of Buster's. As they came beside the table of the McClains and Baileys, the man made eye contact with Tim, and then with Margo. He smiled and said, "Good evening, Professor Bailey, and Professor Layne!"

Tim responded, "Hey, Detective Yazzie! It's nice to see you again." He smiled and said, "And I'm happy to say that Margo is now, like me, 'Professor *Bailey*.' We were married last June."

"Well! Congratulations, and best wishes," the tall detective offered cheerily.

Margo returned, "Thank you. How nice to see you after . . . gee, what has it been—ten months or so?"

"Yes. It was in February, last year."

As Tim and Margo smiled at his companion, Detective Yazzie said, "Let me introduce you to Vella Bonally."

Both Tim and Margo said, "Hey, Vella," and the petite young woman chuckled and responded, "Hi guys."

"Psych and geology are in the same building, so we know Vella," Margo assured Yazzie. "But I'd like you to meet our friends from Ohio. Emerson and Vella, this is Jennifer, and this is Redmond, McClain."

They exchanged greetings, and Redmond asked, "Detective Yazzie, are you by any chance related to Jim Yazzie, who was a Park Ranger at Grand Canyon Park back in 2005?"

Yazzie was surprised by the question, but he smiled and said, "Yes. Jim's my brother. He's now working at Yosemite. How do you know Jim?"

"Well," Redmond answered, "in 2005, about a week before Christmas, Jennifer and I had a harrowing experience at the Canyon, and your brother was very helpful and supportive."

"Oh!" Yazzie smiled and said, "The *McClains*! You're the couple that got yourselves into danger because of a murder in Pittsburgh! Right?"

"Yes, we were the ones," Jennifer responded.

"Jim told me all about that. It was a very unusual and interesting case. Fortunately, nothing terrible happened to you."

"Fortunately," Jennifer said with a happy smile.

"It's really nice to meet you two," Yazzie said. "I'll have to tell Jim we met, and that you had nice things to say about him."

"Please do," Redmond urged. "Tell him we'll always remember his kindness at the Canyon."

Emerson and Vella bid goodnight to the seated foursome and moved off toward the exit from Buster's. Margo volunteered, "We met Detective Yazzie last February, when he interviewed us about that intoxicated man we overheard in the Half Moon Saloon—the one that boasted about committing a murder."

"Oh," Jennifer responded, "so that's how you met him."

"Yes," Margo said. "He and his partner, Detective Healy, interviewed us at that time. And sadly, I recently learned from Vella that Nizhoni Lydecker was a cousin of Emerson. His dad and Nizhoni's dad are brothers. She told me Emerson was just a year younger than Nizhoni, and that they were sort of buddies. She mentioned it just after Nizhoni's skeleton was found. She said Emerson was very upset when he and Healy were assigned the job of verifying the existence of a makeshift grave off Fort Valley Road. He saw a ring on an exposed finger segment and knew it was Nizhoni's."

"*Wow*—talk about tough duty," Redmond commented softly. "Damn! That had to be really painful for him." He paused before asking, "Have there been any new developments in that case?"

Margo grimaced slightly and nodded negatively. "Afraid not, Mac. The DNA analysis confirmed that the skeleton was Nizhoni's, but there haven't been any reports of progress toward identifying a perpetrator. They don't have much to go on, apparently. There was a police artist sketch of the man Nizhoni sat with at Chester's Pub that night. The club manager was the one that gave the police artist information about the man's appearance, and worked with him to produce a drawing of the man's face. It never led to anything."

Jennifer commented, "We read in the *Daily Sun* that the manager that night was named Chris Larrabee. I wonder if he still lives in Flag?"

"No, Jen. Erin told me Larrabee was a realtor that occasionally worked at Chester's Pub, on the side, and that he moved away from Flag. I imagine the police had him look through photo files of men that had a history of assaults against young women. But it apparently never proved helpful."

Jennifer was tempted to relate that she and Redmond thought the police artist's drawing looked somewhat like George Clooney, but thought better of it. She didn't want to get into specious speculation that the drawing looked like a saxophone player they had seen in a jazz club in Seattle. Instead, she said only, "That's too bad. I guess the likelihood of solving such a crime decreases over time. And it's been over seven years since the night of the disappearance."

"Still, Jen," Tim responded, "no one expected her remains to be found. So some other surprising development could lead them to the person that did it."

"I suppose it could happen," Jennifer allowed. "But it seems a long shot, doesn't it?"

Three heads nodded agreements, and Margo said, "Let's talk about skiing or some other more pleasant topic . . . you guys will be skiing in Colorado, too, at Telluride—right?"

"Yes," Redmond replied. And for the rest of their pleasant evening together, they enjoyed their food and a variety of pleasant topics of conversation.

CHAPTER 23

━━━━━━━━ ▼ ━━━━━━━━

At three o'clock on Sunday afternoon, the twentieth day of December, Jennifer and Redmond were unpacking their bags in their second floor *El Tovar* room. They had found the Cheshire Heights house they'd seen yesterday very tempting. Redmond had taken a number of pictures of the inside and outside of the house. They felt they could safely postpone a decision on it until the holiday season was behind them. Now, they eagerly anticipated an invigorating stroll, enhanced by softly falling large snowflakes, along their beloved Rim Walk just outside *El Tovar*.

While Jennifer and Redmond were strolling along the rim of the Grand Canyon, Lindsey Marston was in Pleasanton putting her Fontanelli garment bag and matching wheeled suitcase into her Mercedes. This was in preparation for her drive to the Columbus Airport the following morning. Having positioned the luggage to her satisfaction, she returned to the house. She was in a happy mood, and feeling the excitement she always experienced when preparing to go to her hometown for the holiday break. She was also pleased that she would be getting out of Pleasanton a day before the first heavy snowfall of the Christmas season would be bearing down on southern Ohio.

During her married years she and Chris had usually spent semester breaks in Europe, mostly in England. She didn't miss the trips to England. During those years she had researched and visited the locales of the preeminent women writers of the eighteenth and nineteenth centuries. Though she now sometimes felt a bit guilty for not using the semester break for studious pursuits, she was able to quell such incipient self-condemnation by assuring herself that she knew all there was to know about early English women writers. It was, after all, *history*, and she knew the history inside and out.

What was important about the women writers, she thought, was that they defied and fought the prejudices against their literary ambitions. Still, she believed they should have been much braver than they were, and that she would certainly have been more courageous. She granted that many of them were burdened with children, and raised in a stifling atmosphere that stressed submissive gentility, duty, and subservience to their fathers, husbands, and the church. I would never have submitted, she thought. I would never have accepted the rotten fate those miserable old men inflicted on their women. I would have known what I wanted, and I would have had it. A little arsenic judiciously dispensed over time to the dinners of a sanctimonious bible-quoting old bastard of a husband wouldn't have been amiss for some of those poor ladies—no one should have to accept the *regular abuse* of others. She thought their devotion to their craft was essentially an escape from their burdensome and unromantic everyday lives. She was pleased to think her own life was not burdensome, and that it *was* romantic. And, she told herself, it's romantic on my terms.

Her thoughts returned to her upcoming three-week escape from the everyday routine. She truly loved her life as a professor, but she also greatly enjoyed her semester breaks, and especially the semester break at Christmas time. It was her escape from academic preoccupations, and it allowed her to feel alive and rejuvenated, ready for the spring semester. And then she'd happily return to the life that nurtured her self-image and gave her satisfaction and fulfillment. What had she told Jennifer McClain? Yes . . . that was it: "If for some reason I couldn't teach or write, my life wouldn't be worth living." She smiled, recollecting Jennifer's raised eyebrow in response to her statement. It does sound melodramatic, she granted, but it was *the truth*. I didn't say it idly.

She went to her office at the back of the house and retrieved her airline tickets. She checked the time of her flight, though she knew it was for nine-fifty out of Columbus. She calculated the flight time to Reno to be three hours and fifty minutes. She had earlier checked the weather and was happy to find it would be cold, and she imagined herself looking sinfully sensuous in her long natural mink coat and glamorous gowns as she swept into and out of Dominic's big Lexus sedan, the high stakes casinos, the five star restaurants, and their elegant suite.

She took her airline tickets to her bedroom and slipped them into her Gucci alligator handbag. As she zipped the bag closed she imaged the shock some of the good people of Pleasanton would feel to know how much she craved her annual Christmas indulgence with Dominic Gambrino . . . and the thought of their shock gave her a little rush of pleasure.

CHAPTER 24

▼

On Tuesday, January thirteenth, the second day of the new term at Ravenslake, Jennifer worked her two-hour stint at Grounds for Thinking, and then met Eve at the Coffee-in-Ya shop for their Tuesday afternoon coffee and conversation session. Both Eve and Jennifer told the other of their activities during the Christmas Break. In addition, Jennifer showed Eve a number of photos of the house on Blue Spruce Road. She confided that she and Redmond had made an offer on the house just last Friday, and were now nervously awaiting a response to their offer.

Eve said, "The pictures show that both the house and setting are really beautiful." She smiled and tapped an index finger on the table for emphasis as she stated, "I want you to know, Jen, that Ted and I *expect* to be invited to visit it."

Jennifer laughingly replied, "Of course, Eve! You and Ted have a standing invitation. But first, the present owners have to accept our offer."

Thirty minutes later, after enjoyable conversation and coffee, the two friends said their goodbyes, and headed for their residences. When Jennifer got home she changed into casual clothes, and checked to see if she had any phone messages. Finding none, she went upstairs to the studio/office and checked her emails. Disappointingly, there was no word from Shirley Evans. She turned her attention to dinner preparations. She planned to have baked ziti with a tossed salad, onion rolls, and a California *Cabernet Sauvignon*. She'd done the prep work for the meal before going uptown, and now she only needed to pop the ziti into the oven around five-ten, for a six o'clock meal.

When Redmond came in the front door at five of five he asked anxiously, "Any word from Shirley?"

"Not yet, darling."

"All right, then. I'm putting it out of my mind." As he stowed his coat and gloves in the front hall closet, he asked, "What's for dinner?"

Jennifer related the menu.

"Great," he said. "I'm going to change clothes." He mounted the stairs, two at a time and then changed into jeans, a navy blue turtleneck, and old running shoes. Though he tried to resist the urge, he went to the computer to check his email. Maybe Shirley had *just* sent word of the owner's decision. But he was disappointed—no message from Flagstaff.

He put the computer on standby, descended the stairs, and glanced into the family room. Jennifer was seated on the sofa, browsing a thin home furnishings catalogue. He said, "I'm going to have a ginger ale. Would you like anything to drink, hon?"

"No, sweetheart," she said without looking up from the catalogue.

When he returned with his drink, he asked, "Looking for furniture for the Cheshire Heights house already?"

"Not seriously, Mac—just browsing, trying to get some ideas." She closed the catalogue, smiled, and asked, "How was your day? Getting back into the grind?"

"Just another day in the life of Redmond McClain . . . nothing special. I had lunch with Tony and Steve. We talked about the usual sorts of things—how great it was that the Ravens won their bowl game, and how the men's and women's basketball teams are off to good starts." He paused, trying to recall other topics they'd discussed at lunch. He chuckled and said, "And Tony brought up the topic of a UFO being seen along Lake Erie, near Lorain, a week or so ago."

Jennifer smiled and said, "I didn't know Tony was interested in UFOs."

"Oh, I don't think he is, particularly. Apparently, it was reported in the Columbus paper. It was the usual kind of sighting—something in the sky with blue and red lights in the shape of a triangle. It was thought to be no more than a thousand feet above the ground or the lake, whichever it was."

"It could have been a star, just misjudged as to distance."

"Well, it supposedly sat there for twenty minutes or so before zooming off at rocket speed to the north."

"Then it wasn't a star!" She asked, "Why do people want to believe that these things are spaceships piloted by extraterrestrials from distant planets, and that governments around the world are suppressing knowledge about UFOs? Do you think it's reasonable to believe they could be the space ships of extra-terrestrials, Mac?"

"I don't know. The distances to other star systems are so very great that it would take thousands of years for them to get to earth, even in real souped-up, super-duper fast spaceships. That makes it seem impossible unless the aliens are incredibly long-lived and don't have to eat . . . how much food would you need on board for a thousand year trip? Still, I keep reading claims that Neil Armstrong and Buzz Aldrin saw two huge UFOs sitting on the edge of a crater and watching them the whole time they were on the moon. But until one of those guys says it's true, on live television, count me among the non-believers."

"Right! So why do people seem to want to believe in them?"

"I suppose people would like to know that chemistry, physics, and climate created things like us on at least some of the trillions of planets out there. And maybe aliens could provide proof that 'worm holes' or other shortcuts for getting around the universe really do exist. Perhaps they could teach us that there's some clever way for a space ship to 'warp' the space-time fabric in front of it to dramatically shorten the distance it has to cover to get to its destination. I think people want to believe in extraterrestrials because it could mean that we have the potential for finding other places to live when earth begins to show signs of being unable to support life into the future."

"That makes sense, Mac. Carl Sagan said we have to be a *two planet* species if *Homo sapiens* are to survive into the distant future. Life on earth will be ended sometime by the alteration of our climate or atmosphere, asteroid collision, super-volcanic eruptions, super-diseases, religious wars, or whatnot. The conditions that allowed sensate life to emerge and evolve on this planet will change. And I read that a rough estimate of the number of earth-like planets *just in our galaxy* would be ten billion!"

Redmond nodded agreement and said, "There have to be incalculably huge numbers of older and more advanced planets out there! After all, the same elemental stuff that's here is also out there, and the same principals of physics and laws of chemistry that apply here also apply out there. Therefore, given the right conditions, and enough time, life is inevitable. Clear back in 1953 a University of Chicago grad student named Stanley Miller connected two flasks, one filled with water, and the other with a mixture of gases probably present in the early atmosphere of earth. He sent an occasional electric current through them to simulate lightning. After just a few days there was an abundance of amino acids, sugars, and other organic compounds in the flasks."

"Really?"

"Yes. So, the precursors of proteins seem to have been quite easy to make. Of course, humans are made up of a huge number of different proteins. But given enough time and cooperative conditions, such as the presence of abundant liquid water and an oxygenated atmosphere, complex organisms seem certain to develop without the need for a human-like 'god' to make them. And Stephen Hawking and Leonard Mlodinow have just said the same thing in a new book. Hawking also said that mankind's survival as a species demands that we find a new star with a habitable planet."

Jennifer said, "You have to admire Hawking's courage in the way he has dealt with his motor neuron disease, and how hard he has continued to work at his profession."

"Yeah—it would have been so easy for him to give up. Hawking believes humans have to find a new planet within 200 years, max, if mankind is to survive into the future. He says we're depleting or contaminating the resources that make human life possible on this planet; and, of course, life could become unsustainable on earth much sooner than that. He believes a 'matter-antimatter' propulsion system could conceivably be perfected within that time frame, and could propel spaceships at speeds approaching the speed of light. That would give humans a shot at long term survival as a species."

Jennifer smiled and said, "Well, Mac, we won't be around to see it, but I hope our species manages to continue its development and avoids the fate of the dinosaurs and other extinguished species. But, far more *urgently*, I've got to put the ziti in the oven."

By the time Jennifer returned from that task she found Redmond looking through the CD collection. She suggested, "I wouldn't mind hearing a nice romantic piano concerto, sweetheart."

"How about Rocky two or three, or the Grieg?"

"Rachmaninov's *Concerto Number 2* sounds perfect to me."

Redmond set the volume low and they allowed the familiar music to be atmospheric, rather than an object of their attention. They sat together on the sofa, and Redmond, having just noticed his Trujillo discs while locating their Pierre Entremont Rocky 2 recording, said, "You know, hon, we haven't followed up on our resolution to find out more about Duke Hartsfield."

"I know. That crossed my mind yesterday sometime. Maybe after dinner you could send Johnny an email and ask if he's heard anything about Hartsfield."

"Well, Johnny thought Duke was pursuing his talent in Paris, or somewhere else in Europe."

"Right."

"I could tell Johnny I'm interested in knowing more about Duke because I like his playing so much. I could inquire about where Duke is from and if he has any CDs as a leader."

"Don't tell him your wife wants to know if Duke is capable of being a killer," Jennifer said with a soft chuckle. She added, "Sorry, Mac. I couldn't resist!"

By seven o'clock the McClains had enjoyed a tasty dinner, cleaned up the kitchen, and retired to different endeavors. Jennifer, having earlier finished *The Benton Hall Affair*, began reading a classic Agatha Christie murder mystery, while Redmond went upstairs to send an email to Johnny Trujillo. Before composing his note to Trujillo, he checked to see if Shirley Evans had dropped them their much-awaited news, but alas, still no message from Flagstaff. Redmond recalled that Johnny Trujillo's email address was straightforward—johnnytrujillo@hotmail.com. He typed a simple note to the veteran tenor sax man:

> Dear Johnny,
>   I'm sure you remember meeting my wife Jennifer and me, and the pleasant conversation we had at "The Jazz Interlude" last October. We recently bought your *Johnny Trujillo at Hermosa Beach* and *Johnny Trujillo at The Jazz Interlude* CDs. They're great! You had so many wonderful solos on these discs—and the vocalists were terrific, too!

You may recall that I liked the playing of Duke Hartsfield when we heard your group at the Lighthouse in Seattle back in the summer of 1999. You told us you thought he'd gone to Europe to play with Chet Condoli, and that he was somewhat disenchanted with the jazz scene in the U.S. Have you heard anything new about Duke? And I was wondering, too, if he ever recorded as a leader and has a recording for sale? Anything you could tell us about Duke, like what part of the country he comes from, would be appreciated. We don't know much about him or his career.

Your loyal fan,
Redmond McClain

While Redmond was rereading his message, Jennifer came into the room and said, "I'm making some tea, sweetheart. Like a cup?"

"Sure, I'd love it, hon." He added, "I just finished this note to Johnny Trujillo. See if you think it's okay."

Jennifer read it over his shoulder. "It's good, Mac. Johnny should like all the nice things you said. He'll know we're serious fans."

"Now, you'll notice I didn't mention, 'Jennifer wants to know if Duke could be a killer.'"

"Good. But just between us, Jennifer would *really* like to know about that."

CHAPTER 25

▼

It wasn't until five-thirty on Thursday, the fifteenth, that Redmond and Jennifer received and opened Shirley Evans' email message. Together, they read:

> Dear Jennifer and Redmond,
>
> I just got off the phone with Harold Johnson. They accepted your offer! Sorry it took so long, but Mr. Johnson was out of town during the week and was preoccupied with business matters. The acceptance is totally clean—no counter offer, and no quibbles.
>
> Our office will handle the closing details. These will be straightforward since no loan is involved. Even so, this will take about three weeks of getting papers to and from you and the Johnsons for signatures and fees.
>
> Congratulations! It's a beautiful home. I know you'll love it as a wonderful vacation residence.
>
> Sincerely,
> Shirley Evans

Jennifer startled Redmond with a vigorous, "*Yahoo*! We got it at our price!"

"All right! Great news," Redmond said, and then added, "But now I wonder if we could have got it for less?"

"Oh Mac, don't go second-guessing the price. We offered what we thought was fair. And it's all accomplished, except for getting a bank check to Shirley for the closing, and other necessary paperwork. I'm so excited to actually have the vacation house we've talked about for so long. We have a house in Flag that offers a beautiful view of The Peaks, that's surrounded by pines, and is just a couple of miles from downtown. And, it's only sixty-eight miles or so from the South Rim."

"It's all terrific, sweetie!"

They embraced, and Jennifer noted, "This is another milestone for us, Mac! I'll have to email the kids later. Right now, I'm too excited to compose a calm and coherent letter."

"And Jen, I'm too excited to eat the dinner you started to prepare. Let's walk uptown to the Colonial Inn for a simple dinner and a celebratory glass, or two, of wine."

"Great idea! We need to get out in the chilled air and work off some of the excitement. It'll only take a few minutes to put the food back in the refrigerator. I hadn't started cooking anything."

Ten minutes later as they walked along their familiar East High Street route they talked about the possibility of spending virtually all of their upcoming summer vacation time in Flag. They also spoke of the likelihood that there might be times when their kids would want to vacation in Flag with them, and certainly the Gundersens and Muirs might like to spend a little time in Flagstaff. Jennifer said, "And maybe we could take on the responsibility for some family gatherings at Thanksgiving, Christmas, or school breaks. It would be a vacation money saver for our kids."

"And when we have some grandchildren they could spend some vacation time with us. We could try to get them interested in geology, or archeology, or astronomy, or history—all realms of knowledge and interest that Northern Arizona can stimulate and nourish."

"Yes. I hope they can find all those things interesting enough that they'll want to know more about them."

"Also, Jen, I guess this means we should plan on spending our spring break in Flag. That's a possibility we discussed before, but now it seems to be required. We need to buy furniture, and make sure everything is ship-shape and secure until we return in mid-May. We'll probably be at the house sometime during every summer, and for part of the semester break, and for some of the spring and fall breaks. Still, the house will be empty a good deal of the time. I suppose that could be a worry."

"Well, Mac, let's 'Worry Later,' as the Thelonious Monk tune title advises. Maybe, after we've vacationed in Flag a lot, in five years or something, we'll come to spend less time there. But Jeremy and Vanessa, and Kate and Drew—and hopefully, their little ones—will like to get away on their own sometimes to experience that great part of the country, and they can use our vacation house as home base. Other than upkeep and taxes, it's a free ride for us. And if at some point we ever chose to sell it, we can. And there are so many magnificent landscapes in Northern Arizona, Mac—and given the luxury of having ample time to be there, I mean to paint a lot of them."

"And maybe I could find some kind of hobby."

"Maybe I could teach you to paint," Jennifer offered with a little smile.

"That would probably prove too painful for you, hon."

By the time they entered the Colonial Inn the outdoor thermometer at the Pleasanton Savings Bank across the street told them it was cold in Pleasanton—fifteen degrees, to be exact. They found a table for two, ordered simple food and wine, and enjoyed the celebration of their acquisition of a second home.

An hour and half later they reentered 134 Shadowy Lane, and as Redmond removed his gloves he said, "Man! The temperature must have dropped a few degrees while we were eating. My fingers are stinging."

"Mine, too. I'm going to turn the heat up a bit." Jennifer went to the living room and adjusted the thermostat. When she returned, she said, "I think I've got my excitement under control now, thanks, perhaps, to the sedative effects of the wine. So, I'm going to send a note to the kids to tell them about the new house."

"Good idea, hon. I think I'll catch the news on CNN, in the family room."

Twenty-five minutes later Redmond heard Jennifer call his name and say something. He walked to the foot of the stairs and asked, "What'd you say, sweetie?"

"Come up here!"

As Redmond entered the studio/office he asked, "What did you want, Jen?"

"An email came in from Johnny Trujillo while we were out. I didn't open it until I finished writing to Kate and Jeremy. It's interesting. It's about Hartsfield."

Redmond pulled the side chair around to the front of the desk and read Johnny's message:

Dear Redmond and Jennifer,

First off, of course I remember our conversation, and it was great to get your nice email. Second, thanks for buying the CDs. I'm happy you liked them.

Now, I asked around about Duke Hartsfield, but I only found one guy that had any idea where he might have gone. The guy said he went to Europe.

Also, Duke is a good photographer, as well as an outstanding player. He had a studio here in Vegas for a time. He could have decided to do photography, in addition to playing for a living in Europe. It's talking out of school a bit, I suppose, but I can tell you, confidentially, that Duke had a bit of a problem with gambling. Like I say, he's a complicated guy. His "Is as strange a maze as e'er men trod," as the bard put it.

You might contact Billie Hamilton, who used to sing with my band. Duke was interested in her, but it wasn't reciprocal—still, she might know where he is. She owns a little club, Billie's Music Bar, in Toledo these days. I played there a couple of years ago. I don't know how far that is from where you live.

And as far as Duke's background is concerned, he said he and an older brother grew up with foster parents in Detroit, and he told me he never had so much as a thought about the foster parents once he got out on his own. And "Duke" isn't his real name—it's Weldon or Wesley, something like that. And Duke never made a recording where he was the leader.

Keep grooving,
Johnny

"Well," Redmond observed, "that's a very good response to my letter. Of course, it doesn't tell us much about Duke, or Weldon, or whatever."

"Duke sounds complicated, doesn't he? Raised by foster parents, but he never really bonded with them; he has a natural aptitude for music and photography, but also has a gambling problem. On the whole, Mac, I think this information is kind of a mixed bag as far as being consistent with a hypothesis that Duke could be a killer."

"But to me Jen, this information reinforces my inclination to think well of Duke Hartsfield. After all, you can find *something* unflattering, like gambling, about most everyone."

"Not you, darling."

"Well, I'm fortunate to have a wife who's blind to my faults. But, it sounds like Duke came up the hard way. Johnny seems to regard Duke as a talented and artistic guy. And I think Johnny understands what's artistic and what isn't. He throws out little bits and pieces by the Bard, or by great lyricists like Larry Hart, and he does it cogently, you could say. Hartsfield doesn't sound like a killer to me. Yes, he apparently has a gambling problem, but that doesn't make him a dangerous type. And the bottom line for me is that Johnny has a very high regard for Duke's musicianship. I believe that suggests a fundamentally warm hearted temperament."

"You know, Mac, we've been living in Ohio for over two and half years now," Jennifer said, very innocently. "And do you know where we've never even been?"

Redmond smiled slightly as he ventured a guess. "Gee, I don't know, maybe . . . Toledo?"

"Couldn't we make a little weekend trip to Toledo to see the University of Toledo, or the city's famous art museum? Perhaps we could stop in to hear some music at Billie's Music Bar. Billie sang so great with Johnny's group. It would be nice to meet her."

"Well, it's not a really long drive—certainly less than three hours. We *should* try to learn more about our new home state. We could make the trip, and stay overnight in The Glass City."

"What a wonderful suggestion, Mac," Jennifer said with a grin.

"You know, my dad and I visited Toledo once when I was about twelve. We came down from Grand Rapids to see the Toledo Mudhens play the Louisville Colonels. A neighborhood kid, Jimmy Russell, was a first baseman for the Colonels. Jimmy was a nice guy, and all of us young kids looked up to him."

"Really? Did Jimmy Russell ever get to the bigs?"

"Yes, but only for a year or two, with the Pirates. But that night in Toledo he went three for five and had a home run."

"And you remember *that*? I tell ya, Mac, you men remember sports minutia as if it happened yesterday, but you can't remember where you put your sunglasses."

"Hey! I can *usually* find my glasses."

"Usually," Jennifer conceded with a smile.

"Anyway, my dad and I pulled for Jimmy, and that was a real feel-good night. That's why I remember it, I suppose."

After a brief pause, Jennifer said, "We should check to see if Billie's Music Bar is still in business."

"Right. I'll google the bar and hopefully get a phone number. Then I can call and see if it's still operating and if Billie will be there."

"You might get Billie on the phone."

"Maybe, but most people aren't comfortable being interrogated by a person they don't know and have never even seen. If we go to Billie's club that could give us a leg up, because it'd let her know we're fans of her singing, *and* we'd be spending money in her club."

"Good point! It sounds like a nice little trip."

CHAPTER 26

▼

At four-thirty on Friday afternoon, the twenty-third day of 2009, Tyler Lydecker sat at the desk of his third floor office in the Jankowski Sciences Building of Humphreys University. He stared vacantly through the window above his desk, and through a gathering dusk he sensed the swirling of snowflakes carried by the leading edge of a weather front expected to dump fifteen-inches of snow by mid-morning. He was accustomed to prodigious January snowfalls in Flagstaff, and he was totally indifferent to this one because his thoughts were about his life, and not about the weather. His mind had chosen this time to once again assail him with thoughts about how he had screwed up his life by being weak and selfish. Why, he asked himself, does it all still haunt me? Why do I sometimes hear her voice in the kitchen when I wake up in the morning, or when I open the front door of our house?

His thoughts ran a familiar pattern of internal conversation. "It didn't have to happen. She was so terribly angry, and so threatening . . . and so *hurt*. And every bit of it was my fault. I was having an affair, or a bit more than one affair. Niz discovered the major affair. I had no discipline. I wanted to stop it, but I was too flattered, too mentally immature to stop it. Niz said I didn't want to break off the relationship and just tried to put *all* the blame on the woman."

His inner voice continued, "Still, divorce could have been the right choice for both of us. It could have worked. But Niz was so hostile and demanding, and so unreasonable about the terms of the divorce. She demanded I sign the house over to her—just fork over an eight hundred thousand dollar house to her! She knew I wasn't financially or emotionally able to give up the house we inherited from my parents! She demanded the house *only* to hurt me. And she wanted alimony on top of that! Hell's fire, she even got promoted before I did—she was making more money than I was. She just meant to hurt me and have the upper hand, and all because of her wounded pride . . . her anger about my infidelity. She should have known I

- 119 -

couldn't afford to give her the house and the amount of money she demanded. I just couldn't allow her to abuse me like that, to *squash* me like I was some mindless, repulsive, bug. She wasn't fair—and she made me *crazy*!"

He knew the script next leapt to thoughts that unleashed overwhelming anxiety and guilt, so he stopped the script and shifted his thoughts away from Nizhoni and his personal transgressions.

And now, he thought disconsolately, Ridley has told me to get lost. His thoughts stalled and his mind became a vacuous pit into which he seemed to fall unanchored and disoriented for several seconds—he bit his lip and then murmured, "Well, god damn it! I *am* lost! I'm paying the costs for what I have done."

There was a knock at his door. He hesitated, but swallowed hard and lifted his hands to the computer keyboard. "Come in," he said, hoping his voice didn't betray his emotion.

His colleague, Chuck Thompson, cracked the door and without entering said, "Still slaving away, I see, Ty."

Tyler didn't turn to address Thompson. He didn't want him to see the distress in his face.

His friend continued, "Gibson, Cowen, and I are gonna stop at Buster's bar for a beer or two. Want to join us? The snow's not expected to get heavy till later tonight."

"Sure, Bill," Tyler replied over his shoulder. "Meet you there soon as I finish transcribing a few more field notes."

"Good," his colleague replied, and closed the door.

In the ensuing silence the word 'good' persisted in Tyler's echoic memory like an assailing taunt from a knowing specter, one sent to inform him that he could never again regain the wonderful state of actually feeling *good* about being what he was.

CHAPTER 27

▼

At seven o'clock on Friday evening, the penultimate day of January, Redmond and Jennifer set out from their home for Brice Arena, the splendid basketball venue of the Ravens. The twenty-eight degree temperature was bracing, but the air hung absolutely still while a low waxing crescent moon shone softly on its appointed course to an early ten-thirty setting.

As they strode past the home of their neighbors and good friends, Giselle and Earl Hanford, Jennifer commented, "I visited with Giselle for an hour or so this afternoon. She told me Haylie sleeps through the nights now. She doesn't fuss, is easily engaged, and she smiles and gurgles a lot. She was awake while I was there, and I held her for ten minutes or so. She's such a pretty baby."

"Hardly a surprise. Giselle is renowned in Pleasanton for her beauty, as well as for her generosity to the town and to Ravenslake."

At seven twenty they entered the sixty-five hundred-seat Brice Arena where the pep band was pumping out the fight song, "Stand Up and Yell," and the students were standing up and singing it at the top of their lungs. They found their seats next to Steve and Ellen and Tony and Maria Carmazzi, and they settled-in just five minutes before the tip-off. It proved to be a hard fought game, with neither team ever getting more than six points ahead of the other. As the final buzzer rasped, the big scoreboard over center court read RU 86, BG 83. The students cheered and poured onto the floor, the band played two choruses of the fight song, *double forte*, and the place rocked.

Jennifer's voice was nearly lost beneath the noise as she vigorously semi-yelled to her companions, "Great game! Now let's get out of this din!" The three couples headed for the nearest exit and a few minutes later they stepped out into the cool fresh air.

"Jen and I would like to head uptown to Mac and Joes for a beer. Want to join us?" Redmond asked.

The others answered in the positive, and Steve offered, "My car's parked in the Red and White Club lot. Anybody want a ride uptown?"

The McClains declined, with thanks, saying they wanted to enjoy the walk; but Maria and Tony accepted Steve's offer.

"See you there," Redmond called, as he and Jennifer headed up Tallawanda Road. As they walked they chatted about the game, about how Ellen was just as fervent a cheerleader for the Ravens basketball team as she was for the football team, and about what a nice night it was for their stroll. They passed the Sigma Nu and Phi Delt houses on Tallawanda, turned right at Church Street and passed the Pi Kap and Sig Ep houses. Ten minutes later they arrived at Mac and Joe's, the little bar and restaurant known so well to RU students over the past sixty-three years.

When they entered they saw that Mac and Joe's was quite busy. "There's our group," Jennifer said, nodding to the back left of the main room. They wended their way to their destination. Langston Wallingford was sharing a neighboring table with an English department colleague, Tom Bennett, and Tom's wife, Glenda. They exchanged greetings with the McClains, and Langston said, "Damned good game tonight, wasn't it?"

"Terrific! Nip and tuck all the way," Redmond returned.

Steve and Tony had already ordered and poured their beers, and a waitress quickly arrived to take the McClain's order for a pitcher of Budweiser. As they waited for their beer to be delivered, Maria said to them, "Steve and Ellen mentioned that you guys just bought a vacation home in Flagstaff. Congratulations! We knew you'd been looking for a place there."

"Thanks, Maria," Jennifer responded. "It was, maybe, a bit impulsive on our part, but we do love the area. And the house is nice."

"So," Tony asked, "are you planning to spend a lot of your summers out there?"

"Yeah, we are, Tony," Redmond answered. He added, "We now have a place to escape the Pleasanton summer heat and humidity. Flagstaff, at seven thousand feet, has a near perfect summer climate."

For the next fifty minutes they enjoyed good beer and conversation about a number of subjects of interest to Ravenslake faculty and Pleasanton residents. Then Steve and Ellen announced it was time for them to head home. Maria and Tony concurred, and accepted Steve's offer of a ride, but Redmond and Jennifer chose to linger a little longer before walking back to Shadowy Lane. Redmond noted, "We just got this third pitcher and we'll have to finish it off. We can't allow good beer to go to waste," he said with a smile.

The Muirs and Carmazzis bid them goodnight and headed off, picking their way through the still congested Mac and Joe's. A few minutes later, the Bennetts also called it a night and began preparing to leave. Redmond, observing that Langston had a nearly full mug of beer in front of him, said, "Langston, you've still got beer there. Join us, please."

Langston gladly accepted the offer, and as the Bennetts exited the bar Langston lowered his six foot-three frame onto a chair at the McClains table. He remarked, "What was that I heard about you two purchasing a home in Arizona—Flagstaff, wasn't it?"

"Yes, that's right, Langston," Redmond answered. "We plan to use it as a summer and holiday vacation house."

"Well, congratulations on that. Now, correct me if I'm wrong, but you guys did a sabbatical year out there at Humphreys some years back?"

"Right," Jennifer answered. "It was in '99/2000. We really liked the area. We've visited it a lot during the past few years. We decided, since we enjoy it so much, that it would be a good place for a vacation home. I spoke with Lindsey Marston about the various residential areas of Flagstaff, and she suggested the area where we bought as a good choice."

Langston smoothed his mustache and goatee by gently running his hand down over them before saying, "That was a good idea on your part, Jen. Lindsey lived there a while, even after Chris Marston was killed." He paused, and then asked uncertainly and in a confidential tone, "You *do* know about that, don't you?"

"Oh yes," Jennifer replied. "Lindsey told me about it one day when she and I had lunch at the Alexander House. It was a terrible tragedy."

Langston nodded, and continued in a wistful vein, "Marston was an extremely talented writer, and so young." Langston's normally lively blue eyes now seemed clouded and fixed on some disturbing distant imagery as he said, "You know, I was at the meeting in Salzburg, the one Marston was attending when he was killed in the car accident. It was an occasion of high tragedy and pathos—cast a pall over the entire proceedings and everyone in attendance. But, I'm proud of Lindsey for the way she bounced back from that horrific experience. She's a remarkable woman. And Chris Marston was a stellar, absolutely *stellar*, writer. I'm happy Lindsey chose to keep his name as a reminder of the man, a man whose greatest works where probably still ahead of him. Lindsey told me she considered going back to her maiden name, Lindsey Lavery, but she made the right choice. It honors Chris, and it serves Lindsey well, too." He paused before concluding, "The poor gal has been through a hell of a lot, and more than just once in her life."

Jennifer decided this line of conversation was a downer. It's truly sad, she thought, but I don't want us to be literally crying in our beers. She took a generous drink of her Bud and turned to a topic she knew would shift Langston's conversation to pleasanter themes. She said, with her best engaging smile, "Langston, I heard that your new World War II novel is out, and that it's getting *great* reviews. Congratulations!"

"Oh, well," he replied with well-practiced calculated modesty, "The book has had rather good *early* reviews, Jennifer, to be sure. I'm pleased with it all. My publisher will be launching a major publicity and promotional tour for me in May."

"It must feel good to have that book out," Redmond commented. "I know you've been working on it quite a while."

"Yes . . . started it in early two thousand-four. It didn't come easily, Mac. I wrote it in fits and starts, with a lot of indecision at times about the sequence, and the ending. It finally came together last summer."

"I've got to remember to order the book," Jennifer offered brightly.

For the next fifteen minutes Langston held forth on the vagaries of writing as a career, replete with quotations from Mark Twain and William Faulkner on the subject, while the McClains interspersed appropriate smiles, chuckles, and comments.

Then, their beers consumed, the three left Mac and Joe's. At Campus Avenue Langston bid them goodnight and headed toward his Church Street home, and Redmond and Jennifer began their descent from the hillcrest. Redmond, feeling the effects of the three pitchers of beer they had enjoyed, tripped slightly when his right foot partially wandered off the curb, but he caught his balance without falling. As they moved away from the lights of uptown toward the darker wooded east campus areas, Redmond commented on the clarity of the many stars visible in the now black and moonless sky.

Jennifer asked, "Mac, do you suppose that on some of the planets of those billions of suns some intelligent creatures might be wondering if there are intelligent creatures on planets such as ours?"

"Sweetie, I think I've had too much beer to think my way through suppositions about the wonderings of distant conceptualizing creatures. But, as you know, Carl Sagan did say, and others have calculated that he was correct, that there are more suns and planets out there than there are grains of sand on *all* the beaches of our planet. So, I have to believe it's likely that some sensate and reasoning beings are out there, strolling and wondering, just as we are."

"Yep! I think so, too."

"But, they probably aren't thinking about something specific that I'm thinking about just now, Jen."

"Yeah? What?"

"What Langston meant in saying, in reference to Lindsey, that 'the poor gal has been through a hell of a lot, and *more than just once*, in her life.' What do you think that meant?"

"Don't know, Mac. Didn't pay much attention beyond the fact that the conversation was getting a bit morbid for Mac and Joe's. So I brought up Langston's latest book. You suppose he meant she had a boyfriend who was also trag-hic . . . ally kilt?"

Redmond chuckled and said, "I think you've had a little too much beer, Jen." He paused before adding, "I suppose it could have been a boyfriend."

"More likely a parent, or a sibling, I should think."

"But you told me she was an only child, Jen. Remember?"

"Oh! Right—couldn't have been a sibling. So I don't know what Langston meant by 'more than just once in her life.' The woman had every 'vantage in life, including a melodious moniker—Lindsey Lavery."

They strolled along quietly, and as they turned onto University Avenue, Redmond asked, "Do you suppose some couple could be strolling down a gentle hillcrest on a planet of one of those billions of suns, and wondering something about some female acquaintance of *theirs*?"

Jennifer replied, with just enough of a slur to show she'd imbibed more than she was used to, "Well, if the universe is infinite—and it jus' might be, darling—then it seems to me there are prolaby a lotta couples wandering about wondering about,"—she hesitated, confused by her sentence, but then continued, "bout some female quaintance of theirs, out there. Jus stands to reason," she said definitively.

They walked on a few more steps before Redmond suggested, "Next time we go to Mac and Joe's, hon, let's limit ourselves to no more than two pitchers of beer."

"Az a good idea. Three's prolaby too many for you, sweedheart."

CHAPTER 28

▼

Redmond found the phone number of Billie's Music Bar on Saturday, January thirty-first, and he called it at six-thirty that evening. He was happy to learn the bar was still in business, that Billie Hamilton was still the owner, and that the next jazz program, featuring the David Hazeltine Trio, was due in Toledo on Saturday, February seventh. He made a reservation at the Crown-Plaza Hotel, located just a few blocks from Billie's Music Bar.

And now, at five-fifteen on the seventh, Redmond steered the well-traveled red Sable off I-75 at exit 201-B, executed a left onto Erie Street, a right onto Monroe, and the forced left onto North Summit Street. Three tenths of a mile down Summit he turned into the circular driveway of the hotel, and parked at its entrance. As he retrieved their small overnight bag from the trunk he commented, "The Toledo Crown Plaza looks pretty nice, Jen. And the Maumee River is, as advertised, located just behind it."

"Truth in advertising is *not* a thing of the past in Toledo," Jennifer noted approvingly.

Redmond told the doorman they were staying for just one night. The doorman called a parking garage attendant to park the Sable, and gave Redmond a ticket he'd need to reclaim his car. Ten minutes later they entered their tenth floor room. Jennifer went immediately to the river-facing window and said happily, "Look Mac, the Maumee is wide, and there's a park across the river."

Redmond joined her in surveying the scene, and he noted, "There's a nice paved walkway along the river, and it looks like there are a lot of restaurants along the shore, over to the right. I saw pictures of that area on the Toledo website. The park is called 'Promenade Park,' and there's a good view of the Toledo skyline from the park and from the restaurants along the river." He added, "I made a seven o'clock dinner reservation at one of the restaurants, Bandini's Bistro, down at the far end of the restaurant row."

"It looks like we'll have to drive to the restaurant. There is a bridge just a block or so to our left, but it'd be a long walk, and it's going to be dark by dinner time."

"Yeah, I checked the area out on the map. That's the Cherry Street Bridge. It's a drawbridge that allows sailing ships with high masts to come into the Toledo Marina from Lake Erie. A little farther out the river is the Port of Toledo. It unloads and loads cargo from and to countries all around the world."

"It's surprising to know that Toledo has such active relationships with the whole world!"

"It does seem miraculous that Great Lake city ports have shipping access to the whole world, thanks to the Saint Lawrence Seaway. I'm sure most people don't think of Toledo as a 'world port city,' but it is."

Jennifer smiled and suggested, "Lets take a quick turn around this general area and get a bit of a feel for The Glass City."

"I'm for that. You know, the new Toledo Mudhens baseball park is reputedly the nicest non-major league baseball venue in the country, and it's just a few blocks from here. I'd like to have a look at it."

"Let's go," Jennifer said.

*   *   *

At eight forty Redmond pulled the Sable into the well-paved and nicely treed parking lot that sat smack on the south shore of the Maumee River and immediately behind the Water Street site of Billie's Music Bar. They had enjoyed an excellent dinner at Bandini's and were now looking forward to hearing the David Hazeltine Trio. And, of course, they hoped to speak with Billie Hamilton and to learn something more about the enigmatic alto saxophonist, Duke Hartsfield.

The entrance to the establishment sat above the parking lot and faced the river. They climbed a short exterior stairway to the entrance of Billie's Music Bar and as they entered they were pleased to see that the jazz club projected a welcoming and sophisticated air. It was moderately spacious, clean and uncluttered, with windows that faced the river. Jennifer noticed, and was drawn to inspect, two large oil paintings hung at the end of the L-shaped entry. One was of Art Tatum, the great jazz pianist of the nineteen forties and beyond, and the other was of the pianist-turned vocalist, Jon Hendricks, the master of the art of creating clever lyrics fitted precisely to immortal jazz instrumental solos, a genre sometimes called "vocalise."

"These are really well executed portraits, Mac," Jennifer remarked. She sighed and said, "There are just so *many* talented painters in the world!"

"Including Jennifer McClain," he replied, and gave his wife a brief one-armed hug.

"Thank you, darling."

Redmond, looking at the painting of Tatum, said, "Toledo is rightly proud of Art Tatum and Jon Hendricks—hometown Toledo men. Of course, Tatum is long passed, but I believe

Hendricks still lives here. I know he was directing the Jazz Studies Program at the University of Toledo, but he may be retired now. And according to those most qualified to make such assessments, Tatum was unmatched in his ability to 'get around' on the eighty-eight keys. A talented young Oscar Petersen, who was no slouch in that regard himself, on first hearing a Tatum recording on the radio said to his dad, quite seriously, that they were hearing an interesting *piano-duo*! That tells you something about the fluidity and speed Tatum could bring to the instrument."

A strikingly attractive young woman wearing a finely fitted skirt and stylish short flared jacket greeted them with, "Good evening, and welcome to my club. I'm Billie Hamilton. Thank you for coming."

Redmond and Jennifer responded with warm smiles, and Redmond said, "We know, of course, who you are, and we're fans of your singing. We have a CD of you singing, terrifically, two great songs with the Johnny Trujillo Septet—'Cute,' and 'Lover Man.'" He paused momentarily before adding, "I'm Redmond McClain and this is my wife, Jennifer."

Billie responded, "Oh! Thank you so much, Redmond, and Jennifer."

Jennifer said, "Please, just call us Mac and Jen."

"Mac and Jen are easier," Billie said with a beguiling grin. "It's nice to hear that some people still know of my days with Johnny's band."

Jennifer said, "We saw Johnny and his group in Vegas last August, and had a nice conversation with him. And we exchange emails with him, occasionally. We also saw his group in our former hometown of Seattle in the summer of 1999. We're fans of his, *and of yours*, as well. In fact, Johnny was the one that told us you have this beautiful jazz club. He told us he'd played here."

Billie was obviously pleased by this. She said, rather apologetically, "I haven't recorded anything since that session with Johnny, but I still perform here from time to time. I confess I do think somewhat nostalgically about my days with Johnny's band and Vegas, at times. It was musically challenging, and very rewarding. But, I love Toledo, too."

"Well Billie," Redmond offered as other customers approached from behind them, "You have patrons to greet here. But we'd love to talk with you a bit between sets if we could."

"For fans, and friends of Johnny, I always have time to chat."

"Great," Redmond said.

Billie summoned a waitress and directed her to seat the McClains at a table near and just to the left of center stage. They ordered drinks, and at nine-ten the David Hazeltine Trio came on stage and launched into a swinging version of "You Make Me Feel So Young." Over the course of the first set, the group played a tasty mix of jazz classics, beautifully embellished versions of eternally meaningful songs from the Great American Songbook, and new compositions. Hazeltine amply demonstrated the mastery of the piano and the jazz repertory that have justly earned him star status.

An hour and ten minutes after the music began the trio left the bandstand to appreciative applause. Billie stopped to talk with several of her customers before taking a chair at the McClain's table. She asked a waitress to bring her a drink, and then asked, "Isn't David's trio terrific?"

"It is, indeed!" Jennifer responded. "I loved the ballads, especially 'The Night We Called It A Day.' It's a favorite song of mine. It has such unexpected, but beautiful, minor chords and unusual melodic patterns. And Hazeltine handled it all so facilely."

Billie smiled in recognition of the fact that the McClains were knowledgeable fans, and said, "I'd love to be able to record a vocal album with David's group. We've talked about it."

"Well," Redmond quickly responded, "we'll keep tabs on that possibility via Google. We'd really like to have a whole CD of yours. The way you sang on that *Johnny Trujillo at the Jazz Interlude* recording knocked us out."

"You have a wonderful voice," Jennifer said. "You make the lyrics so meaningful. Songwriters should love to have you interpret their songs."

Billie expressed her thanks for the kind comments and asked, "Do you live in Toledo?"

"No," Jennifer responded. "Mac's a psychology professor at Ravenslake University, in Pleasanton. And I'm an artist. This is our third year at Ravenslake, and before that we were at Bain-Cottrell University in Seattle."

Redmond added, "And we now have a summer home in Flagstaff, Arizona—so, being fairly close to Vegas, we plan to go there a bit more during the summers than we've been able to in the past. There are still a lot of great jazz players in the area."

"It sounds like you are dedicated fans. Do you visit Toledo often?"

"No," Jennifer answered. "In fact, this is our first visit to the city. We felt a need to get away from Pleasanton for a weekend. Johnny told us about your club in an email, and Mac and I had talked before about acquainting ourselves with The Glass City and other places in Ohio. I'm glad we decided to visit Toledo, because it seems like an interesting town. And having seen and talked with Johnny a couple of times, and having his CDs, we've gotten interested in some of the people who have been in his band, like you, and June Connor, and one of Redmond's favorite alto saxophone players, Duke Hartsfield."

Billie said, "June is a wonderful singer, and she still lives and works in Vegas. We keep in touch. She's devoting a good deal of her free time to writing children's stories, nowadays."

"Really?" Jennifer asked in surprise.

"Yes, she writes children's stories by day, and sings beautifully, I'm sure, by night! She's quite a gal."

"Well, that's interesting." Redmond said. "Do you, by any chance, know anything about Duke Hartsfield and what he's been doing? I love his playing, especially on ballads. Johnny told us he's lost touch with Duke and doesn't know what he's doing now, or even where he is."

"I haven't heard anything about Duke since I left the band," Billie said. "Duke and I weren't close," and she hesitated before adding, "I mean, frankly, we didn't get along too well."

She took a swill of her drink, and said with an apologetic smile, "Duke *is* a fine player, and I don't mean to criticize one of your favorite musicians."

Jennifer said, reassuringly, "We understand, Billie. No one is perfect. We all know that. In fact, Johnny told us Duke has something of a gambling problem."

"Well, Johnny told you right about that. Duke was always in debt to one gambler or another."

"And you didn't approve of that, I'm sure," Jennifer ventured. "It must have been very frustrating to see someone work hard for his pay, and then throw it away by gambling."

Billie's lips formed a sardonic half smile. She said, "Well, Jen, I didn't care about Duke's gambling. In Vegas, gambling problems are as common as tits and glitz in the chorus lines."

Redmond smiled.

"The problem," Billie said in a confidential tone, "was that Duke couldn't keep his hands off young women . . . and that included me."

"My goodness," Jennifer said. "Was it a real problem, or like, just a minor annoyance?"

"Believe me, it was a very *real* problem. I had to threaten Duke by telling him I was going to tell Johnny I'd leave the band if he didn't stop mauling me. Fortunately, that did the trick." Billie took a little sip of her drink before adding, "And I knew a dancer, a showgirl from New York City, who once warned me to be careful not to be alone with Duke. She said she had to threaten him with a restraining order to get him to leave her alone."

Redmond said, in a tone of understanding, "Well, Billie, a lot of great jazz players, like people in all walks of life, have had some personal failings. I guess we still have to respect their musicianship, whatever personal problems they might have." Then, after a pause, he changed the subject by asking, "Are you from Toledo, yourself?"

"Yes. Born and bred, as they say." She glanced at her watch and said, "Oh! I'm sorry. I have a couple of things to take care of at the bar. Are you staying for the second set?"

"Of course," Redmond answered.

She rose to attend to her responsibilities. She said, with a broad and endearing smile, "It's been really nice meeting you, Mac, and Jen. Thanks for coming, and for the compliments about my singing. I really do appreciate that. And just keep an eye out for my possible CD!"

"We shall!" Redmond assured her. They watched Billie return to the bar and instruct the bartender about something.

Redmond took a drink of his scotch and water, and inquired softly, "Well Jen, what do you make of Billie's comments about Duke?"

"Not what we hoped to hear. I assumed we'd learn he was a warm and fuzzy type of guy, a fitting personality for one with a talent for interpreting sentimental love songs. But now, we know he could be aggressive toward attractive young women."

"It's troubling, I think, Jen. Maybe we should try to find an email address for Chris Larrabee and send him a copy of Duke Hartsfield's photo. The portrait from the Hermosa Beach CD is a pretty good shot of Duke. We could ask Larrabee if it looks like his memory of the mystery man of Chester's Pub."

"That's a good idea, Mac. Larrabee worked for Realty Execs, the same company Shirley Evans works with now. Maybe she'd know where he lives. Maybe she can even find an email address for him if he's kept in touch with any of his former co-workers."

"Good idea."

"Suppose Larrabee says the photo *is* of the mystery man—what then?"

"Ah . . . indeed! What then? Well, sweetie, I'd say let's not worry about that supposition till we actually know Larrabee's reaction. For now, let's just dig the great music—the trio's coming back on stage."

CHAPTER 29

▼

When Chris Larrabee checked his electronic mail on Tuesday, February tenth, he was puzzled to see an email from a "Redmond McClain," and that the indicated subject of the message was "Nizhoni Lydecker Disappearance." The name, Nizhoni Lydecker, re-evoked a tinge of the sadness he'd felt following her disappearance, and again, following the eventual discovery of her remains. He pushed these recollections aside and noted that the message was marked as safe by his computer, so he opened it and began reading:

Dear Mr. Larrabee,

Let me introduce myself. My name is Redmond McClain and I am a Professor of Psychology at Ravenslake University in Pleasanton, Ohio. My wife, Jennifer, and I had a one-year sabbatical to Humphreys University for the academic year of 1999/2000. Since then we have vacationed frequently in Flagstaff, and we recently bought a vacation home there. Shirley Evans, our realtor, and as we have recently learned, a former co-worker of yours, directed me to your Kingman Reality Office website.

While on vacation in Flag last summer my wife and I learned of the tragic 2001 disappearance of Professor Nizhoni Lydecker, and we read the *Daily Sun* accounts of that event. We tend to find such cases interesting. We have no standing for investigating crimes other than as citizens interested in helping the authorities find the perpetrators of criminal acts. We did not know Professor Lydecker, though we have recently met one of her cousins, Emerson Yazzie, a detective with the Coconino County Sheriff's Office.

Now, the reason for my contacting you is that my wife, a portrait and landscape artist, and I, saw the police artist's sketch of the so-called mystery man who shared a table with Nizhoni during the jazz performance at Chesters's Pub on the night of her disappearance. Of course, we don't know if you felt it was an accurate depiction of the man you saw that night or not, but we know of a person who has some resemblance to the drawing and who also has a history of making somewhat aggressive (though not criminal) sexual advances toward attractive young women. Additionally, we know he has an interest in jazz performances. I don't believe it would be fair to that man to reveal his name at this point, since the likelihood that he is the mystery man could be low. But, I have attached a photo of this person for your examination. What my wife and I are asking is whether or not this person bears a strong resemblance to the man you saw that evening. Should you wish to contact me, please do so by email. Should you wish to contact Emerson Yazzie at the Coconino County Sheriff's Department regarding who I am, before you respond to this email, I have no objection to that.

Sincerely,
Redmond McClain, Ph.D.

A wry smile crossed Chris Larrabee's round face. "A psych prof playing detective with the Lydecker case," he muttered. He reread the letter and allowed himself to briefly recollect the sad event that had befallen Professor Lydecker on that turbulent April twentieth evening. In response to the question about his personal assessment as to the accuracy of the police artist's sketch, Larrabee spoke, internally, to the author of the email—"Well, Professor McClain, for what it's worth, I've always felt the police sketch was pretty damned good."

He clicked on the attachment and opened it. When the electronic photo solidified before him he uttered, "*Oh!*" In just a second Chris Larrabee was transported back into Chester's Pub, into the smell and feel and sounds of the place, and the pictured man was asking if a seat could be found for him. It was all instantaneously there as a total reintegration of time, place, emotion, and actions, rendered in their full range of fine and coarse-grained elements—a tableau summoned as by magic from long dormant but exquisitely intact memory traces. He felt a brief wave of disorientation and dizziness, the not unexpected effects of sudden time and space travel. He blinked spasmodically, took a deep breath, and leaned closer to the monitor. "That's him," he muttered. "By God, *that's him!*"

*   *   *

At nine-fifteen that evening Redmond saw that he'd received an email from Chris Larrabee, the subject line simply titled, "Response." He called to Jennifer, "Come up here, Jen. Larrabee has answered our inquiry!"

Jennifer soon arrived in the office, and as she pulled a chair over beside his she asked, "Well, aren't you going to open it?"

"Yeah. I was just waiting for you. I thought we should open this together."

"Really, Mac! It's just a response to your question, and most likely a non-committal answer, or a totally negative response."

"Well, here we go!" He opened the email, and they read the message.

> Dear Professor McClain,
>
> I received your letter, with the attachment you sent. I do not feel a need to contact Detective Yazzie and have him vouch for you.
>
> I believe, absolutely, that your photo is of the man I seated with Professor Lydecker on April 20, 2001. When I saw his face on my screen I immediately knew I was looking at that man. The certainty I felt was overwhelming. I'd thought the artist's sketch was a good one, but it never gave me the feeling I was actually seeing the face of the man who was in Chester's Pub that night. In looking at the photograph I feel I'm looking at that man! I was totally unprepared for the emotional wallop your photo packed for me.
>
> I assume you will contact Detective Yazzie. I feel I should also contact him and tell him what I have told you here. In fact, I will definitely contact him tomorrow morning. You apparently know the identity of the man in the photo, and therefore the authorities can interrogate him. Maybe the questions about Professor Lydecker's brutal death will finally be answered. I'm very hopeful that the killer will be found and punished.
>
> Chris Larrabee
> Larrabee Realty
> Kingman, AZ

"Damn!" Redmond uttered in disappointment.

A few seconds later Jennifer said, "Larrabee sounds really convinced that Duke Hartsfield *is* the mystery man."

"Yeah," Redmond conceded. "I guess we should give Emerson a call tomorrow, and tell him what we know about Duke."

"Which isn't really much, Mac. We just know that Duke is a great saxophone player, a photographer, a gambler, and supposedly a man who can be sexually aggressive with women. Still, it seems sure to be encouraging to Emerson. He's had little to go on till now."

"But Hartsfield has fled the country, gone to Paris or some other place in Europe. That won't make things easy for Emerson."

Jennifer, trying to soften Redmond's disappointment concerning Duke Hartsfield, said playfully, "Maybe there's some detective in France, a sort of Hercule Poirot type, who'll find him for Emerson."

Her little comment had a calming effect on Redmond. In kind, he gently jested, "But maybe Emerson will have to rely on someone more like Inspector Clouseau."

Jennifer chuckled.

"Well, Jen, all we can do now is to tell Emerson what we know about Duke Hartsfield, and hope it helps his investigation. I'm sure it'll give him a lift. I'll call him tomorrow."

CHAPTER 30

▼

The following morning, at eleven-fifty Pleasanton time and nine-fifty Flagstaff time, Redmond placed a phone call from his office to Flagstaff. A pleasant female voice answered, "Good morning. Coconino County Sheriff's Office."

Redmond asked to speak to Detective Emerson Yazzie, but was told the detective had left his office and wouldn't be back till late afternoon. Redmond requested that Yazzie call him at his home in Pleasanton, Ohio, anytime after three o'clock Flagstaff time. He gave the woman his home phone number.

"Could you tell me what you wish to speak with the detective about?" the pleasant voice asked.

"Well, yes," Redmond replied. "It has to do with a case he's interested in."

"Can you tell me what case that is?"

"The Nizhoni Lydecker case."

"Oh! He'll certainly be interested in that. I'll leave the message for him."

"Thanks," Redmond said.

At nearly the same time Redmond ended his call to Flagstaff, Jennifer strolled into the Lange Library, returned a book, and she and Ellen headed off for lunch at the Colonial Inn. As they exited the Lange, Jennifer was saying, "I stopped by the Follett's and DuBois bookstores on my walk uptown to see if they'd sold any of my prints. Happily, both stores have sold about fifteen percent of their supply. That's pretty good for the short time they've been on sale. And I stopped at Phil Regan's Shop. He also said the prints have been selling pretty well. We talked a bit about creating some new prints."

Ellen said, "Steve and I bought your Covered Bridge print at Follett's. Have you got other scenes in mind, Jen."

"Yes. I'm planning to do something with the Beta Theta Pi Campanile as the focus. I have to find a unique way of presenting that bell tower—I mean, its been done to death, and it's such a familiar landmark to everyone. So, I'm thinking that instead of depicting it as seen from High Street, I might show it as viewed from the little circle between Harrison and Elliott Halls, with a wider angle of view, like, maybe I'll include Tuffy's and a bit of Tallawanda Road as background. I don't want to have just another print of the tower. I might even include a slightly defocused background view of the Swing Hall cupola above some tree branches."

"I think showing a more diverse landscape is a great idea, Jen. Most of the campus prints offered in the past have concentrated exclusively on a single building or structure like Harrison Hall, or Benton Hall. I think more complex scenes would better communicate 'Ravenslake' to alums, and consequently, they'd sell better . . . you know, put *more* Ravenslake into the painting."

"Exactly," Jennifer said, and she then switched the topic with, "Sally Diebold, at Follett's, told me the Ravenslake University history book you co-edited is now on her shelves and has been selling well."

"It has, Jen. It has a lot of appeal to alums, and faculty. There was a nice review of the book in the Ravenslake Alumni Magazine, and that really helped."

As they entered the Colonial Inn they saw that it was fairly busy, but they found a small table near the middle of the restaurant. As Ellen seated herself she waved to someone a few tables behind Jennifer, and then said, "It's Langston, Lindsey, and Muriel Seachrist, the English department chair. Do you know Muriel?"

"I've met her, of course. I don't really know her."

"She's nice. Steve and I golfed a few times at Johannsen Lake State Park with her and her husband, Paul. She's a darned good golfer. Steve and Muriel led the way around the course, while Paul and I just struggled along. Fortunately, none of us takes the game too seriously." She asked, "Do you play, Jen?"

"I do, but it's not my game, either. I prefer tennis, and Mac and I sometimes play on the courts behind Swing Hall."

They ordered simple light lunches. Ellen asked, "Has your Flagstaff house closed yet?"

"First of March," Jennifer replied. "And Spring Break's coming up, so we plan to be in Flag from March sixth to the fifteenth. We need to buy some furniture during that time. We'll try to get the place furnished to the point that on our next visit we'll be able to stay in our own home."

"Knowing you, Jen, I'm sure you have a list of furnishings and appliances you'd like."

"You do know me, El," Jennifer said with a smile. "I have a *very detailed* list. Mac, of course, is easy to please, though I do ask his opinions on furniture."

"So your trip should be enjoyable, with no distractions about murder mysteries, or environmental threats to The Peaks, to worry yourselves about," Ellen said lightly and with a smile.

"That's right. Of course, we may need to talk to a detective in Flagstaff."

"Really? What for?"

"Well, the detective is Emerson Yazzie. He's a cousin of the HU astrophysicist, Nizhoni Lydecker."

Ellen nodded and said, "The Navajo professor whose skeletal remains were found in early September."

"Yes."

"Why might you have to talk to Detective Yazzie?"

"Well El, it seems Mac and I may have discovered the identity of the 'mystery man' that sat with Nizhoni at Chester's Pub the night she disappeared. You remember that part of the story?"

"Yeah—*wow*! Who is he?"

Jennifer said in subdued tones, "His name is Duke Hartsfield, and *that's* confidential."

Ellen looked incredulous, and asked, "Now, just how in the hell could you find that out?"

Jennifer then told Ellen about the police drawing, how she and Mac thought the drawing looked rather like George Clooney, how a picture of one of Mac's favorite alto sax players also looked like George Clooney, and how they had located Billie Hamilton, a jazz singer in Toledo who had worked with Duke Hartsfield in Johnny Trujillo's band in Las Vegas.

Ellen listened to this recitation in wide-eyed amazement. "And you found Billie what's-her-name in *Toledo*?"

"Yes. We spent one night there earlier this month. She owns a nice jazz club on the Maumee River, downtown."

"And what did Billie tell you about Duke?"

"That he was sometimes aggressive with attractive young women and found it difficult to keep his hands off them. So much so, in fact, that a chorus girl told Billie she had to threaten Duke with a restraining order before he left her alone."

"It certainly doesn't sound like Pleasanton, does it?"

"It's Vegas, baby. Sin City, as they say." Jennifer was, by now, getting a kick out of Ellen's amazement regarding her and Redmond's detective-like sleuthing. Jennifer continued, "Still, we thought it was unlikely that the man that sat with Nizhoni that night, and may have left Chester's Pub with her, could have been Duke Hartsfield. So, we found an email address for Chris Larrabee, the man that seated the mystery man with Nizhoni. Actually, we got his email address from our Flagstaff realtor, Shirley Evans. Larrabee once worked in the same reality office with Shirley."

"Okay," Ellen responded with a tell-me-more stare.

"So, Mac contacted Larrabee. Remember that Larrabee was not only the person that spoke with the mystery man and seated him with Nizhoni, he was also the person that worked with the police sketch artist to make a drawing of the man."

"Right."

"Well, Mac and I had a pretty clear photo of Duke in a liner notes booklet that came with a Johnny Trujillo CD that was recorded back in 1999, and Mac emailed that picture of Duke Hartsfield to Larrabee."

Ellen said, somewhat breathlessly, "To see if Larrabee thought Duke could be the man that might have left the club with Nizhoni the night she vanished!"

Jennifer nodded.

"So, what did Larrabee say?"

"That he was emotionally *shocked* when he saw Duke's picture, and he's convinced Duke is the man he talked to and seated at Nizhoni's table. And then, Larrabee contacted Detective Yazzie."

Ellen took a deep breath before offering, "And that's the reason you might have to meet with Detective Yazzie during Spring Break!"

"Yes. To tell him what we know about Duke, and to be kept up-to-date. Emerson's good about that. And he's very nice."

Ellen chuckled, and said matter-of-factly, "You two can't leave mysteries alone. Of course, I do recall how upset *you* were when you learned what had happened to the unfortunate professor. I guess this guy's history of coming on to young women makes it seem possible he could have abducted and sexually attacked Nizhoni."

"Yes . . . *possible.*"

"So you have to see if Yazzie wants to meet with you in Flag?"

"Right. Mac's going to phone Detective Yazzie today. And Larrabee told us in an email yesterday he was going to talk with Yazzie today, too."

They switched the conversation to other topics, and at twelve-fifty they took their checks to the cashier. Langston, Lindsey, and Muriel were paying their bills when Jennifer and Ellen arrived behind them. They overheard Lindsey say, "Langston, I'm driving Muriel back to Upham Hall. Can I give you a lift?"

"Thanks for the offer, Lindsey," Langston responded, "but I'm heading home for the afternoon. I've got a lot of personal correspondence I must attend to, and I do that best at home."

While Jennifer and Ellen were paying their bills, Langston was saying goodbye to his colleagues. Jennifer said, "Langston, I'm hoofing it home, too. Could we walk together?"

"Certainly, my dear! I'd be delighted to have the company. Of course, I'll be turning off of High, at Campus."

Jennifer and Ellen exchanged goodbyes. Ellen headed west to return to the Lange Library, while Jennifer and Langston headed east. They chatted briefly about the unusually warm February weather Pleasanton was experiencing. Then Jennifer mentioned how she and Redmond had walked to Campus Avenue with Langston just a couple of weeks earlier, after celebrating the Ravens basketball win at Mac and Joe's.

"Ah yes," Langston said. "I think I had a bit too much to drink that night, Jen. But it was a pleasant time."

"Yes. Mac and I imbibed a bit more beer than usual that night, too. And, in fact, it occurred to me later that the beer might have made me forget to ask you about something you said that night."

"Really? What was it?"

"You were telling us about the great talent Chris Marston possessed, and how tragic his death had been."

"Assuredly . . . *terribly* tragic."

"And you praised Lindsey for how well she managed to deal with the tragedy."

"Indeed . . . *admirable* fortitude!"

"And you said something then that I was curious about, but," Jennifer chuckled, "the beer must have made me forget to ask about it."

Langston smiled and asked solicitously, "What did I say?"

"Well, after you expressed admiration for Lindsey's pluck in the face of tragedy, you said something like, 'She's been through a hell of a lot, and more than just once in her life.' Now, I can't imagine anyone having to deal with a second crisis anywhere near comparable to what she must have suffered and overcome in relation to Marston's tragic demise."

"And you wanted to know what other tragedy she experienced? Is that it?"

"Yes. I was curious about that."

Langston suggested, "That could require a little longer than it'll take us to walk to my turnoff at Campus, Jen. Since we're approaching our quaint little Uptown Park here, we can relax on a bench while I tell you of that."

"Fine."

They sat partially turned toward each other on a slat-back wooden bench in the little park, as picturesque as if Currier and Ives had placed them as they were, their earnest and interesting faces softly illumined by the February sun as earth's unfelt rotation spun little Pleasanton toward its evening darkness at an approximate speed of eight hundred miles per hour.

Langston said, "Though I don't recall exactly what I said that night, I'm sure I know what I had in mind, because I've thought it more than once in relation to Lindsey. To have looked tragedy in the eye and dealt so unblinkingly with Marston's death was remarkable. And then, I always recall that while she and Chris were at Colorado State, she a grad student and Chris a professor, she had to deal with the deaths of her mother and father."

"Oh my, Langston! What happened to them?"

"They were on vacation in Southern California. It was in December of 1995. They'd spent the day at a ski area in Wrightwood, and were returning to their hotel in Pasadena. The ski area is in the San Gabriel Mountains, just northeast of Los Angeles. They left the ski area on California Route 2."

"Oh, that's the Angeles Crest Highway. I know exactly where that is, Langston. Mac and I were on a Sports Car Club of America national time and distance rally in that area, in our carefree youthful days. It's incredibly scenic, overlooking the Mohave on the north side of the Angeles Crest, and the Los Angeles basin once you cross the summit of the road and start the narrow curvy downgrade into Pasadena."

"Exactly. And it was a steep blind curve that proved their undoing. Ellis Lavery was driving, and for whatever reason, he missed a turn—most likely just driving too fast. The car plunged a hundred feet before hitting the ground, and then it rolled over and over down the mountain slope."

"My goodness," Jennifer said softly. "How very tragic. How *awful* for Lindsey."

"So . . . that was the point of my comment at Mac and Joe's. It was, certainly, a terrible thing. But Chris Marston told me Lindsey never let herself go to pieces. She took the winter academic quarter off from her studies, but she was as solid as Gibraltar. She dealt with lawyers and complicated business matters. She had a surprising knack for business and legal affairs, and she made informed decisions."

"Lindsey did mention to me that her dad owned a lumber and paper company in Reno. Did she inherit the business, or was it sold?"

"It was an *international* company, Jen. Since both of her parents were deceased, and she had no siblings, Lindsey was the sole heir. The Lavery's had a very sizeable fortune. Ellis and Lillian Lavery had set-up a number of very generous trusts, mostly for the arts. You often see their names associated with some of our great orchestras, institutes, festivals, and such. The paper and lumbering business went lock, stock, and barrel to Lindsey. She then sold it to a group of her father's major executives." Langston confided, *sotto voce*, "She's *extremely* well off, Jen. She owns a very expensive condo in Reno and an elaborate home at the Oxnard Marina in California, where she keeps a nice thirty-foot Sea Ray Sundancer power yacht. She told me she didn't buy a bigger *twin engine* Sundancer because she wanted to be comfortable piloting it herself."

"Well, fate has been very cruel to Lindsey in some ways, but quite generous in others, I guess."

"Yes. But the point I had in mind at Mac and Joe's was probably just how resilient Lindsey proved herself to be—*tres formidable*, as they say."

"She certainly had more than her share of very sad things to deal with."

"Certainly. But she's stuck to what's important to her. You know, she's very dedicated to teaching, writing, and researching in her area, Jen. I think she lives for her work, really. She dates a lot of men, and likes to be flirtatious, but it's *mostly* just fun making on her part. And, of course, men like her. She keeps very fit through regular workouts at the Rec Center. She's solid as a rock. There isn't a soft spot on her body."

Just as Jennifer was wondering how Langston could say this with such an air of certainty, he appended, "It would seem," to his description of Lindsey's muscle tone. He continued, on a higher level, "I believe her work and her humor are the things that saved her from despair."

Jennifer nodded her agreement. "I suppose the family business has continued to prosper for those that bought it?"

"Apparently so. I don't think Lindsey was ever much inclined to worry about the family businesses, nor to covet them. Of course, her father also owned a major hotel-casino, the Silver Castle, in Reno. He willed that whole enterprise to Dominic Gambrino, who'd managed it. Gambrino was just barely into his thirties when he got the Silver Castle. That all seems to have been fine with Lindsey."

"Well, Lindsey never mentioned to me that her father owned a hotel-casino." Jennifer paused before asking, "Does Gambrino still own the hotel-casino?"

"Yes, he does. He's something of a phenomenon in the hotel-casino industry, I believe. Lindsey told me he spends most of his time in Vegas, where he owns and runs one of the classiest casinos there—the new Babylonian Gardens. He's a famous entrepreneur these days, with his very successful casinos. And Lindsey seems to be very fond of him. They go back a long way as friends, I gathered."

Possibly more than friends, Jennifer thought. There was a short pause before she said, "So, Lindsey has, as you've so rightly said, shown real strength in dealing with not just one, but two, terrible personal tragedies."

Langston took the statement to signal the end of Jennifer's interest in his previously unexplained Mac and Joe's reference to Lindsey's indomitable grit. They stood and resumed their stroll, commenting along the way on the prettiness of East High Street on this pleasant afternoon. At the intersection of High and Campus, they exchanged friendly farewells.

Jennifer crossed the street and headed down Old Slant Walk, the original pathway to the only classroom building on the campus at the time of Ravenslake's founding over two centuries ago. When she reached the little memorial circle between Harrison and Elliott Halls she withdrew a small sketchpad from her coat pocket, and quickly sketched an outline of the Beta Bell Tower and the Swing Hall Cupola in the background. Then she proceeded on to 134 Shadowy Lane.

Redmond, arriving home at four-forty, found Jennifer sitting in the family room and talking on the phone with Eve. Jennifer was saying, "Well, Eve, we're planning to do some essential appliance and furniture shopping."

He hung his coat in the entry closet, went to the kitchen, and poured a large glass of ginger ale. He ambled back to the family room just as Jennifer ended her phone conversation with, "Okay. Talk to you later, Eve."

"Telling Eve about some of our upcoming chores in Flag, I gather."

"Yes."

He sat on the couch beside Jennifer, and asked, "How was your day, sweetie?"

"It's been an interesting day," she answered with a smile. "This morning I checked on the sales of my prints and found they're selling reasonably well for this time of year."

"Good!"

"So that was encouraging. And I had lunch with El at the Colonial Inn." She smiled and said, "I told her about the house and our need to buy some furnishings while we're there during Spring Break. I also mentioned that we might need to meet with Detective Yazzie, and she asked why."

Redmond said, "Not to interpret you, sweetheart, but I called Yazzie's number in Flag around eleven-thirty and was told he wouldn't be in till 'late afternoon.' I requested he call me here, after three their time."

"Good!" She paused before continuing, "Anyway, I explained how our possible need to see Detective Yazzie in Flagstaff had come about. El was kind of nonplussed about how that had all gone down—you know, about how we learned of Duke Hartsfield, Johnny Trujillo, Billie Hamilton, our trip to Toledo, and so on. She was very surprised by it all, and interested in it. Of course, she commented that it was more evidence that you and I, as she put it, 'Can't leave mysteries alone'—sort of like we're mystery *addicts*. But, you know, I think El is a little envious of our sleuthing and has a bit of a desire to be in on it. You know, she reads a lot of mystery stories, too."

Redmond smiled, took a short swig of his drink, and responded, "She's a dear. Unfortunately, we can't form a 'Nizhoni murder solution club.'"

"No, we can't. Oh—and Lindsey, Langston, and Muriel Seachrist were also having lunch at the Colonial Inn. We all left at the same time, but Lindsey and Muriel were returning to Upham Hall by car, and Langston was planning to work at home. So I walked with him to Campus Avenue. I wanted to ask him about his remark at Mac and Joe's—you know, about Lindsey having dealt with tragedy 'more than once in her life.'"

"Oh yeah! What did you learn?"

Jennifer related all the things Langston told her in Uptown Park, and Redmond was interested in her account. He said, "So Langston's comment at Mac and Joe's was certainly not an exaggeration. Lindsey has been through really challenging tragedies—the deaths of both her parents, and her husband, in fatal car accidents."

"Yes. And I learned her father's business interests were rather diverse—lumber and paper on the one hand, and a Reno hotel-casino on the other. He willed his international lumber and paper business to Lindsey. She sold it to company executives. But her dad *willed* the hotel-casino to Dominic Gambrino, the very young manager at the casino. And that suggests he was very fond of this Gambrino, Mac."

"I've heard of Gambrino."

"He owns hotel-casinos in both Reno and Vegas, now." Jennifer added, "When Lindsey and I had lunch she didn't mention Gambrino's name, but Langston said she's 'very fond of Gambrino,' and that their friendship goes back a long way."

"Hmm," Redmond responded.

"Yeah. I, too, wondered if there could be more than just friendship between them."

Redmond shrugged, but suggested, "I suppose her father knew Gambrino was good at managing the business. Maybe he thought of the young man as something like a son. And, no doubt he thought it wasn't a business for a young woman interested in writing and teaching."

"Right. And Langston told me that Lindsey is, and I quote, '*extremely* well off.' She has an expensive condo in Reno, a home at the Oxnard Marina in Southern California, where she keeps a nice power yacht, and no doubt, she has a lot of other ritzy stuff."

Redmond smiled. "Sounds like, 'Ain't No Misery in Me,' that old song Gene Roland wrote for June Christy in their days with the Kenton Orchestra—you know, 'I've got a ranch in Arizona, a yacht in LA, a house in San Francisco overlooking the Bay,' and so on."

"Ain't no misery in Lindsey these days, and that's for sure. Langston also volunteered that she works out at the Rec Center regularly, is very fit, and to quote Langston, 'There isn't a soft spot on her body.' I thought he said it with surprising certitude," she said with a smile.

Before Redmond could respond, the phone rang. "Could be Yazzie," he said. He picked up the phone and said, "Hello. This is Redmond McClain."

"Hi, Professor McClain. This is Emerson Yazzie."

"Yes, Detective Yazzie. I've been expecting your call. I assume you've spoken with Chris Larrabee sometime today?"

"He called me early this morning, before I left the office to run up to Tuba City. He told me about you sending him the photograph of a man you thought resembled the police artist's sketch of the guy Nizhoni sat with during the jazz set at Chester's. He forwarded the photo to me, as well."

"That's good."

"He believes, with high confidence, the photograph *is* of the man he seated with Nizhoni on the night she disappeared."

"That's what he wrote to us in his email last night."

"He assumes you know the name of that man."

"Yes, Jen and I do. It happens that he's a jazz musician whose recordings I've admired. But let me tell you what I know about him. His name is Duke Hartsfield, although the 'Duke' part is probably a nickname, not his birth name."

"That's Duke . . . *Hartsfield*?"

"Right." Redmond spelled the last name.

"Do you know his first name?"

"No, but a bandleader he worked for told us he thought Duke's real first name is Weldon or something like that, but he wasn't really sure what the first name is. You know, you might be able to check with the American Federation of Musicians Union in Vegas about that. I'm sure Duke lived and worked there. The bandleader who told us about Duke is still active in Vegas. His name is Johnny Trujillo, and he's a solid citizen and a nice man. Jen and I know him, and are fans of his band. We have his email address and phone number. They're given on his website. Just goggle 'Johnny Trujillo' and you'll find his website."

"How's he spell his name?"

Redmond spelled both of Johnny's names for Yazzie.

Yazzie asked, "What do you know about this Duke Hartsfield guy, Professor McClain?"

"We've never spoken to him, but we did see and hear him play with Johnny's band in Seattle in the summer of 1999. We know he's a talented jazz player. We also learned from Trujillo that Duke grew up in Detroit, and was raised by foster parents, but wasn't close to them. Johnny also said Duke's a good photographer, and he once had a photography studio in Vegas. And a female singer, Billie Hamilton, who worked with Johnny's band while Duke was in it, told us, and I quote, 'Duke couldn't keep his hands off young women.' That included Billie Hamilton, herself. Billie also said a showgirl in Vegas warned her not to be alone with Duke, and the showgirl had to threaten Duke with a restraining order to get him to leave her alone—and Billie had to threaten to tell Johnny she'd leave the band if Johnny couldn't stop Duke from harassing her."

"*Well* . . . certainly interesting!"

"And both Johnny Trujillo and Billie Hamilton said Hartsfield had a gambling problem."

Redmond paused before concluding, "That's about the sum total of what we know about the guy."

"Do you have any idea where this man could be now?"

"No. Johnny Trujillo and Billie Hamilton both said they haven't seen Duke for a good while. Trujillo remembered hearing that Hartsfield was going to Paris to work because he didn't feel Americans appreciated him as much as they should have. It's a fact that classic jazz is more popular in Europe than in America these days."

"That's too bad—I mean, that we may have a hard time finding him."

"Yes, but at least you have someone to look for."

"And don't think I don't appreciate the lead! Frankly, we've had *nothing* in the way of a lead until now. This is the first possible breakthrough since the disappearance. That's going on eight years now!"

Redmond volunteered, "Jen and I will be in Flag for Spring Break during the week of March eighth. We just bought a vacation home out in Cheshire Heights and we're going to take possession of the house and be busy buying some furniture for it. But we can meet with you if you'd like."

"That's good, professor. Could we meet on, let's see . . . Tuesday, the tenth, for lunch?"

"Yes, of course. How about at Buster's."

"That would be fine." Yazzie paused briefly before asking, "Could I have your email address?"

"Sure." They exchanged email addresses.

Then Redmond said, "We'll see you on the tenth of March. And just out of curiosity, did you tell your brother Jim that you met us at Buster's?"

"Yes, I did. He said nice things about you—told me you were both strong in the face of a challenge."

Redmond chuckled. "Well, that was really a nice compliment, Detective Yazzie."

"Maybe we could drop the titles of 'detective' and 'professor,'" Yazzie suggested with a smile in his voice.

"I'm all for that. Please call me 'Mac,' and my wife likes to be called, 'Jen.'"

"And I'm 'Emerson.'"

"All right, Emerson. Jen and I will see you at Buster's. If you need to get in touch with us before that, you can call or email."

"That's good, Mac. In the meantime, I'll see if I can find out anything more about this Duke guy."

Redmond hung up the phone and said to Jennifer, "He sounds pretty excited about Duke Hartsfield. He said this is the first real lead on the mystery man in the nearly eight years since Nizhoni vanished."

"Yes, darling. But it's still possible that it wasn't really Duke Hartsfield Larrabee saw that night. Larrabee could be wrong, no matter how strongly he feels about it. And even if it were Duke who sat with Nizhoni that fateful night, no one saw them leave together."

"That's true, hon. Lots of people have gone to prison because a witness identified them as having been at a crime scene, or having been an assailant, only to have later evidence prove them innocent. But, it's a lead that has to be followed up."

CHAPTER 31

───────────── ▼ ─────────────

It wasn't until the evening of Friday, February twenty-seventh, that the McClains heard any news from Emerson Yazzie. It came in an email they found at eight o'clock, after returning home from dining uptown with Ellen and Steve. Redmond opened the message. It read:

Jen and Mac,

Thought I'd update you on what I've learned so far about Duke (real name, *Wallace*) Hartsfield. I've been getting excellent cooperation from the Las Vegas Sheriff's Office. I spent two days in Vegas with one of their detectives, Dan Crocker, who accompanied me on my rounds.

I've learned that The American Federation of Musicians, Local 369, allows musicians to be members on a quarterly basis, and they often drop out and rejoin in accordance with the job market. Duke used that kind of irregular membership in order to save money when he was on the road or had no prospect of gigs scheduled in Vegas for a few months. Duke didn't renew his membership after it expired at the end of June 2001.

I found there were a few traffic warrants on Duke—speeding or parking tickets. There were no felony charges against him in Vegas.

The president of Local 369 made it clear that he considers Duke to be a truly outstanding musician—the guy sounded like a real fan of Duke's. He did allow, however, that Duke liked to gamble and, like most gamblers, he lost more than he won.

I'm looking forward to seeing you two for lunch at noon on Tuesday, March tenth, at Buster's. Then we can go to my office. I'd like to have you dictate an account of how you came to suspect that Duke Hartsfield could be the man Nizhoni sat with on the night of her disappearance, and how you came to contact Chris Larrabee.

Regards,
Emerson

"So," Redmond said happily, "Duke Hartsfield sounds like a generally law abiding citizen, except for driving too fast, and parking where he shouldn't. And though he's fond of gambling, that's not a crime."

"Don't forget his trouble keeping his hands off attractive young women," Jennifer countered.

"Yes. But not to the point of getting the law involved."

"Well, lots of young women might fail to report such incidents out of embarrassment or fear."

"You can't assume a man's guilty of such activities when there's no real evidence of it," Redmond asserted.

"That's right, of course, darling. Emerson will have to learn more about Duke and his past before we should believe anything truly negative about him."

CHAPTER 32

▼

On Saturday, March seventh, the McClains began their Spring Break by flying to Phoenix. From there, they drove their rental car to Flagstaff, and arrived at the Hilton at six fifteen in the evening.

As Redmond removed their suitcases from the trunk, he commented, "Just think, this will be our last time staying at a hotel in Flag, hon. On future trips we'll just head to our home in Cheshire Heights."

"Right. But for now, we have some shopping to do. We have eight days to find, order, and receive essential appliances and some furniture. I'd like to have at least one bedroom furnished before we leave." She paused before adding, "We can pick up our house keys from Shirley on Monday morning. That's going to be a thrill for me!"

"Me too, hon."

They checked into the Hilton, and as Jennifer surveyed the view of The Peaks that room 512 provided, she commented softly, "The Peaks are beginning to fade into darkness. It's strange that I somehow think of them as alive, as though they could know night is falling and be aware of what's happening in their city—of its street and window lights, and the many restaurant signs and headlights turning on."

Redmond smiled and said, "Well, there's certainly a lot of life on The Peaks. But I don't think they can 'cognize' about what goes on beneath them."

"I don't think they can, either, but maybe in some microscopic cellular way they can sense what's going on around them. I don't believe the Peaks carry on an internal conversation, but maybe they're somehow *aware* of us."

Redmond mockingly voiced his imagined version of the Peaks' internal observation by saying slowly and in as bass a voice as he could effect, "Oh, I *sense* Mac and Jen are at the Hilton, in Room 512." Then he said, "I think you need some food and drink, sweetie."

Jennifer laughed, and punched him on the chest.

"Well," he granted, "I'll concede that there is something about great natural phenomena that somehow suggests a living quality. After all, the Navajo and Hopi regard the Peaks as a *living god*. Anything that inspires some sense of awe carries a mystical tinge for most humans, it seems. It doesn't mean that mystical tinge is in any sense 'humanoid' or conscious. Mostly, it means humans like to imagine things."

"I find it much easier to think the very real Peaks are living and, in some sense, aware of what happens beneath them, than to think Zeus, Amun-Ra, Jupiter, or the scores of other fantasized man-like deities are sitting out in the infinite, dynamic, and incredibly explosive universe keeping tabs on every single thought and action of every human on this little planet, in order to either punish or reward them. To think *that* you have to be totally bonkers!"

"Yeah, well sweetie, I think we could use some sustenance. How about Josephine's on North Humphreys? I'll call and make a reservation."

"Good! I need to shower and get out of these travelin' duds."

At seven-thirty the McClains arrived at Josephine's, and ten minutes later were shown to a table. They ordered their food, and a glass of Chardonnay. As Jennifer swirled her wine in a gentle slow arc she commented, "This is the third time we've eaten here. It's a very relaxing atmosphere."

"Something like the Alexander House, don't you think?"

"Yes, but cozier."

"And it's busy tonight. I checked HU's academic calendar online last week. Their Spring Break doesn't begin until the sixteenth. And it looks like there are a lot of faculty types, and some students here tonight."

"You know, Mac, we've been in Flag so much I feel I recognize a number of people in town, even though I don't know who they are."

"Me, too. Of course, it's possible that we're just recognizing 'types,' I suppose. After all, Flagstaff has so many more visitors than Pleasanton, and three times as many residents. We're pretty much bound to see a few people who look familiar to us."

Jennifer agreed, then said contentedly, "Well, despite the fact we have a lot to do this week, I'm totally relaxed."

"We have lots of time to accomplish our main goals for the house. And we have to see Emerson on Tuesday."

"Oh, I forgot to tell you that I exchanged emails with Margo before we left. They'd like to see the house later this week."

"Great. We should try to firm that up. Maybe we could go to dinner with them."

"I'll call Margo and try to arrange something."

*   *   *

On Monday morning Jennifer and Redmond had a minimal breakfast at the Hilton breakfast bar before stopping in at Realty Execs to see Shirley Evans. They picked up the keys to their new home, as well as two electronic garage door openers, and they chatted with Shirley for about fifteen minutes before heading out to the Flagstaff Mall area.

The first items to purchase, according to Jennifer's list, were a refrigerator, a dishwasher, a microwave oven, a washing machine, and a dryer. She knew exactly what makes and models of appliances she wanted, and they found them at The Home Depot. They were pleased to learn the items could be delivered and hooked up on Wednesday afternoon. Then they turned their attention to finding a bed for the master bedroom. After visiting three furniture stores, each in a different area of town, Jennifer was still undecided. "I'll have to think about the choices, Mac," she said.

"Well, hon, it *would* be nice to be able to sleep in our house by, maybe, Thursday."

Jennifer responded, "Yes, I know. I'm inclined to favor the king sized sleigh bed we saw at Babbitt's, but it was the most expensive."

"That's my choice, too. Let's just order it."

"All right, Mac. Let's go back to Babbitt's Furniture after lunch, and see how quickly they can deliver it."

"Good." He consulted his watch and noted, "I'm thinking the Call of the Canyon for lunch, but it's only eleven-fifteen, Jen."

"Actually, that's fine, because I'd like to drop by the *Daily Sun* and look through their papers for the week leading up to Saturday, April twentieth, 2001."

"That would be the week Nizhoni Lydecker vanished." Redmond smiled and asked, "And just what do you have in mind, Jen?"

"Well, as I was falling asleep last night I thought it might be interesting to know who performed at Chester's on April twentieth of 2001. Chester would have taken out an ad sometime during the week leading up to the band's appearance—right?"

"I suppose he would, Sherlock," he replied with a smile.

"So, I'm thinking that if the mystery man were really Duke Hartsfield, maybe he could have known some of the guys in the band. In fact, maybe that could have been the reason for Duke, if it were Duke, to come to Chester's in the first place. Emerson could interview the band members and ask if they knew Duke and remembered seeing him at Chester's. It could end any remaining uncertainty as to whether the 'mystery man' was *definitely* Duke Hartsfield."

"Hmm . . . damned good thought, babe! Let's check it out."

Thirty minutes later the McClains exited the *Daily Sun* office, and Jennifer said exuberantly, "Now we know the band that played in Chester's Pub on that awful April night of 2001! More importantly, we know June Connor was there, and, of course, we know that June Connor and Duke Hartsfield knew each other."

"Absolutely! They'd been together on Johnny Trujillo's Hermosa Beach recording date, and both worked and lived in Vegas. So, if Duke Hartsfield were the mystery man in Chester's

Pub, Connor would certainly have seen him. I mean, it's a small and intimate venue. And, if she didn't see him it would mean Duke is *not* the mystery man, even though he may look something like Duke."

"And, conversely, Mac, if Connor says she recalls seeing Duke in Chester's Pub it would leave no doubt that Duke was there. It would absolutely document Larrabee's belief that Duke *is* the man he seated with Nizhoni."

"Exactly. We need to tell Emerson about this tomorrow. And let's hope June Connor has a good memory."

"Right. For now, let's have lunch, and then drive back out to Babbitt's and buy our bed."

CHAPTER 33

───────── ▼ ─────────

On Tuesday morning Redmond told the Flagstaff Hilton desk clerk he and Jennifer would be leaving the hotel on Thursday morning. As they prepared to go meet Emerson Yazzie at Busters, Redmond commented, "Well Jen, we'll be able to have breakfast at home on Friday, Saturday, and Sunday. Of course we'll be heading down the hill early on Sunday morning for our flight back to Pleasanton."

"Oh, that reminds me—Margo and I agreed to dinner on Friday evening. There's a new Italian restaurant on East Aspen we're going to try."

"Great."

When they entered Buster's at noon they immediately encountered the dignified and well-dressed Emerson Yazzie standing in the vestibule of the busy establishment. He greeted them with a smile and, "Hey guys. Good to see ya."

The McClains reciprocated the sentiment. Emerson informed the young woman at the reservation desk that his party had arrived, and she summoned a waitress who showed them to a table on the quieter upper level of the restaurant.

As they took their seats Jennifer commented to Emerson, "I believe this is the table Mac and I shared with Tim and Margo the night we met you and Vella Bonally back in December, and we told you about our knowing your brother, Jim."

"Yes, I believe it is," Emerson returned. He added, with a smile, "I'll have to tell Vella you remembered her name."

"Please do," Jennifer said. "And I'm glad to know you two are still dating. Vella seems like a very nice young woman, and very attractive, as well."

"She is all of that," Emerson said with a grin, and following a brief pause, he asked, "So how's the shopping for your new house going?"

"Well," Redmond replied, "we've bought the 'necessities' so far, just enough to allow us to move in on Thursday afternoon. The complete furnishing of the house is something we'll get around to over the summer."

They ordered their food, and as the waitress left, Redmond asked Emerson, "So, anything new regarding Duke Hartsfield?"

"Unfortunately no, Mac. Johnny Trujillo is doing a bunch of one-nighters back east, but his wife says he'll be home this weekend. Dan Crocker and I plan to interview him on the sixteenth, or as soon after that as we can arrange. We're hoping he'll recall something more about Hartsfield's family or friends, someone who might know where he is and how we can get in touch with him."

"Seems worthy of a shot," Jennifer said.

"Yeah, Jen," Emerson said, "but you know, I've been thinking a lot about Hartsfield, and it occurred to me that it's always possible Larrabee is wrong about him being the mystery man. Chris seems totally convinced Hartsfield's the guy, but when you get down to the nitty-gritty of it, a lot of people look like a lot of people. Facial resemblance is too weak a factor to convince a jury the guy was Hartsfield if he says he wasn't there. Still, it's the only thing we've got to go on for now."

Redmond smiled and said, in a confidential tone, "Emerson, Jen found a way to get definitive evidence as to whether Duke was in Chester's that night or not."

Emerson managed to look both pleased and perplexed. His dark eyes suggested doubt, but his questioning smile suggested encouragement. "Ah . . . what *evidence?*"

Jennifer explained, "We found out from a *Daily Sun* advertisement that the jazz performance Nizhoni attended the night she disappeared included a singer named June Connor. And, we know that June Connor worked and recorded with Johnny Trujillo during the time Duke Hartsfield was in the band! June Connor still lives and works in Vegas." She smiled at Emerson and asked, "See?"

Emerson didn't "see" for a few seconds, but then he put the picture together. "Yeah. That'll work, Jen! If Hartsfield was in the club that night, and this June Connor saw him there, it would absolutely confirm that he *is* the guy that sat with Nizhoni—just as Larrabee says." He looked from Jennifer to Redmond and back, and asked, "Anybody ever tell you guys you oughta be detectives?"

Jennifer said, "Well, a Pittsburgh detective named Sean Driscoll said that to us once. We do have curiosity, especially about disappearances, I guess. Such cases intrigue us, as they do many other people."

Their food was delivered and as the waitress left, Emerson said, "Well, your information about June Connor being at Chester's that night is just *great* news. If Connor says Hartsfield was there it'll require that I continue looking into his background. On the other hand, if she says she's sure she didn't see him it'll leave our mystery man the enigma he's been, despite

Larrabee's conviction. So, I've got to call Dan Crocker and have him set up an appointment for us to talk with June Connor, as well as with Johnny Trujillo."

"We'll be back in Pleasanton on Monday, the sixteenth," Redmond noted. "Please let us know what you find out after you see Connor and Trujillo."

"I'll keep you informed," Emerson assured. He paused before continuing in a rather confiding tone, "You know, my dad's brother, Douglas Yazzie, was Nizhoni's dad. This isn't just another case to me. Niz and I weren't just cousins—we were good *friends*! She was a year older than I was. She gave me a lot of good advice about college, advice that I put to good use at U of A. She encouraged me to be a serious student. She was an incredibly kind and brilliant person. Niz thought a lot about the universe, but she was a down-to-earth, good-natured, warm hearted, soul. And there are a lot of fine people whose lives have been permanently scarred by what was done to Nizhoni."

Jennifer replied, "We understand," and the soft quaver in her voice was testament to her words.

Emerson nodded. "I truly appreciate your interest and help in this matter."

"We're happy to help where we can," Redmond replied.

CHAPTER 34

▼

At six-fifty on Friday evening, Margo and Tim Bailey left their Mount Elden condo in Tim's red Wrangler, and headed to Muselli's Italian Restaurant on East Aspen. They were going to meet the McClains for dinner at the fairly new and very popular downtown eatery, and they'd been invited to visit the McClain's new vacation home for coffee and dessert following dinner. As the Jeep exited the condo development Margo said blithely, "It's nice to find a restaurant none of us has tried yet. Erin told me she and Dean Suder had dinner at Muselli's last weekend, and they thought it was great."

"Looking forward to it," Tim said. "And, with respect to Erin, are she and Dean Suder getting serious about one another? I thought their dating hadn't jelled into anything significant."

"I guess it's been simmering on a low flame," Margo answered with a grin and a slight chuckle. "I remember Erin telling me back in July of last year that they'd had a date, but didn't hit it off too well. But yesterday I got the impression they might be getting serious about each other. She's usually very skittish when it comes to talking about her personal life, or anyone else's for that matter."

"You had lunch with her yesterday?"

"Yes, at the *San Felipe Cantina*. She was in an unusually expansive and revelatory mood—well, revelatory *for Erin*, that is. She says their relationship is 'developing.'"

"Good to hear she's showing an interest in something more than just her work."

They soon arrived at the lot behind Muselli's, parked the Jeep, and shortly thereafter found that Redmond and Jennifer were already there. The couples exchanged greetings, and Redmond said, "We just got here a few minutes ago, but I've been told our table is ready."

They were promptly shown to their table, were seated, and given menus. Jennifer was pleased with the restaurant's menu. She chose the *Linguini Da Vinci*, and Redmond requested the Chicken Caesar. Margo favored the Scrod Muselli, while Tim preferred the Veal Romano.

They agreed to share a bottle of 2002 *Castello Di Queceto Chianti Classico*. Redmond performed the duties of inspecting the cork, accepting and swirling a dram of the libation, and subjecting it to a considered sniffing, tasting, and final approval. The waiter poured wine for Redmond and departed, leaving Redmond to dispense the wine to the others.

As Redmond finished pouring, Margo suggested, "Let's have a toast."

"Of course," Jennifer agreed. "Let's have a toast, Margo."

Margo, her delicate features relaxed and reverent in the soft lighting of the room, raised her glass, and with an air of enchantment, said, "To truth, and to reason."

The others smiled and lightly clicked their fragile stemmed glasses while repeating, "To truth, and to reason," and took a sip of the wine.

Redmond said approvingly, "That's a quite noble salutation, and you said it with such an ethereal touch, Margo. It's an excellent choice. Truth and reason are the most basic guides to understanding this existence we all share, and they're basic to fairness and justice, as well."

Margo smiled. She said, "I'm in a high minded mood tonight, I guess. I'd thought of toasting Spring Break," she said with a chuckle, "but decided to go for something more precious and meaningful than that."

Redmond turned the conversation to Margo's rejected toasting topic. He asked, "Are you guys heading anywhere for the break?"

"Yes," Tim answered, "we're leaving in the morning. You remember how we told you about the Ojai Valley Inn we stayed at last summer, and how, if we ever got enough money, we'd go back?"

"Sure do," Jennifer said. "So you acquired the money to afford it!"

"Unfortunately . . . no," Tim replied easily. "We haven't come into that sort of extra money. But there are lots of places to stay in Ojai that aren't so expensive, and we're staying three nights in one of those. As you know, we really liked the area and we want to see more of the backcountry between Ojai and Santa Barbara. We're staying four days, and then we'll come home. We're planning to camp out one night at Wheeler's Hot Springs, just a few miles from Ojai. It's on a stream that comes down from the Los Padres National Forest." Their meals were brought and thoroughly enjoyed while the four talked animatedly of their work and their progress. Margo and Tim spoke of their research efforts, and Redmond expressed pleasure that both Baileys were succeeding so well in their young careers. Jennifer shared with the Baileys the news about her artistic endeavors, especially her giclée archival print sales and plans.

They finished their meals, all deemed to have been excellent. Redmond had already paid the bill before Tim could protest his generosity, and Tim expressed his thanks.

At eight forty the Bailey's Wrangler followed the McClain's rented Taurus to their newly purchased home at 257 Blue Spruce Road in Cheshire Heights. Redmond parked the Taurus in the garage, and Tim parked his Jeep in the driveway.

As they approached the front door, Tim said, "Geez, this is a really wooded area, and the road is so winding and up-and-down. It's fun to drive it." He surveyed the scene along the road, and noted, "You can only see one house to the left and maybe two houses to the right of your home. It's great!"

"Well," Redmond responded, "it's pretty dark out here right now, Tim. In the daylight you can see a few more houses on this road from here. But we're up on the ridgeline, and the houses between us and Mount Humphreys are all lower down."

Margo asked, "So you got the great view of the Peaks you wanted?"

"Oh, yes," Jennifer answered. "We have an outstanding view of the Peaks. It's a somewhat moonlit night, so I hope you can see it." She unlocked the front door and the others filed in behind her. They passed through the entryway and the large family room to the door that opened onto the back deck.

Redmond opened the door and clicked on just enough of the outdoor lighting to allow them to see the immediate area of the deck. They stepped out onto the spacious platform that jutted out above shrubs and granite outcroppings below, and provided an unobstructed view of the Humphreys and Agassiz peaks.

"Hey! Take a look at that," Margo said enthusiastically. "With this moonlight and the clear sky, it's just gorgeous. And in the daytime you'll be able to see the trees and the tree line, and the detailed three-dimensionality of the mountain."

They admired the nocturnal view and imagined how much more detail would be visible under clear blue daytime skies. Then Jennifer conducted a tour of the interior of the dwelling.

Redmond pointed out the obvious fact that they hadn't had time to buy much in the way of furnishings. "We've got a bed, a few dishes and cups, a simple table in the dining room that will go into our studio-slash-office upstairs, four chairs, and essential appliances. We've done about as much as was possible during this week. We want to have more time to really consider what we want in the way of the feel of the house."

"Well, I'm sure it's going to look terrific by the end of the upcoming summer," Tim offered. "You guys *are* planning to spend most of the summer here, right?"

"That's right, Tim," Redmond answered. "We plan to be here from mid-May until August twentieth or so. Jen wants to have some of the rooms professionally painted, and we hope to have everything done by the end of our summer stay. And we plan to have time for some mini-vacations, as well."

"For now," Jennifer suggested, "let's use the dining room for our dessert and coffee service. I brought some coffee from Grounds for Thinking, our favorite coffee shop in Pleasanton. It's called Carolina Mountain Blend. And for our dessert I have a cake with an interesting name—Midnight in Venice, to compliment our fine Muselli's dinner. It has three layers of vanilla and chocolate cake, soaked in rum syrup, with two layers of cannoli filling, all covered with bitter-sweet chocolate, and almonds!"

Margo smiled and said, "*Well*—that sounds about right to me! Where did you get such an opulent cake, Jen?"

"From the new Cathy LuCerne Bakery. They have wonderful things there. Our realtor, Shirley Evans, put me onto it."

They chatted about the ample sizes of the rooms of the house, and the handsome granite counter tops and backsplashes of the kitchen while they prepared the coffee and cut the cake. They joked about using coffee mugs for their coffee and mismatched large plates for their fancy dessert.

They greatly enjoyed the Cathy LuCerne cake creation and the mellow coffee. Jennifer then topped up their coffees, and when she reseated herself beside Redmond and across from the Baileys, Tim asked, "You're heading back to Ohio on Sunday?"

"Yes," Redmond answered. "And our spring term will end in early May. We'll have some things to take care of around our home before we can come back to Flag. We'll try to get the lawn, shrubs, and flowers off on a good footing for summer. Once we leave Pleasanton we'll have a lawn service look after the yard. This'll be the first summer I won't have to mow our grass. Actually, I'll miss that, though I'll do some of it through late August and up until mid-October. And, of course, we have prodigious amounts of tree leaves to deal with in October, so I'll eventually get my fill of yard work."

"Well, you guys have had a productive week here, getting some of the basics into the house," Tim noted. "I'm sure you've given a lot of thought to paint colors, types of furniture, and so forth."

"We have," Jennifer acknowledged. "And today, we also had to meet with Emerson Yazzie at Buster's. And after lunch we went to the Sheriff's Department to dictate some information about Duke Hartsfield possibly being the mysterious stranger that sat with Nizhoni Lydecker on the night she disappeared."

Tim looked mystified, and he asked, "Who is Duke Hartsfield? And how do you know that he might be the mysterious stranger?"

Margo asked eagerly, "You mean there's new information about Nizhoni's disappearance?"

Redmond put a hand to his forehead and gave it a rub or two as he said, "Holy smoke! We've been so preoccupied with this house we didn't realize we hadn't told you about the possible Duke Hartsfield connection."

Redmond and Jennifer spent the next ten minutes describing elements of the story of how they came to think the jazz saxophonist, Duke Hartsfield, might have been the man that sat with Nizhoni on the fateful evening of April twentieth, 2001.

Margo said, "So you put together information from Johnny Trujillo, Billie Hamilton, a photograph of Duke, Chris Larrabee's positive identification of Duke's picture as being the guy in Chester's that night, and how June Connor might be able to really nail down that identification?"

Jennifer said apologetically, "Yes, we did. Sorry we didn't let you know."

Tim chuckled and said, "Heck, that's okay, Jen! As we've said, you had lots of things about this house on your mind. But what you learned regarding Duke Hartsfield adds up to great investigative stuff—damned impressive!"

Redmond said modestly, "It just fell together, Tim. And Emerson isn't going to be able to talk to June Connor until Monday, or maybe later for all we know. He was planning to see her and Johnny Trujillo in Vegas, assuming she's in town and not performing somewhere on the road. It's entirely possible that all our speculation about Hartsfield could amount to *nothing* if Connor doesn't remember seeing him at Chester's that night."

"Well, that's all really fascinating," Margo observed. Then she said, somewhat tentatively, "I learned something from Erin James yesterday that's related to Nizhoni Lydecker and her divorce."

"Well, let's hear it," Jennifer said eagerly.

"I told you before, I think, that Erin and Nizhoni were friends?"

"You did—at Chester's," Jennifer confirmed.

"Well, Erin told me that she's dating the Business School dean. I was surprised to learn they're still dating, since Erin is very closed mouth about her personal life. And I was surprised when she admitted to being rather serious about him. The last time we'd talked about Dean Suder was last summer when we were having lunch in the Lumberjack Room of the Union. At that time Erin said she'd been on a date with Suder, but wasn't much interested in him because they hadn't 'hit it off' too well. I reminded her of that yesterday and she smiled, a *bit* uncomfortably, and said, 'Well, things have changed since then.' I could see she didn't want to talk about it any further. So I switched the conversation, subtly, I thought. I mentioned that we had also spoken at that luncheon about Nizhoni Lydecker's disappearance and her marital troubles.

"Erin responded with a sort of resigned grimace and said, 'Yes, Lindsey Marston sure broke up that marriage.' Well! I was startled to hear her say that, because she'd made it clear last summer that she didn't want to get into gossiping about her friend Nizhoni, or Tyler Lydecker. So, knowing how reticent Erin tends to be about gossiping, I didn't want to inquire further about her slip. I changed the subject, and I felt that Erin was relieved that I did. I'd heard of Professor Marston, but I never met her. I understand she left Humphreys last year."

Margo noticed that both Redmond and Jennifer were staring at her with widened eyes and slackened jaws!

Jennifer said, "*Holy cow*, Margo! Lindsey Marston *did* leave Humphreys last year—and she came to Ravenslake. We know her." Then Jennifer continued, just a bit more calmly, "And I'm not altogether surprised by that odd bit of news about Lindsey being involved with Tyler Lydecker, because, frankly, from almost the moment I laid eyes on her I've thought she's a chronic flirt!"

Redmond smiled and said, "In fact, Jen thinks Lindsey sometimes flirts with *me*. And, of course, she's right about Lindsey, generally, because the woman does seem to like to play up to men."

And don't I know it? Jennifer thought. She said, "And Lindsey has dated a goodly number of men since she arrived in town. But one of the men, a colleague of hers, told me her flirting is mostly harmless and that she does it just for fun."

"Well," Margo replied, "apparently her relationship with Tyler Lydecker went way beyond flirtatious fun to the *seriously* smarmy level, Jen."

"Yes," Jennifer conceded, with a sour expression.

The group changed the conversation to more personal themes, including the Bailey's hopes to buy a house in about a year. Tim related that he had a buyer for the Mount Elden Condo he'd bought when he first arrived in Flag, and Redmond and Jennifer were pleased to learn that Tim was getting what he regarded as a good price for it.

Then, saying how much they'd enjoyed their evening, the two couples bid each other goodnight. As the exhaust note of Tim's Jeep faded down Blue Spruce Road the McClains turned their attention to rinsing the dishes and silverware and putting them in the new dishwasher.

Redmond commented, "Well, that was a very enjoyable get together. Muselli's certainly lived up to its billing, and your dessert and coffee were *outstanding*, sweetie."

As she closed the dishwasher door Jennifer said, "Yes, and I learned I'd better keep an eye on an itinerant home wrecker."

Redmond asked, "Why?"

"Because, darling," she said with a little smile, "I've learned a *truth* about Lindsey Marston, and I can *reason.*"

CHAPTER 35

▼

The McClains returned to Pleasanton on Sunday, quite satisfied with the progress they'd made on their new home, and thoroughly reassured that the decision to purchase it was a sound one. On Monday, March sixteenth, they defied both the twenty-nine degree temperature and a mild case of travel-induced languor by getting back to their regular routine of running before breakfast. As they strode resolutely along, Jennifer observed, "Boy, it feels more like mid-January than March sixteenth."

"Yeah it does! So, contrary to the Rodgers and Hart song title, 'Spring *Isn't* Here!'"

"No, it isn't, Mac. But Dorothy Parker wrote that, 'Every year back spring comes, with nasty little birds yapping their fool heads off and the ground all mucked up with plants!' So, we have Dorothy's assurance that spring does come *every* year."

Redmond grinned and said, "Dorothy wasn't all that enamored of spring, I guess. But we do have something to look forward to today—Emerson might see June Connor and learn whether or not she saw Duke Hartsfield in Chester's."

"Yes, but that doesn't mean he'll have time to contact us about it today."

"True enough. But I'd like to hear from him today."

"Of course. But I'll be busy with other things. I've got to write to the kids, have lunch with Ellen, buy groceries, and at two I'm meeting with the manager of the University Bookstore."

"Oh?"

Jennifer took a deep breath before saying, "He wants to stock more of my prints, and talk about maybe doing a painting for his office or his home."

"Sounds good."

When they reached 134 Shadowy Lane they were happy to escape the chilled air. They showered, dressed, and prepared their breakfast of oatmeal, eggbeaters, whole-wheat toast, orange juice, and coffee. Jennifer remarked, "This tastes so *very* good . . . simple pleasures, as they say."

Redmond agreed, and then asked, "I was wondering if you planned to share with Ellen what we learned about Lindsey?"

"Absolutely not, Mac. I don't want to be a common gossip any more than Margo's friend, Erin James, does. You know, I'd like to think that Lindsey probably carries some psychological scars and guilt from her escapade with Lydecker."

"You credit her with that much conscience?"

"Sure. She has a fresh start here, and heaven knows there are lots of people that get involved in ill-advised relationships. Those mistakes shouldn't be allowed to dog them all their lives."

"I share your view, sweetheart. As George Costanza or Jerry would say on the old Seinfeld show, we'll put that story *in the vault.*"

"Yeah," Jennifer said with a smile, "We'll vault it."

They filled their day performing required and chosen tasks, and over a simple dinner at home Jennifer shared information about her activities. The most interesting tidbit was that Jim Sampson, the manager of the RU Student Union Bookstore, had been very cordial and encouraging to Jennifer. He said he'd like a new supply of her archival prints—specifically, a dozen of each. Jennifer noted happily, "The initial order was for only six of each print, and he sold all of the DeWitt Cabin ones, and four of the Covered Bridge prints. He figures they'll sell well during Alumni Week this June."

"That's terrific, sweetie."

"I told him of my plans for 'extended scene' paintings of the Beta Bell Campanile and maybe the Wilson Tower Carillon, and he thought those would appeal to alums. He also asked if I could provide a kind of composite painting of the Union—not the front view that's been done in the past, but of the back of the Union, with the fountain and reflecting pool, and the back entrance to the bookstore."

"That would be nice."

"He seems to want something a bit more impressionistic than the almost photographic renderings of campus buildings other artists have favored. And I think he wants a painting for his office."

"I'm sure you said you could provide that," Redmond said with a relaxed smile.

"I suggested I could do some sketches and we could discuss them."

"Good. I suppose you stopped at the Lange and chatted with Ellen a bit about what we did in Flag."

"Yes. And I invited her and Steve to visit us anytime we're there."

"Excellent."

After dinner, Jennifer retired to the family room to read from the volume of Sherlock Holmes novelettes she'd checked out at the Lange earlier in the day. Redmond went to the upstairs office to try to locate a neuropsychological article he'd seen mentioned in the

Columbus Dispatch. He found it quickly. The article reported the latest news about a vaccine aimed at preventing the accumulation of beta-amyloid plaque in the brains of very early stage Alzheimer's cases. He was interested to see that the vaccine had been remarkably effective in preventing plaque formation, but it had not prevented the progression of Alzheimer's disease in the patient sample. So, he mused, beta-amyloid plaque formation is *not* responsible for the impairment the patients suffer. It's disappointing, but it focuses attention on the other chief suspect, the tau tangles within the neurons, as the likely mechanism for the disease. This work has been tremendous, he thought. It suggests the possible efficacy of the vaccine approach utilizing tau tangle material, down the road.

He clicked back to the MSN Homepage, then onto his email site, and found he had no messages. He put the computer to sleep and headed back downstairs.

As he came down the steps he glanced into the family room, and asked, "Would you like a drink of anything, sweetie? I'm going to make some tea."

Without looking up from her reading Jennifer replied, "I'd like a cup of tea, with a little honey, honey." She did look up then, with a smile, and said, "I mean with a little honey, *sweetheart*."

Just as Redmond was retrieving two cups for their teas, the kitchen phone rang. He answered with a simple "Hello," and was pleased to hear Emerson's voice respond, "Hey Mac."

"Hold on a sec, Emerson, so Jen can get on the family room phone," Redmond requested.

They soon heard Jennifer say, "Hi Emerson."

"Hi Jen. I wanted to let you guys know I talked with Johnny Trujillo and June Connor at their homes earlier today. Johnny was very friendly, although he didn't tell me anything I didn't know. June Connor, on the other hand, says she clearly remembers conversing with Duke Hartsfield right after the first set at Chester's. I told her Duke might have some information in relation to a crime, and that I couldn't tell her anything more specific than that. After all, we've got no evidence that he committed a crime, and I wouldn't want to unfairly damage his reputation."

Redmond said, "Right. But was Connor definite about seeing Duke in Chester's?"

"Oh yeah. She remembers he said he was moving to Paris and planned to apply for citizenship. He told Connor he was going to play in the band of an old buddy."

"So," Jennifer responded, "now we know absolutely—Duke *is* the mystery man!"

"Yes. I ask June Connor if she could tell me anything about Duke and what kind of guy he is. She said he's a bit of a womanizer, and that he was often broke because of gambling loses. She recalled one time when Duke was beaten up pretty bad because he couldn't come up with the money he owed someone. It left him in no condition to go on the road with Johnny's band. Johnny had to scramble to find a replacement."

Redmond asked, "So, what's the next step?"

"I've got to try to find Duke Hartsfield. Of course, we don't know that he had any contact with Nizhoni beyond sitting with her that night. But even at that, he could have been the last person to speak with her. We need to talk to him. You never know what you might learn."

"But finding him could be more difficult than it sounds," Jennifer noted.

"Well, Jen, we do know he might have a brother, and maybe some living ex-foster parents in the Detroit area. We can try to locate them, and hope they'll know how to contact him. Getting information about foster-child placements from Child Protective Services is notoriously difficult. Now . . . we might be able to get a check of his passport for activity, although I've heard that could take a long time these days what with the concerns about 'watch lists' and terrorism. It's not like we can argue he's a criminal or a threat to the nation. I'm going to have to ask Sheriff Slater how I should proceed. Since this is a relatively old case and there's no real evidence that Duke's guilty of anything, Slater may not see it as an urgent matter."

"All right, Emerson," Redmond said. "Thanks for letting us know that the mystery man *is* Duke Hartsfield! If you come up with anything, we'd like to hear about it, if that's okay with you."

"Mac, without you and Jen we'd never have known, *for sure*, who the mystery man is. I'll certainly let you know anything we learn that Sheriff Slater says I can tell you."

"Fair enough." Redmond said. "And good luck with your investigation."

"Thanks, guys."

They hung up the phones, and Jennifer exalted, "We were right! Duke is the mystery man!" She added, with evaporating enthusiasm, "That means Duke could have been the killer."

"Well Jen, it's one hell of a big leap from knowing that Duke sat with Nizhoni in Chester's to proving he left with her, maybe accepted a ride from her, stripped, suffocated, and buried her off a Forest Service Road, and then went blithely off to Paris to play music."

Jennifer shuddered. "That's just a whole lot more graphic than I want to hear, Mac."

"Yeah . . . sorry."

They were quiet for ten seconds or so before Jennifer said, "Well, there's nothing we can do to help Emerson any further. It's up to him to find out if Duke is the villain or not."

"That's true. But, you know, hon, Duke just improvises so beautifully on ballads. It's hard for me to believe he could do something so brutal."

"People can be chock-full of contradictions, Mac."

"Sadly, that's the truth."

CHAPTER 36

▼

At four-fifteen on Tuesday afternoon, April seventh, Jennifer had just returned home from uptown Pleasanton. She'd done her stint at Grounds, and she and Eve had met for coffee, scones, and conversation at The Coffee House.

Now she set about assembling the ingredients for the chicken, pasta, and salad dinner she planned for tonight. As was her wont while performing such familiar tasks, she reflected on her day. Quite enjoyable, she judged. She'd received more good feedback regarding the sales of her prints, had been happy to have the opportunity for a pleasant conversation with realtor Tierney Thornhill, at Grounds, and she and Eve had enjoyed their light-hearted get together. Pleasanton *is* pleasant, she thought approvingly. It occurred to her that in only about a month she and Redmond would head off to their Flagstaff home. She smiled to think they now had a vacation home in the pines on Blue Spruce Road, with a great view of The Peaks. She assured herself it wasn't a selfish indulgence, and would allow her time to try her hand at painting western scenes, and attempting to capture the subtleties of the high blue skies, the quality of the light, the feel of space—all different than those of the Midwest. These thoughts aroused an incipient impulse to go look through her book of paintings by southwestern artists, but she dismissed the thought. One thing at a time she told herself, echoing a frequent admonition from her mother. If only I could master the western landscape and its light and textures the way Maynard Dixon did, she thought wistfully.

By seven o'clock she and Redmond had enjoyed their dinners and exchanged accounts of their activities of the day. While putting the dishes in the dishwasher, Redmond said, "Like you, hon, I had a thought or two today about our first full time summer in Flagstaff."

"Oh," Jennifer responded with a hint of feigned concern, "I hope you aren't thinking of hiking the Canyon, or white water rafting through it."

"No, sweetheart. Relax. I was just thinking that I'm going to do pretty much *nothing*. Of course, we'll run, and maybe play some golf or tennis, but outside of that I'm going to just become a townie . . . just enjoy the local culture. And we can take a few short car trips to places that are interesting. I thought maybe a couple of days in Chinle to see the Canyon de Chelly again. And maybe explore some of the more westerly Grand Canyon area."

"Sounds great to me," Jennifer allowed.

"Good. I'm thinking we should spend a lot of time together, just the two of us, doing things we like to do."

"Sounds romantic," she said slowly, while locking eyes with Redmond's, smiling warmly, and tossing her head most perkily.

"According to what I've learned, I'd say you're *flirting* with me, sweetie."

"Congratulations, darling."

They laughed, but before they could say anything further, the kitchen phone rang. Redmond answered it with, "Hello."

"Hello, Mac."

Redmond responded, "Hey, Emerson. What's up?"

"Nizhoni's Cherokee has been found!"

Redmond inhaled sharply before blurting, "I'll be damned! After all these years! Wow! Who found the Jeep? Where was it?"

Jennifer exclaimed, "*Holy Toledo*!" She dashed to the phone in the family room.

"A retired rich guy named Wes Bullock spotted a brief light reflection in the high desert while flying over west-central Nevada, just east of the Mono Lake area of east-central California. Light reflections in that high desert only come from man made objects or materials. Bullock had to be at just the right altitude and angle to see that reflection, and he got a satellite fix on it. The point from which the reflection came is just west of Hawthorne, Nevada, and about a mile and half off an unpaved road named Lucky Boy Pass Road. That spot is about five hundred-sixty miles from Flagstaff. Bullock and a buddy named Don Winert investigated the area where Bullock saw the reflection. They were hoping it might be the crash of Major Armstrong's plane—you know, the Viet Nam War hero that disappeared back in 2004."

"Yeah. Armstrong disappeared on Labor Day of 2004. We read about it, and found it interesting."

"They first checked it out by chopper, but they could only see a strip of shiny blue painted metal between a stony ledge and some boulders in front of the ledge. So, last Saturday they took a Land Rover to the site and discovered the Jeep. It had been pushed off the sloped ledge, smashed against huge, well-grounded and tall boulders, and most of the Jeep bounced back beneath the stone ledge. The elevation there is around eight thousand feet!"

"So the Jeep was smashed up?"

"Oh yeah. When they got to it they found it wasn't Armstrong's little blue and white acrobatics plane, but a blue '97 XJ Jeep Cherokee. There were no plates on it, and the VIN had been removed from the side of the dash. They notified the Mineral County Sheriff's Office of the find. A paper parking tag, the kind you hang on a mirror, was found wedged beneath a carpet edge, under a seat. It was a Humphreys University parking permit."

"*Geez*," Redmond uttered softly.

"They located the VIN number that's stamped into an undercarriage member, and they searched the records for a missing '97 XJ Jeep Cherokee. They found it was Nizhoni's. That Jeep was a big vehicle, with four seats plus a storage area, and it was well equipped to handle the rugged off-road terrain in the area. Tyler Lydecker had used it in his field research in that remote back country, so it was up to the job of getting from Lucky Boy Pass Road to its hiding place."

"That's interesting!" Jennifer commented, and quickly appended, "Hi Emerson. I'm on an extension. I heard what you were saying."

"Hi Jen. It's a surprising development, to put it mildly."

"Is it likely," Redmond asked, "that the forensics folks can find evidence of who drove the Jeep there—fingerprints, or DNA?"

"I don't know, Mac. The Jeep has probably been there since April twenty-first of 2001 or thereabout. The body was smashed down, but I understand it was pretty well protected from water and large animals by being back in what was virtually a cave formed by the ledge and the tall boulders just in front of the ledge. There was no breach of the interior of vehicle. So, we're hoping for evidence from it."

Jennifer offered, "If they can find DNA in the Jeep, maybe some of it could be matched to DNA from Duke's brother to find out if Duke was ever in the Jeep."

"Well, Jen," Emerson responded, "there won't be any problem finding Duke Hartsfield's DNA—skeletal remains in the Jeep appear to be those of Duke Hartsfield".

"Oh no!" Jennifer said.

"Aw, damn!" Redmond exclaimed.

"Afraid so, guys. There was no soft tissue, some skin, hair, and the skull and all of the major bones were there. There were also clothing remnants, including parts of a herringbone pattern sports coat. And they found a small notebook. It contained musical notations, and brief self-reminders or comments by the writer. One of them said, 'Take all small group arrangements, finished and unfinished, to Paris.'"

"Ah man! It's gotta be Duke," Redmond said grimly.

"There's something else. There was a shattered rib bone from both his chest and back, consistent with a bullet to and through his body. No bullet was found. Apparently, he was shot outside the Jeep."

"Poor Duke," Jennifer lamented.

There was a silence of several seconds before Redmond observed, "Now we know the 'mysterious stranger' *wasn't* a vicious murderer. He was just a second victim."

"Yeah," Emerson said. He made a conscious effort to sound upbeat, by adding, "So, we have a better understanding of what happened to Nizhoni and Duke. Somebody took both of them when they came down that alley from Chester's."

"Now," Redmond observed, "you have to wonder if it was Nizhoni *or* Duke the killer was after, because Duke and Nizhoni had no relationship. They were strangers to one another."

"Sounds right to me, Mac." Emerson paused briefly before continuing, "We're still in the dark about a lot of things, but at least we know more than we did. The Reno FBI Resident Agency investigates cases in Mineral County, where the Jeep was found. They're going over it with great care. They're hoping to find at least some 'touch DNA.' A single touch of the skin on a surface leaves hundreds of microscopic skin cells."

"That's good," Redmond commented.

"I'll keep you informed of any developments. News that the Jeep was found is gonna be released to the news media tomorrow."

"We'll keep it to ourselves long after that, Emerson," Redmond said. "We plan to go to Flag around the middle of May and work at getting our new home furnished. We'll be there through most of August. I'll give you our phone number when we get one."

"Okay guys."

"Thanks for all the information," Redmond said.

Redmond walked to the family room and slowly lowered himself onto the sofa beside Jennifer, who said, "Man—Nizhoni *and* Duke. What kind of monster could do that? It just raises more questions about what happened on that April night of 2001. Still I guess it's good news in some sense. It's factual, even though it's horrible. It's a truth." She looked at Redmond and said, "We now know that *both* Nizhoni and Duke were murdered. You were right about Duke not being a killer, Mac."

"Yes, and what was assumed to be a single murder was a double murder. Maybe the most logical theory would be that Duke was the intended victim, and Nizhoni just had the misfortune of being in his company when he was abducted. Since Nizhoni saw the crime, she'd have to be killed, too. Maybe the killer was clever, and wanted it to look like an opportunistic sex killing committed by a wandering serial killer. Maybe he removed all her clothing to make it look that way in case the body should ever be found. It could throw the police off his trail, and disguise the fact that the killer might be an 'enforcer' hired by some gambler Duke had stiffed."

"Or," Jennifer suggested, "a killer hired by Lydecker to get rid of Nizhoni. The killer could have suffocated her, removed her clothes to make it look like a sex crime, buried her, put Duke's body in the cargo area of the Jeep, covered it with a blanket or something, and then driven to a remote Nevada location to dispose of Duke's body and the Jeep . . . and then he could hike out and hitch a ride. Still, its entirely possible Nizhoni *was* the target and that sexual motivation *was* the reason for her abduction. In that case, Duke would have been killed just because he was in the way." She paused, wrinkled her forehead, and asked, "But isn't it just too damned *weird* that Duke's body and the Jeep were driven to *Nevada* to be hidden away?"

"Hell yes! I'd call it extremely weird. Emerson said the site is five hundred and sixty miles from Flagstaff! You'd think that would have been an unnecessary risk for the killer. He could have been stopped by the highway patrol for a traffic violation, a brake light that didn't work, or being in an accident."

"Driving a dead body to the middle of nowhere just doesn't seem to make much sense." She sat briefly silent before conjecturing, "On the other hand, maybe this killer wanted to make Duke appear to be the likely *suspect*. Maybe he was smart enough to figure Duke would be the last person seen with Nizhoni, and if Duke disappeared people would think he must have been Nizhoni's killer. He made Duke *and* the Jeep disappear so detectives would continue to think Duke was out there, without them considering other scenarios. Maybe the killer knew the Jeep was the most dangerous possible clue the cops could find—that it had the potential for yielding fingerprints, DNA, or evidence from some future investigative methodology. Maybe he thought that remote and far away spot, behind boulders and beneath a ledge, was a place the Jeep might *never* be found."

They sat quietly for ten seconds or so before Redmond asked, "So, how many theories have we generated here? Let's say Theory One is that Duke was the targeted victim because of his gambling debts, and Nizhoni was sexually attacked—or not—and then murdered, because she witnessed Duke's killing. And then, Duke was transported way off to Nevada to be hidden away with the Jeep. Let's call it, *The Kill Duke Theory*. The killer would have targeted Duke."

"Theory Two," Jennifer expounded, "holds that Nizhoni was targeted for sexual reasons, and Duke was killed because he was in the way. The killer could have followed her to Chester's, and then, when she and Duke left, followed them to her vehicle. Duke could have been killed in the Jeep or on the Forest Service Road. Then Nizhoni could have been raped, and killed. Let's call it, *The Sex Predator Theory.*"

Redmond said, "And theory three could be that Nizhoni was targeted *by her husband* because he was filled with rage over her divorce demands, so he hired someone to do the murder . . . and poor Duke just happened to be there. We can call that *The Husband Arranged It Theory*. Emerson has always suspected Lydecker could have been behind it."

"With respect to Nizhoni's death, theory three seems the most dreadful to me, Mac."

"It's hard to choose the *most* or th*e least* dreadful, Jen."

"I guess. Still, in the first theory no one was evil enough to *plan* Nizhoni's death. Duke's murder was planned, and the killer followed him to Chester's. But Nizhoni's death would seem to have been determined just by her being there. In the second theory, *The Sex Predator Theory,* her killing could have been determined by fairly short-term circumstances. The killer saw her, wanted her, tracked, abducted, raped, and killed her. Duke was in the way and had to be shot. But in *The Husband Arranged It* theory there would have been a *lot* of planning, the hiring of a killer or killers, a post-killing plan to bury her and get rid of her Jeep—a plan to make it appear she just disappeared from the face of the earth. And if her naked body should ever be found, the crime would look like a sexually motivated murder, and not a murder motivated by intense anger over her aggressive divorce settlement demands."

"It seems your judgment as to the most dreadful scenario takes the view that the theory that includes the most *planning* for Nizhoni's death would be most dreadful."

"Well, it's not that an 'impulsive murder' for sexual thrills or to silence a potential witness to Duke's killing aren't ghoulish, but the careful planning of the killing of Nizhoni Lydecker would require a terribly cold and calculating mind. It's possible her husband could have such a mind. The act of planning shows a corruption of something that should be incorruptible—'Thou shall not kill!' It's murder *aforethought* for Nizhoni. It means applying the analytical and planning powers of the human mind to something really dreadful—the wanton killing of *a spouse*. And while Duke's being with Nizhoni must have been unexpected, the killer was smart enough to make it look like the probable killer was Duke, by making him vanish with the Jeep. It would keep the police looking for Duke, and neglecting to look for the real killer." She paused before asking, "Could Lydecker be that deviant?"

"Well hon, we know that stable minds can lose their stability under sufficient stress, so I'm willing to consider Lydecker a suspect. Theory three is interesting. But maybe it's too elaborate. Maybe you grant the killer more cleverness than he possessed. Perhaps the motive behind these crimes is pretty simple. It could have been to show Duke and other gamblers they have to pay their gambling debts—our theory number one. Nizhoni could have been killed *solely* because she witnessed Duke's killing."

"Well, it's all just theorizing, of course. But if Duke's murder were a punishment for failure to pay his gambling debts, wouldn't it have been better to get Duke when he was alone, and not have to kill a woman he just happened to be walking with?"

Redmond considered the question, and answered, "Yes. That's a damned good point, Jen. If Duke were targeted, the killer could certainly have found some time to get him when he was alone. And that holds true for the killing of Nizhoni, too. If she were a target for murder and not sexual attack, why wouldn't the killer just opt to wait till she was alone?"

"Hmm . . . so maybe the killer wasn't that smart after all. One killing should have sufficed, whether the target was Duke or Nizhoni. And yet, once he made the sick decision to kill them both, he did an effective job of making both bodies disappear."

Redmond sighed wearily as he thought of Nizhoni and the grief her death had brought to her family. Theorizing about murderers was interesting, but it wasn't pleasant. "Well," he said, "we've kicked around a lot of coulda and mighta possibilities. But they don't seem to have gotten us anywhere. Let's just hope Emerson thinks more clearly about this case than we do. Let's hope he solves this double murder soon."

CHAPTER 37

▼

May proved to be a lovely month in Pleasanton. Commencement Weekend came and went at Ravenslake University, and students headed home for the summer. The weather was pleasant, and Jennifer and Redmond enjoyed many activities. They planted a variety of annual flowers, played tennis on the nearby courts behind Swing Hall Dormitory, and took regular twilight walks around the beautiful campus and charming town. Three weeks before they were to leave Pleasanton Jennifer advised Terry Wilson that she and Redmond would be away most of the summer. Terry said he would price the second-hand books over the relatively slow period of the summer months. Redmond made arrangements for the care of their lawn and flower gardens during the time they would be in Northern Arizona.

On Monday, June eighth, Redmond drove their old gray Taurus to the Columbus Airport and parked it in the long-term parking lot. Then they flew to Flagstaff, via Phoenix. At Pulliam Field in Flag they rented a car, and drove to their new home on Blue Spruce Road.

There they immersed themselves in the task of sprucing up and furnishing their new home. The pace of their work was steady, but not pressured. Rooms were professionally painted, and furnishings, including a good music system, were purchased and placed. The twenty by sixteen foot second floor office/studio at the rear of the house was fitted with a new desk and chair, a full complement of computer-related electronics, two storage cabinets for painting supplies, two easels of differing size, and a modest general purpose table with chair. The oversized two-car garage below the office/studio now housed a newly purchased, low mileage, 2007 Mercury Montero.

At nine in the morning of Wednesday, June seventeenth, Redmond was preparing to resume the job he'd worked at for four hours on Tuesday—applying wood preservative to the extensive cedar deck at the back of the house. He popped into the office/studio to tell Jennifer, "I'm going to finish up the deck, hon."

- 172 -

Without looking away from the computer, she replied, "Good, sweetheart. I'm answering the letter I just got from El."

"Oh? What news from the heartland?"

"Hot and muggy."

"I meant like, anything *interesting*?"

Jennifer stopped typing, and replied, "Nothing unusual. Tony, Maria and their boys have gone to Mackinaw Island for three weeks; Eve and Ted are pleased with the ongoing renovation of The Huddle and looking forward to their northern Michigan getaway. Tierney Thornhill and Chip Craddock had a grand wedding at the Methodist Church uptown, and *yes*, El delivered our nice wedding gift to them. Steve and El are looking forward to their touring vacation of northern California and Oregon. And, lets see . . . Langston has gone to Provincetown for the summer, renting a century old ocean-front bungalow, to work on a novel about" . . .

"*The Old Man and the Sea,* perhaps?"

"No, something to do with the hardships of three brothers, two of whom recently returned to Boston after suffering serious wounds in World War I."

"Well, sounds cheery enough, as Langston's historical novels go."

"And, Lindsey escaped Pleasanton to her Oxnard Marina home for the summer, ostensibly to work on a novel, too. She announced her intention of having a *real go* at writing a mystery novel."

"So, old Ravenslake now has dedicated authors working both the Atlantic and Pacific shores, their ears perked for whispers of inspiration within lapping waves and crashing surf, their eyes staring into shifting folds of morning mist in search of haunting spectral characters."

"*Purportedly* working, Mac. Who knows what they're really doing. I expect Langston has found himself a picturesque old tavern for drinking and pontificating to chummy vacationers and colorful local denizens—you know, the famous writer, raconteur, hail fellow well met! And I'd be surprised if Lindsey hasn't hooked an attractive man or two to take out to the Channel Islands for picnics and 'to appreciate nature,' as she might put it. But maybe I'm being unfair. They are, after all, highly committed to their work."

"True. And not to be outdone, I too, am committed to my *painting* work, as mundane as it is, Jen. I think I'll call it, *Preservative on Cedar.*"

By eleven forty-five Jennifer was ready to take a break from the demands of the house by meeting Margo Bailey for lunch. As she prepared to leave she poked her head out the door to the deck and called, "There's a chicken salad sandwich in the fridge, and I put a can of tomato soup in a pan for you, sweetheart. Just heat it up. Coffee's in the pot, and there are brownies in the square Tupperware container."

"Great, hon. Say hello to Margo for me."

By twelve-thirty Redmond had finished his "masterpiece." He resealed the last can of preservative stain he'd used, spent annoyingly longer than expected in cleaning the large brush and thoroughly removing the stickiness from his hands (he had failed in his vow to keep his working gloves on at all times). Then he enjoyed the simple lunch Jennifer left him. He washed and dried the few dishes he'd used, and returned them to the cupboard. He decided to check his emails. While ascending the stairs to the office/studio he softly whistled the theme from his favorite *film noir* classic, 'Laura.' He glanced through the Peaks-side window next to the computer desk, opened it, and inhaled the cool Ponderosa-scented air. Then he seated himself before the new Hewlett Packard computer, got online, and went to his email inbox. The only message of interest was from Emerson. Redmond recalled that the last they'd heard from Emerson was the April seventh call about Nizhoni's Jeep being found. He opened and read the new message:

> Jen and Mac,
>
> I'm figuring you two are in Flag by now. I thought I'd fill you in on the investigation. The Nevada FBI didn't find any useful fingerprints because the steering wheel and doors were wiped clean, and where they did find prints they were what they called "inchoate," that is, partial prints from many people that overlapped other prints. But they did find touch DNA on what appears to have been a new tarpaulin that was apparently used to cover Duke's body during its long drive to Nevada. They got more than enough skin cells to get a DNA profile, but because of the backlog of cases it could be months before they can get to it. The second thing I've learned is that the place where Niz's Jeep was found is within twenty-five miles of the ancient Anasazi site Tyler Lydecker discovered near Walker Lake back in '96. And Niz had told me he spent some of his time there every summer, scouring a wide area around Walker Lake for possible other sites. So, for what it's worth, it would seem Lydecker really knows his way around the area where the Jeep was found.
>
> Regards,
> Emerson

Redmond sent a brief "thanks for the update" note and included his and Jen's new Flagstaff phone number. He pushed back from the desk and swiveled to a position that allowed a view of the Peaks through the open window. His gaze fell on a section of Coconino Pines he knew to be the approximate location where Nizhoni Lydecker's remains were discovered. Redmond found it hard to imagine Lydecker being a killer, but his imagination conjured up Humphrey Bogart as Sam Spade, looking world-weary and haggard, and spitting his words through tensed lips and a haze of cigarette smoke—"Sometimes, sweetheart, it ain't so much a question of who buried the stiff, but *who ordered the hit*." Bogey's pithy aphorism elicited a tense-lipped half-smile from Redmond.

He heard the garage door activate below him. "Jen's home," he muttered. He was eager to tell her of Emerson's news, so he hustled downstairs to greet her. As she exited the short hallway from the garage and entered the family room he asked, "So, how was your lunch with Margo?"

"Well, it was very pleasant."

"Good." He paused only a moment before launching into his news. "We just got an email from Emerson. He wanted to update us on the FBI forensic team's work on Nizhoni's Jeep. They didn't find any usable fingerprints, but they recovered enough touch DNA from a tarpaulin in the Jeep to generate a profile. He says it'll be a good while before they get results."

"Really! That's good news."

"And get this, Jen. The hiding place of the Jeep *is within twenty-five miles* of the ancient Anasazi site Tyler Lydecker discovered—a place he worked every summer after he'd first found it in '96. He combed all over that desolate high mountain desert of west-central Nevada looking for other possible ancient Anasazi sites. He could have known of that cave-like remote place where Nizhoni's Jeep was so well hidden."

Jennifer noted, "We've always speculated he could have bought the crime."

"Yeah. And Bogey thinks so, too." He smiled.

"Been conversing with Bogey about it, have you?"

Redmond laughed. "Bogey says, 'Sometimes, sweetheart, it ain't so much a question of who buried the stiff, but who ordered the hit.'"

"Bogey knows a lot about crimes."

"Yes, he does," Redmond agreed, with a little smile. "And I sent Emerson a 'thanks for the update' message, and gave him our phone number."

"Good! Any soda in the refrigerator?"

"Yes—some bottles of regular Dr. Pepper. I'll get you one and join you in that. We can sit on our deck, but only on the part that's had *two* days to dry. We'll relax while we enjoy the view. I'll pipe some cool jazz out to the deck."

Five minutes later Redmond set two tall glasses of iced soda on the cedar table, and as he did, Jennifer said, "You know, Mac, Lydecker could have been every bit as angry with Nizhoni as she was with him. It makes you wonder."

With Stan Getz's tenor sax providing the dark and haunting Kern-Harback C-minor tune "Yesterdays" for background, Redmond said, "Makes you wonder, all right. Lydecker and his *paramour*, Lindsey Marston, could have partnered up in the crime—long as we're playing detective fantasy. It could have been like in *Double Indemnity*, but without the insurance angle. In this case the murderous spouse, Lydecker, wanted to *protect* his money and his house, whereas in *Double Indemnity* Barbara Stanwyck wanted to *get* money by having Fred McMurray bump off her boring old husband."

Jennifer smiled, and went along, saying, "Lindsey could have partnered with Lydecker because she didn't want Nizhoni tossing her name around to reporters who could cover the Lydecker's divorce, if it went to a trial. She could have told Lydecker he had to protect her identity and not let Nizhoni make public the fact that she was the marriage-busting mistress. And like McMurray and Stanwyck, Lydecker and Lindsey were *hot*" (she put a searing sensuous emphasis on the word, and raised an eyebrow as she said it) "for each other. And they could have felt even closer cause they were both being threatened by Nizhoni."

"So," Redmond proceeded, "Lydecker and Lindsey shadowed the exotic doll to Chester's jazz joint. Lydecker had a key to his old rock climber, so they lets themselves in, hide behind the front seats, and wait for the slinky dish. They ain't figured on her pickin' up a suit in Chester's dive, but when the doll and her pickup slide inta the front seats the thugs know the die is cast—they gotta act. Lydecker plugs Duke, drags Nizhoni into the back seat and shoots her up with knockout serum. Then he finishes off the job with a plastic bag over her head, while his doll drives the Jeep outta the lot and hightails it to the grave they got prepared for their trouble maker."

Jennifer jumped in, "When the deadly duo gets the mouse to the forest they strip her clothes cause they want it to look like a sex crime, not the angry husband/sexy lover killing it is. The doll says, 'It's gonna look like a sex fiend did it—steada us!'"

Redmond responded, "As Lydecker finishes up the spade work he mutters, 'We was smart to pick this spot for the frail. But now we gotta get rid of this here lug she latched onta.' He snaps his fingers as he says, 'Hold on, doll face! I know *just* the place to stash this Jeep and this creep—and it's only a five hundred-sixty mile drive from here!'"

Jennifer stifled a laugh and said, "Now the skirt's eyes flash like lightnin' bolts strikin' out to sizzle right through Lydecker. Her kisser looks like an angry mule's as she spits out, '*Five hundred-sixty miles*? Are you freakin' crazy?'"

Redmond says, "Lydecker chews his lip, then lifts a muddy paw to his mug and rubs doubt away. He smiles that crazed twisted smile that only a life of hard knocks and bein' left dockside by the ship to Easy Street kin chisel into the kisser of a poor sap. He says, 'Yeah, angel—I'm crazy all right—*crazy like a fox*! Cause they ain't no shamus gonna ever get wise ta the hidin' hole I got in mind fer this here Jeep. Not Elliott Ness, not even the Big Guy upstairs is gonna be able ta find where I'll stash this heap.'"

By this point they were both laughing too hard to continue their film noir parody. Gaining control over his chuckling, Redmond said, "Well, of course, this crime isn't funny, really."

"No, it certainly isn't. And our little sketch is so far out. We don't really know Lydecker, but it's a bit of a stretch to think he and Lindsey could even arrange for such things, let alone do them."

"Yeah. But our little sketch was fun, even if a bit gruesome."

"It was, Mac. But enough frivolity! I have to get busy organizing my share of our office/ studio."

"And I have to clean out the storage shed behind the garage. Jim Niyol, the roofer, will be here to replace the patch of missing shingles on the back of the garage tomorrow morning. The extra shingles the Johnson's left us are in the shed, but there are boxes and screens I need to move so Niyol can get to them easily."

"Did you get an estimate from Mr. Nile when he looked at the roof last week?"

"Yes, and I showed him the shingles in the shed. He said they're in good condition, and there are more than needed. He quoted me a price of three hundred-fifty bucks. Very reasonable, I thought. And by the way, his name is Niyol, *N-i-y-o-l*, not Nile. He's Navajo, looks to be in his mid-forties, and seems like a nice guy. He's very sociable, and he likes to chat. He told me he grew up in Ganado, but lives in Flag because that's where the work is. I told him a little about us, as well."

"That's good, sweetheart."

CHAPTER 38

▼

When the doorbell chimed at nine-thirty on Wednesday morning Redmond opened the door and greeted Jim Niyol with a cheery, "Good Morning, Jim."

Jim Niyol, an alert looking lanky man with a rather round face and a thick head of the blackest hair imaginable, smiled and returned Redmond's greeting. He added, "I'm ready to get to work, Mr. McClain. We got a great day for roofin'."

"It's a *perfect* day, Jim. You know the shingles are in the storage shed out back. I cleaned up the shed so you can get to them easily."

"Good. I'll hop right to it."

Redmond closed the door, and went up to the office. He found Jennifer typing away at the computer. When she paused, he asked, "An e-mail to the kids?"

"No, just a short letter for Eve."

"Well, Jim Niyol will be hammering in a bit, hon."

Jennifer slowed her typing just enough to say, "Won't bother me, Mac."

"Okay. I'm going to make a pot of Joe and read yesterday's rag." As he descended the stairs he smiled to think he'd called coffee "Joe" and the newspaper a "rag." Still being influenced by yesterday's *noir* film lingo, he thought. He made the coffee and chose his favorite coffee mug, the one with the figure of Kokopelli, the hump-backed flute playing Hopi kachina. He filled the mug with decaffeinated Highlander Cream coffee. Then he cued up their CD of Samuel Barber's *Adagio for Strings* and *Second Essay for Orchestra*, set the volume very low, boosted the lowest frequency range so as not to lose the low bass, settled into his comfortable armchair, and turned his attention to the paper. And despite the fact he'd had a sound night's sleep, an invigorating run through Cheshire Heights with Jennifer, and a wholesome breakfast, Redmond fell asleep before the *Adagio* was completed, and early into the *Second Essay* he began to dream.

In his dream he and Jen stood in a small clearing within a dense pine forest, admiring a solitary house. "Isn't it beautiful?" Jennifer asked softly.

"Yes. Reminds me of the lovely house in Malibu."

Suddenly the house crumbled before their eyes and dissolved into the ground, with not a vestige of it to be seen. Jennifer lamented, "Oh, how sad! It was such a pretty house."

"How could that happen?" Redmond asked in a bewildered tone.

Jennifer didn't answer the question, but said, "Look Mac, someone's coming through the trees!"

"It's not human, Jen. It's some kind of Navajo shape-shifter. Maybe it's coming to explain how this house disappeared."

Before the spirit could speak, Redmond began to waken in response to the ringing of the doorbell. He oriented himself quickly, removed the newspaper from his chest, and went to the door. On opening it he found Jim Niyol there. Redmond said, "Hey Jim. Finished *already*?"

The roofer smiled apologetically. "No, not yet. It'll be another hour or so. It's just that I forgot to bring any bottled water this morning. I . . ."

Redmond forestalled further explanation, saying, "We've got bottled waters in the refrigerator, and I just made a pot of coffee, too. Which do you prefer?"

"Cold water would be fine."

Redmond brought two bottles of water and gave them to Niyol. "How's the work going?" he asked.

"No problems, Mr. McClain. Bout thirty percent done, and it'll go fast now. Wanna take a look at it?"

"Sure. I need to get out in the fresh air and move around a bit."

They walked to the back of the garage and Redmond surveyed the area of the roof being repaired. "Hey! It looks *real good*, Jim. I can hardly see the difference between the old and new shingles."

"Yeah. And once the new shingles get a bit of weatherin' on em they'll get darker, and blend in perfect."

Niyol took a long swig of water and then gazed across the backyard of the house, and said, "This is a real nice property you got here. The way the land drops away from the back of the house gives your deck elevation, so you can look down on the yard. Real nice," he repeated. He unbuttoned a shirt pocket, removed a pack of cigarettes, and offered one to Redmond.

"No thanks, Jim. It's a habit I never developed."

"Sensible," Niyol assured him. "I'd quit em if I could." He continued, "I gotta take a little break. The ole legs get cramped workin' on an inclined area. And I got a pretty good sweat up. Ya just gotta take breaks in this line ah work."

"I understand."

Niyol was happy Redmond wasn't the type to expect him to take no breaks from the job. He smiled and asked, "So you're gonna be workin' at Humphreys when fall rolls round?"

"Oh no, Jim. My job is at Ravenslake University, back in Ohio. I mentioned to you that I worked at Humphreys, but that was just for a year. I was here on a sabbatical leave in the 1999-2000 school year. This," he motioned to the house, "is just a vacation home for us."

"I see," Niyol said. He took a drag on his cigarette before volunteering, "Well, I always thought HU had a pretty campus. I wished I coulda gone to HU. I didn't have the money . . . but I got a cousin, Gilbert Samm, who graduated from HU. And after he graduated he even started workin' on a master's degree there, but . . . well, he had some trouble with the teacher he worked for. So he dropped outta HU and went down to ASU. He's a teacher now, up at Tuba City High. Doin' real well, so he is."

"Good for him. Too bad he had trouble at Humphreys."

Niyol smiled ambivalently, but then said in a confiding way, "Yeah, damnedest thing, ya know. He was, whadda they call it . . . a graduate assistant, to the teacher he couldn't get along with."

"That's pretty unusual, Jim. Professors are usually nice to students."

Niyol chuckled, and said, "Well, I told him he was just too good-lookin' for his own good. See, this teacher, she kept putting the make on Gilbert. She let him know if he wanted to get his degree he'd better find some time for her—and *regular*, too. He said she was single, real good-lookin', and in her twenties. I told him he was one lucky dude, but Gilbert . . . well, he was a good kid, ya know. He was only twenty-two. He just kinda freaked out. Said he talked, confidential, to some advisor or something at HU bout it. Told the advisor he just wanted to get away and change schools . . . didn't wanna make no trouble."

Redmond found himself interested in Gilbert's problem. He asked, "What was Gilbert's field of study?"

"He wanted to be a high school English teacher. And that's what he is, now. Doing real good."

"Did Gilbert ever mention the name of his good-looking teacher?"

Niyol thought earnestly for a few moments before saying, "Nah . . . never said her name ta me. Didn't wanna make no trouble," he reiterated.

Redmond nodded his approval of Gilbert's decision.

Niyol carefully extinguished his cigarette against a granite outcrop, and slipped the butt into his cigarette pack as he cautioned, "With all these pine needles you got on the ground here, ya gotta be real careful with fire, ya know."

"Absolutely, Jim." But, Redmond thought, you just dropped something seriously incendiary into our backyard, Jim.

When Redmond entered the house Jennifer was in the kitchen pouring a cup of coffee. She looked up and asked cheerily, "How's the roofing going? I haven't heard any pounding for a while. Is Mr. Niyol finished with the work?"

"No, sweetie. It's moving along, but he was taking a needed break, so I *inspected* the work. He's doing a nice job."

"Good."

"Have a chair at the table, Jen. I'll have coffee with you, and I have a bit of a story to tell you. I learned it from Niyol."

"I'm always in the mood for a story."

As he poured his coffee he said, "Good, because I'm dying to tell you this one."

Jennifer's forehead creased in momentary perplexity, but quickly smoothed as Redmond began, "Jim and I chatted a bit after I approved his work. He thought I was going to be teaching at HU. I explained that I worked at HU for one year back at the turn of the century, but that my job is in Ohio, and that this is just a vacation home."

"Like many other nice homes here," Jennifer said a bit defensively.

"He wasn't put off by that, Jen. And he said he thought HU has a nice campus, and he always wished he could have gone to HU. But, he didn't have the money."

"It's unfortunate," she empathized.

"Yes, but he isn't *sad* about that. Anyway, he mentioned that he has a cousin, Gilbert, who graduated from HU . . ."

"That's nice."

"And Gilbert started on a masters degree at HU, but he ran into a problem with the 'teacher' he worked for. Seems his teacher, to quote Niyol, 'put the *make* on' Gilbert and told him if he wanted to get his degree he'd better find regular time for her."

"Good grief! What happened?"

"Well, Jim said Gilbert was 'a good kid,' and only twenty-two. He told Jim the teacher was single, in her twenties, and real good looking. So," Redmond smiled, "Jim told Gilbert he was one lucky dude and shouldn't complain about his good fortune."

"Yuk! Men!"

"But Jim said Gilbert was 'freaked out' by the prof's advances. Gilbert talked to a faculty member about his predicament, but decided to drop out of HU and go to ASU. Gilbert didn't want to cause trouble for the woman. He didn't want to bring a sexual harassment charge against her. He transferred to ASU, got his masters, and now he teaches at Tuba City High." Redmond paused before slowly appending, "He's an *English* teacher."

Jennifer continued to look patiently interested for a few seconds, but then Redmond saw the proverbial light bulb go on over her head. "Good grief, Mac! Do you think it could have been Lindsey Marston?"

"Don't know, but it seems a possibility. As I said, according to Jim, Gilbert talked to some faculty member about his situation. Could that have been Nizhoni? Could she have tried to threaten Lindsey about what certainly sounds like a case of sexual harassment, with serious consequences for the student—Gilbert lost time and money in transferring. And even though Gilbert didn't want to, quote, 'make no trouble,' could Nizhoni have tried to scare Lindsey by threatening her with a sexual harassment complaint? Could she have found it an irresistible way to further badger the woman who'd destroyed her marriage?"

"What a question! Now, we've *got* to tell Emerson about the need to ask Erin James about the harassment case she mentioned to Margo, but refused to detail."

"Right. We'll do that."

Having told Jennifer of his possibly portentous chat with Jim Niyol, Redmond relaxed and took a slug of his coffee. And then he recalled the dream he'd had. He said, "You know sweetie, just before Jim came to the house I fell asleep listening to the *Adagio for Strings*."

"Well, it's hypnotic and beautiful." She tossed a teasing smile his way, and added, "And maybe I taxed you too much on our run this morning—or last night."

"Probably both, hon. But when I fell asleep, I had a dream."

"Oh?" She had often found Redmond's dreams unusual and interesting.

"Yes. In my dream you and I were in a dense pine forest."

"Coconino or Ponderosa?"

"Just *generic* pines; but they were all around us, as far as the eye could see. And there was a house, the *only* house in the entire forest, and we were looking at it. You commented on how beautiful it was, and I agreed. I said it reminded me of the lovely house we saw in Malibu—*of all places*!"

"I see. Go on." She took a small sip of coffee.

"And all of a sudden the house just sank into the ground and *totally* disappeared. You said, 'How sad. It was such a pretty house.' And I asked, 'How could that have happened?'"

"Interesting," she commented.

"And you said, 'Look at the trees. Someone's coming through them.' It was some kind of diaphanous *something*."

"How exciting!"

"I said, very calmly, 'It's not human, Jen. It's some kind of Navajo shape-shifter. Maybe it's going to explain why this house disappeared into the ground.'" After a slight pause, Redmond concluded, "And that was pretty much all of the dream, because Jim Niyol rang the doorbell and woke me up."

"Well, that's a very interesting dream, Mac! Would you like me to interpret it for you?" she asked with a subtle smile that Redmond found captivating.

He looked into her eyes and chuckled. "You know I don't believe in Freudian dream interpretation. It was just an interesting and bizarre sort of dream. Still . . . I'd like to hear your 'interpretation.'"

"Well, as I recall, Freud said that houses, or any types of enclosures, were very often symbols of females. So, when you and I commented on how pretty the house was, we were speaking of a pretty woman."

"Okay."

"And *further*, of course . . . I *must* conjecture," she said as she slipped into the oddly accented speech pattern the late actor Jeremy Brett used when portraying Sherlock Holmes, "that the house *represented*—Nizhoni Lydecker!"

Redmond displayed only the briefest minimal smile and hint of a raised left eyebrow. He didn't want to interfere with Jen's Sherlockian performance.

"You see, in your dream I said the house was beautiful, and you agreed. And you added that the house looked like the lovely one we saw in *Malibu*. Perhaps you were saying Nizhoni resembled Jennifer Jones, the actress, and you may *associate* Malibu with famous actresses, for there are many movie stars with homes there."

"Ah, this is good, Jen," he smilingly assured her.

"But then the house disappeared into the ground, just as Nizhoni had disappeared beneath the pines. I said it was sad, and that the house had been so pretty. And you asked how the disappearance of the house could have happened. Then you saw a Navajo shape-shifter, a spirit capable of transforming itself into animal and human forms, and also capable of informing, *or* deceiving, humans. You said to me, 'Maybe it's going to explain why this house disappeared.' That was an element about your *wish* to know what happened to Nizhoni. And then, in wakeful reality, Jim Niyol, a *Navajo*, though probably not a shape shifter, told you a story about his cousin Gilbert, a story that might, to some extent, explain why Nizhoni disappeared. You see, Mac, it may even have been a prophetic dream."

Redmond laughed heartily, slapped his hands on his thighs, and said, "Damned good, Jen! Really good! You could make a living of dream interpretation. We could set you up in a little shop on North Humphreys, next to the Palm Reader's place there. I don't believe in prophetic dreams or other supernatural events or processes, of course, but I do believe in your ability to weave a credible scenario out of odd information."

She smiled and asked, "So, you think my interpretation was pretty good?"

"Oh yeah! It has logic to it, hon. I certainly credit your cleverness. In fact, I think Sigmund Freud himself would probably endorse your interpretation, except maybe for the prophetic idea. Sigmund wasn't big on supernatural stuff, either."

"Well, alright then," she said with a satisfied smile. "If Freud could endorse my interpretation I have to be happy with that. But, I must say your interesting dream is less compelling than Jim Niyol's story. Could Gilbert Samm have told Nizhoni about his harassment by Lindsey Marston? The story raises the possibility that Nizhoni could have had a valid reason for threatening Lindsey with a sexual harassment charge. It makes me wonder if our playful takeoff on *Double Indemnity* yesterday could have some truth to it. Even if Nizhoni threatened Lindsey just for the satisfaction of frightening *the other woman*, and without any intention of actually encouraging Gilbert Samm to lodge a complaint, Lindsey could have felt very abused by the threat. And she's not someone who'd willingly suffer abuse."

"Yes, but I can't imagine Lindsey finding such abuse a sufficient motive for having Nizhoni murdered. I have to believe Duke and Nizhoni were killed by people who were after Duke—our 'Kill Duke Theory.'"

"Possibly, Mac. But sexual harassment could have been a very potent threat to Lindsey. I told you how she said, at the Alexander House, 'If for some reason I couldn't teach and write, my life wouldn't be worth living.' She said it with such a stark sense of finality, as if it were a vow, or a threat. I was startled. Maybe it was a thought she'd had in relation to Nizhoni's badgering. Lindsey could have imagined that a sexual harassment complaint would leave her disgraced and reviled. She could have felt that even if she weren't fired, she'd be devalued, warned, and put on some sort of watch list like an unworthy second class academic. And don't forget, Lindsey could have put a lot of pressure on Lydecker to protect her from being exposed as the other woman in Nizhoni's threatened lawsuit, and that in turn, could have put Tyler under pressure to surrender his house—or to help get rid of Nizhoni. Could Lindsey have been angry enough to feel Nizhoni had to be killed? I can picture Bette Davis making such a cold and imperious decision, and I can imagine Lindsey Marston doing the same thing. She's a woman that goes after what she wants, as when she said, in relation to Chris Marston, 'I decided that I wanted him, and I got what I wanted.' Maybe she had that same decisiveness when it came to wanting Lydecker, and wanting her graduate assistant. She's a very wealthy woman, and a somewhat offbeat and adventuresome one. She has an air of entitlement. And it would require a great sense of entitlement to go after Nizhoni's husband, and a young grad assistant. And maybe, to go *at* a vengeful tormentor, to boot."

Redmond sat, silently considering Jennifer's thesis regarding Lindsey, while Jennifer patiently awaited his response. Finally, he said, "That's a momentous formulation, Jen; and it's an alternative to the hypothesis that Duke was the intended victim. But we have no definitive evidence that Lindsey was, in fact, the professor that demanded a sexual relationship of Niyol's cousin. And, come to think of it, Emerson isn't even aware that it was Lindsey who was Lydecker's illicit lover; and apparently, he doesn't know about Nizhoni's possible sexual harassment complaint that Erin James, in an unguarded moment, mentioned, but would not explain, to Margo."

Jennifer nodded agreement. "Emerson needs to interview Erin. And Erin needs to understand the possible importance of information she's been reluctant to reveal. Let's give Emerson a call."

CHAPTER 39

▼

At nine-fifty on the morning of Wednesday, June seventeenth, Emerson Yazzie phoned the McClains. Redmond answered, and Emerson said, "Hey Mac, I thought you'd like to know what I found out from Erin James and Gilbert Samm."

"Yes, of course, Emerson."

"I spoke with Professor James in her office on Tuesday. I learned she was definitely a friend of Niz and that Niz felt comfortable confiding in her at times, and letting a little steam off. As you suggested last Thursday, Lindsey Marston *was* the woman Niz blamed for the breakup of her marriage. And Professor James knew quite a bit about the possible harassment complaint against Lindsey Marston. It did concern the student, Gilbert Samm. Niz was the faculty adviser to the Navajo Student Club at Humphreys, and Gilbert had been president of the club when he was an undergrad. And, in addition to that, he's from Many Farms, Niz's hometown."

"I see. That explains why he could have chosen to take his problem to Nizhoni."

"When I told Professor James I'd learned that the complaint concerned Gilbert Samm, she reluctantly opened up and told me what she knew about it. Apparently, Gilbert was very distressed about the harassment and sought Niz out. According to Professor James, Niz was outraged about Gilbert's situation and she and Marston had a stormy confrontation over it in Marston's office—but then Gilbert told Niz he was planning to drop out of school, and wanted to go to ASU. He asked Niz not to file any harassment charges against Marston. Now, this was all contemporaneous with Niz's divorce action against Lydecker. So, maybe she wanted to threaten Marston with the harassment complaint partly out of her anger over the relationship Marston had with her husband. She sure as hell couldn't have had any respect for the woman."

Emerson paused briefly before noting, "This Marston babe . . . er, professor, obviously had an eye for men. She didn't mind going after a married man and a young masters program student, and, perhaps other men we don't know about."

Redmond couldn't disagree. "Yeah. She's still a flirty woman who knows, and rather revels in the fact, that she can turn men on. And you couldn't blame Nizhoni for wanting to give Lindsey some anxiety about the Gilbert episode. Had Nizhoni lived, she may well have started some kind of action against Lindsey, within the university. You know Emerson, reporting blatant sexual harassment is something academics now regard as an ethical requirement once they learn of it. Although there was no terribly blatant sexual exploitation of her student, some expression of concern or even a stern reprimand would have been in order. That reprimand could have gone into her personnel file in the Arts and Sciences dean's office."

Emerson conjectured, "So, Niz may have been happy to have something on this Marston woman, over and above her personal beef with her. And you're saying Niz would have been expected to report it to, like a dean?"

"Yes, or maybe to Lindsey's department chair, who might then report it to the dean of Arts and Sciences."

"I see. Niz had information that this Marston woman had clearly crossed the line with Gilbert Samm. She had every reason to feel she should report it, then?"

"No question." Redmond paused before asking, "You got corroboration from Gilbert?"

"Oh yeah. I drove up to Tuba City yesterday to talk to him. He confirmed the harassment, but said it had done him no permanent harm. She had told him if he wanted to have her sponsor his M. A. thesis he'd better be 'friendly' with her. And Gilbert told me Marston did more than just talk sexy to him. She put her hands on him, very inappropriately, and that's when he went to talk to Niz."

"*Well!* That would have made a harassment charge more compelling, for sure."

"It caused Gilbert to transfer to ASU, and it cost him both time and money in getting his M.A. Fortunately, he says he really liked ASU and he's doing fine. He's a popular teacher at Tuba City High."

"Nice to know he's doing well."

"I owe you and Jen a lot for putting me onto this. If nothing else, it tells me more about what was going on in Niz's world at that time. It makes me wonder if Lindsey Marston could have been involved in what happened to Niz. And Lydecker really knew the high desert territory where the Jeep was hidden." Emerson realized he was beginning to contemplate Marston and Lydecker being together in more than just their affair. He asked, "You see where I'm going here, Mac? Does this all sound, you know . . . too far out?"

"Well, it's hard to imagine that Lindsey could be involved in murder. Still, Jen and I recently kicked that idea around in wondering about the case. We playfully imagined Lindsey and Lydecker as involved in the crime as part of a little take-off on an old *film noir* type movie plot, roughly like in *Double Indemnity*. It was just a screwball fun thing. We sometimes do whacky things like that for amusement, when we're trying to figure something out."

"Well, you guys have contributed to the solution of several murders. Maybe Vella and I should develop that kind of pastime!"

"It can be fun," Redmond allowed. "It can generate some laughs, if nothing else."

"Can you tell me a little about this Marston woman? Do people in Pleasanton like her?"

"I'd have to say they do. She's regarded as a good addition to the faculty and has established a solid reputation as an excellent teacher, particularly among her female students. She's written some influential books in her field. She's sociable, and, yes, she does seem to like men—she's gone through a few in the year she's been at Ravenslake, but she's restricted herself to single and mature men far as I know. Let's see . . . what else? She probably gets some good income from her books, including the ones she wrote with her late husband, Christopher Marston. He taught at HU along with Lindsey for a time. He was a very successful writer. He was killed in a car accident in Germany back in 1998." Redmond paused briefly, then continued, "And, additionally, she has very considerable inherited wealth. Her father owned an international paper and forestry company, and when he died she inherited the business. She then sold it to a group of her dad's major executives, and she apparently has done well by the fortune she got for it. I'm sure she'd have made good investments."

"Some people have all the breaks, don't they?"

"Well Emerson, Lindsey's father *also* owned a successful hotel-casino in Reno."

"Really!"

"But as it turned out, her dad didn't leave the hotel-casino to Lindsey. He willed it to a very young man who'd been managing it—a man named Dominic Gambrino."

"The guy that owns the *Babylonian Gardens* in Vegas?"

"That's the guy."

"This woman's dad must have had the Midas touch," he observed. "But I gotta get to a meeting, Mac. Again, thanks for the lead, and give my thanks to Jen, too."

"Okay. We appreciate the update."

Redmond headed upstairs to the office to relate the news to Jennifer. As he came into the room Jennifer swiveled around from the computer and asked, "Who called?"

"It was Emerson."

"Oh good! What'd he say?"

Redmond then conveyed, with no interruptions other than Jennifer's several single word condemnations of Lindsey Marston, all of Emerson's new information.

She said scornfully, "It's clear that Lindsey engaged in egregious sexual harassment of Gilbert Samm. Margo thought Erin had hinted about *a man* that sexually harassed Nizhoni, but it was actually a case of Nizhoni threatening Lindsey with the harassment complaint *on behalf* of Gilbert Samm." She pursed her lips, pushed her hair back from her face, and conjectured, "Let's suppose Nizhoni was appropriately principled about Lindsey's misbehavior and felt an ethical responsibility to bring it to the attention of someone up the administrative ladder. Suppose further, that when Nizhoni had her 'stormy confrontation' with Lindsey she laid down some heavy threats in relation to the misbehavior toward Gilbert." With an air of inspiration, Jennifer proposed, "Maybe the university president or the dean of A&S was out of town for a time, and Nizhoni made it clear she intended to inform him of Lindsey's misbehavior as soon as he returned. *That* could explain why the killer didn't wait until he could get Nizhoni alone. Maybe there was a deadline, and time was running out. So it had to be done *now*."

"Well, that's interesting, sweetie. The time's running out postulate would strengthen our Theory Four—the *Vengeful Woman Theory*. It's a stronger scenario with that. And Theory Four could be relabeled the *Fearful and Vengeful Woman Theory.*"

Jennifer was pleased with her new 'postulate.' She felt she was on a roll, and continued, "So, suppose the president, or dean, is due back at HU on Monday, April twenty-second. What might she do?"

Redmond considered the question for no more than three seconds before answering, "Maybe she'd call Fred McMurray . . . I mean, Tyler Lydecker, and say, 'Ty, we gotta get rid of that trouble-making Nizhoni *now*. Time's runnin' out.'"

His answer was rejected. "No, I don't think so. Maybe she'd call Dominic Gambrino, the man who owed his fortune to her family. Maybe she'd want a referral to someone who could end Nizhoni's abuse, and fully punish her for having the colossal gall to threaten the daughter of Ellis Lavery!"

Jennifer's twist took Redmond by surprise. "That's getting a bit away from classic *film noir*, hon—closer to *The Godfather*. But there *does* seem to be a flavor of mobsters and Vegas and gambling problems being somehow involved in the deaths of Nizhoni and Duke. You could be onto something."

"Still, Mac, while there's no question that Lindsey has been smarmy, it's hard to believe she could be murderously evil—or that a prominent guy like Dominic Gambrino maintains a stable of deadly thugs to loan out to ex-girlfriends."

"But Jen, Lindsey isn't just a possible ex-girlfriend of Gambrino. She's the only child of the man who just outright *gave* Gambrino the Silver Castle in Reno and launched him on a fabulously successful career—the man who gifted him, at a rather tender age, the instrument that secured his success in life. Maybe there's a deep sense of gratitude and loyalty there. Maybe in addition to his personal history with Lindsey, there actually is a protective sense of *family*."

"You really think so?"

"It's possible."

"So, you think Gambrino might recommend a killer to get rid of Nizhoni?"

Redmond looked uncertain. "You know sweetie, it sounds so harsh and unlikely when you put it that way. But somebody brutally killed Nizhoni Lydecker and Duke Hartsfield. You have to wonder who could have wanted her or him dead—wanted it so much they arranged for it. Someone had to have a strong enough motive to decide that Nizhoni or Duke *had to be* killed. And, except for the hypothetical gambler of Theory One, and the sex psychopath of Theory Two, it's difficult to imagine that our other three suspects, namely, Lydecker, Lindsey, and Joshua Usher, could be killers."

Jennifer wondered, "Do you suppose a faithful follower of The Prophet could have found the 'mistreatment' of the Prophet's son a reason to actually kill Nizhoni?"

"Man! It's mind-blowing to think that, Jen, but, hell—who knows?" He paused briefly before suggesting, "Just out of curiosity, let's see what we can learn about the House of the Ascension."

"Right," Jennifer said. She swiveled her chair back around to the computer, and typed, "Jimmy Usher's House of the Ascension near Lake Havasu City," into the Google Search box. The very first item to appear was Usher's website, The House of the Ascension Settlement. On the opening page there was a photo of Jimmy Usher gazing super-compassionately at the viewer. He looked to be a robust mid-fifties man of western European ancestry. Redmond and Jennifer read materials from the website with interest. These described the settlement and its history. Usher started it in May of 1994, with just seven people from two families. By 2008 it boasted a community of one hundred and twenty-eight members from thirty-eight families.

Redmond and Jennifer were impressed by the quality of the website. There were extensive written materials, including advertisements for two older books authored by Usher, both described as "best sellers," and a third book, *The Coming Apocalypse and Salvation,* soon to be published. Some color photos of the settlement were included. There were photographs of the original small "Worship Building," hardly more than a shed, on the grounds; and there were five other buildings, including a substantial and attractive dormitory and a modest, but new schoolhouse. A trend for newer and larger buildings on the settlement suggested a trajectory of increasing affluence for the sect.

Having finished reading the half page devoted to characterizing the purpose of the settlement, Redmond commented, "It's strange to me, Jen, that these people have put so much of their money and energy into a place that's just the waiting station, as it were, for The Rapture. It's like they'll be at the station waiting for *The Twenty-first Century Rapture*, and the Rapture sounds like a space ship bound for heaven."

"Reminds me of *Porgy and Bess*—the song that goes" (here Jennifer softly sang and perfectly hit all eighteen notes of the fourteen word phrase), "Oh, the train is at the station and it's headin' for the Promised Land."

"Hey, sweetie! You sang that really well . . . but, unlike the folks on Catfish Row, in this case only those that have their tickets punched by the Prophet get to go."

Jennifer clicked on other results for "Jimmy Usher." They showed him to be an active preacher who gave sermons in a number of small and medium sized cities. But on the second page of the listing of materials containing the words "Jimmy Usher," there was one that jolted Jennifer. It was the opening lines of a September twenty-sixth, 1988, article from the Tonopah

Sentinel Tribune. It reported the arrest of the Reverend Jimmy Usher for having shot a physician named Phillip Webster, outside the town's Family Planning and Medical Services Building.

"Good grief, Mac! Look at this."

They read the article silently, and when both had finished, Jennifer said, "Well! Usher and a group of followers had been harassing this clinic and damning this particular doctor for 'murdering God's unborn children.'"

Redmond said, "And Dr. Webster was coming to work, walking the gauntlet of so-called righteous fundamentalists, when Usher whipped out a pistol and shot him. The bullet hit Webster in the left thigh, and it sounds like Usher came up to him and could have been preparing to finish the doctor off when the male nurse, Ted Martin, flattened Usher and got the gun from him."

"This is very interesting, Mac." Jennifer clicked back to the listing of items and ran through half of the next page before finding one reporting a judge's sentencing of Usher to prison. She clicked on the article and they read it. Redmond said, "So, Usher was charged with assault *with* a weapon—a first-degree manslaughter offense. The defense argued that Usher hadn't meant to wound or kill the doctor, and had meant only to frighten him. They claimed the doctor was wounded only because Usher was a man of peace and unaccustomed to handling guns. And they tried hard to paint the doctor as an evil abortionist."

"Even though," Jennifer noted, "the doctor had never performed an abortion at that particular clinic."

"And even though abortion is legal in America. The prosecution argued that Usher intended to kill the doctor, had guns in his home, and the only thing that kept Usher from killing him was the heroic action of the male nurse."

"Martin was a brave guy," Redmond observed.

"The jury came in with a guilty verdict and the judge sentenced Usher to six years," Jennifer noted.

She soon found a later brief article reporting Usher's release from The Nevada State Prison in Carson City. She skimmed the article, noting along the way, "He was released in February of '94, having served just five years of his six year sentence. The parole panel took into consideration the fact that he'd organized a bible study group for prisoners, and was considered a model prisoner. Apparently, he left Tonopah shortly after his release and moved to the site near Lake Havasu City. And we know he started the House of the Ascension settlement there in May of '94."

She printed out the relevant articles and put them in a file she labeled, "The Prophet." Then she and Redmond went down to the kitchen to make a pot of English Tea Time black tea. They busied themselves with the tea preparation and delayed discussing the things that'd learned. When the tea was brewed and Jennifer filled their cups, they moved to the back deck and seated themselves at the table.

Redmond leaned back in his chair and savored a welcome swig of his favorite tea before saying, "According to Margo, some people wrote letters to the *Daily Sun* in support of Joshua Usher. I wonder if any of them expressed outrage against Nizhoni's teaching 'atheism,' as Joshua put it. We could run by the *Daily Sun* and check on that."

"Okay, I'm up for that. Let's grab a quick lunch at *La Bellavia*, and drop by the *Daily Sun* after that, hon."

"Let's."

*   *   *

At three-fifteen Redmond steered the Montero north on Humphreys as he said, "Searching through those old copies of the *Daily Sun* was tedious and hard on the eyes, but we found what we were looking for."

"We did," Jennifer said. "But, there were only five letters to the editor for the three weeks following Usher's talk. And the letter writers weren't terribly angry with Nizhoni, although several of them suggested that astronomy and biology courses should include creationism."

"Well, Jen, it's always possible that someone who didn't write a letter could have been 'terribly angry' and done the crime."

"Right. But the only person we *know* to have been really angered by Nizhoni's teachings was Joshua Usher. And Joshua's father has a history that shows he can get worked up enough to shoot those he defines as servants of the Anti-Christ. So, now our list of suspects starts with a gangster who was after Duke. Then there are five others, all with conceivable motives for going after Nizhoni: a sex psychopath, Tyler Lydecker, Lindsey Marston, Joshua, and the prophet; and, as in our little *film noir* script of yesterday, Lydecker and Lindsey could have been a team. But our 'script' was just fantasy, and it isn't clear how we could find real support for any of our theories."

"Well, Jen, we've imagined lots of suspects, but we have absolutely no evidence. I think we've devoted quite enough time to this tragedy for one day! What say we think of something more pleasant?"

"I'm with you on that! Actually, this ole gal is plumb thought weary on the topic of murder." Her manner brightened as more appealing thoughts presented themselves. "I've been thinking we could plan a few of our little trips around northern Arizona, and maybe southern California."

"Yeah! That sure sounds good to me."

CHAPTER 40

▼

At nine-forty on Tuesday, August eleventh, Emerson Yazzie sat in his austere little office, casually perusing the old file of his and Chief Hansen's April, 2001 interview of Joshua Usher. Joshua had been painfully nervous and uncertain when questioned about his activities ten days after the abduction. Joshua said that on the night in question he ate late, and alone, at the Lumberjack Pizza shop, less than a block north of The Wexford. He said that while he waited for the traffic light at North Leroux and East Aspen to turn green, he saw Dr. Lydecker turning down the alley next to the hotel. Asked if he saw a man accompanying Dr. Lydecker, he said he didn't, but that it was possible she could have been with a man who had turned the corner a step ahead of her. He said he was disappointed to see Professor Lydecker turn down the alley because it was part of his shortcut to his dorm, and because of the rain, he didn't want to take the longer route. Instead, he said, he ducked into the Wexford lobby for a minute or two because he didn't want to overtake them and have to exchange a "hello" with her. Finally, Joshua said that by the time the lot came into his view the Jeep was exiting the lot behind the Wexford.

Emerson had always felt that Joshua was truthful in the interview. Joshua had been just eighteen years old and out of his depth at HU. He had felt compelled to challenge a professor, and that brought him a lot of attention he didn't welcome. Emerson never really considered Joshua a suspect in the disappearance of Nizhoni, and during the ensuing years he'd occasionally wondered how Joshua's life had progressed after his painful interaction with the wider world of HU, and the city of Flagstaff. As he turned these thoughts over he told himself it might be somehow informative to contact Joshua; but he knew he was really just curious as to how Joshua's life had unfolded since he left HU. Emerson had a secretary find the phone number of the House of the Ascension, and when she supplied it he placed the call. He asked to speak with Joshua Usher, and was promptly connected with "Mr. Usher."

The voice at the other end of the connection said, "This is Joshua Usher."

Emerson responded pleasantly, "Hello Joshua. This is Detective Emerson Yazzie, in Flagstaff."

There was a slight delay before Joshua replied, "Good morning! It's been a long time since I heard your voice, Detective Yazzie, but I do recognize it." He asked cordially, "How are you?"

"I'm fine, thank you. I was just filing away notes from some of my old cases, including those from our conversation back in 2001, and it made me curious as to how you are these days. I've wondered about you from time to time, hoping you're doing okay. I know it was a pretty traumatic experience for you at that time, and I imagine you've thought about it now and then."

"It's very Christian of you to have thought of me, Detective Yazzie. I've been very busy since I left Humphreys University. Our precious settlement has grown abundantly. We've just begun a big construction project—a new group of townhouses for our people. I have a lot of responsibility connected to that right now."

"Well," Emerson said in a relaxed and unhurried voice, "it sounds like you and your settlement are doing well."

"It is so—praise the Lord. Our new Seventh Seal Complex will be the third construction project we've built in the past six years."

"Your settlement sounds very prosperous."

"Well, we don't covet monetary success, Detective Yazzie. We're grateful for what the Lord decrees we should receive. All of our people donate money regularly, and The Prophet donates the money from his best selling books. And the Lord gave us a blessed donor that helped us with the costs of construction on the new complex." Joshua mentioned the name of the donor, and then quickly added, "We are mostly self-sustaining."

Emerson sensed a hint of nervousness in Joshua's voice and concluded that perhaps the young man, in his eagerness to impress, had violated a settlement rule against revealing donor's names. Emerson said, "It's good that you have so many resources."

"Well, Detective Yazzie, we are *blessed*. And I'm preparing myself to lead our flock in the event anything should happen to our Prophet before The End of Days." He appended, "Lord protect him."

"Is your father well?"

"Bless you for asking after his health. The Prophet is at the Seattle Clinic right now for his annual check-up. We're all praying that he'll get a clean bill of health. The Lord does protect and look after him. He's very vigorous and labors mightily for our settlement. He still has his famous memory ability and optimism. He can recite every word of the *Book of Revelation* and the works of the other prophets. In fact, he can recite any sermon he's ever heard, if it's one he wants to remember. The Lord endowed him with that special gift that he might better serve his flock. And he has a new book out, *The Coming Apocalypse and Salvation*. He'll be on a nation-wide speaking and book tour in two weeks."

"Well, that's very impressive, Joshua. Now, I just had one thing from our 2001 conversation I needed to check, just to make sure I got it right before I file these old papers away."

"I see."

"Do you remember the night of April twentieth, 2001? That was the night Professor Lydecker went to Chester's, and disappeared."

"Yes, I know. It was all so shocking. I remember that I left The Lumberjack Pizza shop late that night. When I crossed East Aspen and came to the door of the Wexford I saw Dr. Lydecker ahead of me. I saw her turn the corner of the building and head down the alley. I was disappointed to see her going down the alley by the hotel because that was the short cut I used to get back to my dorm, especially if it was raining hard. I ducked into the Wexford for a minute or two because . . . well, I didn't want to overtake Dr. Lydecker and have to speak to her. Looking back on it, I feel a bit guilty about that, because maybe if I hadn't felt that way I could have prevented what happened."

"I understand," Emerson said. "My notes say that you told us you didn't see a man with Dr. Lydecker, but that the man could have made the turn around the corner a step ahead of Dr. Lydecker."

"Yes. That's right."

"So what happened next?"

"When I went back out and headed down the alley to where the parking lot came into view I saw Dr. Lydecker's Jeep leaving the lot."

"So you don't know what might have happened to Dr. Lydecker during that minute or two while you were in the Wexford lobby and then walking down the alley?"

"No. When the lot came into my view her Jeep was leaving the lot."

"I see."

Joshua was silent for five seconds or so before saying, "And yet, I've *dreamed* of watching them from the corner of the Wexford. But the dreams aren't always the same. Sometimes I dream that when Dr. Lydecker goes to her Jeep, two men jump out of it. One man steps out on the passenger side, and he has a gun. He pushes Dr. Lydecker's friend into the front seat, and I hear her friend say the word 'money,' but I don't hear other words I can understand. Then the other man, on the other side of the Jeep, pushes Dr. Lydecker into the back seat and I imagine he hits her and pushes her over so he can get in. In my dreams, I sometimes hear her . . . scream."

Emerson heard the catch in Joshua's voice on the word "scream." He said, "But you didn't actually see or hear any of the things you dream?"

"No, I didn't—that's just in a dream. In reality, I'm sure that by the time I could see the parking lot, the Jeep was already turning onto East Aspen. But I've had so many dreams, or parts of dreams, about it."

"So, in your dreams you think there were two men who attacked Dr. Lydecker *and* her companion?"

"Sometimes I dream that. I read about the man that was seated with Dr. Lydecker at Chester's, and I guess that's why the man is in some of my dreams. I know that on that real night, Dr. Lydecker's Jeep was leaving the lot when I first saw it. It's just that my dreams have extra things that I know didn't happen. I always hope I never dream anything like it again, but the dreams still come sometimes."

"Okay, Joshua. I understand. It was a terrible thing." Emerson surmised, once again, that Joshua didn't really know what had unfolded in that dark and rainy space behind the Wexford. His recollections were just an uncertain mix of dreams and the now well-known fact that Nizhoni and her male companion were abducted in her vehicle. There was nothing substantially different from what Joshua had said back in his 2001 interview, except that he now had a collection of dreams to deal with. He had said, back then, that all he saw was Nizhoni's Jeep leaving the lot, and he still feels that was the simple realty.

They said their goodbyes. Emerson was pleased that Joshua sounded so much more confident than he had eight years earlier, and that his father's settlement was doing well. Emerson wasn't religious, but he accepted the fact that many people turn in that direction as they try, in a rather simple way, to make sense of the world.

His mind returned to the inscrutable mystery of that April night of 2001. The new information about Lindsey Marston and her several entanglements with Nizhoni are interesting, he mused. I owe Jen and Mac for putting me onto that. Come to think of it, I haven't seen them since March tenth! That's when they told me about June Connor, and Connor absolutely nailed down the identification of Duke Hartsfield as the mystery man. So, I owe them for that, as well. I'll give them a call and see if they'd like to meet for a drink or two after work today, and the drinks will be on me. And I've got a bit of news for them.

*   *   *

At five-fifteen the McClains and Emerson Yazzie arrived simultaneously at the Half Moon Saloon parking lot on South Beaver Street. As he got out of the car Redmond smilingly called to Emerson, "When we say five-fifteen, we three are damned serious about it."

"Yes. Hopelessly *compulsive* people, some would say," Emerson jested.

The Half Moon was only moderately busy. They chose a table in an unoccupied area, and Emerson informed his friends that the drinks were on him as deserved rewards for Mac and Jen's work on the Nizhoni case. They ordered beers and pretzels, and chatted briefly about the McClain's progress in getting their new home furnished. Redmond also mentioned the various places they'd visited over the past month.

"Well, that's one of the nice things about Flag," Emerson noted. "There are a lot of spectacular places to visit, all within a day's drive."

"There sure are," Redmond said. After a brief pause he asked, "Any news about the DNA analysis?"

To the McClain's surprise, Emerson said, "Well, as a matter of fact, there is. But the information isn't being released, so I have to tell you now, this is *absolutely* confidential. You can't share it with *anybody*."

"There's no one we would share it with . . . word of honor," Redmond said.

"Ditto," Jennifer assured.

"Well, the Nevada FBI forensics unit found some touch DNA on the inside of the front doors and dashboard, but it was all mixed up. It's from lots of people, so, like the fingerprints they found, it's contaminated."

"Too bad," Redmond offered.

"Yeah—*but*, they did get the DNA of two people from a tarp, people that must have pulled the rough-textured canvas over Duke's body for its drive to Nevada. The tarp could have been bought by Niz or Lydecker, or by the killers, and must have still been new—like fresh out of a box. It was basically free of touch DNA except around each side edge along the one end of it—the end they must have pulled up over Duke's body for the trip north. *And*," Emerson cast a furtive glance around the room before saying very softly, "the DNA obtained from one top side-edge matches that of a convict named Henry Schmidt. He served time in The Nevada State Prison in Carson City from March of 2002 through March 2004, and Nevada's DNA archive started for prisoners jailed in the year 2000. He was in for assault, a second-degree manslaughter rap. He beat a man over a gambling debt. Schmidt died of a heart attack in late 2004, at the age of thirty-nine."

Jennifer glumly commented, "*Cripes!* In other words, this Schmidt bastard got away with murder."

"Yes Jen, sad to say," Emerson answered. "Anyway, that's all we know right now; but I'm expecting a copy of Schmidt's rap sheet and personal history soon."

Redmond asked, "What about the touch DNA from the opposite side-edge of the tarp?"

"Also a male, but there was no match in criminal records. I think Schmidt's partner will turn out to be someone a lot like Schmidt. When we catch him we'll try to determine who put them up to this crime. Who ordered the hit on Hartsfield will be the next question."

"Well," Redmond noted, "this Schmidt guy does tie right in with the likelihood that Duke was the real target of the crime. Schmidt seems to have been an enforcer who beat up on gamblers that didn't pay their debts. It would seem Nizhoni was just unfortunate to have been in the company of a gambler."

"Looks that way," Emerson agreed. He paused before saying, "You know, I want to tell you guys that you've been great in working this case. You discovered that the mysterious stranger looked like Duke Hartsfield. You had Chris Larrabee declare that Duke Hartsfield *was* the mysterious stranger. You found out that June Connor sang at Chester's the night of the disappearance, and then Connor confirmed that Duke was actually in the house that night at Chester's. And, you put us onto talking with the Musicians Union in Vegas, and with Johnny Trujillo. You nailed down the suspicion that Duke could be rough with women, by going to

Toledo and talking with Billie Hamilton. In other words, you guys went to some trouble to do all those things. And it was all *damned good* investigative work."

"Well," Jennifer said, "actually, it was all fun."

Redmond noted, "And, the way it turned out, the things we did weren't really all that important. They all seemed to be pointing to Duke as the person who did the crime. But when Nizhoni's Jeep was found, it became crystal clear that Duke *wasn't* the perpetrator of the crime."

"Yes, Mac. But that doesn't mean you two didn't do *great* work on this case. Finding the Jeep was a lucky break where a pilot, flying at just the right altitude and in just the right spot, saw a reflection of sunlight from the ground and thought it could have come from the wreckage of Armstrong's plane. It was dumb luck, but it did end the possibility of Duke being responsible for Nizhoni's death."

"Of course," Jennifer noted, "we've had a hood who was after Duke, a sex psychopath who was after Nizhoni, and then Lindsey Marston, Tyler Lydecker, Joshua Usher, and the Prophet Usher as persons who could conceivably have had a motive for the crime. But I have to agree that the identification of Schmidt as one of the perpetrators of the crime argues strongly that Duke was the target, and that pretty much clears our other suspects. So, we seem to have come down to the hood theory, and were wrong about our generous sample of other suspects."

Emerson said, "Guys, you have to understand that cases are like this. You have to follow leads, and sometimes the leads take you in the wrong direction. It's the nature of investigative work. What I'm saying is, I want you to know you did a lot of *first-rate* work on this case. In fact, I think you both missed your calling . . . you guys should have pursued degrees in criminology."

"Oh no!" Jennifer laughingly protested. "I was born to be an artist, and Mac was born to be a scientist and teacher. Now, I will admit we do greatly admire detectives, such as *Emerson Yazzie*; and we *do* have something of a fascination with mysteries of all sorts."

Yazzie replied, "And murder mysteries must be high up on your list of fascinations. But, I never bought into one of your theoretical suspects—Joshua Usher may have had some anger or resentment toward Niz, but I never thought for a minute that he had that inward sense of entitlement a killer has to have. He was very confused, and scared nearly witless when I first interviewed him back in 2001. I've often wondered how the young man's life has gone. And, in fact, I called Joshua just this morning. I told him I was filing away some of my notes from the interview we had, and I just wanted to make sure I had things right. Just routine old paperwork, I told him."

Jennifer was surprised. She asked, "You called him just to find out how he's *doing*?"

Emerson smiled. "Yeah. I guess that's right."

"Well, I think you're a very good-hearted person, Emerson," she said approvingly. She smiled and said, "In fact, I think *you* should have got a degree in psychology."

"Oh no! I was born to be a detective," he proclaimed, mimicking Jennifer's example. They all laughed. Emerson said, "I will grant that I'm not a *bad*-hearted person, at least. I was just curious about the effect the crime had on the kid. I mean, in a way, Joshua was a victim of the crime, too. So, I called The House of the Ascension settlement and asked to speak with him. A secretary connected me with Joshua.

"Of course, Joshua was damned surprised that I called. But he sounded very confident. He told me his father was at the Seattle Clinic for a regular checkup, making sure he's up to the demands of a national book promotion tour he's going on. Joshua will be in charge while his father's away, it seems.

"You know, old Chief Hansen and I questioned Joshua shortly after the crime. Joshua said he ate late and alone that night at the Lumberjack Pizza shop, just half a block from the Wexford. When he left the Lumberjack and approached the hotel he saw Niz turn the corner of the hotel and head down the alley. Asked if he saw a man with her, Joshua said he hadn't, but he pointed out that Nizhoni could have been with a man who had just turned the corner a step ahead of her. He said he ducked into the hotel for a couple of minutes because he didn't want to overtake Niz and have to speak to her, or snub her—he still had hard feelings toward her because she'd dismissed him from her Intro to Astronomy class. Then he went down the alley—it was his shortcut route back to his dorm on that stormy night. He said that by the time the Wexford parking lot came into his view Niz's Jeep was already leaving the lot."

"So," Redmond asked, "he didn't see anything that happened before the Jeep left the lot?"

"That's right, Mac. And he told me the same things today that he said back in 2001. But today, he added that he has *dreamed* about that night many times, and the dreams distress him. In his dreams he sometimes sees two men come out of the Jeep just after Niz opens the driver's door. One man goes to Duke and orders him into the front seat. Joshua says he sometimes hears Duke say the word 'money' to his attacker, but he doesn't hear any other words. A second man pushes Niz into the back seat. Sometimes he also hears Niz scream, and then he sees the Jeep leaving the lot."

Redmond remarked, "Well, that's pretty interesting. The 'money' comment might suggest that Duke was the target and was trying to assure the assailant that he had, or would get, the money he owed somebody."

Emerson said, "Yeah, but hell's fire, guys, its *all* ethereal, just light and shadow—ify, pify, maybe stuff. Joshua doesn't know what actually happened. He just knows what he dreams, and there's nothing solid there. It's fantasy. He didn't claim he saw the abduction at the time we interviewed him, and his story today is entirely consistent with that. The only thing new is that he says he is plagued by dreams about it. And the idea that Niz and Duke were assaulted and driven off in the Jeep is obvious, given what's now known about their fate."

Redmond mused, "Well, Joshua's thinking that Duke said something about money would be consistent with our gambling enforcer theory. Maybe Duke recognized this guy Schmidt, and tried to assure him he had the money he owed, and would pay him."

"But, Mac, that's *just* in Joshua's dreams. He denies having seen the attackers and what they said or did," Emerson noted.

Redmond said, "Well, I don't want to get too psychoanalytic about it, but if Freud were having a beer with us here, he might wonder if Joshua actually witnessed what he describes as the dream material. It could be a defense against anxiety—he could have repressed the actual witnessing of the abductions that night, and that repressed material could now be expressed in his dreams. It could be his way of protecting himself from anxiety about what he saw."

Emerson chuckled and said, "And if Freud were here I'd tell him, 'Sigmund, stick to your own line of work, and I'll stick to mine.'"

They laughed, and Redmond responded, "Well, it sounds like the impact of the crime has stuck with Joshua all this time."

"Yeah," Emerson said, "a long time. But, far as I'm concerned, I never believed Joshua Usher could kill anything. Now, Joshua's old man is a different kettle of fish. He has that sense of grandiosity and empowerment to harm those he sees as defying God's wishes. He believes he's a Prophet. The guy shot a doctor for the Lord. You know about that?"

"Yes. Mac and I read about it on Google, back in June. That crime was a long time ago, and before Usher started his successful 'House of the Ascension.'"

"So," Redmond said, "we've got a hit man named Schmidt, and an unknown accomplice who's DNA was on the tarp. And the assumption that Duke was the target because of his unpaid gambling debts is rather persuasive to me because Schmidt *was* an enforcer—a guy that punished gamblers for not paying their debts. Still, for a time we all believed Duke could have been the killer, and that was wrong. It's still possible that the hit wasn't about Duke's gambling debts. We can still make the case that a sex psychopath, or Lydecker and our other suspects could have bought the hit."

Jennifer said, "It's unfortunate that Schmidt never had to pay for his crimes. We have to assume there's an accomplice out there that hasn't been caught. Let's hope he's still alive, and that he'll be apprehended. It would be really unfortunate if *two* killers never had to face appropriate punishment for their murders of Nizhoni and Duke."

Emerson nodded affirmatively and said, "We have to hope we'll catch a break somehow, and find out who the second bastard is. Maybe a break is coming."

Jennifer thought of the optimistic line from the *West Side Story* song that says, "*Something's Coming*, something good." Could it be? Yes it could, she told herself.

They were briefly silent before Emerson asked, "So, when are you heading back to the Buckeye State?"

"Sunday morning," Redmond answered. "But we've had a great summer here."

"Well, if anything like a break in this case comes along, I'll certainly let you guys know about it."

"Thanks, Emerson," Jennifer said, and added, "Speaking of breaks, we'll be here for about three weeks on Christmas Break. We'd love to get together with you and Vella, and the Baileys."

Emerson was pleased at the thought. He smiled and said, "Definitely! Let's all get together for dinner. Maybe we'll be able to celebrate the arrest of the second killer by then."

They stood and moved away from the table. Jennifer said softly to Redmond, "I have to hit the Ladies' Room, Mac. Be right out."

"Okay hon. I'll be outside."

As the two men headed for the exit Redmond remarked, "So, I gather you feel that Joshua Usher wasn't too badly damaged by his experiences at HU."

"Yeah. He seems to be doing okay, Mac. He said he has a lot of responsibilities now."

CHAPTER 41

▼

Early on Sunday morning, August sixteenth, the McClains took a cab to Flagstaff's Pulliam Field for their forty-minute flight to Sky Harbor, and from there they flew non-stop to Columbus. They located their grit-encrusted second car, and were relieved to have it fire right up. "Glad we had the new battery installed in our trusty old Taurus," Redmond said with a smile.

After copious applications of wiper fluid and wiper action, Redmond directed the car onto I-270. Fifteen minutes later they turned onto State Route 33, and settled back for the relaxing ride to Pleasanton. As they rolled along they enjoyed the beauty of the late afternoon in south-central Ohio. Jennifer remarked, "It's so nice to see the green grass, the flowers, and the variety of trees on this rolling countryside. It's all just so lush."

"Between our two houses, we're privileged to see two very different types of landscapes, and each is beautiful," Redmond noted.

"We accomplished so much at our new house, and additionally, we had a very real vacation. Think of the things we did. We visited Many Farms and Chaco Canyon, swam at Havasupi Falls, and had the conviction that we were walking on a *trustworthy* surface and not on air at the Skywalk!"

Redmond chuckled. "That was just a hell of a lot scarier than I expected. It was hard for my mind to overrule the information my eyes were giving me."

"Our two-day stay at the North Rim was great. The Ojai Valley Inn was everything Tim and Margo said of it. Ventura was nice, too. And learning that the Oxnard Marina was only fifteen minutes down Shore Road from the Ventura Pier was a pleasant surprise. I think we were right not to look for Lindsey's home, but we did get to see where she spends her summer vacation. There were so many large homes and beautiful big yachts there. The beach and the ocean views were fantastic. That whole scene was just so entirely *posh*—so very *The Great Gatsby*."

Redmond said, "Well, that suits Lindsey Marston—so very *the flapper*. But while we've tried to give her a shot at being a villain in relation to Nizhoni, I just can't imagine her being that evil."

"Well, Mac," Jennifer said with a taunt little smile and squinted eyes, "I have a *good* imagination. And I'm not ready to abandon the theory that Lindsey could be involved in the Nizhoni case."

They drove along silently for a few minutes. Then Jennifer returned the conversation to their stay in Flag, noting, "The only negative of our trip was that I didn't do much painting."

"And I hardly looked at the data I'd planned to analyze."

"But we worked hard on the house! And now, it's all in order."

"And we were able to see Margo and Tim, and Emerson, and that was all nice; and we learned from Emerson that there's *some* possibility of solving the Nizhoni and Duke murders."

"We can hope," Jennifer said.

"And we learned some things about Lindsey that, frankly, we'd have preferred not to know, such as her relationship with Lydecker, and her sexual harassment of her young grad assistant. It would seem Lindsey wasn't attracted *just* to men of her age, such as Nizhoni's husband. Your woman's intuition that led you to be 'put off' by Lindsey shortly after you met her seems to have been well founded."

"Score another accurate hunch for woman's intuition," Jennifer said with a smile. "But lets also assume that she is now appropriately ashamed of both her relationship with Lydecker and her harassment of Gilbert Samm, and is determined to walk the straight and narrow."

"Let's hope so."

"And I was pleased that Emerson allowed us to tell Margo and Tim the full details about the sexual harassment. After all, it's thanks to Margo that we learned of Erin's saying Nizhoni was angry toward somebody because of sexual harassment. Emerson did insist we tell Tim and Margo not to share that information with anyone. I think Emerson knows Tim and Margo are trustworthy. They provided him with very valuable information in relation to that North Rim murder back in 2007."

"They sure did." After a brief pause, Redmond said, "And now a new semester awaits us. The first football game, against Kentucky, is only three Saturdays away."

"I'm really looking forward to fall, and the fall sports. You know, I'm so glad I married a professor. I could have married someone who'd have me living in a big smog and traffic filled city, going to wrestling matches and demolition derbies, and listening to songs with lyrics that are swallowed, growled, or otherwise rendered incomprehensible." She leaned closer to him and purred, "Off coors . . . I vood hafe marrit chew, darlink, naw madder vot yur hoccupation vas."

Redmond chuckled and said, "Of course, Greta. How could anyone doubt that?"

CHAPTER 42

▼

At eleven sharp on the following Monday morning Jennifer set out on her walk to uptown Pleasanton. She hoped to find Phil Regan in his shop, and to see how her prints had sold over the course of the summer. It was a fine Monday morning for a stroll. High Street was largely devoid of cars and people, a pleasant state soon to be ended when forty-five hundred freshman students and their families rolled into town for freshman week. Still, she looked forward to the liveliness of the academic year.

She entered Regan's Art Shop and was happy to see Phil ringing up a sale for a young couple. As the couple left, Phil said, "Hey, Jen! Welcome back to town. I trust you had a great time in Flagstaff?"

Jennifer, happy to see the bearded and sociable proprietor, smiled and replied, "Yes, Phil, we *did* have a great time. First, we had to get our new house in order; but after that we really vacationed. We went to the Canyon de Chelly, the North Rim, Havasupi Falls, and to Ojai and Ventura, California."

"Ah, Ojai! It's a place Jill and I love to visit. We haven't been there in six or seven years, but we're thinking we'll hit Santa Fe, Sedona, Ojai, and Santa Barbara next summer."

"All places with lots of artists and art galleries," Jennifer observed.

"Yes. We'll buy some things for the shop, of course; and we'll earn a little tax deduction from the trip."

They chatted about local news, scant as it was, and then Phil said, "We had some sales of your prints during Alumni Week in June." He withdrew a folder from beneath the counter. "Let's see—two of the Covered Bridge, and six of the DeWitt Cabin. So, I'll write you a check for eight times your one hundred-twenty-five dollars per sale, and . . . that's exactly one thousand dollars."

"That's great," Jennifer said happily. She added, "Sounds like alums prefer the DeWitt Cabin to the Covered Bridge print."

"I think so, Jen. They're more familiar with the cabin, what with it being close to the University Stables and Tawee Creek. And it ties in directly with the history of RU, while the old Covered Bridge area is remembered by only *some* of we alums as a great place for springtime beer parties."

"I do plan to stick with familiar campus scenes in the future."

"Good idea. I think the expanded Beta Bell scene we've talked about could be a strong seller."

Phil wrote a check, handed it to Jennifer, and noted, "We still have a good supply of the first two prints. We should sell some this weekend, since lots of the parents of the new students are RU grads."

"Let's hope so," Jennifer responded. "See you later Phil. Say hello to Jill for me."

She headed west to the Lange Library, entered, ascended the stairs to the second floor, and proceeded to Ellen's work area. Ellen, sitting at her desk, looked up and said, "Hey girl! Good to see you, Jen." She smiled broadly and said, "You look great!"

"And so do you, El. Can we do lunch?"

"Of course. And it's so good to have you back in town." She consulted the clock on the sidewall and said, "I've got something here I have to finish. It'll take ten minutes or so."

"Not a problem. I'll just look through some mysteries and wait for you in the reading room."

Jennifer went to the first floor and browsed a number of new mystery stories, none of which appealed to her. By the time she chose and checked out a well-worn volume of Edgar Allen Poe short stories, Ellen came trippingly down the stairs. The two friends headed back down High Street toward the many restaurants of Uptown Pleasanton. As they entered The Appointment, Jennifer was finishing the account of her and Redmond's return trip to town, and her visit with Phil Regan. They were shown to a table near the back of the restaurant, and they ordered simple lunches and coffee.

"So," Ellen asked, "your Flagstaff home is all painted and furnished as planned?"

"Yep. And we had some minor roof repairs done. Then, we went to the North Rim for two days, spent two days at Canyon de Chelly, followed by two days at the beautiful Havasupi Falls area on the western side of the Grand Canyon. We swam and camped there."

"Romantic," Ellen said with a smile.

"And idyllic—made us feel like Tarzan and Jane," Jennifer responded with a grin. "And, we visited the Canyon Skywalk. That was scary, but I suppose you'd have been unfazed by it."

"I think I could handle walking on 'air' above the Grand Canyon," Ellen said with a chuckle.

"I'm sure you could, Miss Fearless. But, enough about Arizona! What's been happening in Pleasanton."

"Well, very little. Everyone has been somewhere or other. Steve and I loved Tahoe and our tour of Oregon and Washington. That was great. And we spent four days in Chicago with my sisters and brothers-in-law—saw the Cubs, went to the aquarium, and enjoyed a wonderful local production of a slightly rewritten old Gershwin musical. And we ate in some good restaurants. All in all, it was wonderful!"

"Sounds great."

"Yes. And now we're looking forward to the students being back in town, and the football season." She paused briefly before noting, "Eve and Ted just got back from Lake Bellaire last Wednesday. The dining room at The Huddle was closed all summer, what with the renovation work. They brightened up the dining room with new colors, new furniture and paintings, as well as new flooring. They gave it an upscale modern look, sort of like a Ruth's Chris Steakhouse. It's really nice."

"They didn't change anything on the casual dining side, did they?"

"No."

"Good. I like it just the way it is. We'll be having our game day brunch there in a few weeks."

"And the Ravens are opening with Kentucky this year—should be a good game."

"Has Langston returned from Cape Cod?"

"Last Thursday. Word is he made good progress on a new novel."

"And has our new *fiction* writer, Lindsey, returned as well?"

"Don't know. Haven't seen or heard about her."

"Oh, I forgot to tell you that in addition to going to interesting places in Northern Arizona, we also went to southern California, and visited Ojai and environs. We stayed at the Ojai Valley Inn, and that was wonderful."

"I've heard nice things about Ojai. They have a major music festival there each summer, featuring the Los Angeles Symphony and various great virtuosi."

"Yes. But that was over before we got there. And that was just fine, because the real charm of the place is its insularity and sense of tranquility."

"Close to the ocean, isn't it?"

"Just twenty minutes from Ventura, and Ventura is right on Pierpont Bay. So, we visited Ventura and had a delicious dinner at a restaurant on the city pier. And we saw the most spectacular sunset *ever*, with the gigantic-looking red sun sinking into the ocean." She paused before adding, "And we learned that Oxnard, where Lindsey Marston has her marina home, is only a short drive from the Ventura Pier. So, next day, we drove over to the Oxnard Marina to see where Lindsey spends her summers. We didn't try to contact her, of course. We just wanted to see the marina and beach. It's *very* beautiful, with lots of great homes, magnificent yachts, and great scenery."

"Well, Lindsey fits right in there, I'm sure."

"Yes. A first magnitude star in the small firmament of the *extremely* well-to-do."

"I suppose you saw the Baileys?"

"Oh sure, several times. And just before we left we had a few drinks with Emerson Yazzie."

"Has he discovered anything new in the Nizhoni case?"

"No, not really." Jennifer felt guilty saying it, but was honor-bound to keep the DNA information inviolate. She thought, I can't even tell El our vaulted story of Lindsey Marston being the *other woman* in Nizhoni's divorce action—I've become a really reluctant repository of secrets.

*   *   *

At three in the afternoon Redmond left his office in Stoddard Hall, and softly whistling the melody of "When I Fall in Love," he headed home. As he walked he thought of the opening lines of the very sentimental lyric Edward Heyman set to Victor Young's pretty melody—"When I Fall in Love, it will be forever." What a great sentiment, he thought, one that Jen and I so happily share. He asked himself how many of his colleagues were twice, even thrice, divorced. Too many, he knew. He let go that line of thought, and simply enjoyed the sunny day, the beautiful campus, and the friendly greetings he exchanged with passing faculty and students.

When he arrived home he found Jennifer casually dressed in shorts, a tee shirt, and sandals, seated on one of the living room sofas and reading a book. "Hey sweetheart," he said. They shared a brief kiss. "You look very relaxed. What ya reading?"

"The Cask of Amontillado."

"Ah! Poe at his darkest."

Jennifer quibbled, "I think his darkest has to be 'The Raven.' This is a dark story, but it can't match the haunting hopeless heartbreak over the lost Lenore, and the arcane omniscience of the enigmatic spectral Raven with its knowledge and insistence that the speaker shall *nevermore* find reunion with his love in heaven. *The Cask* is cold blooded, but devoid of the dense bleakness that's wrapped within the profound and tenebrous mystery of Poe's brilliant rhythmic poesy." She smiled. She loved tossing pedantic paragraphs Redmond's way, because she knew he really liked them.

He grinned, and said, "I guess that's right . . . and, I think *you* could write literary reviews for the *Pleasanton Press*. But, isn't '*poesy*' considered an archaic word nowadays."

She fielded the question as smoothly as Derek Jeter would field a soft one-hop grounder. "It is, but it shouldn't be. What better word for the art of poetic construction than that three syllable, five-letter, word? We shouldn't throw such useful words away." She then enounced authoritatively, "Thus spake Jennifer!"

Redmond chuckled and said, "No argument from me, sweetie." He paused before asking, "I assume you saw El today?"

"Yes. I checked out this book, and we lunched at The Appointment. Prior to that, I stopped by Phil Regan's shop. While we were enjoying Flag, Phil sold eight of my prints . . . gave me a check for *one thousand bucks*!"

"Hey, that's terrific! Congratulations, hon."

"And I told El all about our stay in Flag. She asked if we saw Tim and Margo, and Emerson, and I told her we did. She also asked if there were any developments in the Nizhoni case. I had to tell her there weren't. I couldn't tell her about the DNA finding on the deceased Schmidt, or that Emerson was expecting news about Schmidt's background."

The phone rang.

"Probably Eve," Jennifer said as she leaned over toward the end table for the phone. "I called her earlier, but no one was home." She lifted the phone and said, "Hi."

She was surprised to hear Emerson respond, "Hey Jen."

"Emerson! My goodness—we were just talking about you expecting information on Schmidt's background."

"Whoa," Emerson replied, "there's gotta be some ESP going on here, because that's why I'm calling."

"Psychic forces are at play," Jennifer said with a chuckle. "What's the news?"

"Well, I got some stuff on Schmidt this morning."

Redmond went to the kitchen, picked up the phone, and said, "Hey Emerson, I'm on the other line."

"Good to hear your voice, Mac. I was just telling Jen I got some info from Nevada regarding Schmidt's history."

"Good. Let's hear it."

"Well, Schmidt was born in Reno. He was a pretty good student in high school, and a good athlete. After high school he attended a community college in Reno for two years. Then he got a job with the Silver Castle Casino when he was twenty-one."

"The Silver Castle was owned by Lindsey Marston's father in those days," Jennifer volunteered.

"That's right, Jen. Schmidt was an assistant to more-senior employees in the casino's Customer Relations Department. He worked there till he was twenty-seven. That's when he got shipped off to The Nevada State Prison for the *first* time. He got a two-year sentence—from March of '92 through March of '94. He'd stolen some sports memorabilia from a dealer in Reno. His theft included an autographed baseball uniform jersey of Eddie Mathews, and a signed group photograph of Mathews, Warren Spahn, Johnny Sain, and Hank Aaron, all from back when the Braves played in Milwaukee."

"Milwaukee Braves memorabilia," Redmond observed, "could have been worth some serious bucks by '92. But, what else did you learn about Schmidt?"

"When he got out of prison in '94 he was twenty-nine, and he moved to Vegas. Since he had a criminal record, he couldn't get work in a licensed casino. At that point he started working at anything he could get. His history isn't totally clear in the first month or two after his release, but he began working as a waiter in an up-scale hotel restaurant in Vegas that summer. He also seemed to have some friends who were gamblers. It's thought he did some strong-arming of deadbeats for bosses that ran floating card or craps games in Vegas.

"In 2003 he was convicted of second-degree assault, and returned to The Nevada State Prison in Carson City. The state had collected DNA samples on all prisoners starting in 2000. That's what allowed us to identify Schmidt's involvement in Nizhoni's case. He got out of prison in late October of '05. He died of a heart attack on December sixteenth of 2005, just short of two months after getting out of prison, and just a week short of his fortieth birthday."

"Well," Jennifer said staunchly, "don't expect me to feel *sorry* for Mr. Schmidt! Nizhoni was only thirty, and Duke was in his mid-thirties, when their precious and productive lives were terminated by Schmidt and his accomplice."

Both men said, "Right."

Jennifer asked, "Did he have a wife or kids?"

"Prison records had him listed as single. His mother's maiden name was Emma Slagle. She moved to Reno in '64, and married Schmidt's father in '65. Henry came along in late '65. Henry listed his father as deceased on forms he filled out when he entered prison in 2003. His mother operated a flower shop called, 'Flowers to Everywhere,' in the Silver Castle Casino and Hotel; and according to a longtime employee and friend at the hotel, Mrs. Schmidt passed away back in 2003, while her son was in prison."

"How sad, for his mother," Jennifer said sympathetically.

"Yes. Being a parent isn't always fulfilling. Anyway, Sheriff Slater has approved a trip for me to go to Reno on Tuesday, the fifteenth, to talk with the Reno detective that apprehended Schmidt in the assault case. And I'm going to try to meet with the flower shop employee that knew Mrs. Schmidt. I'm hoping she can give me some insight into this guys background."

Redmond said, "Let's hope you learn something useful, Emerson." He paused briefly before asking, "Everything about the case is still a 'dark operation'—right?"

"Absolutely, Mac. We don't want Schmidt's accomplice, assuming the bastard's still alive, to catch wind of our progress and have him pull a disappearing act on us."

"Our lips are sealed," Jennifer promised.

"Okay, guys. At least we have some things to try to figure out. Personally, I believe Duke was the intended target, and that Schmidt and his companion got paid for that hit. I think Nizhoni was an unforeseen complication the killers had to scramble to deal with."

"Right," Redmond said.

"We'll keep grinding," Emerson assured.

They said their goodbyes.

Redmond returned to the family room, dropped onto the sofa beside Jennifer and said, "At least we know who *one* of the killers was. And maybe Emerson can turn up some leads in Reno."

"Yes. Let's hope," Jennifer said.

CHAPTER 43

───────────▼───────────

September fourth of 2009 finally arrived in Pleasanton, bringing with it the annual excitement of the opening football game of the season. As the McClains, Gundersens, and Muirs filed through the south end zone exit amid a mass of jocund Ravens fans, Ted said, in his deep and now roughened voice, "I tell ya guys, *that's* the way to start the season—win a hard fought 27-21 struggle of a game against a quality opponent like the Wildcats! This could set the tone for our whole season."

The others offered similar optimistic comments as they bustled along toward The Ravenslake Inn. As usual, they were the first group of Ravens fans to arrive at the Inn's Colonial Room. Tierney and Skip Suter were expected to arrive presently, so they took possession of an eight-person table near the giant fireplace that, on this warm afternoon, held no fire. They ordered beers and pretzels and greeted later-arriving Ravens fans with smiles and calls of approval for the Raven's achievements of the day. Tierney and Skip soon arrived, closely followed by the usual boisterous group of English Department faculty that included Langston Wallingford, Lindsey Marston, and Lindsey's latest companion, Cameron Whitman, of the Biology Department.

Langston called over, "Wonderful way to start the season, wasn't it?"

"Sure was," Ellen answered, and then she asked, "Langston, do you think this team could become as good as the '67 Ravens?"

Everyone at Ellen's table smiled at the question, for it was well established that in Wallingford's frequently stated opinion, no team could *ever* rival the unbeaten '67 squad of his senior year at Ravenslake.

Langston smiled broadly, knowing Ellen's question to be a good-natured gibe. "Well Ellen," he replied, "one can always hope."

At four o'clock, Tierney and Skip left to fulfill other social obligations, and when Ellen and Eve headed off to the Ladies Room, Lindsey Marston, looking vivacious, and with a glass of beer in her hand, slipped into a vacated chair next to Jennifer, and said, "Hey, Jennifer. How have you been? Did you have a good summer?"

"Oh, I've been fine, Lindsey; and Mac and I had a *great* summer. We spent two months in Flag getting our new vacation house in order." She went on to briefly describe some of things about the new house, and the traveling they did once the house was painted and furnished. She chose not to mention their trip to Ojai and environs since she didn't wish to evoke an awkward, 'You should have called me' routine.

"Sounds like a great summer," Lindsey said.

"What about you? I heard you were planning to write a mystery novel over the summer."

Lindsey's expressive face fashioned a brief frown as she said, "Well . . . that *was* my plan, but I didn't make much headway on it. The social scene at Oxnard Shores is always so very *demanding*—attending so many elegant parties, meeting interesting and attractive people, sending your yacht cutting through the waves . . . delightful diversions simply abound! I did manage to write six chapters, but they're *very* loosely written at this point. It's a first person story, and my heroine is a gorgeous young woman attorney who becomes intrigued by an old unsolved crime. She's smart, strong, single, and sexy."

"The four esses," Jennifer observed.

Lindsey smiled and said, "Yes. She's got the whole package. And she has *two* lovers who complicate her life."

The words 'surprise, surprise' rested briefly on Jennifer's tongue, but she swallowed them and said, "Oh, that sounds interesting."

"One is a detective named Tanner Doyle; and the other's a lawyer colleague and former All-American football player—he had been her first lover. I haven't settled on a name for him yet."

"How about," Jennifer suggested with a rakish leer, 'Hank.'"

Lindsey's expression was initially one of puzzlement, but then she laughed and said, "You *do* have a good memory, Jennifer. You know, after we left the Alexander House that day, I wondered if my mentioning that Henry Schmidt was my first lover shocked you."

"No, no, of course not," Jennifer laughingly replied. "I saw it as just a natural and spontaneous part of your recollections about your Reno days and The Reno Rock Crawlers Club, and their trips into the Mountains around the area."

"Yes, it was," she said. "Anyway, I'm sure there has to be a more engaging name than Henry Schmidt, but it hasn't revealed itself to me just yet."

At that point Ellen and Eve returned to the table and engaged Lindsey in friendly greetings, and light conversation. Lindsey then headed back to her English faculty group, though not before making it a point to chat briefly with Redmond. Fifteen minutes later the McClains, Gundersens, and Muirs headed out of the Ravenslake Inn. Eve said, "I wish Ted and I could dine with you guys tonight, but we'll be really busy at The Huddle; big wins bring big crowds at our 'new' old eatery." They said their goodbyes to the McClains and Muirs, and set off for their Sycamore Street home.

Redmond said to the Muirs, "See you guys at Amalfi's," and then he and Jennifer walked the mere eighty or so yards to 134 Shadowy Lane. As they entered the house, Redmond commented, "Today *was* a great day—a quality win for the Ravens, gorgeous weather, and good friends to talk, cheer, and laugh with."

"It was all *lovely*," Jennifer responded. She headed for the kitchen while asking, "Would you like some tea, sweetheart? I'm going to make some."

"Sure."

"Put some music on, please."

"Classical? Jazz?" He added, with a grin, "Polkas?"

"How about Miles Davis and his Sketches of Spain, and set the loudness level low enough that we can talk."

"You got it, sweetie."

Jennifer soon returned with their teas, and set them on the coffee table in front of the sofa that directly faced what they liked to call "our great and venerable JBL speakers." Then she sat down and snuggled up beside Redmond.

They listened to the music and sipped their teas. Jennifer said, "Lindsey seemed to enjoy her conversation with you at the Inn, sweetheart."

Redmond, too relaxed to attempt a clever response, said, "I suppose." He added, "And she didn't do *any* of the components of flirting behavior."

"I noticed that. Guess she's lost her need to flirt with ya."

"More likely she was just afraid you'd pummel her in the school cafeteria if she did."

Jennifer chuckled, and let it go at that.

Redmond said, "I asked her how her summer had been. She said the summer was nice, and that she started writing a first-person mystery novel, but hadn't gotten very far with it."

"Yeah. I also mentioned I'd heard she was writing a mystery. She told me a little about the characters she's inventing. And it proved to be *extremely* interesting."

"*Extremely?* That interesting?"

"Yep. Her heroine is a smart, strong, single, and sexy attorney who decides to pursue an old unsolved case."

"Yeah?"

"Uh huh. Her heroine has two lovers. One is a detective named Tanner Doyle."

"Kinda cool name—Irish, I guess."

"The other is a fellow attorney who was an All-American college football player. He was her first lover."

"Well . . . why not?"

"She hasn't decided on a name for the guy."

"Gonna be classy I suppose—Reginald Lecroix, or something," he said sleepily.

"I suggested she should name him, 'Hank.'"

"Ah . . . well, sweetie, it's kinda mundane. Couldn't you come up with something less . . . mundane?"

"Oh sure, Mac. But I was being duplicitous."

"Ya lost me babe."

"Well, the attorney was her heroine's *first lover*. So, when she said she hadn't settled on a name for him, I smiled and said, 'How about Hank' as his first name."

"Why Hank?"

"Because, when Lindsey and I had our luncheon at the Alexander House last fall, she told me she and *her* first lover, 'Hank,' used to get purposely lost in remote mountain areas while on the Reno Rock Crawlers Club's four-wheeling rally-type events—just so they could make out in the wild. And she said she was only eighteen, and he was somewhat older than she was. I thought, at the time, she was trying to shock me."

"Shocks *me*, I must say," Redmond offered while producing his notion of a shocked expression.

"When I suggested 'Hank' as a name for her heroine's first lover, the All-American, now attorney guy, it took her a few seconds, but then she made the connection, and she laughed."

"I don't get it, Jen."

"Well, here's the point, Mac—when she told me last fall about her first lover she used just the nickname for Henry, that is, 'Hank.' Today, when I threw that name out there for her, she laughed and said she didn't think 'Henry Schmidt' would be the right name for her fictional attorney. So it would seem that her 'Hank' was Henry Schmidt—the name of the man whose *DNA* was found on the tarp that covered Duke Hartsfield's body in Nizhoni's Jeep.*"

Redmond's drowsy look was instantly transformed into active attention as he sat bolt upright while saying, "*Holy crap*! Lindsey's first lover was one of the guys that murdered Duke and Nizhoni?"

"Seems possible . . . Schmidt's age is about right for Lindsey's first lover. Lindsey said her Schmidt was "a bit" older than she."

"Man! How did you think to suggest 'Hank' as the name for the attorney's first lover?"

"I don't know. I'd thought of the fact that Hank was really just a nickname for Henry when she first told me about 'Hank.' And when Emerson told us that Henry Schmidt was one of the killers of Nizhoni and Duke, and that he was from Reno, I again had the *passing* thought of the Henry-Hank connection. Today, I knew Schmidt's age was about right to be Lindsey's Hank from Reno, and I just threw it out there. I had no real expectation it would lead her to reveal Hank's full name, and yet, when she said that her Hank was named Henry Schmidt, I wasn't terribly surprised. I can't really explain it, Mac. I just had a feeling. Some part of my brain was keeping track of possibilities I wasn't fully aware of—I guess it was what people call intuition."

"Wow! And Lindsey had plenty of bucks she could have paid to Schmidt for his service—a service that could have prevented Nizhoni from making Lindsey's role in the Lydecker divorce case public, *and* prevented Nizhoni from taking the Gilbert Samm harassment complaint to the upper administration at HU."

"Yes, but Lindsey was very relaxed in acknowledging her relationship with Schmidt, Mac. I can't imagine her having that level of *comfort* had she paid him to get rid of her Nizhoni problem." She paused before continuing, "But*, on the other hand*, Lindsey is unaware that we know anything about the case beyond having heard about a 'strange disappearance' at Humphreys University. And she can't know that Schmidt's DNA was found in Nizhoni's Jeep. Given those facts, Lindsey might have had no felt need to be guarded or *wary* with me."

"Yeah, that could be! Schmidt was one of the killers, and Lindsey admits to having had an intimate relationship with *her* Henry Schmidt when she was just eighteen. What that relationship could have been in 2001 is a mystery in itself."

"Well, Lindsey's money and her youthful intimacy with Schmidt could have persuaded him to solve her Nizhoni problem. Lindsey is clearly a suspect, Mac."

"Yeah . . . gotta be. And there's still Lydecker and the *Husband Arranged It* theory. Lydecker knew the area where Nizhoni's Jeep was so well hidden away. Still, as we've always said, it seems *unlikely* that Lydecker could have been involved in the physical act of killing his wife; but in our Lydecker and Lindsey cooperation theory he could have gone along with Lindsey's choice of Schmidt and someone else to commit the murder."

"Awfully *gruesome* to think, though!"

"Yes. But we still have other possible killers, Jen. There's the Prophet Usher, and maybe even the ex-student, Joshua Usher, in our pantheon of possible villains. For all of these suspects we assume Nizhoni would be the intended victim. Yet Schmidt was an ex-con that worked for people operating floating gaming operations, and his second trip to the big house, the one in '03, was for assault on a gambler who hadn't paid his debts. Duke Hartsfield had a gambling problem, and was once seriously battered for failure to pay a gambling debt on time. And Joshua Usher thought he heard Duke use the word 'money' when Duke and Nizhoni were being abducted—if you can put any faith in Joshua's 'dreams' as possible instances of Freudian repression of the abduction scene Joshua might actually have witnessed. So, we keep coming back to the question of whether the targeted person was Nizhoni or Duke."

Jennifer frowned and grouched, "Why does the plot always seem to thicken up, rather than thinning down?"

They sat quietly, just thinking about possible motives for the murders of Duke and Nizhoni. Redmond broke the silence, saying, "Emerson feels Joshua Usher doesn't have the spine for murder. He sees Joshua as a hard working young man who's devoted to his father's House of the Ascension settlement and its growth. He has responsibilities now, like overseeing the construction of a new housing facility at the settlement."

"Well, Mac, that settlement does seem to prosper. I gathered, in reading about it, that new members have to give-over a good chunk of their income to Usher, in order to sustain and grow the colony. And we know Usher makes lots of money from his best selling books."

"Right. Emerson said they also have some benefactors—people that approve of the settlement, but don't want to live there. Joshua told him their new building is being paid for partly by an endowment from an apparently wealthy woman named Lillian Lehmann."

Jennifer turned more fully toward Redmond and simultaneously turned slightly pale, as she asked in an unusually calm flat voice, "Are you sure that was the name Emerson told you?"

"Well, yeah! See, it made me think of *Lotte* Lehmann, the great, long-lived German soprano. And 'Lillian Lehmann' also struck me as, I don't know . . . graceful, I guess."

"Lillian Lehmann. You're *sure* about that?"

Redmond said earnestly, "Sweetheart, I'm still a bit young for you to be so doubting as to the integrity of my memory. Yes, I'm sure!"

"When did Emerson tell you this?"

"While we were walking to our cars at the Half Moon Saloon. You were visiting the ladies room." He leaned back against the sofa and jokingly asked, "Do you *remember*?"

"Yes, Mac. But I also remember that Lillian Lehmann was the maiden name of Lindsey Marston's mother!"

Redmond's head spun fully toward Jennifer at nearly the speed equivalent of a hundred-mile an hour fastball, and he blurted, "No shit? . . . I mean, *really*?"

"Yes! Lindsey told me that fact when we were at the Alexander House last November. But Lillian and her husband, Ellis Lavery, died in a car crash in Pasadena in December of 1995. Langston told me about that. So, how could a woman who died in '95 give money to Usher for a building being constructed now, in 2009? And, if this Lillian Lehmann were Lindsey's mother, why in the world would she donate money to Usher's settlement?"

They sat briefly silent before Redmond ventured, "The name *could* be a coincidence—though that seems a really long shot. Or, it's not inconceivable, that Lillian Lehmann could have been some kind of fundamentalist that approved of Usher's theology."

"Possible, I suppose." Jennifer replied.

Redmond glanced at his watch, then said, "Well, let's save our conjectures about this revelation for later. We have to meet Ellen and Steve at Amalfi's in an hour. Let's drop the topic for now, take our showers, get dressed, stroll uptown, enjoy a good dinner and pleasant conversation with our friends, and celebrate a satisfying Raven's win."

"Good. We'll just put this stuff out of our minds, for now."

*   *   *

By seven-forty five the McClains and Muirs had enjoyed their dinners and conversations about the Ravens big win over Kentucky, the seasonal prospects for the football and hockey teams, new faculty members in the psych department, bits of interesting salacious gossip concerning Pleasanton's mayor, and concerns over recent national and world events. Now they paid for their meals, exchanged cheery "goodnights" with Pete Amalfi, and exited the restaurant. As they stepped out onto East High the couples agreed it had been a great day, and that they were too tired to stop for drinks anywhere. Steve offered to drive the McClains to 134 Shadowy Lane, but the offer was declined, with thanks. "The walk will do us good," Jennifer said. The couples bid one another a good evening, and Jennifer and Redmond set off on their twilight stroll down the hillcrest.

Once home, they opted to relax on the back deck. The light of just a few stars had become visible in the darkening sky. Jennifer commented, "I read that there are roughly eighty four hundred stars visible to the naked eye, from earth; and only about twenty five hundred are visible from any *one place* on our planet."

"Well," Redmond said, "estimates of how many stars and planets there might be out there, and not just in our galaxy, are incomprehensibly large. Carl Sagan estimated there are ten *billion trillion* planets in the universe. And two astronomers from New South Wales University recently estimated there are roughly thirty billion exoplanets, that is, planets potentially favorable for life, in just *our* relatively smallish galaxy. Life, of nearly infinite variety, has to exist on many planets throughout the universe."

"Staggers the mind," Jennifer granted. "But, we have a different kind of mystery to contemplate tonight—namely, who decided that Duke Hartsfield, or Nizhoni Lydecker, had to be killed?"

"Yes," Redmond said. "What a grizzly thing to have to consider on such a great night as this!"

"I know, Mac. But Henry Schmidt and someone else committed those killings, and they can't be allowed to get away with that." She punched a determined index finger through the air, as she said sternly, "Not on this planet, buster!"

Her energetic exclamation made Redmond chuckle. He said, "Yeah! What the hell kind of a planet do the killers think they're on. We gotta be able to have some home planet pride, dammit!"

"Damned right," Jennifer said, with a grin.

"Well, when we met with Emerson at the Half Moon Saloon it seemed clear that The Kill Duke Theory seemed the most likely of our theories to be valid. It seemed pretty cut and dry. But thanks to your excellent memory, and your ingenious *stratagem*, we learned today that it was Henry Schmidt, not just some random 'Hank' guy, that had a youthful sexual relationship with Lindsey. But if Duke were the real target, the Lindsey/Schmidt relationship of roughly twenty years ago would have no relevance to the homicide. On the other hand, if Nizhoni were the target, the Lindsey/Schmidt relationship could be crucial to understanding the crime. Lindsey would have known where to find herself a possible killer, and she'd have no trouble buying the hit—as Bogey would say."

"Right. Schmidt could have been in need of a big payday, what with having to scramble just to make a living once he had a prison record."

"That all seems to makes sense, Jen. Nizhoni threatened, if necessary, to make Lindsey's affair with Lydecker a prominent point in her divorce action; and additionally, Nizhoni was very angry about Lindsey's sexual harassment of Gilbert Samm. Lindsey could have felt her career would be terribly damaged by Nizhoni's threatened harassment complaint. And although we don't know when Nizhoni might have planned to reveal Lindsey's transgression to someone in HU's upper administration, it's possible she told Lindsey she was going to reveal it on Monday, the twenty third of April. As you postulated in our *Fearful and Vengeful Woman Theory*, that could explain why the crime went forward when it did, despite the complication of Duke being there with Nizhoni."

"And Lindsey told me her life *wouldn't be worth living* if she were unable to teach and write. Her academic life and reputation are so precious to her. If she felt convinced that Nizhoni had to be silenced in order to keep her own life from becoming 'not worth living,' couldn't she have bought the hit?"

They were silent for perhaps fifteen seconds before Jennifer said, "And knowing that Schmidt and another man were involved in the crime puts the kibosh on our old theory two—the *Sex Predator Theory*. Schmidt apparently had no history of sex crimes; and sex psychopaths don't work with a partner. They're lone wolves. Therefore, we have to reject the sex predator theory."

"We *also* hypothesized that the Prophet Usher could have been angered enough by Nizhoni's dismissal of Joshua from her class that he could have thought the Lord would want her to be punished."

"Well," Jennifer said doubtfully, "that seems a bit far-fetched, don't you think? Usher is busy building up his settlement, writing exciting best selling religious books with covers showing such things as Christ mounted on a white war horse, a sword in his teeth, leading his army against the forces of the Anti-Christ. Usher is looking forward to the final glorious ascendance of living and resurrected true believers to a state of endless life in heaven. And when he finishes one of his thrillers, he gears up and goes on tour to sell himself and his book, to encourage donations, and to recruit new members to The House of the Ascension."

"That's all true, Jen. The guy's on a roll. But Usher's old time religion didn't keep him from shooting Dr. Philip Webster in '88. He shot, and quite possibly meant to *kill* Webster, because he thought God wanted him to do it. He served five years of his six year sentence and got out in '94 . . . I think it was '94, or am I confusing his release date with Schmidt's first release?"

"No, you're right, Mac. I remember that Usher got out of The Nevada State Prison in February of '94."

"Yeah, that's what I thought, Jen." Redmond was briefly silent, but then said, "There are lots of possibilities to think about."

"Yes. And I'm thinking right with you, Mac. We may want to talk with Emerson about all this. I'll make us some tea."

CHAPTER 44

▼

By two o'clock on the afternoon of Wednesday, September sixteenth, Emerson Yazzie had already talked to, and lunched with, Mark Nolan, the Washoe County detective who made the 2003 bust that landed Henry Schmidt in The Nevada State Prison. Emerson learned that Schmidt was the type of man that made acquaintances scratch their heads and wonder how a guy like this—handsome, athletic, bright, and socially adept—could end up serving two terms in the Big House. Emerson knew the answer resided in what Freud would call a weak super-ego, and your mom would call callous selfishness. Schmidt was a sociopathic personality. He was all surface sheen, polite and affable. But beneath the sheen there lurked a totally self-centered man, one incapable of real empathy or concern for others. Henry Schmidt, so charming, lively, and attractive on the surface, was, at his deep core, only about "me." What he wanted he wanted intensely, and if you were in the way of his getting it, he would charm, connive, calculate, finagle, or fabricate to get around you; and if these tools proved inadequate, he would cheat you or steal from you. For a sufficient price, he'd physically beat you. Emerson learned that Mr. Henry Schmidt was, at his core, one damned nasty piece of work.

And, Emerson thought, Schmidt could probably kill, were that required for him to possess that which he so deeply or urgently coveted. On the surface he seemed a disarming Farley Granger or Robert Redford sort of fellow—smooth, ingratiating, considerate, and handsome. But, in reality, he was the sort of man Joseph Cotton portrayed in the movie *Uncle Charley*—a paragon of kindness and consideration on the surface, but capable of killing if that were the only way to get what he felt he had to have.

Now, at three o'clock in the afternoon, Emerson rang the doorbell of Mrs. Emily Hewson, a woman he'd phoned the previous Friday and made an appointment to visit. A woman opened the door, and Emerson inquired, "Mrs. Hewson?"

Mrs. Hewson, a rather short, neat, and very cheery looking woman who appeared to be in her sixties, smiled and replied, "Yes, I'm Mrs. Emily Hewson. And you must be Detective Emerson Yazzie, from Flagstaff, *I presume* . . . as Sherlock Holmes might say." She chuckled and said, "Actually, I recognize your voice from your call last week."

Emerson smiled and answered, "Yes, ma'am. I am Detective Yazzie."

Mrs. Hewson invited the detective into her home, and led him to a comfortably furnished living room. She suggested he'd find a heavily upholstered armchair comfortable, and she seated herself on a matching sofa, across from him.

Emerson began, "It's very generous of you to see me, Mrs. Hewson. I appreciate it greatly. The fact is that I am assigned to a case in Arizona, and we think it's possible that the late Henry Schmidt could be relevant to it in some way. I'm not free to discuss the nature of the case, but it might prove helpful to our investigation to know a bit about Mr. Schmidt and his background. I understand you worked with his mother in a flower shop at the Silver Castle?"

"Oh, yes. I worked with Emma in her 'Flowers to Everywhere' shop for thirty years, give or take. She was from Germany, you know, and her maiden name was Emma Slagle. And I came from England. We both came to the states in our twenties, though Emma was six years older than me. So we had that in common—immigrants, I mean. She was always nice to me, and we were friends. She was a good soul." Mrs. Hewson added in a softer voicing, "And she had a hard life, she did."

"In what way did she have a hard life?"

"Well, her husband was an American." She laughed and said, "Heavens, I don't mean to say having an American husband makes for a hard life! I got one myself, and he's a gem."

Emerson gave a little chuckle.

"Mr. Schmidt had some sort of heart condition that ran in his family, and he died of it in 1996. He was an insurance man, and had an office downtown. He was a nice chap. He liked to joke and to laugh—popped into the shop time to time. Loved Emma, I'm sure."

"I see," Emerson said. It was apparent that Mrs. Hewson didn't need him to ask a lot of questions.

Mrs. Hewson continued, "So, Emma's husband's heart trouble worried her. It acted up and caused him problems now and again, sad to say."

"Unfortunate," Emerson allowed.

"I think another thing that troubled Emma deeply was that she couldn't move in the same circles, you could say, as her childhood friend, Mrs. Lavery, did. Mrs. Lavery was the wife of Ellis Lavery, and he owned the Silver Castle and a whole lot more. He was a millionaire many, many, times over, so he was."

Emerson allowed, "I suppose it *would* be difficult for the wife of an insurance salesman to live the kind of life Mrs. Lavery must have had."

"Oh yes, and that's a fact! You see, Mrs. Lavery and Emma had been close friends and neighbors growing up in Germany. Emma's family had money, though not quite so much as Mrs. Lavery's folks had—but it was pretty close, you could say. They were equals in that sense of it. Now, because they'd been chums throughout school, and lived next to each other, I believe Emma wanted to come to Reno thinking she'd be reunited with her school chum, and they'd be close friends, do lots of things together, you see. Emma hadn't quite realized just how wealthy a woman Lillian Lavery had become, and what a different life she had to lead."

"I see," Emerson said.

"But, I feel it was the problems with her son that weighed on her most heavy . . . broke her heart, is what I say. Henry—'Hank' he was called—seemed a nice enough lad in some ways. He was a handsome boy. Played sports in high school, and made his old Dad proud of that. He was popular with the girls—even squired Mrs. Lavery's daughter round here and there during the summer after she graduated high school. But then she went off to a fancy college back east, and married an older man soon as she graduated. And, later on, poor Henry got in trouble with the law. You must know he was sent to prison in the early nineties for a couple of years, and then again, about six or seven years ago."

"Yes."

"Emma tried to get him interested in going to church before he got in trouble with the law and was sent to prison in the nineties. She felt it might help keep him on the straight and narrow, you see. But, he didn't want to do it. And then, to her surprise, he got religion in prison! When he got out he wanted to turn his life around. He wanted to spend some time living in a religious colony that was starting up near Lake Havasu City, down in Arizona. But the minister needed money to get it going. So, Emma's boy asked her to work up the courage to ask her old friend, Mrs. Lavery, if she could help the minister out . . . Mrs. Lavery gave lots of money to lots of different things, you see."

"Certainly."

"I think Mrs. Lavery felt deeply sorry for her childhood chum. So she met with the minister, looked at the plans for his colony, set down some conditions, I should suppose, and gave him money to help get him started."

"Mrs. Lavery sounds like a very generous and caring woman."

"Oh, yes. She had that reputation. Still, Detective Yazzie, if you or I was to have the kind of money as she had, we could afford to be just as generous, don't you know!"

"Of course. Now, was Hank helped by participating in this colony?"

"Well, not really, I would say. It was in the spring or summer of 1994 that Mrs. Lavery gave the money, and Emma's boy went down to that colony. Anyway, Hank left the colony and moved himself to Las Vegas. I don't believe he stayed down in Arizona more than two or three months. That was a disappointment to Emma, and a bit of an embarrassment after having had Mrs. Lavery give money to that colony. Emma worried about Hank all the time. It just wore her down. She got high blood pressure, and died of a stroke in August of 2003. Now, I don't like to speak ill of the deceased, but I do feel she died of heartbreak and worry caused by her son. She had such high hopes for him, you see. But he didn't do well. Emma was constantly sending him money to keep him afloat, so to say. It's terrible sad when a child makes his poor old mom suffer." Mrs. Hewson sat silent and sorrowful for ten seconds or so before saying, "And then, Henry died of a heart attack, and him just going into his forties. I suppose it was the same thing killed his dad."

"I see . . . bloody hard to find a silver lining in all that . . . a sad tale."

"It was, truly, Detective Yazzie."

Emerson moved to the front of the overstuffed chair, and said, "I believe you've given me helpful information, Mrs. Hewson. Thank you very much."

She smiled and said, "I'm happy if it helps you, Detective Yazzie."

"It certainly does, ma'am," Emerson replied. He experienced a strange transient feeling that he might be Detective Chief Inspector Morse, and that he was in Oxford, England.

They stood, and Mrs. Hewson accompanied Yazzie to the door. She smiled and said, "It was wonderful nice to talk with you. You're *such* a good listener." She chuckled and said, "Of course, I've been accused, by my husband, of talkin' the ears off people."

Emerson raised his hands to his ears, and said, "My ears are still in place. So . . . no damage done!"

The jolly lady laughed.

"Thank you, again, Mrs. Hewson. I enjoyed our talk. You've been very helpful," Emerson assured her. And he really meant it.

CHAPTER 45

▼

On Saturday afternoon, September nineteenth, Jimmy Usher arrived at Beverly's Book Store in Youngstown, Ohio. He spent some time talking to the store manager, assuring her that the podium for his talk, and the table and chair arrangement for his book signings, were fine. At three o'clock he began his standard sermon about the coming End Time and The Apocalypse. This was the last stop on his book tour, and he really had the fire in his belly this afternoon. His sermon drew many robust "Praise the Lord" and "Thank you Jesus" acclamations from the assembled. Most in the audience were of fundamentalist faiths, and were deeply thrilled by the Prophet's lively and dramatic presentation. They were moved by the deep resonance of his powerful voice, especially when he quoted the very words God had spoken to the Prophet Usher himself. More than a few were moved to tears. The Prophet gave a detailed explanation of just what the Apocalypse would be like, and how Christ would select the final group of living and resurrected faithful that would dwell in heaven forever.

There was a twenty-minute break between the end of Usher's stirring presentation and the beginning of the book signing session. When everything was arranged, the Prophet seated himself, smiled benevolently, and motioned the first person in line to advance with his book to the signing table. He asked each person if he or she would like an inscription, in addition to his flowing signature, and he patiently fulfilled each buyer's request. Some of the buyers had two or even three books for him to sign. It took fully fifty minutes before the last person in line thanked the Prophet extravagantly and left the bookstore feeling, like so many of the others, happier and more optimistic for having heard Usher's message. They had gained knowledge of what they should expect in the Apocalypse, and then in their heaven. They would be able to remember his vivid sermon, read his exciting book, and treasure the inscriptions he had written just for them in *The Coming Apocalypse and Salvation*.

Usher was very pleased with his afternoon's work. He estimated he had signed one book for about fifty people, and multiple books for twenty-five others. He silently complimented himself for his lively delivery of the sermon, and he just knew God had given him the power to help those in the audience this afternoon.

When he returned to his hotel he still felt elated, but he no longer felt quite so energized. "I'm getting too old for the road," he murmured. He had only to spend the night at his Youngstown hotel, and drive his rental car to the Pittsburgh Airport in the morning. I'll be home tomorrow night, he assured himself. I'll be able to control my diet better, and be with Joshua, and my flock. Working for God is no job for a lazy man. There are always things to plan, to initiate, and to finish. He looked forward to seeing the progress on the Seventh Seal Complex when he got home.

He knew the endowment he'd received toward the Complex would be exhausted upon completion of the structure. The Settlement is now as big as I want it to be, he thought with satisfaction. Soon Joshua will be able to begin taking control of the flock, for he's already quite capable of delivering energizing sermons and projecting the appropriate demeanor of a man of God.

So, Usher thought, with the new complex completed I'll be able to concentrate on deciphering the biblical clues as to precisely when the Apocalypse will come. I'll have time to count all the earthquakes, volcanic eruptions, and great fires we've had. I know they've been increasing, so the Sixth Seal has broken. Soon we can expect the souls of all the tribes of Israel to be sealed, and the Great Tribulation to begin. Of course, he told himself, John wrote *The Book of Revelation* around 79 AD, but the Lord *told me* that John meant it as a prediction of the future. It really wasn't about the tribes of Israel. It's about our Lord's true believers and our approaching victory in the Apocalypse. We shall be ready!

CHAPTER 46

‚ñº

At two-twenty on the afternoon of Thursday, October fifteenth, Detective Emerson Yazzie placed a telephone call to the Reverend Jimmy Usher. Emerson told the woman who answered that he would like to speak with Reverend Usher. Emerson next heard a deep and confident voice say, "This is Reverend Usher."

"Good afternoon, Mr. Usher," Emerson responded. "This is Coconino County Detective, Emerson Yazzie. I'm here to charge and arrest you for the murders of Nizhoni Marie Yazzie, and Wallace Gary Hartsfield."

There was a brief silence before Jimmy Usher, his voice pinched and tremulous, responded, "Why, why . . . that's *preposterous*! And *just* where are you? This must be some kind of sick joke."

"I'm calling from one of two Coconino County Sheriff's Department patrol cars parked just outside the entrance to your property. There is also a Mohave County Sheriff's Department patrol car here. Now, you can either come out, be cuffed, and get in a cruiser, or we can come in, cuff you, and walk you out to one of the cruisers. Just tell me which way you want to do it."

"Well, I'll come out, but first, I need to call my lawyer, Dennis Packard, in Flagstaff—this is just *outrageous*!"

"All right, Mr. Usher. If you're not here in ten minutes we're coming in to cuff you and walk you out here."

"I'll be out in ten minutes. I don't want you to upset my flock. This is all some kind of horrible mistake. *I'm a man of the Lord*!"

"Ten minutes, Mr. Usher," the man of the law replied.

Eight minutes later Usher came out and walked to the patrol cars. An officer patted him down, and then Emerson cuffed him. A burly officer directed Usher into the back seat of the first Coconino County patrol car, and seated himself next to Usher. The Mohave County Sheriff's Office patrol car then accompanied the Coconino County cars to the county line, and the latter continued on to the Coconino County Jail in Flagstaff.

* * *

At nine-ten that evening Jennifer McClain answered the phone at 134 Shadowy Lane. She was pleased to hear the voice of Emerson Yazzie. He said, "Hey, Jen. I've got some news for you and Mac."

"Okay," she said, "but wait a second. Mac wants to get on the other phone."

Redmond soon said, "Hi, Emerson. What's up?"

"Well, guys, we arrested Jimmy Usher at two-thirty this afternoon."

"*Geezoopeasy!*" Jennifer exclaimed.

"He's going to be formally charged tomorrow with the murders of Nizhoni and Duke Hartsfield. The DNA from the pages Usher inscribed and autographed in the four copies of *The Coming Apocalypse and Salvation* that you guys bought in Youngstown matched the DNA from the tarp in Niz's Jeep. We just got the results of the tests yesterday afternoon—and we got our man today."

"The touch DNA matched?" Redmond asked incredulously.

"It matched absolutely, Mac—no doubt about it! *Our break has come*—and you two made it happen."

Redmond exclaimed, "All right! But, *we three* made it happen, Emerson!"

"Right. We three."

Jennifer followed with, "Holey Moley! We got the second killer!"

"It seemed worthy of a shot," Redmond said. "When we realized that Usher and Schmidt were in the same prison for a year and eleven months, we had to wonder if they'd come to know each other there."

Jennifer continued, "And when you learned from Mrs. Hewson that Lillian Lavery had created a fund for Usher's settlement, in the vain hope it might help Mrs. Schmidt's son, we had to wonder if Schmidt's partner in the murders of Nizhoni and Duke could have been Usher."

"From there," Redmond happily added, "it was a short step to realizing that Usher's DNA could be garnered and compared to that of Schmidt's partner in the crime. You got Sheriff Slater to approve our Youngstown escapade, and Jen and I, separately, went through the book signing line. We each bought two of Usher's books. And now we know that Schmidt's partner *was* Jimmy Usher! And, if the DNA hadn't matched, it would have cleared Usher without him ever having to know he'd even been considered a possible suspect."

"Yes, Mac," Emerson responded, "but it *did* match! Usher's books provided the evidence we needed. Usher's attorney, Dennis Packard, knows the DNA match is definitive. Packard will probably be content with trying to avoid the death penalty for Usher. And, of course, the Nevada archival convict DNA match to Schmidt's DNA from the other edge of that tarp was a lock, too. There can be *no doubt* that these two men murdered Nizhoni and Duke. We're going to try to get a confession from Usher, and hopefully, learn the details of what happened, and why."

"Is it possible others could be involved?" Redmond asked.

"We're certainly going to look into that possibility, Mac."

CHAPTER 47

▼

On Monday, October nineteenth, Jimmy Usher was brought to Interview Room Two in the Coconino County Sheriff's Department Building in Flagstaff. His lawyer, Dennis Packard, was present. Detectives Jim Healy and Justine O'Hara were there to conduct the interview, and they introduced themselves to Usher and his attorney. Emerson Yazzie, Sheriff Slater, and County Prosecutor, Eldon Sewell watched the interview from behind a one-way vision mirror, with audio piped into their room. Mr. Usher and Mr. Packard were informed that other law enforcement personnel were watching and listening to the proceedings.

Dennis Packard wished to speak prior to any questioning of Jimmy Usher, and he was granted his wish. He stated simply, "My client intends to plead guilty to the crime with which he is charged, and he will freely answer any of your questions. Reverend Usher is fully aware that the DNA evidence against him is definitive in establishing his guilt. He does request, however, that he be allowed ten minutes time to make a statement."

Jim Healy nodded and said, "That will be all right, Mr. Packard. Please make your statement, Mr. Usher."

Jimmy Usher looked energized and eager to speak. He began, "Thank you, detective. I want to state that I did commit the so-called crime with which I'm being charged. I want you to understand that I had *no choice* in the matter. I am, as you must know, a devoutly religious man. The reason for what you consider to be my guilt was, in the eyes of our Lord, an urgently needed counterstrike to end Dr. Lydecker's insidious mission, a mission undertaken at the behest of Satan himself.

"Other than on the night of April twentieth, 2001, my only contact with professor Lydecker took place in her office on the morning of March twenty-second, of 2001. I had arranged to talk to her about her unfairness in making my son, Joshua, withdraw from her class.

"I was *staggered* by what I learned on that day—namely, that I was being confronted by an ally of the Anti-Christ. Oh yes," he said in a rising voice, "she *was* the devil's agent, wrought carnal and sensuous by Satan, and programmed with evil lies about the origins of this world and of the Lord's children, each of her lies designed to pervert our Christian youth, and"—his throat tightened with emotion and he stifled a sob—"turn them away from our precious Lord Almighty."

Usher paused to regain control of his emotion, and then continued, "I arranged to talk with her in her office. She told me that Joshua was an unacceptable distraction in her Introduction to Astronomy class, and that she had to banish him from the course. It was her way of keeping from her students the truth about how God created this world.

"I instructed her that her teachings were shown to be false by the sacred words of God in both *The Usher Bible* and the *King James Bible*. Her preaching that our earth is billions of years old was clearly an evil lie, a lie that is absolutely contradicted by these sacred texts. I tried to make her understand that our Holy Bibles are the sacred words of God himself, spoken directly to we chosen prophets that we might record the exact words the Almighty spoke to us.

"As is widely known, the Lord bestowed upon me a nearly perfect memory. I remember every word that woman said, and how brazenly she said them. Her words provide the *evidence* of her evil mission. When I informed her that the truth of our benevolent Lord should be taught in every science class, she responded without anger, but with a haughty air of superiority!

"She said that the God of our Bible is *not* benevolent. She recited what she claimed were words Mark Twain used to characterize the bible—'Our bible reveals to us the character of our God with minute and remorseless exactness . . . it is perhaps the most damnatory biography that exists in print anywhere. It makes Nero an angel of light and leading, by contrast.'

"What she said was sinful!" He grunted in disgust. "I told her Mark Twain was a corrupt and evil writer of trash, a man that didn't understand the fact that ours is a Christian Nation. Well, that Navajo girl didn't take what I'd said well at all . . . she had the *gall* to lecture *me*, a man of *God!*

"I could see all the practiced seductive movements of her face and torso as she said, 'James Madison, the Father of our Constitution, and the fourth president of our country, wrote: Religious bondage shackles and debilitates the mind and unfits it for every noble enterprise. And Thomas Jefferson, the Father of our Bill of Rights, and our third president, wrote: I do not find in orthodox Christianity one redeeming feature!' She just kept on going, saying, 'John Adams, our second president, wrote: The government of the United States is not, in any sense, founded on the Christian religion. You see, Mr. Usher, our founders were brilliant, perceptive, humane, men like Madison, Jefferson, Adams, Benjamin Franklin, and their fellow patriots. They were educated and thoroughly rational men. They embraced The Enlightenment. They threw superstition and fairy tales aside. They knew that super novae and comets are not messages from a God, that epidemics are not punishments meted out by some all knowing Almighty for this or that person's transgressions, and that there can be nothing holy about Holy Wars.'

"She said, 'If you've never read Thomas Paine's, *The Age of Reason*, Mr. Usher, I urge you to do so. His detailed and extensive analysis of the bible, of its likely real origins, and just when different parts of it had to have been written, are illuminating. The bible is not the words of god, but the words of men who liked to write exciting fantasy stories filled with warfare and supernatural fantasy themes. Our *nation* was founded as a *secular* nation, one that allows all of our people to believe whatever their individual minds tell them about religious stories. Our nation was most certainly *not* founded as a Christian nation. To say it was is quite simply a *gross* distortion of fact. No matter how many times you say it, it will still be untrue.'"

Usher was sweating, and he touched his shirtsleeve to his forehead, and then wiped his hands across his face. He said, defiantly, "Oh *yes*! She spoke her tirade of blasphemies without showing anger, but with conceit and satisfaction written on her face. I could see the gratification her lies were giving her and how she was taking her fill of Satan's strongest narcotic—pleasure! She was finding pleasure in denouncing our Lord. No doubt could remain. Just like the evil doctors that kill God's unborn babies, and the so-called scientists that try to kill God himself, *she was an instrument of Satan*. Satan found and trained that carnal savage to promote his heathen beliefs. I sensed that Satan had her corrupt lots of young men in her boudoir, corrupting them through pleasure, to draw them away from God," he said with trembling lips. "Satan placed her in a position to discredit and silence Joshua, the righteous son of a Prophet—so Satan *had* to be overruled. The Almighty could not allow such evil to go unpunished. She had gone too far! Our Creator instructed *me* as to what had to be done. I was the *chosen one* to do what He commanded. My action saved hundreds and hundreds of students from her future deceits, and pleased *My Lord*. My actions were completely justifiable in the eyes of our Holy Father!"

Usher sat back, and Detective O'Hara asked, "Does that conclude your opening statement, Mr. Usher?

"Yes," he answered weakly. "Yes, it does. It's vital that you understand exactly what she was. She was a minion of the Anti-Christ . . . an extremely dangerous and evil creature."

After a brief silence, Usher smiled weakly and said, "Thank you."

Emerson Yazzi told himself to calm down, to breathe deeply, and realize he had been listening to the grotesque narrative of a tragically and thoroughly delusional man.

Detective Healy asked, "So, Mr. Usher, do you admit to killing Nizhoni Lydecker and Wallace Hartsfield?"

"Oh no! I did *only* what my Heavenly Father instructed me to do. After I got the car key out of her hand, I suffocated Satan's agent with a plastic bag, in the back seat of her Jeep. She struggled for a few minutes, but my precious Lord made me a physically strong man, and she could not save herself. She didn't suffer much," and he added, with a frightful saccharin smile, "And I can assure you, she *wasn't* violated."

Healy said, "You *did* remove her clothing. Why did you do that?"

"Well, Hank, who was a very intelligent person, said that if the grave should ever be discovered, the absence of clothing would suggest that she had been the victim of a sex psychopath, or whatever they call them. He said it could lead the police to go looking for that type of despicable man, rather than for righteous Christians."

Healy asked, "So, Mr. Usher, am I to understand that you killed Nizhoni Lydecker, but *not* Wallace Hartsfield?"

"Yes. I'd been instructed to end the life of Satan's instrument. Hank shot and killed the man at the grave we had prepared for Satan's agent the day before. We hadn't expected Satan's agent to be in the company of a man. Hank saw her go into the Wexford alone, and we assumed she'd return to her Jeep alone." He added, "Hank had kept track of her whereabouts for two days. He had remarked to me that she seemed to be a rather solitary person."

Detective O'Hara asked, "So, Henry Schmidt killed Wallace Hartsfield?"

"That's right, detective. To our surprise, that man Hartsfield knew and recognized Hank. Apparently, Mr. Hartsfield owed money to one of Hank's friends, and Hartsfield initially thought we were there to get that money for Hank's friend. When Mr. Hartsfield saw that I had punished the Lydecker woman, he realized we weren't after *him*. Hank put his gun in the man's face and told him to drive us to the place where we had prepared a grave for Satan's agent. Hank tried to force the man to shovel dirt over the body of that woman, but the man refused. He said to Hank, 'You're going to have to shoot me, you miserable son of a bitch.' Now, *please* understand that is a *quotation*—I would never use that type of language." He paused before resuming, "And he tried to hit Hank with the spade. Hank shot him, just one time. Then Hank and I took turns shoveling the dirt onto the grave we had prepared, at dusk, the day before. We had covered it with pine boughs, and hid the spade there, as well."

Usher smiled and shook his head as he said, "Now, at that point, our work should have been completed; but, instead, we now had to find a place to bury that gambler. Hank looked through a built-in tool chest in the cargo area of the vehicle and found a heavy canvas sheet, in a sealed plastic pouch. We put the man in the cargo area, bent his knees up, folded his arms in, and covered him with the canvas."

Detective Healy asked, "Before we hear about that, Mr. Usher, do you believe God told you to kill Nizhoni Lydecker?"

"Oh yes, *absolutely*! He could not have been clearer on that point."

"I see," Detective Healy said. He then asked, "What about the killing of Wallace Hartsfield? God hadn't instructed you to kill him, had he?"

Usher did not respond quickly. He sighed, and paused for ten seconds or so before saying, "No. You see, we were up against a tight deadline. The Lord had instructed me that Satan's tool had to be punished by that night. We had reconciled ourselves to the fact that if that creature came down the alley with a companion, we had to act against both of them. Hank, who had a skill of unlocking locked car doors, got us into the Jeep. Hank had seen the Lydecker woman go into the Wexford alone, and we assumed, and hoped, that she would return to her vehicle alone. We didn't expect her to pick up a man. It was unfortunate for that fellow, but we had no alternative. The Lord gave me the deadline for ridding the world of Satan's tool, and we had to do what we did." Usher paused before stating, "All that aside, I want to personally assure you that Jesus would not have chosen *either* of these people to survive the coming Apocalypse."

There was an uncomfortably long silence before Detective O'Hara asked, "Mr. Usher, why was Dr. Lydecker's Jeep, with Wallace Hartsfield's body in it, driven to that remote place in the mountains, near Hawthorne, Nevada?"

"Well, you see, we had chosen only the place to bury Satan's agent. We hadn't expected that gambler to be with her. We made no provision for a second burial. Hank suggested the remote Nevada location for the man. He considered it to be the perfect hiding place for the body of the gambler, and for the vehicle that belonged to Satan's agent. I never actually saw the hiding place, but Hank described it to me in some detail. He had the foresight to understand that the vehicle might contain evidence that might somehow identify us sometime in the future, and he believed that the hiding place he picked for the Jeep might never be found in our lifetimes.

"So, when we left the burial site, we swung back through West Flagstaff and I picked up my car from an unmetered space three blocks out on Cherry Street. Hank and I had cell phones and we kept in contact. We made three stops for gasoline along the way. I stayed about two miles or so behind Hank all the way to Hawthorne. Hank kept going on his way to the spot he had chosen for hiding the Jeep, but when I got to Hawthorne I went to the shopping mall they have there. I spent close to four hours at the mall, just waiting for Hank's call, and silently praying for his success. When I got Hank's call telling me the job was done and that he'd hiked back to Lucky Boy Pass Road, I went and picked him up as he walked along that dusty unpaved road. We drove back to Hawthorne, got some drive-through McDonalds food, and then I dropped him at a motel. I went to a different nearby motel. It was late afternoon and we were pretty beat, as you can imagine. We both asked for wake-up calls for three-thirty A.M. I picked Hank up around four, and he drove us back to Las Vegas. Then, at long last, I drove home. I was *very* tired, but I was quietly elated . . . I knew I had conducted a crucial and successful mission that had pleased The Lord Almighty."

Detective O'Hara asked, "So, the decision to transport Mr. Hartsfield's body to that remote site was Henry Schmidt's—is that correct?"

"Yes, detective. It was entirely Hank's decision. He had made love to a girl friend in that shielded cave-like place back when he was in his early twenties. Hank," Usher said in a confiding tone, "like many good people, had been a bit wild as a youth." He paused for a few seconds before reflecting, "It's sometimes difficult to grasp the purpose in the Lord's decisions, but I know He had good reasons for making it work out as it has. He will make the wisdom of his decisions clear to me in the after-life."

O'Hara inquired, "How did you come to know Henry Schmidt?"

"Well, we met in The Nevada State Prison in Carson City in 1992. After I'd been there three years, the warden, a good *Christian* man, allowed me to offer a Bible Study class for interested inmates. Hank joined the class. He was in prison for stealing some baseball memorabilia, as they call it. When he got out in 1994 he joined our new Settlement, and a Mrs. Lavery, a very wealthy Reno woman and close friend of Hank's mother, donated fifty thousand dollars to our colony. We were just getting started then, but we were making it okay without that money. So, I gave Hank the five thousand dollars I had offered him for his assistance in getting the donation, and he left the colony shortly after that and went to Las Vegas . . . you see, Hank, God bless him, always had his own agenda. I put the money from Mrs. Lavery into the tax-free bonds of two hospitals that were affiliated with churchs. That money has grown very considerably over the fifteen years since then, and I've dedicated all of it, along with a portion of my book royalties and our member's contributions, to building our Seventh Seal Complex. It's going to be a *magnificent* structure," he said proudly.

Detective Healy asked, "How did you get Henry Schmidt to take part in the killing of Nizhoni Lydecker?"

"Well, I knew Hank was a good driver, and a resourceful sort of person, you see. There was only one way I could get Hank to help me with my mission—I offered him fifteen thousand dollars. I knew I'd need a way to get Satan's agent to a desolate burial place and to have someone help dig the grave, and I also knew Hank would help give me the resolve to do what my Lord had instructed me to do. Hank wasn't hired to kill anybody, but it worked out that the man Satan's agent picked up in that bar forced him to do it . . . I mean, the man *knew* Hank. And because Hank had to do more than I'd hired him to do, he asked for an additional ten thousand dollars. I had to agree that it was a reasonable request, and I gave him the extra pay. You see, I've never been the type of man to shortchange a person."

Healy inquired, "Was there anyone besides Henry Schmidt that knew about your plan for Nizhoni Lydecker, or was in any way involved in helping you with the . . . mission?"

"Oh yes, of course," Usher replied. "The Lord was with us, and he kept us safe. He had chosen me to carry out his punishment of Satan's minion. I knew that other righteous men had answered the Lord's commands to end the lives of doctors that killed God's unborn babies—justifiable homicides, every one. I could not refuse to follow His command that I terminate the life of another of Satan's agents. She had deeply offended not just me, but our Lord All Mighty, as well."

After a silence, Detective O'Hara asked, "Did any other *living person* know of your planned murder of Nizhoni Lydecker?"

"Oh, no," Usher replied. "The Lord charged me with the responsibility to select a driver and helper, and to remove Satan's agent. It was a very delicate mission, and Hank and I kept it totally secret," he said proudly.

Jim Healy indicated that the time allotted for the interview had expired. "We'll have a second interview at nine o'clock, Thursday morning," he said.

As Usher was led from the room Emerson Yazzie felt satisfied with the results of this initial interview. The details had been painful, but then, the disappearance itself had been painful for eight-plus-years. Nothing could change what had happened to Nizhoni, and Emerson had come to accept that. The silent oath he had sworn so often to his memory of her would be fulfilled. I vowed, he thought, that we'd find the person responsible for the crime and see that he paid the price for his obscene acts. I never imagined it would be a grandiose and delusional man who thought he was so special in god's eyes that he could do whatever he wanted to do, including murder, and ascribe the responsibility for his atrocious actions to god.

But then, Emerson thought, every day there are those that identify themselves as God's people, and hold themselves to be more righteous or worthy than those that worship a different fantasy god, or no manlike god at all. Many consider themselves to be soldiers of their *true God* and feel they must kill those they believe to have offended their god or his teachings. A large proportion of our planet's most highly evolved species, planet earth's vaunted *Homo sapiens*, will kill other Homo sapiens for not worshiping their particular fantasy gods. For these murders they believe their god will grant them admission to his heaven, and will reward them with eternal life in that wonderful place, surrounded forever by loved ones. So deep a dread of endless death possesses them that they are willing to kill non-believers in the hope it will win them a new and endless life after their god terminates their present existence. They choose to kill others to secure *eternal* life, a magical "do over" that their god will grant them following their earthly deaths. Surely, Emerson thought, with a deep sense of desolation, there can be no more terrible and widespread a form of grandiose and despicable delusional madness than this.

CHAPTER 48

───────── ▼ ─────────

The month of October sped by on its journey to ever more distant time, and Redmond and Jennifer felt that the worst of their ordeal-of-attention in relation to the Nizhoni Lydecker/ Wallace Hartsfield murder case was also moving felicitously into the past. At five o'clock on Monday, November ninth, a perfectly gorgeous late autumnal day in Pleasanton, Redmond concluded his walk from Stoddard Hall to 134 Shadowy Lane. He entered the house, called, "Hey, hon," and receiving no response, he went through the kitchen and opened the door to the back yard. He saw Jennifer, dressed in a red turtleneck shirt, faded jeans, and old white running shoes, vigorously raking the likely last of autumn's lavish fall of red and golden leaves.

For a time he just took in what a beautiful scene it was, and then he called, "Hey, sweetie—looks like you've got those unruly leaves corralled. I'll bag them up for you, but first I've got to get into some yard work togs."

She smiled, and said, "I'll hold the bags open for you, sweetheart." She added, as she laid the bamboo rake atop the pile, "But first, I need a glass of cold water."

Twenty minutes later Redmond tied up the eighth and last of his leaf-filled plastic bags and carried it to the front of the house. He laid it with the others, adjacent to the street, for tomorrow's leaf pick-up crew. Then he returned to the back deck and took a seat at the shaded table, across from Jennifer.

He commented, "That should be the last leaf gathering for this year. Any remaining leaves will have to go where the winds take them."

"They'll soon be gone with the wind," Jennifer said. She smiled, and added, "That's the title of a great book, a great film, *and* a pretty darned good 'lost love' song, as well."

Redmond smiled, and then asked, "Any more requests for interviews or statements about the Usher arrest?"

"Happily, not a one, Mac. When they finally get around to Usher's trial we'll undoubtedly be called to testify about how we collected his DNA. I suppose Usher's attorney will carp about 'surreptitious sampling,' but given the crimes Usher committed, no jury would be swayed by such maneuvers. The crimes were horrendous, the evidence incontestable, and Usher can't claim a right of privacy for his books when he *sold* four of his books to us. They were our books, and no longer his."

"Well, Jen, Usher is 'going down,' as they say. When the jury considers what he and Henry Schmidt did, there won't be any doubt that he murdered, with not so much as a tinge of remorse, a very admirable and brilliant young woman; and he abetted the murder of a gifted musician. I suspect he won't get the death sentence, although one could make a pretty good case for it. His defense will, no doubt, argue that his judgment was impaired by his religious beliefs. It should be obvious that he's delusional with respect to his 'duties to god,' and that he experiences auditory, and even visual, hallucinations wherein god tells him to do this or that. Emerson expects Dennis Packard to be content with trying to save Usher from the death penalty, and I think that's what will happen. Usher got off easy when he shot Dr. Webster. He won't get off easy in the hellacious murders of Nizhoni Lydecker and Duke Hartsfield. He'll probably get life in prison. I think he's chronically mentally ill, with such an elaborate, deeply engrained, and self-aggrandizing delusional system that he could never be cured. I'm happy to hear that Joshua Usher has expressed deep and sincere remorse over his father's crimes. He said that religion is a deeply personal matter, and must not include violence against those of different faiths or points of view."

"Good for Joshua," Jennifer said. "I hope he'll prove to be a good leader for The House of the Ascension. Like most of us, he's trying to the right things in life as he sees them."

"Right."

"You know, Mac, our theories about a sex offender being after Nizhoni, a gangster type being after Duke, a vengeful and fearful Lindsey, and/or an angry Lydecker arranging the murder of Nizhoni, and possibly even Joshua going after her, all had one thing in common."

"Yep . . . they were all *wrong*," Redmond said with a chuckle. "Still, they were all theoretically possible. And Usher was certainly included among our possibles, once we found out he was willing to shoot Dr. Webster."

Jennifer said, "We sure were wrong about Lindsey and Lydecker as potential murderers—thank goodness. Some of their behaviors were less than noble, but they weren't criminal. We don't need professors to be murderers, or to donate money to a murderer. It's a relief to know it was Lillian Lavery, and not her professor daughter, that gave Usher financial support, and that it was given only out of a kind wish to assist her longtime friend, Emma Schmidt. And I know Lindsey must be deeply shocked, disappointed, and even freaked-out to learn that Henry Schmidt was a killer. I suspect Lindsey may have some mental anguish in dealing with all that."

Redmond said, "Let's hope we don't have to be involved in any more cases of murder. We can be proud of the fact that we helped solve six murders over the last five years. And in *this* case we did manage to avoid putting ourselves in physical danger. Thinking back, there were a couple of cases where we did put ourselves in great danger, and we had to have real *courage*."

Redmond's emphasis on the word "courage" made Jennifer recall Bert Lahr in his famous role as the cowardly lion of the *Wizard of Oz,* delivering his wonderful oddly rhymed and amusingly confused oration on the deep importance of courage.

She stood, looked into Redmond's eyes, smiled, and then imitated Lahr's fidgety body movements and quirky speech pattern as she asked, "What makes the *Hottentot,* so hot?"

Redmond stood and fidgeted like the lion, and responded, "What puts the *ape,* in ape-ricot?"

"Cur-rich!" they said with fervor, and they laughed heartily.

THE END